THE
GETTING A
grip
DUET

M.E. CARTER

This is a work of fiction. Names, characters, places, brands, media, and incidents are either the product of the author's imagination or are used fictitiously. The author acknowledges the trademarked status and trademark owners of various products referenced in this work of fiction, which have been used without permission. The publication/use of these trademarks is not authorized, associated with, or sponsored by the trademark owners.

Copyright © 2017–2019 by M.E. Carter

All rights reserved.
Without limiting the rights under copyright reserved above, no part of this publication may be reproduced, stored in or introduced into a retrieval system, or transmitted, in any form, or by any means (electronic, mechanical, photocopying, recording, or otherwise) without the prior written permission of the above copyright owner of this book.

First Edition: July 2017
Library of Congress Cataloging-in-Publication Data
The Getting a Grip Duet (#MyNewLife Series) – 1st ed
ISBN-13: 978-1-948852-19-7

GETTING A grip

a
#MyNewLife
romantic comedy

M.E. CARTER

*To My Future Greg
I know you're out there somewhere,
and I can't wait for you to find me.*

CHAPTER
One

"Stop looking at yourself like that."

I glance from the mirror to my BFF sitting in the corner chair of the dressing room. She's scrolling through her Facebook page on her newest iPhone. The iPhone she didn't want but her husband got her anyway, because he has to have all the latest upgrades. Every time. No matter how expensive.

We can't have a conversation anymore without that damn thing distracting her in one way or another.

"I'm looking at the clothes I'm trying on," I say, yanking a horizontal-striped dress over my head and tugging it around my hips.

Horizontal stripes? Who am I kidding? I don't have the figure for this anymore.

Callie huffs and locks the screen of her phone, dropping it into her purse.

"Don't give me that shit," she rebuts, crossing her arms over her chest. "You're doing it again."

"Doing what?" I feign ignorance, twirling around and pretending to care about the cut or fit of the umpteenth dress I've tried on in the last ten minutes.

She cocks an eyebrow at me. "Glaring at yourself and all those so-called imperfections that douche of an ex threw in your face. That's what."

I sigh and yank the offending dress over my head. She's right. Ever since James critiqued almost every square inch of my body as an excuse for trading me in for a younger model, I can't look at myself the same way.

Your hips are so wide now.

Those stretch marks kind of gross me out.

Your stomach wasn't that flabby when I met you.

It wouldn't kill you to have a boob lift to take care of some of the sag.

I'm just not... turned on by you anymore.

It's like small daggers in my gut every time I think about those remarks.

"This one is a no." I throw the dress at Callie's head. She catches it one-handed and starts putting it on the hanger so I don't have to do it later, and she *will* make me do it later. Callie used to work in retail. She's a strong believer in cleaning up after ourselves when we shop.

"Yeah, I hate that horizontal stripes are in style."

Oh good, I think to myself, *we're moving onto a new topic.*

"Seriously, Elena..."

Or not.

"You need to stop letting him get to you."

I grab my shoes, praying I can get out of this dressing room sooner rather than later so the racks of clothing will distract her. I'm hoping to distract myself as well.

When it comes to my body, I've always been my own worst critic. Aren't we all? But eighteen months ago, it got exponentially worse. That's when my husband of fifteen years informed me he was having an affair with his secretary. I was blindsided. I have no idea how I missed the signs. Maybe it's because I was busy raising our three young girls, but I had no clue he was getting a piece of ass on the side.

Before I could even wrap my brain around the information, he dropped another bomb... it wasn't only sex. He was in love with her and wanted a divorce.

I tried to talk some sense into him, but he decided his best defense was to add insult to injury. He threw every insecurity I had in my face and used them as his reasons for not wanting me anymore. Because according to him, it was all my fault.

I've come to realize, over time, what an asshole he was, and continues to be. But that doesn't mean I've gotten a grip on the damage he left behind. I still struggle with the fact that he got married again so quickly, ironically. But mostly, I still struggle with body self-loathing. While I recognize shopping is a necessary evil, it's still a big trigger for me. Even when Callie reminds me of all the reasons I'm being irrational.

"First of all, he was trying to make *you* feel guilty for *him* cheating, which is ridiculous. Second, he's no looker himself. And third, none of it is true. You've had three babies for God's sake. And you're like, a thousand pounds smaller than me."

I snort and roll my eyes. "Poundage doesn't mean anything when you have a husband who adores your body and wants to work it out on a regular basis," I reply, grabbing a handful of clothes from the "no" pile and turn to leave.

"I would be perfectly happy if he *didn't* want my body," she says while following me to the exit. "It's hard to get off when the last thing he says before sexy time is how lazy I am for not cleaning the kitchen after work."

"He said that?" I whip around to look at her. "Even after the therapist told him to back off?"

She purses her lips at me. "Elena, it's going to take more than a few therapy sessions to fix the problems in my husband. Sometimes I envy you for getting two hundred pounds of narcissistic asshole out of your life."

I shake my head and keep browsing through the women's section of Kohl's. Callie introduced the department store to me last year, and now it's our favorite place to shop. "Retail therapy," she calls it. More like "adult time" therapy for me. I usually don't buy anything. I don't see the need to. My weight is like a yo-yo and it always feels like I'm throwing money away. Instead, I come along for the ride as Callie indulges herself.

She likes to shop. A lot. She has more clothes than anyone I've ever known. But she also has a husband that never seems to understand how badly words can wound you. She makes up for it by doing a lot of retail therapy and doesn't feel the least bit guilty about it.

The one thing she does feel guilty about is her weight. Since her son Christopher was born almost three years ago, she hasn't been able to shed the extra pounds. She's tried every diet known to man... Atkins, juicing, some crazy diet about eating according to your blood type. She even went to the gym six days a week last summer and ate a thousand calories a day. She lost one pound.

One.

As soon as summer was over and she went back to work in the high school administrative office, she gained five back.

"I'm not working my ass off to gain five pounds again," she'd said. "I can do that sitting on the couch reading a good book."

While Callie always seems to feel guilty about the weight, she neglects to notice the rest of her.

She's gorgeous. I mean, stunning.

With long, thick dark hair with waves that just won't quit, light brown inviting eyes that shine when she's happy, and the most beautiful smile... I've seen men stop dead in their tracks when they see her. She may be heavyset, but she rocks it.

She is also the funniest person I've ever met, with some of the quickest wit, and that is something to be appreciated. Not everyone gets my sense of humor. But Callie is one of the only people who has ever understood my snark and shoots it right back at me with amazing cleverness.

Sometimes, when we get caught up in something funny, listening to her laugh makes everything hilarious all over again.

But she doesn't notice any of that about herself. Nope. All she sees is the weight.

The good thing about her shopping obsession is that she knows how to hide said weight and that works to my advantage when we have our retail therapy sessions. She always knows what will work on me and what won't. What will hide that flabby gut and show off my arms. With my littlest one's third birthday party next weekend, I'm practically desperate to find something to make me look pretty. Not sexy, or smokin', or anything like that. Just pretty.

James is coming to the party. And he's bringing that little bitch Keri with him. She never lets him out of her sight. It's really annoying. And kind of sad in a weird way.

You know the Barbie aisle at almost any store? If you look closely, you'll see that iconic doll is made up for every occasion or occupation known to man... Veterinarian Barbie, Movie Star Barbie, Home-Wrecking Husband-Stealing Barbie. That's Keri. All plastic and made up and making sure to look and *be* better than anyone else, as if she has something to prove even after she's won the prize. The "prize" being my husband, of course.

But that's the thing about women who steal other women's husbands. They think the fight is getting their claws into the man, but it's not. The fight is keeping your claws in him, because despite winning that round in the game of love, they always seem to forget the most important rule: There is always someone younger and prettier than you.

Callie's phone buzzes in her purse... again.

"Ugh," she says, rolling her eyes. "It's like he can't even take a shit if I'm not there to wipe his ass."

Her husband, Ben, is the neediest man I have ever met in my life. The way she tells it, when they were dating, it meant being wooed. Once the "I do's" were over, it meant her job was to take care of his every whim.

And work full time.

And be the mother of a rambunctious son.

She pulls out her phone and swipes to open it. "Really?" She turns the screen for me to see.

When are you coming home?

It's the same text she gets every time we're out.

"Tell him when we're done shopping," I say, turning back to the rack of tops I'm filtering my way through.

She types for a few seconds. "Done. I swear to you, Elena, if I go home and see he has destroyed the kitchen again, I'm going to go ape shit. I just know it."

I've heard all this before. I'm no stranger to the tumultuous relationship Callie has with her husband. I saw it all firsthand at childbirth classes when we first met. Ben had been a dick then, too. He was just a part-time dick then. When a child was added to the mix of what he considered an already stressful life, it threw him over into the full-time dick category. And when she quit her job this year because Christopher kept getting kicked out of daycare, it made things that much more tense at home. Mostly because according to Ben, being a stay-at-home mom isn't work. Callie, being the one who is trying to raise the most hyper little boy in the world, disagrees.

"Omg," Callie says, throwing her head back like she's shouting to the gods as, yet another, text comes through. "How long will that be? Christopher needs to go to bed," she reads the message aloud.

"You've got to be kidding me," I say.

"I wish I was." She doesn't look up. "So put... him... to bed," she reads out loud as she types. "You're the dad... Man... up." She clicks the phone closed and drops it in her purse. Apparently, she's done with that conversation.

"Callie," I walk over to her, holding a short, strappy black polka dot dress, "remind me again why you stay with him? I get that you're Catholic and such, but I'm pretty sure the priest would forgive you considering all the verbal abuse you take. Probably without even so much as a Hail Mary!"

I'm always poking fun at her about her faith. I respect the hell out of her for being devout, but I don't really understand it. I don't believe that Mother Mary has nothing better to do than stand around and be an answering machine for God. Is

Heaven really that boring? When I get there, I plan to run up and down those streets paved with gold and eat whatever food they have while enjoying my perfect body. I'm sure it's the best food ever. And I love my food.

"You know why I can't leave, Elena," Callie says quietly. "For all his dick-ness, he's still my husband and that counts for something. No," she corrects herself. "It counts for everything. Now try that one on," she says, pointing to the polka dot dress before continuing. "Happiness is only an emotion. It fluctuates due to hormones and weather and what kind of music you're listening to. Sure, I'm not happy all the time in this marriage, but when I made the commitment to him, I didn't expect to be."

"But did you expect to be *un*happy all the time?" I challenge.

She sighs and hands me a beautiful peach tank top. It's covered in rows of ruffles in different peach shades. Perfect for covering that baby gut I'm self-conscious about.

"No, I didn't expect to be unhappy either," she admits. "But reality is, if I leave him, I'll have to get a job and I like my vacation time with Christopher." She winks and walks to another rack.

Her vacation quip is an obvious dig at Ben's belief about what motherhood really is, and it makes me snort a laugh. I love bantering with her. We understand each other well. No, she's not happy in her marriage, but she's not about to leave her husband. She's not ready. And frankly, he hasn't really done anything that can't be fixed.

Is he a dick? Yes. Cheater? No.

Provider? Yes. Best friend? No.

The cons still vastly outweigh the pros on the divorce scale for Callie, and I know it. So I'll never say a negative word about her husband. Will I continue to tell her she deserves better? Absolutely. But I respect her enough to treat Ben courteously as long as they're married.

The whole, "I'm the only one who can say something bad about my sibling" argument applies here, too. Except this one involves her spouse, so I'll quietly keep the names I call him in my head.

Until she's ready to leave him. Then the gloves may come off.

CHAPTER Two

I cringe and freeze as my keys clatter across the table next to the front door. My mom-ears try to hone in on any sounds from upstairs that may have resulted from my noisy mistake.

Around here, bedtime is a very delicate process. If one thing goes awry, all bets are off and there's no guarantee if or when anyone will sleep again. I know everyone says that. But until they've stayed up past two every night for a week because of impromptu dance parties breaking out in my children's bedrooms, they really don't have any idea.

Fortunately, it seems no one is stirring upstairs. "I got lucky," I mumble to myself while practically tiptoeing to the den to greet the babysitter, also known as my mom.

Rounding the corner, I roll my eyes at her choice in television show. "Really, Ma?" I chide as I flop down on the couch next to her. "The Kardashians?"

"Don't judge me." She smacks me on the thigh with one hand and picks up the remote with the other, turning the volume down. "Watching their family makes me feel better about my own."

"Pretty sure that's why most people watch it, Ma. Although I think we have our own brand of crazy around here."

"Doesn't everyone. But this," she points her finger at the television, "this is something else."

"Yeah, as much as you and I butted heads when I was growing up, I'm thankful I didn't end up with Kris Jenner for a mother."

I absentmindedly brush invisible lint off my burnt orange couch. Yes, burnt orange. When my mother first pitched the color idea to me, I thought for sure it was the weirdest color choice. Turns out, it goes great with the slate floors in this room. Really draws out the similar specs of color in the tiles. Go figure. I didn't even realize there was orange in the floor at all until she pointed it out. Visual design is not my strong suit.

"I feel bad for poor Bruce Jenner." She shakes her head and sighs. "It's no wonder that poor man had to become a woman."

"What?" I ask with a laugh. My mother is always spouting off random shit.

"If you had your choice of being married to that woman or wearing a dress for the rest of your life, I'd choose the pantyhose, too."

A laugh barks out of me before I can stop it. "I hope you don't say stuff like that in public."

"Of course not. I may not be politically correct, but I am a lady."

My mother didn't just grow up in a different era. She grew up with a really uppity stepmother. While my mom is one of the least judgmental people I know, and I have literally seen her give someone in need the coat off her back, she's not terribly couth. She subscribes to the belief that because she doesn't offend easily, no one else should either. And she calls it like she sees it.

Behind closed doors.

In public, she's prim and proper and demure.

I guess that's where I get my ability to smile on the outside, even if I'm dying on the inside.

"Well, then," I redirect, "how were the kids tonight? Good for you?"

Her face lights up as she starts telling me about her night as babysitter. Turns out, the same little shits that run me ragged at bedtime were perfect angels for her. They're no dummies. They know who buys all the presents.

"Did Fiona get all her homework done?"

"She did. Oh! And did you sign her up for gymnastics yet? She asked me about it again."

I rub my eyes and groan. "I keep forgetting. It's on my list."

"Elena. You are crushing that poor girl's soul every time you tell her you haven't made it a priority."

"Really, mother," I deadpan. "I crush her soul? Don't you think you're being a bit dramatic?"

She smiles at me playfully and shrugs. "I'm the grandmother. I'm allowed to be dramatic." She taps her finger to her lips like she's thinking. "I may need to sign her up myself."

She knows she's got me now. "Please don't do that," I beg. "You'll sign her up for the wrong day and time, and it'll screw up our whole schedule."

"Well then I guess you better make it a priority."

"You're right. When I take Max to the mommy-and-me class tomorrow, I'll ask about it. I don't think they have classes for her age since they focus on the younger kids. I may have to take her somewhere else. I don't know."

She nods once. Apparently, my answer is acceptable. "Did you have fun with Callie? Did you buy anything?"

"I did. I bought a sundress that I think I'm going to wear to the birthday party."

"You're not dressing up for that jackhole, right?"

"Mother!"

My mother, who has never said a naughty word in her life, has been known to throw around a few cusswords here and there since my divorce. It's a bit jarring since I literally had never heard one dirty word grace her lips until I was thirty-seven years old. But to say she doesn't like James anymore would be the understatement of the year.

"Don't 'mother' me. That's what he is and you know it."

"I know, but can you at least not say it when you're around the kids?"

She waves her hand around like she's presenting the room. "Do you see the kids anywhere? They're asleep."

I sigh and give up. "Ok, fine. He's a jackhole. And no, I didn't buy the dress for him. I bought it for me. I'm tired of feeling frumpy. I want to feel pretty for the party."

"You're pretty all the time."

"You have to say that. You're my mother."

"Regardless. Don't dress up for him."

"I won't."

"And don't dress up for her."

And there it is. She nails it.

I didn't use to care about how I look. And for the most part, I guess I still don't unless his new wife Keri is around. She's young. She's tiny. She's beautiful. And next to her, I just feel... *less*. So when I know we're going to be in the same room together, it helps to have something new to wear. It boosts my confidence a tiny bit.

Not that I have anything to really worry about. She already took what she wanted (my husband and his paycheck) and left the rest for me. "The rest" turned out to be a significant amount.

When we first started the divorce process, James was adamant that I didn't deserve anything more than child support. He argued that I hadn't worked once the girls were born, and I had no financial right over any of our assets. At first, I was worried I'd end up with nothing and we'd have to move in with my mom.

Then he started bringing Keri to all the hearings. And Keri doesn't know how to sit quietly with things that aren't her business. The mediator finally got fed up with her butting her nose into everything and making her opinion known. He threatened to go to the judge with his own recommendations if they didn't shut up and sign off on a more-than-fair split.

I got the house so the kids wouldn't be homeless, the legal amount of child support every month, and half of all the accounts. Checking, savings, retirement… you name it, I got half. James got the other half and a raging Keri who was pissed off that those accounts she was eyeing suddenly shed a little bit of weight.

Fortunately, it's enough money that if I stick to my budget, I have at least a few years to stay home and figure out what I want to do with my life. Because I have no idea. I quit college before I graduated to become a flight attendant, which I loved, but jet setting around the world isn't a good career for a single mom of littles. Now I'm stuck trying to figure out what skills I have that can translate into the work force, while trying to raise a seven-year old, five-year-old, and almost three-year-old. It's one more thing I'm trying to figure out, and I'm not making much progress.

"I'm not dressing up for her, Ma," I finally respond. "I'm dressing up for me. It's time I take more care of myself."

She pats my arm and turns back to the TV. "You and the kids come first in this house. You and the kids. Even if that little wench is in your home."

"Speaking of, the party starts at three. Think you can come early to help me set up? Maybe at about two?"

"Sure yeah. I'll be here at two." She doesn't look away from the TV, so I know she has no idea what she just responded to.

"Ma."

"Shhhh." She waves me off. "Look, there's Bruce as a man."

I roll my eyes and get up from the couch. "I'll let you enjoy watching *Bruce* Jenner. I'm going to get ready for bed."

"Ok, babe. I'll let myself out."

I've got to hand it to my mother. She may have very strong opinions, but they never distract her from a good Kardashian plot twist.

CHAPTER
Three

"Remember to let your children explore their environment!" the instructor yells over all the noise. "It might look like they're only playing, but that's how they learn."

Looking around the gym, I see parents and children working together at the different stations. One mom is chasing her son as they crawl through a tunnel. A dad is teaching his daughter how to do a handstand. There's even a mom helping her child do a forward roll on the high beam. And they're only toddlers.

Max, however (that's my kid), Max is laying head-down on one of the mats shaped like a cheese wedge. I have no idea why. Every time I try to engage her in something, or even move her out of the way, she screams like I'm shoving bamboo shoots through her fingernails.

However, Christopher, Callie's son, hasn't stopped moving since we got here.

"What exactly is he learning?"

Callie looks at me from behind her camera and shoots me a dirty look. "He's learning cause and effect."

"It looks more to me like he's not absorbing the lesson," I tease back.

For a good five minutes, he's been jumping on the bar, swinging out as far as he can, and letting go so he lands on his back. It's not a thick, fluffy mat he's landing on. It's a thin one, and he makes a *thunk* every time he lands. And every time he whines about how it hurts. Then he runs to the bar and does it again.

"He's just determined to do it right." Callie counters, the click of the camera practically a constant hum with as many pictures as she's taking. She's got probably a hundred times more shots of her one child than I do of my three. I must hand it to her, she won't forget a moment of this kid's life. "He can't help that he keeps falling."

"He's letting go, Callie."

"I prefer the term 'dismount'."

"Well his dismount is terrible."

"So was Mary Lou Retton's when she was three."

"Touché," I finally cave, and she smiles at having won that round of battle of the wits. Sarcasm is our favorite form of communication. Sure, we can be serious when there are things to be serious about. But for the most part, we like seeing the joy in everyday life. Even if it means poking fun at ourselves.

As Christopher goes to jump for the bar again, Callie looks to the ceiling, yelling, "Oh come on, now!" and grabs her phone out of her pocket. Somehow, that one forceful statement distracts Christopher, and off he goes, running in circles around the tumbling floor until he falls over.

I look back over at Callie, texting frantically. "What now?"

The irritation is etched all over her face. "I swear to god, Elena, this man's sole purpose in life is to irritate the ever-loving hell out of me."

"Don't say h-e-double hockey sticks in front of other people's kids," I remind her. In front of hers? Fine. In front of mine? I don't care. But not in front of anyone else's. We've gotten way too many dirty looks in public, and a few Bible tracts, because of her mouth. "What's he doing this time?"

"He's mad because I won't go to four different stores to find some random brand of organic, GMO-free, additive-preservative-flavor-free rice cake he says he needs for his new diet."

"New diet? Another one?"

"I swear, Elena, it's never ending. Last time, it was the chicken-only diet. This time, its paleo or some shi… thing like that." I smile because she finally caught herself before we got another stern talking to by the instructor about the use of kid-friendly words. "And I already know what's going to happen. He's going to throw his body into starvation mode, eat everything in the house, gain forty additional pounds when he finally gives up, and blame me because I didn't encourage him enough by doing it with him."

Max finally decides she's done with her very expensive rest time on the cheese and grabs my hands to help her walk on the low beam. The very low beam. Actually, it's pretty much a rectangular log on the floor. But the kids think it's exciting.

"Don't you think you're being a bit theatrical?"

"Uh, no," she says as she looks around until she spots Christopher, who is now spinning in circles until he hits the wall and knocks himself over. What can I say… the kid is weird. "It is exactly what happened the last time he went on a diet and the time before that."

"And it's all your fault he's not successful?"

"Yep."

"Never mind the fact that you don't buy junk food and that he's the one that brings it into the house."

"Yep."

I gasp. With sarcasm, of course. "How dare you bring healthy foods into the household!"

"I know. I'm terrible. And how dare I not drive forty-five minutes to the one store in town where he can find this damn rice cake, or whatever it is."

"I hate the way he treats you," I throw out there, knowing it's not going to change anything.

"I know. But I can't leave, because of that, right there." She points at Christopher as he begins running towards us. "I refuse to let him have weekend visitation. You know how much he engages when he's at home. I'd be terrified Christopher would get hurt if I wasn't there."

Before the words even leave her mouth, he barrels into Max and I, knocking her over and yelling "Mine!" as he wrestles with her on the ground.

"Oh, I don't know," I say as I watch the match on the floor in front of me. Max may be small, but she's scrappy and she's used to Christopher's games. She quickly gets the upperhand. "It seems like pain isn't a huge deterrent to him."

"You know what I mean," she grumbles, as we pull the toddlers away from each other. Christopher has been the stereotypical "all-boy" from the beginning, so tackling Max is nothing new. The first time he did it, I was scared he had hurt her, and Callie was mortified. Very quickly we learned it's just the way they play. Now we monitor it when it happens, which is at least once during our mommy-and-me class every week, and make sure no one else's kid accidentally gets involved.

We've had that "talking to" as well.

As we untangle arms and legs, an unwitting victim toddles up and is promptly knocked over by some flailing limbs. I let go of Max, who immediately body slams Christopher back down on the ground.

Oh well. He started it.

"Are you ok, baby girl?" I ask gently, reaching out for the random tot. She's at least a few months younger than Max with dark ringlets of hair. She almost looks like a mini Shirley Temple, except cuter. She seems a little stunned by the wrestling match in front of her, but she's not crying.

"She's ok," a deep voice says next to me. I look up to see who this little girl belongs to and… *oh my.*

He's tall, like over six feet tall with blond hair. Not like mine which straddles the line between dirty blond and mousy brown. But true, blond. His eyes are a dark blue and he has a beard.

I'm not one of those women who enjoys beards, the longer the better. I can handle scruff. But full-on beards don't turn me on and to be perfectly blunt, I find them unsanitary. But this guy, well, it works for this guy. A lot.

He's giving me an amused look and suddenly I feel really self-conscious about having worn yoga pants and a T-shirt to class. *Way to be prepared for anything, Elena.* The thought is fleeting, though, when I remember his child just got knocked over by the Tasmanian Devil twins.

"I'm sorry they knocked her over," I gush, as he picks up the little girl and she throws her arms around him. "We were trying to break it up before anyone got hurt."

"I saw. You have your hands full." He gently pats the little girl's back and she lays her head on his shoulder. Thirty-minutes of exercise can drain these kiddos quick.

"It was mostly her kid's fault." I gesture to Callie with my thumb and vaguely register a "Hey!" from her in response.

The man chuckles. "You never can trust those boys," he says with a smile.

Is he... *flirting with me*?

I realize how ridiculous my thoughts sound, even though I'm the only one that can hear them. We are in a parent-child gymnastics class and chances are, this man is married. Still, it's kind of nice to have the attention of a man. Even if it's only because your child dragged his child into a WWE match.

"Well, I'm glad she's ok. They can be kind of rough and tumble."

"Speaking of," Callie says behind me, dragging both kids with her, "why don't you give me a hand here and take yours."

I lift Max up into my arms and reprimand her gently. "Max, we don't tackle our friends. That was too rough."

"Too wuf, mommy?" Her eyes are wide as she waits for my response.

"Yes, baby. That was too rough."

"She's fine," Callie cuts in, as Christopher tries to pry her hand off his arm. It's not working and you can tell he's getting frustrated. "This one, on the other hand..." she trails off and gestures her head towards our new friends, "Is she ok?"

The man smiles at Callie, but somehow, it doesn't seem the same as when he smiles at me. Am I making that up in my head? I must be. I guess I've been lonely for too darn long.

"She really is ok. It's good for her to get knocked down every once in a while. That way she can figure out how to get back up."

Callie turns and raises an eyebrow at me. "Hmm. Handsome and wise. He's going to be fun to have in class."

Pretty sure I turn bright red when she says that, and I'm positive my laughter gives away my nerves. But ever the strong one, Callie turns back to the stranger and keeps going.

"Are you guys new here? We haven't seen you in class before."

"We're new to the class, but not new to the area." Callie is the one that asked the question, but he's addressing us both. "She's still really young, so instead of getting my court-ordered Thursday night dinners, I'm doing Thursday morning gymnastics classes instead."

Court-ordered Thursday night dinners? Did he throw that in there so we'd know he was single? Ok, I really am making up stories in my head now.

"Aw. That's fun! I'm Callie." She starts to put her hand out to shake, but loses her grip on Christopher instead. "Shit. I'll be back." She takes off after him, leaving me alone to continue this conversation with a man I have no business being attracted to.

"Is he always that wild?" he questions, as we watch Christopher dodge Callie's grasp multiple times.

"Always," I laugh. "I'm Elena, by the way. And this is Max."

"Greg," he responds. "And this is Peyton."

"How old is she, anyway? I was worried because she's so much smaller than our kiddos."

"Nah. She's really fine," he says dismissively. "She's almost two and a half."

"Ah, that explains it. Max is almost three."

"Then answer me a question," he says conspiratorially. "Do the terrible two's get any better?"

"Uh, no," I laugh. "And if you think two is bad, just wait. It gets worse."

"Until they're how old?"

"About twenty-five."

He smiles at me and I smile at him and we're smiling at each other when Callie strolls back up, Christopher dangling like he just flopped backward when she picked him up.

"Ok, I think it may be in my best interest to get Christopher out of the room and away from all small children walking on the balance beam. Anyone want to join us for McDonald's?"

Max yells, "McDonow!" in response. Even Peyton sits straight up in her dad's arms at the offer.

"I guess we're going for lunch," I say and look over at Greg. "Care to join us?"

"Where did you get the name Max from? That's unusual for a girl." Greg pops a couple of Peyton's fries in his mouth. We tried getting the kids to sit down and eat, but they outlasted us with their tantrums so we finally let them go try their hand at the indoor playground.

Callie laughs under her breath, knowing full well how my child's name came about.

"Her full name is Maxine." I take a sip of my Dr. Pepper and wipe my greasy hands on a napkin. The food seems greasier than normal today. Or I'm more acutely aware that an attractive single man is sitting at the table with us while I shovel a zillion calories in my mouth. "We named her after my grandfather's wife."

"Oh, that's nice," Greg says.

"Yes," Callie interjects. "It was really nice to name her poor daughter after a total witch."

Greg's eyebrows raise. "Really?"

I roll my eyes and throw a napkin at her. "She's not that bad."

"Didn't you call her a gold-digging whore when they got married?"

"I mean, yes." I ignore Callie as she smirks. "But in her defense, she doesn't know she's a gold-digging whore. She thinks she's, um…." I wave my hand trying to come up with the right word to describe my step-grandmother.

"Snobby?" Callie offers.

"No."

"Uppity?"

"No."

"A gold-digger."

"Ok, fine." I give up and start boxing up nuggets to take home for when the kids finally get hungry. "She was looking for a sugar daddy and she found one. But she gives really good presents and she recommended a really good divorce attorney."

"I'll give you that one." Callie shoves the last bite of her burger into her mouth and starts throwing trash in the bags.

"Besides," I continue, "you don't have any room to talk about naming your kid. You named yours after a movie star."

She points a finger at me. "Christopher Reeve is not *just* a movie star. He is Superman."

Greg chuckles.

"What are you laughing at, bucko?" she asks, turning her playful wrath on him.

He throws his hands up in defense, smile still on his face. "Hey, Superman was my favorite. And with as much as that kid throws his muscle around, I think it's perfect."

We all look over to see Christopher tumbling down the slide. And by tumbling, I mean rolling head-over-butt down the enclosed slide until he ends up in a heap on the plastic floor.

"Or maybe not," he retorts.

I laugh as Callie pretends to be offended, which we all know she's not. "Ok, funny guy. Where did the name Peyton come from?"

He smirks. "My ex-wife's favorite show was One Tree Hill. She's a total superfan. Used to go to conventions and all that crap. I guess someone on the show is named Peyton. So there ya go."

Callie snorts. "You are full of crap."

"What?" He tries to keep a straight face, but a smile keeps playing on his lips.

She leans over the table, staring him down. "You're telling me you let your daughter be named after a character on a TV show?"

"Uh, yes?"

"Nope. Tell us why you really didn't put up a fight and before you do, let me remind you that I noticed the Indianapolis Colts bumper sticker on the back of your car."

Greg gives up trying to keep a straight face and starts laughing. It's a deep, throaty laugh. The kind of laugh that makes me happy hearing it, even if I don't know why he's actually doing it.

"Fine. You caught me," he admits. "My ex hated sports so she never put together that Peyton Manning was the quarterback for the Colts for so long."

All three of us laugh at his admission. I forgot what it was like to enjoy the company of a man. He's funny. He's easy going. He's really sweet with his daughter. I like him.

Looking at Callie, I can see she likes him, too. But by the way she cocks an eyebrow at me every once in a while, I can see the gears turning in her brain about what this new friendship could mean for me.

"Mama, Mama, Mama." Max rushes towards me and lays her head on my leg. "Mama, I want my ba."

"Does she still use that thing?" Callie asks, as I pick Max up and rub her back. Her thumb immediately goes to her mouth.

"She hasn't had a bottle in a long time," I reply. "It's her way of saying she's tired."

"Yeah, I think Pey is on her way out, too," Greg remarks. We glance over at where he's looking and sure enough, she's standing on the bottom step of the playscape with her head resting on the next step up and her eyes are closing.

Christopher, on the other hand, is staring out the window roaring at every car that drives by.

"I miss naps," Callie sighs with defeat. I just giggle. She got the short end of the stick with her child's sleeping habits.

"Come on, Pey," Greg calls. "Let's get ready to go bye-bye."

We clear all our trash off the table and Greg insists I take Peyton's left overs, since he's about to drop her back off with her grandmother anyway.

"Thanks again for inviting me to lunch," he says while holding the door for all of us. "Get back here, Superman." He grabs Christopher by the collar when he takes off running for the parking lot. "Stay with your mama."

"Thanks." Callie picks him up and *oofs* again, as he becomes deadweight. "We'll see you next week at gymnastics?"

"Sure will." He looks at me and smiles. "Looking forward to it." Then he turns away and walks to his car.

A single laugh comes out of Callie's mouth. "Oh, he *so* has the hots for you."

I snap my head over to look at her. "He does not."

She nods again with a smirk on her face. "Oh yeah, he does. And I approve my friend. And I want details when you finally get in those pants."

"Ohmygod, you're ridiculous." I laugh and head towards my own car.

I would never admit it, but I kind of hope she's right.

CHAPTER
Four

There it is. The one-eyed monster shaped like a box on the floor of my bathroom. Where that eyeball looks will determine how I feel about myself today.

I hate that thing, but it's a necessary evil, right?

Blowing out the last of the air in my body because surely it'll make a difference, I step up on the scale.

155, 163, 158…. I quickly close my eyes as it swings back and forth to its destination. I can't look anymore.

"Mama?" Maura meanders into the room, pushing her blond ringlets out of her face.

"Hi baby. No don't stand up here with me, honey." I gently push her backward off the scale while I take a gander at the results this morning.

Well, it's not good. But I guess it could be worse.

"What are you doing, Mama?" Maura watches closely as the scale resets itself, now that I've stepped off.

"I'm weighing myself."

"Why?" She stands up on it and starts bouncing up and down, excited that it keeps adjusting over and over again.

"Because I need to see how much more baby fat I need to lose," I answer absentmindedly, grabbing my new dress out of the closet.

"Why?"

I grit my teeth before answering. It's Maura's newest favorite game. Sometimes the "why" game can be funny. Usually, though, she waits until the least opportune times to play it. Getting ready for my ex-husband and his new wife to come over for a birthday party is one of those times.

"Because I'm tired of being fat."

"Why?"

I open my mouth to respond, but realize, I don't have an answer for her. Why *am* I tired of being fat? Looking over, I see Maura has pulled her shirt up and is pinching the skin of her tummy.

That stops me cold.

I hate how my body looks now. I hate that it has lumps and bumps and cellulite. I hate that I'll never wear a bikini and feel confident about it again. And I hate that my husband used my body's changes as an excuse to cheat on me.

But that little girl right there, the one twisting her body so she can look at her rear, like I do when I'm looking at myself in the mirror, she doesn't need me to start her down the rabbit hole of body image regrets. She'll get enough of that from everyday peer pressure.

I don't know if it's seeing the big 4-0 looming in the distance, but it's like I got smacked over the head with some wisdom. Well, shit. Looks like I need to figure out how to make peace with these lumps and bumps if I'm going to raise mentally and emotionally healthy girls.

I hate it when I'm a good mom sometimes!

"You know what, baby?" She untwists her body and looks over at me, big brown eyes full of trust. "Hop down. We don't need this thing anymore."

"How come?" She swings her arms back as far as she can so she can jump the three inches to the floor. This is why kids stay skinny. They overexaggerate all their movements. Every time. I should try that.

Once her feet hit the tile, I pick up the scale and turn to throw it away. "Because it doesn't matter if I'm fat or skinny. It matters if I'm healthy. And this one-eyed monster here isn't going to help with that."

I toss it onto the trashcan. Of course, it won't fit because bathroom trashcans are too small. And because of its bulk, it knocks the trashcan off balance and everything clatters to the floor.

Maura purses her lips and looks up at me. "It doesn't fit, Mama."

"Nope. It sure doesn't."

"Max is taking a nap, Mama."

"Not anymore she's not," I respond.

Sure enough, within seconds, I hear the birthday girl raising holy hell in her bedroom.

Again, this is what I get for being a good mom sometimes.

I throw the dress over my head as I walk down the hallway to her room. Sure enough, snotty face McGee is screaming like her fingers are being cut off. As soon as she sees me, though, the crying stops completely and she smiles.

"Uh huh." I grab her new big-girl panties and rip the sleepy time diaper off. "I'm onto you, you little twerp. You're not *actually* hysterical, you just know I get here faster when you *sound* hysterical, right? Am I right?" I coo at her and tickle her tummy, making her giggle. I love that sound.

A quick glance over at the clock on the nightstand… shit.

1:55

Mom and Callie are going to be here any minute, and I'm still not ready to go.

We race back to the master bathroom, Max content to use the toilet scrubber to clean the bathtub. Not well, mind you. She's only turning three. But that one spot, the spot she scrubs every time she's in here, is starting to look really good.

A swipe of mascara and lip gloss, and some eyebrows painted on because otherwise you can't see them. And now for my signature hair style…

A low messy bun in the back. It's the only "updo" I know how to do when leaving my hair down isn't an option. I don't have time to flat iron. I don't know how to use a curling iron. Scrunchie sprays don't seem to work with my hair anymore. This is the best I've got.

I sigh as I look at myself in the mirror. Not for the first time, I can understand how James could trade me in for a newer model. The exterior package is looking ragged lately.

How did I get here? How did I go from being a pretty woman in my twenties to flat out frumpy and pushing forty?

A knock and the sound of the front door opening pulls me away from the pity party. I've got a different kind of party to focus on now.

Thank goodness my mom and Callie enjoy entertaining because I hate all the planning that goes with birthday parties. I have never been good at throwing parties. I never will be. I would much rather toss some money at Chuck-E-Cheese and let them do it all than implement one myself. And that says a lot because I loathe Chuck-E-Cheese.

Yet somehow, I was convinced that my own backyard would be perfect for a birthday barbeque for all our closest family and friends. That it would be cheaper or more intimate or something like that. Who knows. As long as they spearhead it all, I don't really care.

"Oooh! You look pretty," Callie's carrying a giant cake box through the front door and heads straight for the kitchen. There's no telling what's in that box and I'll admit, I'm almost a little scared.

"You look lovely, honey," my mom reiterates, giving me a kiss on the cheek and carrying several bags of presents. "Is that your new dress? It's really pretty."

I smooth invisible wrinkles out of the front of my outfit. "Yeah. It's not too short, is it? I don't usually show this much leg."

"Not at all. But what shoes are you going to wear?"

"I got your shoes, Mama!" Maura yells as she comes barreling down the stairs, the red Jessica Simpson stilettos that we lovingly refer to as "ketchup shoes" in her hand. Maura started calling them that the first time I wore them because of their color. I didn't notice when I bought them, but they really are the exact shade of ketchup. Now I get hungry for French fries every time I wear them.

My mother shoots me an amused glance. We both know the heels are way too high for this short of a dress. They're going to make me look like a hooker. But the huge smile and look of delight on Maura's face makes it impossible for me to wear anything else.

"Thank you, baby," I coo, as I take the shoes from her. "They're perfect."

By the look of delight on her face as she scampers away, I know I made the right decision.

"You are never going to last through the whole party wearing those shoes." My best friend, folks. Always the realist.

"Shut up," I say, as I stumble a bit, trying to balance on one foot to put the opposite on. Fortunately, my mother catches me and I hold onto her shoulder from that point on. Well, while I'm putting my shoes on, anyway. "And don't give me any shit. You seem to have forgotten about last year's Christmas card and the macaroni necklace you wore in the photo. What was the designer's name again? Christoph? Christy-...."

"Christopher. And yeah, yeah, I get your point," she acquiesces, and begins hanging pink streamers around my living room.

"What's in the giant cake box, anyway? You didn't go overboard did you?"

My mom laughs as she pulls a giant pink Happy Birthday sign out of her shopping bag.

I know that laugh. It means she did exactly the opposite of what I asked. "Oh no. What did you do?"

Callie has the audacity to look offended. "Why do you automatically think I did something?"

I point at my mother. "Because I know that snort laugh, and it means you went overboard."

"It's true," Mom agrees. "It's situation specific laugh."

"You two are weird. It's just a cake, Elena."

"A two-tiered cake with bright pink fondant and a limited-edition Barbie sitting on top," Mom declares.

I throw my hands in the air. "Callie!"

"What? She needed a kick-ass cake," Callie argues.

"When she's three?" I argue back. "Maybe when she's sixteen. I'm gonna have leftovers for weeks."

She waves me off like my concerns are ridiculous. "Whatever. Pass me those streamers?" She points to a purple roll that I pick up and hand to her while she continues to squabble with me. "You've got a lot of people coming to this party and most of them are adults. I guarantee you'll need it."

I narrow my eyes at her. "We'll see, friend. We'll see."

Sure enough, two hours and two dozen people later, it seems she was right about the cake. It's been devoured with almost nothing left over.

I hate when she's right about these things.

The shindig is still in full swing as I try to get things a little more organized. If I thought my mother and Callie overdid it on the food, again, I was wrong. These people can eat! I've already refilled all the trays of food more than once, but they're empty again.

Kids are running around outside, playing on the swing set and shooting squirt guns at each other. James and Ben are manning the grill, which is why Callie and I are avoiding that area. Random neighbors are standing around conversing. It's low-key. It's relaxing. Max is happy she has presents. I got to eat a couple of my beloved hot dogs, *which are my favorite.* So far, there are no complaints from me.

Except that Keri is here.

She's spending most of her time touching James. Rubbing his back while he grills, putting her arm around his waist while he carries on conversations, demanding kisses no matter what's happening and who is watching, the way an insecure high schooler might do. And if I hear her talking about how much she loves my kids one more time, I might deck her.

Ok, that's not true. I've never punched someone in my life. But I might seriously visualize it. Max has never even spent the night with them. I had it written up in the court order… no weekend visits until she turns three.

And now she's three. That means Max's first weekend away from me in the last three years and nine months will be this coming weekend. And she'll be staying with her father and *Keri*. If that little reminder, who keeps shooting ugly stares at me, isn't enough to make me crazy, nothing is. So I avoid coming in close contact with them as much as I can.

For the last year and a half, I've tried really hard to not put the girls in the middle of this divorce, even when my own heart was being shredded to pieces. I've not spoken an ill-word about him in front of them, even if he deserves it. I've not discouraged Fiona and Maura from their visits, even if a little part of me dies each time they walk out the door. I've always tried to make them think I'm excited about them spending time with their dad so they never feel like they have to choose alliances. It's the right thing to do for the girls. But it also means at family events I get to watch Step Monster Barbie play the role of loving stepmother, a title she only gets by default. It can wear on a person after a couple hours.

Now, I'm bustling around the kitchen, refilling bowls with chips and cleaning out the remnants of dip, trying to regroup.

No such luck on that. *Keri* walks in.

"Do you need any help?" Her eyes are wide and she's smiling sweetly at me. If I didn't already know what a homewrecking whore she was, I would think she was genuine. No wonder my husband, *ex*-husband fell for her shit. It's probably the same pure innocent act she used on him.

But I've spent the last two hours catching her shooting daggers at me from a distance while she tries to play like my family is actually hers. I know she's up to something. But I'll play nice.

It's for the girls... it's for the girls... Keep reminding yourself of that, Elena.

"No, I'm ok. Thanks." I brush her off and keep loading the dishwasher, hoping she'll take the hint and go back to her asshole. I mean husband.

She doesn't.

Instead, she saunters right over to the counter and opens a bag of chips. I roll my eyes to the heavens and say a quick prayer for patience. Yes, I allowed James to bring her, but not for us to "hang out".

"It's ok. The guys are talking business anyway," she says pleasantly while I do my best to get this knife in the silverware tray and not launch it at her head. "You know how James is... all business all the time."

"Unless he's screwing his secretary," I mumble under my breath.

She turns to look at me. "I'm sorry? I didn't hear what you said."

"Oh, it's nothing." I give her the same wide eyes and sweet smile she gave me earlier.

She briefly raises an eyebrow in irritation. It happens so fast, if I hadn't been looking for a reaction, I would never have seen it. I admit, I've made a game out of ruffling her feathers sometimes. Knowing I still have at least that much control makes me excessively happy. But isn't that true of every woman scorned? None of us like giving a shit. And for the most part, we don't spend our days fixating on it. But to know you can get a little dig in here and there, it feels like taking back a tiny little piece of the dignity she stole from me when she stole my husband.

Not that he's any prize. At least not anymore. Fifteen years ago, maybe he was. Turns out lying and deceit don't help you age well. Too bad I didn't see it until now.

"Max looks like she's having a good time." Keri tries again to engage me in small talk as she washes her hands of any chip crumbs.

"Hmm," I say noncommittally.

She sighs and leans against the counter, crossing her arms and feet. "Elena, at some point we're going to have to be friends."

And there it is. The dead giveaway that there's more to the sweet smile and puppy-dog eyes. She's here to shake things up a bit. Create some drama. Pretend she has good intentions so I fall for her crap and she gets what she wants, when we all know how self-absorbed she really is.

As I turn around to have this conversation I've been avoiding, just to get it over with, I take a step back and trip over the open dishwasher door. Fortunately, I catch myself by grabbing the counter before I fall over and break the appliance. Forget looking like an idiot. I'm irritated, and maybe a little angry that Bend Me Over Barbie would try to make nice after upending my life, I don't even care.

"What did you say?"

She sighs again, this time like she's annoyed with me... with *me*... never mind that she's a guest in *my* home. "Look, I know I'm not your favorite person…"

"You think?"

"But the reality is, we will be raising these children together. They're my stepchildren. I have a vested interest in their lives." I cock my head in disbelief. Surely, she didn't say that. The anger is starting to take over the irritation.

For the girls… for the girls… for the girls… I keep trying to remind myself, but she won't stop talking.

"And now that Max will be spending the night, it'll work better for everyone if we were friends."

Thank God for my best friend and her impeccable timing. Before I can open my mouth and go against the self-imposed rules I set up for this divorce, Callie walks in carrying an armful of dirty plates. She drops them in the sink, splashing just enough water droplets on our pretty, pretty princess that she squeals.

"Ugh, Callie, be careful! This is a three-hundred-dollar blouse I'm wearing," Keri squeals.

Callie turns slowly and I take another step back… this time very carefully. I'd know that signature move of hers anywhere. It's calculated. It's cold. It means bad, bad words are about to come out of her mouth.

"Since you are now *raising Elena's children*," she emphasizes and I already know this isn't going to go well for my friend. For me? It's going peachy, so far. Especially when she picks up a fork covered in icing and starts running her forefinger over it, smoothing the icing down. "A good rule of thumb is to never wear expensive clothes to a three-year old's birthday party. You never know when someone will accidentally get icing on you." Quickly, Callie flicks the fork. Not hard. Just hard enough that a few tiny specks of icing fly out and land on Keri's shirt.

Of course, Project Runway Barbie squeals again. Only this time she grabs a wet rag from the counter while she does it. "Was that necessary?"

"I have no idea what you're talking about," Callie says with her own fake innocence. I still haven't made a move. Frankly, I'm too entertained by this whole episode. And it's nice having a "bad cop" sidekick so I can stay true to my "good cop" desires.

"I get it, ok?" Keri continues scrubbing at the icing on her shirt. "You're still mad because James chose me."

Simultaneous gasps come from Callie and me. "She did not say that," I whisper.

"Pretty sure she did," Callie whispers back.

Keri rolls her eyes and tosses the rag back in the sink, positioning herself with her hands on her hips like she's making a stand of some sort. "I can hear you, even when you whisper, you know."

"We know," Callie answers. "But it's more fun to pretend we're talking behind your back."

"Look. We have to get along enough that we can help each other raise these kids. That's what co-parenting means."

Callie lets out a cackle and clutches her hand to her heart. "You think… you think first, third and fifth weekends is… is raising children?" She's laughing so hard, she's bent over to catch her breath. I assume this is an exaggerated laugh for dramatic purposes, because it really wasn't all that funny. But knowing Callie, she's about to go in for the kill, so I let it ride.

She finally pulls herself together enough to wipe the invisible tears from her eyes. "Oh, sweetie. Taking the kids to the movies and out to dinner isn't raising them. It's babysitting. You aren't helping raise these children. You're going on play dates so this one here," she gestures to me with her thumb, "can go out and get a little R and R."

Keri narrows her eyes. "That's not fair," she declares. "We do time outs and baths and… and family dinners as much as anyone else. It's not our fault he only gets the kids three times a month and on Thursdays."

Callie and I look at each other and we both start laughing this time.

"You think he takes them on Thursdays?" I ask.

"I *know* he does," she says defensively. "We specifically set up Thursday nights as a night apart so he could go with the kids and I could go to hot box yoga."

My eyebrows shoot up and Callie stops laughing. Suddenly, this conversation isn't funny. As much as I despise Keri, it seems she's becoming a woman scorned way faster than I was. I got almost fifteen years before my relationship caved. They haven't even been married a year yet. "Keri, he hasn't picked the kids up for Thursday dinner since the week before Christmas."

Her face pales. "I don't believe you."

"You don't have to," Callie interjects, "but Elena cancelled her weekly book club meetings because he stopped showing up."

If it's possible, Keri's face pales even further. I sort of feel sorry for her. Well, for a few seconds anyway. Then she straightens her spine, puts her hands on her hips, and opens her mouth.

"You think I'm going to believe what you tell me over what my *husband* tells me? We took vows of honesty and trust."

Callie sniggers. I smack her arm, never looking way from Keri. If she wants to be delusional, that's her problem.

"You are not going to sabotage my marriage by planting seeds of doubt in my mind. He loves me more than he's ever loved anyone. He told me." I cringe at her words. He told me the same thing at one time, too. But, of course, she's not done with her rant.

"First the hooker shoes and short skirt. Now this. I know what you're trying to do and it shows terrible character on your part that you would try to come between a woman and her husband."

"Ok, time for you to go, Delusional Barbie," Callie announces, grabbing Keri by the arm and dragging her to the back door. "You may have a lot of things, but room to judge someone on her integrity is not one of them."

"Let me go!" Keri squeals as Callie opens the door.

"Gladly." She practically shoves Keri out the door and slams it in her face. Through the window, I see her huff and stomp her way to James's side where she demands, yet another kiss in front of the neighbors.

"You ok?"

I blink and jump when she startles me. "Geez, woman. How did you get close to me so fast?"

"I have the super power of speed. Now seriously, don't go back into your head," she warns.

"I'm not." But I'm lying. I am. James used to tell me all the time that he loved me more than he'd ever loved anyone. Even up to a couple of weeks before he left me. Now I question how long ago his eye, and his dick, started wandering.

"Bullshit. I can see your eyes glazing over."

I sigh. "Is this skirt too short? Does it make my legs look fat?"

"What's your definition of fat? Because if you're comparing to chicken legs out there, that's not a fair comparison. I could snap her thigh in half with my pinkie."

I smirk.

"You know I'm telling you the truth." She puts her hand on my forearm and goes into serious mode. It doesn't happen often, but it does happen. "Elena, you're a *woman*, not a child. You're supposed to have curves and scars and embellishments."

"Embellishments? Is that what we're calling cellulite now?"

"Do you really want to drag serious mode out? Stop joking so I can finish my point."

"Sorry." I press my lips together and pretend I'm zipping them closed.

"Like I was saying, you're a woman. A beautiful, desirable woman. You do not let her come in here with her passive aggressive bullshit and make this birthday party about anything other than a celebration of Max. Do you understand?"

I look at the floor and nod. She's right. Today isn't about me. Or Keri. Or James. It's about Max and Max alone.

"What you're saying is, you'd do me if you swung that way?"

"In a heartbeat." We smile, knowing there is no better compliment than a straight woman telling another straight woman she's 'doable'. "Now let's get this food out there to your guests before they mistake her chicken legs for buffalo wings."

Serious mode is officially over. Birthday party mode is back on.

CHAPTER
Five

"When does James pick up the kids?" Callie grabs Christopher before he climbs up the steps to the balance beam and barrels over Max as she walks across it. I could cringe, but it wouldn't be the first time he knocked her off.

I take her little hand and help her walk slowly, while Callie wrestles with Christopher on the stairs. Again.

"Tomorrow after school."

"You ok with him taking Max?"

That is the million-dollar question. Now that she's officially three, he gets the same visitation as he does with the others—first, third, and fifth weekend of the month.

It's been hard letting the older two go with him for their visits. Not because I think he's a bad dad. He's not. He's not as attentive as I'd like, but he's not abusive or anything. It goes against my nature as their mother to be away from them this much. Sending Max away, too, makes it that much harder.

"I'm not thrilled, but there's nothing I can do about it, ya know? I'm trying not to think too much about it." Max gets to the end of the beam and I help her jump down to the floor, pride radiating off her face. "Fiona is old enough that she can report to me if anything goes wrong. And she knows how to make basic sandwiches if Home Wrecker Barbie forgets to feed them."

Callie finally lets Christopher go and he runs across the beam as fast as he can. He trips with just a few feet left to run and tumbles to the ground. Not one adult in the gym even blinks twice. We're all used to his rough and tumble ways. Sure enough, almost as soon as he hits the floor, he's on his feet, racing to a springboard and jumping onto a few stacked-up mats. Max races behind him and, somehow, they end up falling in a heap on top of the springboard.

We meander our way across the room, careful not to get too far away from the kids.

"I hate him," Callie grumbles. "He's such a jerk and of course he married the worst woman in the entire world. I understand how hard it is to raise kids with a deadbeat dad. But I feel like that's better than all this fake shit they do."

"I know. He was such a distant parent when we were married that you know they're eventually going to dump out of my kids' lives at some point. Why put them through all the back and forth now?"

"That's easy. To shove their psychotic relationship in your face."

I roll my eyes. "You think they'll ever figure out that I genuinely don't care that they're together? That if they were hit by a bus tomorrow the only tears I would shed would be for the sad looks on my kids' faces?"

"They're never going to understand that, my friend. They're delusional enough to think none of us see through their games."

It's true. Yes, the betrayal still stings. But any emotion I have towards either of them is gone.

"Mama, Mama!" Max yells from a few feet away. I turn my attention in her direction as she does a forward roll down the cheese-shaped mat. She lands with a flop on her back, spread out like a starfish, but we clap for her improvement anyway—she didn't roll sideways off the mat this time.

As we clap, I feel him come up behind us before he even says anything.

"Hey, uh, Callie?"

I can't help but feel a little jealous that he addresses her first. It's ridiculous, but sometimes I wish a hot guy would be interested in me. Even if it never goes anywhere.

"Oh, hey Greg," she says with a smile. "We didn't see you before. Did you get here late?"

"Yeah, my ex decided Peyton was too sick to come today."

The three of us look over at the young girl happily throwing a scarf in the air and catching it.

"Uh. yeah. She looks really under the weather," I retort.

"She made a miraculous recovery, right? But hey... did you see where Christopher is?" He points to the bars, and we watch as Tarzan shimmies his way up the side to the high bar.

"Hell..." she mutters and stomps away, yelling, "Christopher! You get down from there right now. We've talked about this!"

I laugh under my breath.

"I have no idea how she keeps up with him," Greg remarks.

"She doesn't." Callie stands underneath Christopher, grasping at his feet as he hangs on to the high bar for dear life and flails his legs to get her way from him. If I hadn't seen this happen a million times before, I'd question her ability to contain him.

Oh, who am I kidding. I'd be laughing at her and thanking my lucky stars it wasn't me.

"She baby-proofed pretty much her entire house the minute he started walking," I tell him.

Callie finally gets a good grasp of Christopher and yanks him down, the force throwing them both to the mat. Greg and I both laugh.

"I really wish I would remember to have my camera rolling at all times when they're around."

"Is that funny videos show still on TV?" he asks. "You could probably win serious money by putting together some sort of montage of them."

"I was thinking more like a YouTube channel."

"That could work." I smile at him and notice he's smiling back at me. And not just a friendly smirk when he glances my direction. He's really *looking* at me and grinning. Like Peyton could fall off that weird rock wall thing or get stuck in a hula hoop and he wouldn't even notice because he's looking *at me*.

I get a weird sensation of butterflies in my stomach. Part nervous. Part excited. And a significant part of me that doesn't want to get my hopes up, especially since, once again, I didn't plan to talk to a hot guy and I'm wearing yoga pants and a stained t-shirt. I need to get a grip.

"How much longer do we have in class?" Callie puffs out, as she drags Christopher behind her. I mean "drags" in a very literal sense. He's made himself dead weight behind her and refuses to stand up.

I look at the clock. "We've still got twenty minutes."

She strains as she makes one last effort to lug Christopher to the mat and drops him on the floor. "We doing lunch when we're done?"

"I assumed. Don't we always do lunch?"

"Yes, but this one is extra-hyper today. I'm not sure... Christopher!" she calls out as he starts running back towards the bar. "Good god, will this child ever listen to me?"

"Christopher, stop!" Greg yells after him. And whatdoyouknow... the little shit stops and turns around. "Your mother said stop. Come back here please."

Callie and I watch with our mouths wide open in disbelief, as Christopher walks right over to Greg who squats down in front of the tot. "Your mother said you can't go on that high bar. Do you understand?" Christopher nods. "Good. Now you can walk over and swing on the low bar. But if you try to climb to the top, you will sit against the wall until your mom says you can get up. Do you understand me?" Christopher nods again. This time Greg smiles at him. "Good job, bud. Give me five, right here." Christopher slaps his hand, a smile on his face. "Remember what I said...walk to that low bar."

"Holy. Shit," Callie whispers, as we watch Christopher calmly walk exactly where Greg told him to go. "Are you some kind of magician? No, you're a witch, right? Or warlock. Isn't that what they call a guy witch?"

Greg bends down and picks up Peyton, who pops her thumb in her mouth and lays her head on his shoulder. "Nah. Sometimes little boys just respond better to men."

"He doesn't listen to my husband."

"Your husband doesn't talk to him unless he's disciplining him," I remind her.

"I don't know why he doesn't respond to your husband, but there's a lot of different research on the topic." Greg absentmindedly rubs Peyton's back, and I can't help another twinge of jealousy. Not because I want my back rubbed, but because I know James doesn't do that with my kids. "Some people think it has something to do with testosterone responding to testosterone. But there's also some research that shows a lot of boys hear lower toned voices better, which typically is a man's voice versus a woman's voice."

"Well, whatever the reason, if you can get my kid to respond and obey, you and I are going to become great friends," Callie says with a wink and a smile. "Would you like to join us for lunch again today?"

I swear Greg looks over at me when he answers. "Count me in."

Forty-five minutes later, we're at our favorite post-gym restaurant... McDonalds. The kids are, once again, taking over the playscape. And we are, once again, munching on their forgotten Happy Meals.

"Have you put together your birthday list for your mom yet?" Callie knows my mom refuses to buy birthday or Christmas presents anymore if she doesn't have a list of exact colors, sizes and brands. I suspect it's from hearing my brother bitch one too many times about not getting the right thing, so she gave up. I guess it's nice that we always get what we want. But I like surprises, too.

"Your birthday is coming up?" Greg asks as he licks ketchup off his thumb. I have no idea why I noticed that, but it was actually kind of sexy.

Oh boy. I've hit a new low.

"It's not for a couple of weeks."

"Oh. Do you have big plans?" he asks.

"Not really. I guess birthdays were never really that big of a deal in our house. Now Christmas, we do up Christmas like you've never seen. But birthdays mean celebrating that my parents had sex."

Apparently, he wasn't expecting that response, because he chokes on his drink.

Callie begins banging on his back. "You ok there? Didn't expect our girl to be so blunt?"

He shakes his head back and forth. "Nope," he coughs out.

I shrug with a smile. "Sorry." No, I'm not. "I guess once you hit thirty, no one really pays attention to your birthday anymore," I say once he's pulled himself back together.

Callie points at me with a fry. "No, *you* don't pay attention to your birthday anymore because you don't like drawing that much attention to yourself." The fry flops around as she keeps talking. "Some of us, on the other hand, want to do it up big every year. Cakes and streamers and a giant sign that reads 'Happy Birthday, Calixta' in twinkly lights." She throws her arms out wide in exaggeration and half the fry flies off. It lands on the floor right in front of Max who promptly snags it up and eats it before running to the colorful stairs again.

We're such a classy bunch.

"Calixta, huh?" Greg says, still whacking his chest. "You ever read *The Storm*?"

Callie's eyes widen and her jaw drops open in delight. "By Kate Chopin?"

He nods and smiles.

"Ohmygod, my mother did a paper on it in college. She was fascinated by it. Said it was a revolutionary book for a woman to write in 1898." She smacks him on his arm. "I can't believe you knew that!"

"My mother was a college professor. Taught all kinds of literature classes so the bookshelves were stocked."

A squeal rings out and we all turn simultaneously to stare at the playscape. When no one starts wailing, it's an unspoken determination that no one is bleeding or dead and we return to our conversation.

"Anyway," Greg continues, "when I was nine or ten, my mom wouldn't let me go to a friend's house or ride my bike or something until I finished reading a book. It was this ongoing argument she and I used to have." He pops another fry in his mouth and takes a quick sip of his drink. Seriously. How does a man make a beard look sexy?

"I was determined that I would show her," he says with mock indignation. "So, I grabbed the shortest book I could find." He nods again with an ornery smile. "My mom was pissed when she realized what I had read."

Callie howls with laughter and Greg keeps munching, with an ornery smile on his face.

I look back and forth between them, trying to ignore the weird jealous feelings that have popped up now that they have an inside joke.

"Um, hi," I blurt out. "Anyone want to explain why that's funny?"

Callie wipes a tear from her eye. "The entire book, actually, I wouldn't even call it a book. It's more like an essay. But it's about a woman who is married with children and has an affair."

"Very, very torrid," Greg says.

"Not torrid at all," Callie disputes.

"Torrid to a nine-year-old boy."

Callie looks at me and changes her answer. "Very, very torrid."

"How many times are you guys gonna say torrid?" I jest.

"Until it confuses our brains and loses all meaning." Callie doesn't miss a beat. She can go on like this for hours.

"Pretty sure I'm already there." I wipe my hands on a napkin and lean my elbows on the table. "But what I want to know, Greg, is how many times you read the book for the name to have stuck with you."

A slight blush covers the apples of his cheeks and he ducks his head, still snacking. "A few."

"A few?"

He wipes his own hands and throws the napkin on the table. "Let's just say when I moved away to college, Mom found it under my bed. Dog-eared to a certain page."

Callie and I both laugh this time.

"That's such a guy thing," Callie giggles.

"Get ready," Greg says as he turns to look at the kids again, Max and Christopher rolling down the slide. I can't tell which limbs belong to which kids. "I can tell you right now, you're going to find a lot of porn on that kid's devices when he's in high school."

Callie grimaces. "He better not. The minute I find out he's been looking at nudie pics, I refuse to do his laundry anymore."

"What do those two things have to do with each other?" I ask.

She points another floppy fry at me. "I have a brother. I know what crusty socks mean they've been doing."

Greg chokes on his drink again and Callie reaches over to hit him on the back again. "You really need to get used to the things we sometimes say."

"No kidding," he chokes out the words, as he bangs a fist on his chest, face turning bright red from all the pounding going on. "You two are determined to kill me."

I smirk. He really has no idea how crazy we can get. But I have a feeling he's going to find out.

CHAPTER Six

It's shocking how much a single mom can get done on the weekends her kids aren't home. We're so good at multitasking on a daily basis, having no children under foot means remarkable focus. Not to mention, you only have to pick up toys *once*. Wipe down the bathroom sink *once*. Do the dishes *once*. Most of us forget how easy cleaning house really can be when you're not cleaning the same things eighteen times a day.

Now my house is practically spotless. The laundry is folded and put away. There are even a half dozen pre-made meals in the freezer. To say I've been productive over the last two days would be an understatement.

I don't normally plan these things. I am far from June Cleaver. I don't even have a Pinterest account. The last thing I need is another internet vortex to suck me in.

No, the reality is, I tried very hard to keep busy so my mind didn't wander.

I've never been away from Max this long, and more importantly, she's never been away from *me*. Don't get me wrong, it's been hard having Fiona and Maura gone as well. But they're so much older that it doesn't feel quite the same. They can fend for themselves. Max is just *little*.

When the divorce was being mediated, James wanted her for weekend visits immediately, but I nixed that idea. She wasn't even two and I had been a stay-at-home mom. It was rare that James made it home before she went to bed when we were living in the same house, so by the time we'd been separated for a few months, they didn't know each other hardly at all. Not because I kept the kids from him, but because James kept being James. Nothing is more important to him than, well, him. At the time of mediation, it hardly seemed fair to traumatize a child. It seems everyone else involved agreed.

I negotiated that James have her for a two-hour dinner every Tuesday and Thursday and part of the day Saturday. Of course, he stopped showing up for dinners right after Christmas, so any chance to build a relationship with her before weekend visits started disappeared quickly.

But now she's old enough to stay with him. Turns out, three years old seemed much older during mediation than it does in this moment.

That leads me back to my excessive Betty Crocker weekend. Instead of worrying for two days about if Max was tired or scared or hungry, I focused on getting as much done as possible. That way, when they get home, I will be completely available to them to do whatever damage control is needed.

Now that they'll be here any minute, though, I have nothing left to do, and the worrying is out of control. I've been pacing for the last ten minutes, expecting the worst.

A quiet knock makes me jump, then race over to the door and swing it open.

James has his finger to his lips. "Shhh. She fell asleep in the car." Sure enough, Max has her head on his shoulder, her light brown hair covering her face like she rubbed her head back and forth in her sleep. "I'm gonna...." he whispers and gestures to the stairs. I nod and move out of his way, understanding he's taking her to lay her down.

And then I look down to see the older two. My entire face widens in shock.

What. The. Hell. Happened to my kids?

Maura skips right over to me and hugs my legs tight. "Hi, Mama."

"Hi baby." I hug her back, trying to maintain control of my emotions. But when I try to run my fingers through her hair, there's so much hair spray and goop in it, my nails get stuck.

"I'm gonna go show my Barbies my new dress." She skips away, leaving a smear of lipstick on my pants. My five-year-old daughter is wearing LIPSTICK!

Glancing up in the doorway, there is Fiona, staring at me. She has a full face of make-up, an updo, and a huge scowl on her face. "I look like a Barbie doll."

I nod in agreement, too shocked to even respond, as she stomps over to the couch and plops down, crossing her arms. Before I pull my thoughts together, James saunters back down the stairs, cool as a cucumber. If that cucumber was a jackass that let his five-year-old channel Tammy Faye Baker.

"Max should be down for a while," he says, completely missing the look of horror I'm sure is still on my face. "She had a really busy day and this is the first nap she's had—"

"James—" I interrupt with a blink and wave of my hand. "What the hell did you do?"

"What?" He looks legitimately confused as to what I'm talking about.

"You seriously don't know?" He stares blankly at me. "Why do the girls look like they stepped out of an episode of *Toddlers and Tiaras*?"

"Oh that. Don't they look pretty?" He smiles over at Fiona who narrows her eyes back.

"They look like they should be on the pageant circuit," I practically shout.

He rolls his eyes like I'm the one who over does things. Me. Not his little twat wife who turned my daughters into mini-hookers. *I'm* the one over-exaggerating. "That's not very nice," he reprimands. "The girls in pageants work very hard and win a lot of college scholarships."

I blink rapidly, making sure I heard him correctly.

Yep. I did. He seems to see no problem with his daughters being dressed up like they're trolling for dates in the toy aisle.

"I'm sure pageant contestants do work hard. But to compete requires A," I tick off my arguments on my fingers, "their mother being involved, and B, an actual pageant!"

"Oh calm down, Elena. They look pretty."

"Pretty? They look like two-bit whores!"

"There's no reason to be judgmental," he argues. "You of all people have no room to talk about someone else's looks."

I reel back like I've been slapped. His words shouldn't surprise me. It's not like I haven't heard variations of this from him before. That I'm not pretty enough, and I'm not skinny enough, and I'm not good enough. That doesn't mean it stings any less.

But just like the other week with the scale in the bathroom, I have a lightbulb moment—I'm not married to him anymore. I don't have to put up with this shit.

The realization is freeing. I take a breath and walk to the door, pulling it open. "Ok. Well, on that note, thanks for dropping them off. We'll see you in a couple of weeks."

"Don't be like that, Elena," he whines. "This isn't a big deal."

I cut him off with a raise of my hand. "There is a difference between helping the girls do their hair and making them pedophile bait. If the new missus is looking for someone to play Dress Up Barbie with, give her her own baby."

"You're making a mountain—"

"Bye, James."

He sighs and walks out the door, me slamming it behind him.

"Mom." I look over at Fiona who hasn't said a single word since she walked in. "I don't want to go over there anymore."

"I know, baby. But you don't really have a choice right now."

"No, Mom. You don't understand." I take a seat next to her on the couch and she turns her entire foundation-and-goop-covered body towards me. Is this even my daughter? I can't tell. Her skin has an unnatural orange hue to it. "Keri hates me," Fiona says. "I told her I didn't want to play dress up, and she told me little girls need to look their best to be successful. And I told her that when I do gymnastics, I'm gonna have a ponytail and I won't need hairspray. But she said girls who do gymnastics don't develop so they never get a man. Whatever that means."

"She said that to you?" I gape at her. Turns out, the term *step-monster* wasn't just a snide remark after all.

"Mom, I don't want a man. I have Daddy. I wanna do gymnastics."

Sighing, I pull her to me and rest my cheek on her head. "I know baby. I promise I'll call about getting you signed up tomorrow, ok?"

I feel her nod against my chest.

"Besides being forced to be a life-sized dress-up doll, did you have fun this weekend?" I stroke her hair, but stop when I realize the strands aren't moving and my hand feels waxy. Gross.

"Yeah." She grabs my hand and starts playing with my fingers. It's a habit she picked up as a baby and never stopped. It seems to comfort her, so I don't mind. "We had movie night and made a picnic in the living room. Keri got mad because Max spilled juice on the carpet."

"She didn't give Max a sippy cup?"

She shakes her head. "Daddy doesn't have any."

Somehow, I'm not surprised.

We stay snuggled together on the couch talking about the movie they watched and Keri's dog, who apparently has bladder issues. I'm both disgusted and wildly amused by that information. Before too long, Maura has joined us and after a few minutes of hugs and snuggles, I look like I've been in a paintball fight. Except with make-up balls.

Our conversation must get too loud because Max wakes up way earlier than normal.

"Ok girls." I move Maura off my lap and set her down on the couch next to me so I can get up. "Let me go get your sister and then we'll sit down for a snack, ok? I made something special."

They cheer and clap their hands, not knowing the "something special" is the same old peanut butter and jelly sandwiches they always have, just triangle shaped with the crusts cut off.

I trudge up the stairs and down the hall to Max's room. I'm glad she felt comfortable enough with her dad to fall asleep in the car and not wake up when he carried her in. I think. The vindictive part of me wishes she would hate him and love me more. But for the mom part of me, it's a load off my mind that she wasn't too afraid to sleep.

I'm still a little concerned about how she's going to react to being home. You never know if a three-year-old will be happy to see her mother after a weekend away, or make a point of giving her the cold shoulder. I guess I'll find out.

Opening the door, I peak in and am stunned by what I see.

"Oh. My. Gawd."

CHAPTER
Seven

"Ohmygawd," Callie practically shrieks. "Why does Max look like a twenty-dollar truck stop hooker after a pay-per-view event?"

I snatch my phone away from her and close the picture file. Normally, I'd be pissed about someone eluding to my daughter being a woman of the night. But considering Max woke up from her nap with black eye make-up smudged down her face, red lipstick smeared all over her cheeks, and stiff bed-head hair that looked like she'd been rolling around, the assessment is somewhat valid.

"See what I'm dealing with? The make-up took long enough to get off of her. But do you know how many times I had to wash and condition her hair before I could finally get a comb through it?"

"Five?"

I freeze. "How did you know that?"

"Lucky guess," she shrugs.

I snap out of it and continue my rant. "It was bad, Callie. Walk-of-Shame Barbie better be glad she didn't come with James to drop them off. I would have laid into her so hard."

"No, you wouldn't have." She pulls the door open and we step inside the cool building as I concede her point.

"Ok, fine, I wouldn't have. But I would have thought very strongly about it! I still am."

"We have an appointment with Kristi," Callie says to the sales woman behind the counter, then turns back to me. "I'm glad you told off James, at least. I'm fine with children's pageants. They're not my gig. But what I'm not fine with is making the child dress like an adult to take them out in public."

"Exactly. Teaching them how to dress and act for a performance competition is one thing. But to turn them into performance ponies every single minute of the day? That's where they crossed the line. That's where *Keri* crossed the line. I'm almost surprised none of them showed up with a fluffer in their mouth."

Callie barks a laugh. "A what?"

"A fluffer." I wave my hands in front of my face. "You know, that plastic thing that goes in their mouth. Makes their teeth look good or something."

"Honey, that's not a fluffer." Callie tries really hard to hold herself together, but she's laughing through her words. "That's a flipper."

"That's what I meant. A flipper. Wait... what the hell is a fluffer?"

The sales woman giggles and slaps a hand over her mouth, clearly eavesdropping. Callie gets a huge grin on her face, knowing she has an audience for our banter.

"A fluffer is the woman who primes a porn star before the camera starts rolling." I look at her quizzically. "You know... she gives him a blow job to get him hard so he can perform?"

By now the sales woman isn't even trying to cover up her amusement. If I was a lesser woman, I'd be an offended customer. But I'm not. I'm a hot mess and I know it. At least I'm making her day brighter by being the dull knife in the drawer today.

"Well it's a good thing they didn't come home with that in their mouths either," I respond, making the cashier laugh so hard she has actual tears in her eyes.

"I'm sorry," she says while fanning her face with her fingers. "I'm not trying to listen. I just... oh boy, I needed that laugh. I'll move over to this register now." I watch her move down a couple stations, wiping the wetness from under her eyes.

"I love that you don't get offended when other people laugh at your expense," Callie mentions as a side note.

"What's the point of being offended? If I was going to be offended by anything, it would be you calling my daughter a woman of the night."

"Are you here for a makeover?" a voice inquires behind me. I barely notice the look on Callie's face before turning around. I really should have paid attention.

"Yes." Standing in front of me is a tall woman, maybe five ten or so, with curves that go on for days. She's got a beautiful face.

And she's scary. Really, really scary. Her eye make-up is the darkest black I've ever seen in my life. Like she's trying to look like a demon. There are no less than four piercings on her face. At least a dozen more in her ears. A tattoo of a snake peaks out from under her collar. And her hair is black with some bright white stripes mixed in. She looks like a modern day Cruella de Vil, except one who makes coats out of people instead of dogs.

"I'm Kristi," she announces, and thrusts a tattoo-covered hand in my direction.

I only hesitate for a second before taking it and squeaking out, "Elena".

The Amazon woman who calls herself Kristi shakes my hand once, extra hard, and then drops it like a rock. "Follow me to my station." Then she turns and barrels away. And I do mean barrels away. She looks like a woman on a mission walking through the store and people move out of her way when they see her coming.

Callie and I follow her, a good ten feet behind.

Leaning into Callie, I whisper, "I don't understand. What did you sign me up for?"

"I asked for their best make-up artist," she whispers back. "They said Kristi is it."

"But, I... her make up is... goth. I don't want to be goth."

"Give her a chance," Callie hisses. "She has to be popular for a reason. I paid extra to get you squeezed in today."

Kristi points to a tall chair next to one of the makeup counters. "Sit here," she orders and pulls various brushes out of the apron she's wearing. I do as she says, not quite sure what else to do. "What are we doing today."

"I don't want to be pierced," I blurt out. Callie takes a step back like she's distancing herself from what is sure to be a shit show, the traitor.

Kristi rolls her eyes. "We don't do that here. We do make-up. That's why the store is called *Make Up Alley*, not *Piercing Alley*."

"Sorry," I say sheepishly. "Today is my fortieth birthday and I'm already emotional and my ex-husband made my little girls look like hookers so I have a love/hate relationship with make-up, and I haven't had anyone show me how to do this in at least fifteen years so I have no idea what to expect and I'm afraid I'm going to look like a clown and my ex's new little arm candy will have yet another reason to make snide comments towards me." I finish my rant and take a breath and the strangest thing happens.

Kristi stares at me, arms crossed, and then her face softens.

"I have a dickhead ex, too."

"You do?"

"Asshole cheated on me so I kicked him to the curb. We've been divorced for twelve years and he still hasn't paid a lick of child support." Her voice sounds gruff, but I can tell we're having some sort of a moment. "Yours traded you in for a younger model?"

I nod.

"What a dick. You're turning forty and your skin looks thirty-two. He'll regret that when the new missus ages faster than you do. It's always the way."

I feel my body relax into the chair as we find some common ground. Out of the corner of my eye, I see Callie inch forward as well. Kristi doesn't seem scary anymore. She seems like a woman who has lived and has interesting stories to tell.

"Ok, Elena..." She looks at my face from all angles, assessing me. "What is our goal here? Do you want to be super glam? A nice daytime look? Or something that will knock your ex to his knees so you can kick him while he's down?"

Callie laughs. "I like the way she thinks."

"Honestly, I just want to feel pretty," I admit. "I don't want to feel forty. I want men to look at me. Not ogle or anything. But a double take every now and then would be nice."

"You want a more polished version of you," Kristi clarifies.

"Yes!" I say excitedly. "That's exactly what I want!"

"And you shall have it."

Kristi proceeds to work her way around the store, gathering different supplies. None of the make-up comes from the same brand. It's a mixture of whatever she thinks will look good.

"What do you think?" Callie asks, as we watch her plod around the room. It's almost like watching that proverbial bull in a china shop. Except I'm not worried she's going to break anything. Except possibly my nose if I say the wrong thing.

"I think she's going to do an amazing job. She seems kind of artistic. Plus, she seems to hate any man who falls under the 'ex' category, so I think that will work to my advantage."

"Unless she makes you look like a motor-cycle chick."

"At which time we will smile, nod politely, hand over our money and go to the nearest grocery store to find some scrub brushes for my face."

Callie nods in silent agreement and steps out of the way as Kristi returns and dumps all the products on the table in front of us.

"First lesson," Kristi begins. "Always start with your eyes. That way if you get them wrong, you can redo it without having to fix your whole face. They are your most important feature. Once you get them the way you want them, the rest of your make up will complete the look."

I spend the next fifteen minutes learning about eye primers and watching as Kristi paints one of my eyes, then do my best to mimic her work on the other side. It's not exactly the same, but according to her, it's the only way I'll learn to do it on my own.

"That wingy thing doesn't look right," I mention, looking at the eyeliner I'm trying to master.

"Sisters but not twins," Kristi says. "Good enough for now. You'll get it."

"I hope so." I blink rapidly a few times, getting used to having this much make-up around my eyes. I don't think my eyelashes have ever felt so heavy.

"What made you decide to come get a makeover anyway?" Kristi focuses her attention on the circles under my eyes, brushing concealer this way and that as she tries to cover up several years' worth of sleep deprivation kids bring with them.

Looking at the ceiling to keep my eyes open wide, I try to answer without moving my face too much. "Um, I got a good look at myself in the mirror the other day and started thinking about how I wish I knew how good I looked when I was twenty. Why didn't I flaunt it back then? Why didn't I play it up, ya know?"

"Relax your face." Kristi pulls the brush away from my face. I look around for Callie who seems to have gotten lost in the abyss of never-ending cosmetics.

"I started thinking about what it'll be like when I'm sixty. I don't want to wake up in twenty years and think about how good I had it when I was forty. Why not play it up now?"

"I like that perspective." Kristi hands me the concealer and the same brush she was using. "Here, do what I did."

I look in the round mirror next to me and try to imitate her moves. Three small dots of concealer, and brushing in downward strokes until it's covering the whole circle. Good lord,

I'm carrying around more baggage than I thought and it's all under my eyes.

"Can I ask you a personal question?" I keep stroking, trying to get my under-eyes just right.

"Sure."

"Why did you decide to be a make-up artist? You don't look the part." I catch her eyes in the mirror and the glare I get in return scares me. "Ohmygod, I'm sorry. I didn't mean to sound judgmental. I'm... oh geez..."

Kristi breaks out into a huge grin and starts laughing. "I'm kidding. I'm not offended at all." She takes the brush from my hands and wipes it off on a tissue before grabbing something new and continuing with her work. "I like make-up. I like how you can manipulate it to present any image you want. For me, I like people to think I'm tough. I like people to think I'm intimidating. But I also like when I can help make someone feel pretty. Or more confident because we covered a scar or something. It's like art to me."

And like a true artist, she begins painting foundation on my face. I don't usually like the goop, but I've never tried it with a brush before. It doesn't feel as heavy as I was expecting.

"That's really nice, Kristi. No wonder you're so popular here."

She stops her movements and looks at me quizzically. "You think I'm popular here?"

"That's what the lady who scheduled our appointment said. She said you're the best make-up artist they have."

She whips her head around to look at the same saleswoman who eavesdropped on our fluffer converstion. The same woman who accidentally catches Kristi looking at her, gets wide eyed and quickly looks away. "Huh," Kristi says under her breath. "I guess I better call her by her name now."

"What do you normally call her?"

"What?" she asks, seeming startled that I heard what she had said. "Oh, um, I call her Gretchen. Like Gretchen Weiner from that movie *Mean Girls*. She's always come across as a prissy little bitch. I had no idea she respected my work so much."

I smirk. "Well she's probably too intimidated to tell you to your face. That's what you wanted to present, right?"

"Good to know my art works." She smiles and once again, I can't help but think about how beautiful she really is. I wonder if she even knows, or if anyone has ever told her how stunning she is. Inside and out. I toy with saying something but realize that's probably crossing a really awkward line.

Plus, I genuinely don't trust that she won't shank me just to prove a point about how tough she is, so I let it go.

Thirty minutes later, Callie walks up, handbasket full of products Ben is going to be thrilled to pay for later.

"Holy shit, Elena. You look fucking amazing." She looks shocked, I kind of want to smack her. "Greg is going to shit himself when he sees you."

Now I want to smack her for bringing up my crush that I refuse to admit I have a crush on.

"Greg? Is that the fucker's name?" Kristi growls, making Callie take a step back.

That's what you get for bringing him up, Callie. Of course, I don't say that out loud. Instead I pat Kristi's arm reassuringly. "No. Greg is a friend of ours, right Callie?" I narrow my eyes at her. "He's a *friend*."

She rolls her eyes. "Sure. He's a *friend*."

"Thank you."

"A friend who wants to jump your bones."

"Callie!" I screech.

She turns to Kristi. "It's true. He's tall and handsome and good with his daughter. And he has the hots for her, but she won't admit she has the hots right back."

I gasp in indignation. "I do not have... I don't... He just..."

"See?" Callie raises an eyebrow, and Kristi nods.

"Oh yeah. She's got it bad."

"*Et tu*, Kristi?" I try to give off the most pathetic look I can muster, but neither of them is falling for it.

"Don't try throwing Shakespere at me," Kristi says, as she starts tossing cosmetics into Callie's basket. "I majored in English lit. It doesn't work on me."

I should be surprised by that last comment, but after spending the last hour with her, nothing about Kristi surprises me anymore.

Taking a final glance at myself in the mirror, I climb off the chair, thanking Kristi profusely for making me look like a way better version of me. She quickly moves away and on to the next customer without so much as a good bye.

Ok. I guess we didn't bond as much as I thought we did.

"I can't wait for you to try out your new makeover on lover boy." Callie switches the basket from one hand to the other, grunting as she moves it. It's filled almost all the way to the top.

"I don't know who lover boy is."

She frowns at me. "Greg. I'm talking about Greg."

"Oh. He's not my lover boy. And I'm not wearing this to the kids' gymnastics class anyway."

"I'm not talking about the class." I know that look on her face. She's getting ready to drop some sort of bomb on me. "I mean at Christopher's birthday party."

I stop in my tracks. "He's coming to Christopher's party?"

She turns around and smiles at me. "Sure is. I texted him this morning and he's bringing Peyton."

I'm not sure what to feel first. Excited that he's coming or annoyed that she has his phone number and they apparently text now. I'll stick with indifference for now.

"Pfft… he's coming on Saturday. We're friends. It's no big deal."

Callie threads her arm through mine and drags me to the checkout counter. "Good. That means you can relax and have fun. Even though you're full of shit and are totally into him."

I opt to ignore her accusation. No use in arguing when we both know she's right. I'll make her pay for all the make-up instead.

CHAPTER
Eight

Today is not the day to be running late. I promised Callie I'd be here an hour before Christopher's birthday party started, but of course it's the only day my doctor had an opening for my wellness check for the next two months. And of *course,* he was running forty-five minutes late. And *of course,* he wanted blood work done and the phlebotomist was on break so I had to wait an additional half hour until she got back from lunch.

Of course.

I'm now half an hour late for the party, despite my mother getting the girls ready to go and wrapping the present for me. There's no way they would still be clean with perfect bows in their hair if I had been the one to do it.

Sometimes I think she's a witch.

Fortunately, the weather cooperated. It's a beautiful day for a backyard barbeque. The sun is out, it's not too hot, and there's a light breeze to keep things cool.

I think the birds are chirping as well, but as I stumble my way through the gate, trying not to drop anything, I can't hear them over Christopher. He keeps yelling at the top of his lungs before running and charging into the football training bag he got for his birthday.

Seriously. What three-year-old needs a giant, NFL grade tackle dummy attached to a speed sled? Christopher the Crazy. That's who.

"Need help with that?" a familiar deep voice says behind me, as I struggle with the present I'm carrying, as well as the diaper bag, my purse, and my cell phone that somehow ended up falling on the ground. The girls, who were too excited to help me carry everything because they're "big girls", ditched me the minute they saw a dinosaur-shaped piñata.

Some poor man will be holding their purses in the mall someday while they race away to look at shiny things. I just know it.

"Yeah, thanks." Handing over the gift Callie is going to kill me for later, I push my hair out of my face and smile up at Greg.

He blinks at me a couple of times, a weird look on his face. I have no idea what that expression means and it makes me feel self-conscious. Did I not cover up the concealer correctly? Are my eyebrows painted on crooked? Is that wingy thing that I tried to do with my eyeliner wrong? I thought the whole "sisters but not twins" thing was ok when it came to eye make-up.

Pushing my insecurities deep down, I remind myself that we're friends so it doesn't matter anyway. "Callie told me you'd be here. Did you bring Peyton?"

"Yeah, she's over there trying to master the swings." He gestures towards the swing set with his hand and sure enough, his sweet little girl is on her stomach on a swing, letting it move her back and forth.

"She's such a calm child," I remark. "I don't understand how she gets along so well with Max and Christopher."

Greg places the present on the gift table with a *thunk*. "She's not as calm as she seems. You only see her when it's winding down to naptime."

"Well, she's sweet. You do a great job with her."

"Thanks."

"I'm surprised you didn't have plans already today. Surely you're not the only single dad you know."

Christopher runs by us, yelling, this time with Max hot on his heels. I have no idea what they're running to or from, but I know the backyard is Christopher-proofed, so I don't pay much attention.

"Yeah, well, it seems my ex got custody of all our friends in the divorce so I had nothing better to do. Plus, I enjoy hanging out with you guys. I was glad for the text." I watch for any sign that he's upset by not being with his old friends today, but there's nothing except a hint of playfulness to his tone. It makes sense though. Do I really miss any of the people James used to make us hang out with? Not at all. They were all a bunch of self-absorbed jerks. I guess I was so used to dealing with James all the time I didn't notice.

All of the sudden, it hits me how late I am. I'm supposed to be playing co-hostess. "Oh, shit! I'm sorry. Do you want a drink?" I offer. "I didn't even think to ask you. Callie's going to kill me."

He laughs. "It's ok. Actually, I could go for a drink. Do you know what she has?"

"I'm guessing there's a variety of juice boxes in the cooler. Let me figure out where she set everything up." I look around trying to find any sign of beverages, or even our hostess. "I need to see what Callie needs me to do."

"How about this… you go check in with her and I'll find you after I figure out where the juice is and offer it to the guests. Deal?"

My shoulders relax as he jumps in to help. "Deal."

He turns to walk away and I bite my lip, trying not to smile so big that I split my face in half. I'm trying really hard not to believe that Callie's assessment is true and that Greg is interested in me. He's perfect; I know it would be a total let down if it ended up that we were misinterpreting the whole thing.

Once again, I push my attraction to him aside for my reality. We're friends and that's fantastic. He's a great guy. A perfect, beautiful, Adonis of a guy….

"Callie!" After walking around the yard for several minutes, I finally find her. "I'm sorry we're late. Stupid Dr. Wassman was running behind… Ooh! You got hot dogs!"

"Of course I did," she snaps, fighting with the bag to get it open. Apparently, the "easy-open" package isn't as easy as she thought. She looks frustrated, so I take the bag from her. Mostly, it's to make sure my lunch doesn't get splattered all over the grass, but I pretend it's to be helpful.

"Why are you standing by the grill anyway?" I ask, as I easily pull the tabs apart. "Where's Ben?"

She huffs and blows her bangs out of her face. "He's supposed to be manning the grill, but it ran out of propane because he didn't check it yesterday when I told him to." She waves her hands around, clearly upset by his inability to plan ahead.

I look down longingly at the hot dogs in my hand. "How long until he gets back?"

"Oh, he's back already. Just finished installing it." She tries to turn the grill on and take a step back. I've seen this before in a movie or something. That sucker is about to blow her hair back if she's not careful.

"Have you ever turned on a grill before?"

"No. But I use the stove all the time."

"Um...."

"I got you apple juice, I hope that's ok." Greg pops up out of nowhere and I've never been so grateful.

"Thank god you're here. Do you know how to turn on a grill?" I quickly point in Callie's direction.

He looks confused until he sees her struggling and shoves his own juice box at me to hold as he jumps in to pro-actively rescue her. "Oh shit, Callie, let me get that."

She backs off and I breathe a sigh of relief. Thank goodness he got here in time. I spent way too much time on this make-up job to have soot blown all over it.

"Thanks, Greg. Ben will be back in a second. He went to put the empty propane tank in the garage, we're running behind with lunch now," she sighs. "The kids are about to get restless."

We all look up to see Christopher hanging on for dear life as he sits on top of his new tackle dummy, Max and friends running into it making it move.

"Too late," I remark.

"Fucking hell," she grumbles and stalks away. "Christopher! Get down from there! I don't want to get you stitches for your birthday!" Turning around quickly, she addresses me. "Elena, can you grab the plates off the counter and condiments and stuff while I deal with my devil child?"

"Here. Now listen up..." I thrust the hot dogs at Greg and give him strict instructions. "I like mine medium rare. Make sure there are two of them. They're my favorite."

"Really?" He cocks his eyebrow at me.

"Get your mind out of the gutter, Pervy. It's a favorite American meal that I don't indulge in often. The only thing I'm thinking of right now is getting that sucker in my belly."

"Of course it is." He smirks which makes me blush, which makes him smirk more, and it's a whole big mess of smirking and blushing. I'm really confused by the time I get to the kitchen to start collecting supplies. But maybe it's a good kind of confusion. It's been a long time since I've had butterflies in my stomach. I forgot how nice they can feel.

The door swings open as I stack containers of condiments on a tray, and an exasperated Callie walks in. "Thank god you're here," she rants as she slams the door. "Did you see who came? My mother-in-law. My *mother-in-law*, Elena. The most passive aggressive person I've ever met and the sole reason for my husband's inability to take a shit without texting me about where the toilet paper is."

I giggle, grabbing a bunch of plastic forks and putting them in a red Solo cup. Later, I'll lift it up and we'll have a party.

No, we won't. But now I'll be humming that tune all day.

"She's not that bad."

"She *is* that bad." Callie rips open a bag of chips and shoves a couple in her mouth. Wild eyed and hair disheveled, all she needs is a little bit of smeared black eye make-up and she'd look like a rabid animal. "When the propane tank went out ten minutes before people were supposed to get here, you know what she said?"

I shake my head and open packages of birthday napkins, arranging them on the tray to carry outside.

"She said, 'Oh it's ok, Benny. Things happen. You go on to the store and I'll help Callie finish.' Then the second he took off, she parked her ass in that lounger and hasn't moved. Well, except when she needs a refill and demands I bring her a new martini."

"There are martinis?" I exclaim. Nothing goes better with hot dogs than a dirty martini, extra olives.

"No. We ran out. Now I'm giving her diluted olive juice."

"You are not," I say with a laugh.

"Oh, yes I am. If she wants more vodka, she can take her happy ass to the store herself." She takes a deep breath, having ranted enough to finally be able to relax, and plops down on a stool. "What happened at the doctor anyway? Is everything ok?"

"It was my yearly check up. He wanted to do blood work and of course they were running late. I'm really sorry, Callie. If I had known you were scrambling, I would have rescheduled."

She waves me off and takes a sip of a random juice box sitting on the table. No wonder she never gets sick. Her immune system is constantly getting a work out. "Nah. It was fine. Thankfully Greg was the first one here, and he helped me get the piñata all set up. I couldn't get the damn rope over the tree branch. I needed his height."

Once again, I can't help but feel a twinge of jealous at their obvious friendship. Not that we're not friends, too. But Callie is the one people gravitate towards. This time, I wish our new friend gravitated towards me.

She narrows her eyes. "I knew it."

I look around, trying to figure out what she knows. "What?"

"You have a thing for Greg."

"I do not!" I say a little too quick and a little too loud. That's always proof I'm lying. Callie knows that, and now she knows about my secret crush that is not so secret, I've been keeping it from myself until now, and none of this even makes sense anymore. Shit.

She crosses her arms over her chest and leans back. "You are a rotten, filthy liar. You have a crush on the man and don't you deny it."

"I'm not denying anything because we're not having this conversation." I stand up and grab the tray of supplies off the counter. "Today is about your son's birthday, not about your delusions."

She snorts and slowly peels herself off the chair, opening the door for me. "Whatever you say, but this conversation isn't done."

I swish past her, my knee-length flowy skirt flouncing around me. I make it two steps before I stop. "What the...."

Callie bumps into me from behind. "Hey... what... oh no. Oh no! Christopher, stop!"

He doesn't even notice as he tears through all his presents, tossing all the cards and wrapping paper aside as he opens them all.

"Ben! Ben, where are you? Are you even paying attention...?" She stalks over to her husband, clearly irritated that he didn't stop his son from digging into the gifts before Callie had her camera ready to go or could figure out who brought what gift. In all honestly, I have to side with Ben this time. There's no way to keep Christopher contained. All it took was one brightly colored package to catch his eye and it was over.

"Heads up." Greg sidles up next to me. "We have an injury."

Sure enough, Max is snuggled up in his arms, sniffling. A sudden wave of grief hits me. Not because I miss James. I really don't. It's more because of the life I had planned for and didn't get. It's the loss of the dreams I had. In an ideal world, Max would be snuggling with her father, not my crush.

But I'm grateful for Greg. He has a knack for recognizing when a child needs a man's influence, and he's willing to jump in and be that for them. It takes the sting out of a situation that could make me turn bitter. I really appreciate that about him.

Taking Max from him, she wraps her little arms around my neck. "What happened, sweet girl?"

"Cwistopher hit me," she sniffles.

"Oh no." I gently rub her back. "That wasn't very nice. Why did he hit you?"

She sits up in my arms and gives me a serious look. "Cause he said I can't have a pwesent. I wanna pwesent, Mommy."

"Baby, those are Christopher's presents for his birthday. You already had your birthday, remember?" She nods, her big eyes still looking tearful. "Christopher didn't get any presents on your birthday. Today is his turn."

She nods again and lays her head on my shoulder for a few more minutes. Greg, of course, starts unloading all the supplies onto the table next to the burned hot dogs, not a medium rare in the bunch. Dammit. I knew that would happen as soon as Ben took back over the grill.

"Okay," I finally say and put Max down on the ground. "Why don't you go play for a minute while I make your lunch, ok?"

Max takes off running, not looking back. Well that moment of trauma ended quickly.

"Amazing how fast they recover, isn't it?" Greg's pulling the plastic seals off the top of all the condiments. Every time he licks his thumb, I can't help but have a dirty thought about other things he can lick.

Focus, Elena.

"It must be nice to be a child, when all your problems are made better by a hug from your mom or dad."

"Very true. By the way, I've been meaning to tell you. That's a nice drum set you got Christopher. Callie's never going to forgive you for that one."

I grimace. "I'm hoping our card got lost in the mayhem and she won't know it was me."

"Oh no," he chuckles. "She saw you walk in with the biggest box. Unless you can put it together and dispose of the cardboard before she sees it, you're screwed."

"Eh. I'm not that worried." Glancing up at him, I put on my best conspirator face. "Last year she got Maura a bead set for Christmas. *Beads.* I'm still vacuuming those things up every day. It's like they multiply. She totally deserves this."

"Mama, I'm hungry." Speaking of the devil, Maura tugs on my skirt.

I take that as my cue that it's time for these kids to eat. Callie has her hands full, so I make the executive decision to get this party started.

"Ok, baby, let's get you a hot dog."

Within seconds, a pack of hungry children comes racing at us. Greg and I handle it like champs, while all the other parents sit around and drink. Seriously, do none of these kids have allergies that need to be addressed? We feed all the little beasts before they starve to death. Or at least this is how dire they want us to believe the situation is.

Callie eventually stalks back over, dragging a black garbage bag full of wrapping paper behind her. "Welp, I guess present time is over. You guys fed everyone?"

"Yeah." Suddenly Greg looks really unsure of himself. "Um… that's ok, right?"

"I don't even care anymore," she discloses. "From the time that propane tank ran out, it was all downhill from there. Thank goodness we still have the piñata…" We all look over to see that Christopher has yanked the piñata off the tree and is beating it with a baseball bat. Callie sighs. "There goes that idea." She drops the bag of trash on the ground and turns towards the house. "I'm grabbing the cake. Maybe that one thing will turn out right."

I turn back to Greg. "Sometimes I feel bad for her. She tries really hard."

"Yeah," he says like he's distracted. He's looking at me and he's got that weird look on his face again. It finally bugs me enough, I have to ask.

"What? Why do you keep looking at me like that?"

"What?" He startles, like I snapped him out of a daydream or something. "I'm sorry, I just… you have really pretty eyes."

"Oh… I… Um…." I stumble over my words. That's not at all what I was expecting. "I, uh, had a makeover the other day. The lady, Kristi, she taught me how to play up my eyes. I'm sure that's what you're seeing."

"No, that's not it. I didn't even realize you had a makeover." I swear my heart kicks up a notch when he says that. "I noticed your eyes before. I think the outside light makes them brighter. They're beautiful."

My breath catches. Are we having a moment? I'm not sure what to do or what to say. Thankfully, Callie chooses that moment to set the square red cake down on the table next to us.

"So far so good," she grumbles and then yells, "Christopher! Let's have cake!"

He comes running as my mind continues to reel over the exchange.

Maybe Callie's right, I think as we all sing "Happy Birthday". Maybe Greg gravitates to her as a friend and to me as... more than a friend. Is that possible?

As the song winds down, and it's time to blow out the candles, I refocus on the situation at hand. Participating in this party until Callie and I are alone to over-analyze the entire situation over a bottle of wine. First... I'll have dessert.

I look up just in time for Christopher to take a deep breath...

And sneeze all over the cake.

CHAPTER
Nine

The gym smells like sweat and feet and chalk and air freshener. And it brings back wonderful memories of my childhood.

I spent ages ten through seventeen in this same gym, either on a mat or a bar or a beam or a springboard, for at least ten hours a week. Because being a competitive gymnast is practically a job in itself, even when your bedtime is eight o'clock.

The equipment is all updated, but the set-up is exactly the same, and part of me longs for the good old days. And the tiny little body I had back then.

I have no idea how my mother kept up with my gymnastics schedule, particularly when I was in high school and didn't only compete for the club, but also for the school team. That added extra hours of practice, which meant extra drivetime, to our schedule.

Fortunately for me, Fiona has never taken a class before. One hour a week shouldn't kill me on mileage. I'm saving that free oil change I earned at Quickie Oil when I completed the punch card last month for when I really need it.

Fiona grips my hand a little tighter as we approach the front desk. She's just like me in some ways. We talk big, but in a new situation, we can get really shy.

"Hi, my daughter Fiona is here for the beginner's class."

The woman behind the desk grabs her binder and begins flipping through it. She's petite with a short dark bob and wide smile. "Is this your first time, Fiona?"

My girl nods and tries to hide behind me, one lopsided pigtail peeking out.

"Well, you're going to have lots of fun today." She gives her a wink and Fiona looks up at me, her eyes filled with excitement. My mother was right. I should have done this a long time ago.

"Ok, let's see... Fiona, Fiona, Fiona Monroe, right? Looks like you are going to be with Coach Zach." She stands up and leans over the desk to point across the gym. "You see all those cubbyholes over there? Take your shoes off and put them in one like all the other kids are doing. The coaches will call for your class in just a couple of minutes. Sound good?"

"Sounds really good, right?" I exaggerate my own excitement, hoping to help stave off some of Fi's nervousness. She bites her lip, but she nods. I take that as a good sign.

We wind our way through the maze of hyper children in bright leotards, most of them bouncing, plenty of them cartwheeling, and a few of them doing the splits in the middle of the waiting room. Poor kids. They can see the trampolines, rings, and foam pits... it's all right in front of their wide little eyes... and no one will open the gate to let them in and run free. I get it. I feel that way right before they open the doors at Target during Black Friday every year.

"I'm scared, Mom," Fiona whispers. "I don't know anyone."

I sit down on a bench by the wall and grab her hands so she'll look at me. "I know. But you're about to make a bunch of friends who all love gymnastics like you do. Just follow what the other kids do first when you get in there. You're gonna warm up before you learn any new tricks anyway, ok?"

She nods, but I can still see a bit of fear. It's overpowered, though, by that fierce determination I know is in there. It's the same determination that made her ask to sign up *every single day* for two weeks until I finally remembered to make the call. She isn't going to back down now.

"Ok, beginners!" a baby-faced teenager yells to get the kids' attention. Were the coaches always this young when I came here? "Let's head to the mat and follow the leader. I need everyone to run three laps!"

The bottleneck of children at the gate entrance reminds me of a viral video I saw once of a bunch of piglets all trying to get through a fence at the same time. Their little feet were still moving rapidly even though they weren't going anywhere.

The same thing is happening here, except these kids are basically running in place instead of climbing all over each other. Well, there are a couple of the little boys who can hardly take holding back so they wrestle while they wait. I may or may not have laughed when one of them raised his teeny tiny arms up in a muscle pose showing his victory.

I have to give Fiona credit. For as nervous as she is, she does exactly what I told her to do and she follows the crowd. Soon enough, she runs into a little girl from school.

And I mean that literally. The other girl was running the wrong direction and they smack into each other. Fortunately, the excitement of seeing each other overshadows any injuries.

The warm up hasn't changed all that much since I was a gymnast. Same stretches. Same lunges. Same backbends. Briefly, I feel an urge to run out there myself and start tumbling. But then I remember the last time I jumped on a backyard trampoline with Fiona to show her my front flip, and I peed all down my leg.

They don't tell you about *that* in your health classes in high school. We'd see a huge drop in teenage pregnancy in this country if we only told the poor girls about weak bladders and hemorrhoids. I'm sure of it.

A door next to me closes, and I glance up, only to do a double-take. "Greg?"

He stops and smiles. "Hey, Elena. What are you doing here?"

"I was about to ask you the same thing? Do you work here?"

"Yeah. I thought you knew that." We both stop and think for a second. "It's never come up before has it?"

"I don't think it has. How weird is it that we see each other all the time and I've never asked where you work?"

"We're usually too entertained watching the Callie and Christopher show. I guess we shouldn't be surprised, right?"

"Yeah. But now that I think about it, I don't even know your last name."

A blush creeps up his face. "It's Brady."

"Oh that's... wait..." My lips slowly curl up in amusement. "You're *Greg Brady*?"

"Yep."

"I'm trying really hard not to laugh."

"I appreciate that. And also, no. Despite her obsession with the *Brady Bunch*, my mother didn't hate me. Much."

I have to bite my lip to stop the giggle that wants to escape. Callie is going to have a field day with this one.

"You don't happen to have a weird last name or something that would make me feel like less of a freak, would you?"

I shake my head. "Sorry. My last name is Monroe."

"Elena Monroe," he says. "That's really pretty."

And it's back. That moment that might be a moment but might not be a moment, and I can't tell because I'm freaking neurotic. So I do what I do best... look away and deflect.

"Um," I clear my throat and sever the mood completely, "are you a coach or something?"

"Program director," he corrects me. "But yeah, I coach a lot. Normally it's the team, but Coach Zach called in sick. I'm filling in for him today."

"Oh, Fiona's going to love that! Today's her first day, and she's really nervous." I peek out onto the floor and find her cutting up with her new friend, laughing her head off when she's supposed to be stretching. "Well, she *was* nervous. She looks okay now."

I look back over at Greg and he hasn't taken his eyes off me. "I'm sure she'll be fine. If she's anything like you, she's resilient."

I'm not sure how to respond to that compliment, except to blush. Sometimes I feel like I'm going through the motions of my life and forget how strong I truly am. It's nice hearing that someone else besides my mother and Callie can see my strengths.

"Anyway," he says, pushing away from the wall, "I'm gonna go get my class moving. You're sticking around the whole hour?"

I nod. "Wouldn't miss it. It's bringing back all my childhood memories."

"Cool." He keeps talking as he walks backward. "I'll make sure to come talk to you after class is over."

"Ok."

He smiles and I smile and he's still backpedaling until he smacks into the gate, making him stumble and me laugh. But in true gymnast fashion, he hops around and rights himself quickly as he jogs towards the kids.

Suddenly, I'm extremely disappointed in myself for waiting this long to bring Fiona. I could have spent weeks ogling him from afar without Callie giving me any shit about it.

Pretending I'm busy texting, I try to take a super stealth picture of Greg in action. Open camera. Zoom in. Click.

And the flash goes off.

Several parents turn my direction and glare.

"Sorry. It's our first day." I point at Fiona who waves at me. "See?" My explanation seems acceptable to the uppity parents who turn back to their own tasks, but I happen to glance up at Greg who has his arms crossed and is smirking at me.

Dammit. Busted.

Ignoring my embarrassment over the faux pas, I open my text messages and pull up Callie's info.

Me: *It's Fiona's first day of gymnastics.*

Callie: *Fun! Does she love it?*

Me: *She does. Of course, it helps that she likes her coach.*

I attach the picture, press send, and wait.

It doesn't take long for the shouty capitals message I expect to come through.

Callie: *NO FUCKING WAY!!! He's a gymnastics coach?*

Me: *Program director. But he coaches the team.*

Callie: *How did we not know that?*

Me: *Because we're self-absorbed and have eleventy billion children?*

Callie: *Exactly. But now you get to watch him from a distance and he'll never know you're staring.*

Me: *I'm leaving now.*

Callie: *If he flashes his abs, get a pic for me!*

Me: *Already tried stealth mode. It didn't go well.*

Callie: *Lol. Rule #1: Always make sure your flash is turned off. How do you forget every time?*

Me: *Shut up. I'm busy watching my kid.*

Callie: *Sure you are. Tell Greg I said hi.*

Me: *Will do.*

Clicking my phone off, I search the gym for my child. I find her and a few other little girls around her age rotating through stations on the floor. Some are doing backbends on the cheese. Some are doing handstands. Fiona is with Greg, working on her cartwheel.

Her little arms are high in the air, one foot out in front, as she listens closely to what he is telling her. She nods, he claps, and she pushes off, throwing her legs in the air, hands on the ground.

And in a split second, somehow she's fallen and ended up on her butt. I smile, because it's too much fun seeing my girl learn all the tricks she dreams about every time she watches a competition on TV. Thank goodness we can find most meets On-Demand. It's tough tearing her away from the boob tube at bedtime before the final competitors perform.

Fi rubs her head as she stands up, making her lopsided pigtails even more disheveled. Greg then does something I never expected. He stands behind her, pulls the hair ties out, runs his fingers through her hair until she has a high ponytail on top of her head, and ties it all back together like a champ.

And if seeing a hot single dad do a little girl's hair didn't just make my ovaries explode, what happens when she walks away does.

He lifts his shirt to wipe his brow.

My jaw drops and I blink several times.

Holy. Mother. Of abs.

Not only is Greg handsome, and tall, and kind… he's ripped. I've never noticed before but he's really muscular. The biceps peeking out of his sleeves are bulging. His shoulders are broad. From behind, when he stretches to demonstrate a technique, his back muscles are rippling. All of those adjectives people use to describe an attractive muscular man apply here.

"Ohmygod," I say under my breath. No way I can deny my secret crush now. He has catapulted to a new level of sexy in my book.

I spend the last thirty minutes of class trying really hard to watch my daughter, but my eyes keep gravitating back to her coach. He's so good with the kids. Encouraging and motivating and smiling all the time. How in the world this perfect man is divorced is beyond me.

As the classes wind down and the kids trickle back out the gate, smiles on their sweaty little faces, Fiona bounds up to me. She looks elated and it puts me in a good mood, too.

"Did you have fun?"

"Mama, it was so fun!" she exclaims. "Did you see me flip on the bar? Did you?"

"I did! Your pullover looked great!"

"Coach Greg said my handstand is super high, too!" She jumps up as high as she can. "Did you see me do my handstand?"

"I did!"

"Can we come back next time?" she interjects, not even listening to any of my responses because she is way too excited. "Please, Mama? I wanna do gymnastics again!"

"Of course you can."

"She really did do a great job, especially for her first time." I look up and my breath hitches a bit. Now that he's exponentially sexier to me, my puppy dog eyes could become a problem. He has officially succeeded in dazzling me today.

"I'm gonna come back next time!" Fiona yells and continues to bounce.

"Okay, okay, calm down kid." I pat her arm lovingly. "I don't want to have to Benadryl you when we get home."

Greg chuckles. "Hey Fiona, why don't you go get your shoes on so I can talk to your mom."

She bounds away, leaving him and I alone to chat. Well, as alone as you can be in a room full of people thinking they're training their kids for the Olympics in eight years.

"Thank you for coaching her today. I mean... I know it's your job and all, but you're amazing. I mean... you're amazing with the kids. Not that you're not amazing anyway... Oh geez." I blush and he smiles. It seems that blushing and smiling are the only things we do these days.

"She's a natural. I hope you bring her back."

"She's officially signed up for this class so we'll be here every week at this time."

"Good, good." He clears his throat. "Um, I've been thinking. Ok... I'm just gonna say it... Can I make you dinner some time?"

I... wait... what.... Did he ask me out on a date?

"Did you just ask me out on a date?" I blurt out.

"Yeah. Is that ok?"

"Yeah, it's totally fine. I ..." I pause to gather my thoughts. "Sorry, I wasn't expecting that. Are you serious?"

He scratches his beard. "About the date or about cooking?"

"Both, I guess. I haven't been asked out for a long time, so I guess I'm trying to make sure I'm not misunderstanding. Or dreaming." I squeeze my eyes shut with embarrassment. "Or say stupid things like that out loud."

He leans towards me and I swear he is tossing smoldering looks my direction. "You're not misunderstanding, and you're not saying stupid things. I would like to take you on a date, but I also like to cook sometimes. Would you like to come over to my place? I can cook for you."

His baby blues are locked on mine and I lose all ability to speak temporarily as I'm sucked into his web. Or maybe my hormones kicked up a notch. Either way, I have to shake my head to break myself of the fog.

"Yes. Yes, I'd like to go on a date with you. And I'd love to not have to do the cooking for once."

He smiles and begins to back away. "Great. I'll grab your cell number off Fiona's registration paperwork and text you this weekend so we can make plans."

"Sounds good. And thanks."

He turns and jogs back onto the mat, clapping his hands to take over warming up the next group of classes.

"Mama, can we go?" Fiona tugs on my hand as I stare at my future date. "I'm getting hungry."

"Yeah, um, ok. Let's go, baby cakes."

We turn and make our way back through the crowd and out the door.

We certainly got more out of her new class than I ever anticipated.

CHAPTER
Ten

"**Y**ou've got to be kidding me." Callie turns her phone to show me the latest text from Ben, who continues to prove himself incompetent.

Ben: *Where are the frozen fish sticks?*
Callie: *In the freezer.*
Ben: *Which freezer?*

I try to keep a straight face, knowing she's annoyed. "I guess he forgot the one in the garage broke."

"Ugh." She quickly types out a response and tosses her phone in her purse. "It was last month, and he's the one who dragged it to the curb. How did he forget that?"

We slam the car doors and make our way into the newest salon in town. When my mother asked what I wanted for my fortieth birthday, I finally fessed up. I want a new me. I don't think I realized it until I had my makeover, but I really have enjoyed seeing myself look pretty, and I want to continue to find ways to do that.

"I'm still wondering why you don't leave Ben," I toss out there, hoping not to hit a nerve.

She shrugs, which I take as a sign that she's not offended. "Because when he's not being a total dillweed, he's kind and caring and affectionate. He genuinely loves us, even though he's completely inept about getting things done. Besides…" the evil smirk comes out and I know she's about to share something juicy. "… it's more fun to cut a hole in his favorite socks when he's not looking than go to divorce court."

"Did you really do that?"

"Sure did. It was just a tiny hole. But when he pushed his foot into his sock, his big toe went right through. I haven't heard him cuss like that in a while. It set the whole tone for my wonderful day."

"You're diabolical," I laugh. "I'm impressed. How come I'm not clever enough to come up with these passive aggressive things?"

"Because you are way too sweet and kind. I'm jaded from years of him stepping over dog poop and pretending not to see it so I have to clean it up." We stop in front of a check-in desk, a petite twenty-something with a sleek blond bob and perfect make-up looking professionally indignant at our arrival. "And now we're going to stop talking about this because we're seeing Ben's sister's niece and I don't want my cover blown."

I mimic zipping my lips and throwing away the key, before meandering around the room. It's all greens and browns and whites. It's a very open concept. All the hairdresser stations are in the same big room. A row of sinks is lined up in the back, complete with reclining chairs. Several of the hair dryer stations are off to the side. There's even a coffee bar. It's all very swanky and looks very expensive.

"Are you Elena?" A petite brunette with long flowy hair and a tiny little waist approaches me. "I'm Jordan, your stylist." The first thing I notice is she has a high-pitched, almost baby voice. This is going to get annoying.

The second thing I notice is that she puts out her hand and when I think she's about to shake mine, she goes straight for my hair instead. That's not awkward or anything. "Hmm. What are we doing with you today anyway?"

"I don't really know. I hadn't thought about it. I was hoping you'd have some ideas."

"Uh huh," she says with a blank smile. The lights are on, but I'm seriously not sure how many people are home. "Come with me."

I hesitate but follow her to her station, which is right next to the coffee bar. Her mirror has the standard things taped to it… her stylist license, some ads for styling products, a price list. But all of that is overpowered by dozens of pictures of her with some guy. They're making googly eyes at each other in some. Kissing in others. Some of them have post its with love notes written on them and things like "J+C" written in swirly letters. It's like a shrine to their relationship.

"How long have you been dating?" I gesture to the mirror/shrine.

"Chad? Um… about six weeks."

That's… surprising. "Oh. I thought with all the pictures, it was longer than that."

She giggles. Not like a shy giggle. But like an I'm-barely-out-of-high-school-and-don't-know-what-I'm-doing giggle.

I have a bad feeling I won't be getting out of this chair with any dignity left intact.

She pulls the hair tie out making my messy bun fall around my shoulders and begins combing through my hair with her fingers. "Callie said I could do whatever it takes to make you feel beautiful. I have some ideas. How much time do you have?"

"Wow. I didn't realize my hair was that bad." And I can't believe I'm letting a teenager take scissors to my head.

"It's not bad, exactly. It's really healthy. It's kind of… well, you look like my mom."

"I didn't know being a mom was a bad thing," I say defensively.

"No, silly." She rolls her eyes and already I'm having visions of ripping her voice box out of her throat. Her voice is slightly too high pitched and bubbly. "It's not bad to *be* a mom. You don't want to *look* like one, ya know?"

I honestly don't know, but I let her blather on and try to ignore the dig on how insignificant and unimportant my entire life for the past eight years has been and how I should be doing my best to not look the part. Someday, she'll get it. The more babies she has, the more she'll get it.

I make a mental note to pray she'll have triplets someday.

And then she says the magic words….

"What do you think of having a keratin treatment?"

My face immediately brightens. I know, because I see it happen in the mirror. I go from scowling to excited in a split second.

"I've always wanted a keratin treatment, but I was afraid it wouldn't work on me."

Jordan stops and gets a very serious look on her face. "Elena, keratin treatments were made for people like you. For people who have lots of hair, but battle frizz because your hair isn't quite curly enough to hold curl, but isn't quite straight enough to stay straight."

"Yes. That's it exactly. I want my hair to be sleek and stylish."

She smiles like this new plan is going to change the course of history. As long as it changes the course of *my* history, that's good enough for me. "Then you came to the right place. First, we'll start with your color. You have a good base with your natural color. Let's add some dimension…."

She rambles on for the next ten minutes about what all we're going to do, and it sounds good to me. I haven't gotten more than a *Super Cut* in years, so even if it looks like shit, I can at least claim it's stylish.

"Hey Jordan, I'm going to run a couple of errands. How long do you guys need?" Callie grabs a cookie off the coffee bar and takes a bite, handing me the rest of it.

"Oh, it's going to be a while. Do you think you can bring us some lunch?"

"It's only nine in the morning," I mumble through some crumbs.

Jordan turns to me and smiles. "I know, silly. But beauty takes time. And we're going to make sure you are the best version of you, you can be."

Ok, this teeny-bopper is starting to grow on me.

"I guess I'll be bringing lunch," Callie shrugs. "Burgers work?"

"Make it Chinese," Jordan shoots back.

Callie wasn't expecting that response. Apparently, her husband's sister's niece has a little more bite to her than Callie knew.

"I'll grab some *Panda Express*."

"I'd rather *Cho-Min Chow* down the street."

Callie gives me a look that tells me she really wants to wring Jordan's neck, but she won't for my sake. You don't want to piss off the woman who could "accidentally" mix chemicals that burn all your hair off.

"Ooookay. I'll be back in a few."

As soon as Callie walks away, Jordan gets to work. Listening to her talk non-stop about Chad, her boyfriend of six weeks, and how as soon as he graduates from college and gets a job, they're going to get married, is really annoying. Especially since Chad is undecided on his major and spends a significant chunk of his time planning frat parties.

Sounds like Chad might have a future in event coordination.

When I mention it to Jordan, she stares at me blankly. I guess she doesn't agree.

While her voice continues to grate my nerves, watching her work isn't annoying at all. Quite the contrary, surprisingly. Her fingers move quickly and efficiently. She watches the clock like a hawk, and says it's to make sure she doesn't over-process. When Callie drops off our lunch, Jordan never stops checking my foils. And even more interesting, several times, other stylists approach her and ask for advice on mixing a color or a special cutting technique.

This ditzy, stereotypical hairdresser who could be a stand-in for Minnie Mouse voiceovers is actually a master of her craft. After Kristi gave me my makeover, I should have learned never to judge a person's abilities by their personality. But did that lesson compute? No. I'm continually surprised by how competent some professionals can be.

Five hours later, yes five *hours,* I am highlighted, lowlighted, deep conditioned, cut, keratined, trimmed again, blow-dried, flat-ironed, and I'm about to see the new me. Because at some point during the cut, Jordan decided I needed a big reveal instead of watching as the process happens.

"Are you ready?" She giggles and claps her hands, which I've strangely gotten used to over the day. She spins me around and...

"Oh no, why are you crying?" she asks. "Is it the color? We can change that. Or if it's the cut we can do something different or..."

I put my hand on her arm to stop her from working herself into a panic. "It's beautiful."

"Oh, that's all." She puts her hand over her chest and breathes out. "Don't scare me like that, silly. You like it?"

Like doesn't even begin to describe it. My normally frizzy not-quite-curly, not-quite-straight hair is sleek and shiny. The color is almost what I remember my hair being like as a teenager, except with more definition to it. The bangs I swore I would never have are swept to the side, covering my giant forehead.

I look like me. Only better.

"I love it," I finally reassure her. "It's perfect."

"Well good." She takes the cape off my shoulders and does one additional quick sweep of my hair with her fingers. "Let's go get you checked out and make your next appointment."

Callie looks up as we round the corner and her jaw drops open. "Holy shit, Elena. Your hair is gorgeous."

"It's good, huh?"

"It's great. Wow. I knew Jordan was good with hair, but if I knew she was this good, I would have started making appointments with her instead of the lady I've been seeing since high school."

"Maybe it's time for you to make a change as well." Jordan punches some buttons on the register while Callie keeps touching my hair. I feel like things are finally falling into place. I'm feeling confident and strong. I have an actual date. I'm on the path to taking my life back and making it whatever I want it to be.

"Your total is four hundred and twenty-three dollars."

And just like that, the new path I'm on goes right over a proverbial cliff.

CHAPTER
Eleven

If the look on her face was any indictor, my mother was as shocked as we were when she saw that receipt. The squeak she made was a dead giveaway that she never expected to get me a five-hundred-dollar visit to the salon for my birthday.

But then she looked back over at me and caught me staring at myself in the mirror again. Very quickly she forgot about the cost and said it was the best birthday present she had ever gotten me.

Well, she didn't totally forget about the cost. She said it's also the best Christmas present, because she'll still be paying this gift off around the holidays so I'm not getting anything else.

It's still totally worth it. Especially as I walk up the sidewalk to Greg's condo.

I feel all jittery and nervous, smoothing down my skirt and running my hands over my hair. It's not like he hasn't seen me in yoga pants and a messy bun before. Why am I anxious?

Because I like this guy. And I can't for the life of me figure out why he likes me, but I really, really want to be attractive to him. Not in a she-has-such-a-great-personality way, but in a I'm-really-hot-for-her way. Is it too much to ask for your date to be turned on by you? I think not.

One more smooth down of my skirt. One more fluff of the hair. One more rub of my finger over my teeth to make sure my lipstick doesn't make me look like I've been punched in the mouth when I smile. And I push the doorbell.

He opens the door and stops. And then he stares. And he stares some more.

"What?" I'm not sure why he's looking intently at me. "Shit, do I have a stain on my shirt?" I pull at the soft fabric, trying to find the spot which is probably on my shoulder. "I told Max not to lay her head down on me after eating peanut butter. Is it bad?"

"No. There's nothing on your shoulder. Sorry, I didn't mean to stare…" he opens the door a little wider. "Come in."

Stepping inside, the first thing I notice is how bright and airy his apartment is. There's quite a few windows and the blinds are all open, letting the natural light in. The second thing I notice is the aroma.

"Wow, it smells great in here." Dropping my purse on the couch, I look around at his pictures. They're everywhere. Some are artsy landscape looking pictures. Some are snapshots of family and friends. But most of them are Peyton over the last two years.

"I'm making pasta primavera," he calls over his shoulder as he walks toward the back of the room, where I'm assuming the kitchen is. "I hope you don't mind lots of sauce."

I laugh and gesture to myself. "I think it's pretty obvious that I'm not a picky eater. The more sauce the better."

"Good." I can see him over the counter, tossing a salad. "Nothing irritates me more than heating up leftovers and the pasta's too dry because there's not enough sauce. So I always overdo it."

"You also need a few more calories than the average person for your job." I situate myself on the bar stool and watch him work. How in the world does he make chopping lettuce sexy? I need to make an appointment with my ob/gyn. Clearly, I need some sort of hormone therapy. Mine are out of whack. "I still feel terrible that I didn't know you were a coach."

"Why?" He throws the salad into a big white bowl and starts chopping up hard boiled eggs.

"I don't know. I feel like you know so much about me and Callie, and we haven't made enough effort to know you. Makes me feel like we haven't really been good friends to you."

"I kind of like that you didn't know about my job right away." A few eggs get added into the bowl along with some dried cranberries. "I like that we can hold fun conversations without bringing work into the discussion. I talk about work all day long. It's much more fun to talk about things like what a perv Callie's mother really was before she had *Calixta*." He emphasizes her given name, referring to the character she was named after, which makes me laugh. Callie's mom really is kind of kooky.

"Shoot! I forgot the wine." He turns toward the fridge and grabs a bottle of something pink.

"You got us wine?" A slow smile crosses my face.

He looks surprised I would even ask. "Of course I did. What kind of date would this be if I didn't splurge at least a little?"

It's been a long time since anyone has made that kind of effort for me, and I can't help but wonder, of all the people in the world he could have asked out, why me? I'm nothing special. No that's not right. I'm special to my family and friends. I'm just nothing overly remarkable. I'm kind of... average. Average height, average weight, average number of kids. He's got a good job, is a loving father, and is pretty much the prettiest man I've ever met in person. I can't quite see how we'd be on equal footing if this went any further than one date.

Well, that's depressing.

Putting those thoughts out of my head again, I concentrate on having a fun evening.

"How did Fiona like her first class anyway?" He pulls the cork out of the bottle with ease and pours two glasses.

"I thought you didn't want to talk about work," I chide, taking a sip of the crisp Moscato. It's good. Sweet and not too dry.

"I don't. But I'd like to get to know you better and part of that means getting to know your kids."

I hold his stare and see nothing but sincerity in his gaze. It's a little frightening when he says things like this. It makes me feel good, but also makes me nervous. What if I say or do something wrong? Will he stop liking me? And why the hell do I sound like an overly dramatic high schooler? Did Jordan's immaturity rub off on me while I was at the salon?

I'm disappointed in myself for always going back to my insecurities. I'm a nice woman. I have a lot going for me and I have a lot to give. If someone can't see that, even Mr. Perfect here, that's not my problem.

"She had a great time. She's been wanting to take classes for a while now, but I kept dropping the ball."

He tsks playfully at me. "How could you keep forgetting?"

"I know, I know. I'm the world's worst mom. You would think being a former gymnast myself, I would've gotten her in there the minute she showed an interest."

"I knew you were a gymnast the minute I set eyes on you." He moves around the kitchen when the timer buzzes, finishing up our dinner. For as tall as he is, he's not lanky. He doesn't slink around the room. He's way more graceful.

"How could you tell?"

"Every former gymnast looks the same when they see the equipment," he says, waving away the steam as he drains the pasta. "It's like they're trying not to run over to the bars and climb on. Even if they're little bars like Peyton and Max use."

"Guilty." I raise my hand in the air. "I had to hold myself back from running out on the mat with Fiona the other day. It looked like a lot of fun."

"I wouldn't recommend it. I can't tell you how many times I've almost thrown my back out demonstrating a move. Getting old is kind of shitty sometimes."

"Were you a gymnast growing up?" My mouth starts watering as I watch him mix the sauce into the pasta and dish out our servings. It smells really good, and I have a soft spot for carbs, as my waist line reminds me on a daily basis.

"I wasn't. Is this enough?" He holds up the plate full of steamy goodness. I nod and take it from him, following him to the small table off the kitchen. He refills our wine glasses and makes sure we have everything we need before digging in.

"If you weren't a gymnast..." I ask around a bite of my food. Good lord, this is good. "How did you get into coaching?"

He chews and swallows his bite before answering. "My sister, Joie, was a gymnast." He gestures to a picture on his wall. I'm pretty sure it's his family, but none of them look anything alike. The older couple, I'm assuming are his parents, both have an olive complexion and dark hair. They're average height. The woman, I guess is his sister, is short and looks to be Hispanic. She's standing next to a dark haired teenage boy. He's a good-looking kid. And then there's Greg, holding Peyton. He's taller than anyone else by at least a few inches, and blond with blue eyes. "I spent a lot of time at the gym during her practices when I was young, so the coaches knew my family pretty well. By the time I was in high school, I was over six feet, and when they needed to hire some big, strong guys to learn how to spot, they called me."

"Wait... did your sister train here?"

He shakes his head and wipes his mouth. "No. Most of my family is in San Antonio. I moved here when I was in college and my boss happened to be friends with Dave, the owner here. They needed a coach. I needed a job. I've been there ever since."

"That's really cool. It's almost like you fell into your calling."

"Yep. I realized pretty quickly how much I loved it. But I also knew there isn't much room for advancement as a coach, so I got a business degree. Now, I run most of the operations."

"That's really awesome."

"I think so." He stacks our plates and leans back in his chair, sipping his wine and flashing that flirty smile. "What about you? Did you get a scholarship to a Big 10 university?"

"Hardly," I say, playing with my hair. This is literally the only flirty move I know, and since my new 'do makes me feel pretty confident, I go for it. "I got to Level 9. I have no idea what that means anymore since they changed the levelling system."

"It's still almost elite level. You were pretty good."

"Yeah, I held my own. I just couldn't get past that mental block."

"What do you mean?" His eyes hold so much interest in what I'm saying. I don't remember anyone ever really hearing me talk about my gymnastics days. It's either something that interests you or it doesn't. I don't know if he's interested because it's his career or because he's interested in *me*.

"Um... it's like the harder the skills got, the more fear I started feeling. It's hard to explain, but I started visualizing crashing and burning my release moves."

"And you couldn't do them anymore?"

"Exactly. I did everything I could think of to visualize sticking my landings and completing the moves, but I hit a wall."

What I don't tell him is that I still struggle with this part of myself. It doesn't affect my normal day-to-day life, but if I start to feel anxiety about a situation, if I don't get a grip on it quickly, it can become debilitating. Like people who run from a four-centimeter spider, or women who refuse to have their picture taken. It doesn't really affect anything externally, but internally the struggle is real.

"It happens to the best of them," he responds. "I can't tell you the number of athletes we've had to get into hypnosis or some other therapy to help get past that. Want something else to drink?" He stands and gathers our plates, taking them to the sink.

"I think I'll stick with water now. Two glasses of wine is my limit these days."

He begins cleaning the kitchen and I jump in to help. It's nice working side by side with him as we talk. I got used to doing all the clean up by myself over the years, having an adult conversation while getting something accomplished almost makes doing the dishes, dare I say, fun.

I definitely need to stick to water the rest of the night.

We talk more about the gym, and I'm shocked by how much political drama happens behind the scenes. From stage moms to employee hook-ups, it makes me glad I've never tried to run a business.

I tell him about my job as a flight attendant before having kids and the favorite places I've traveled.

We laugh about Christopher's antics and "aww" over the stories of our kids' accomplishments. It's all so... *easy*. The conversation is entertaining and doesn't feel forced. I can feel myself relaxing, and not wondering if I'm going to say the wrong thing. It's different than I remember past relationships being. Even my marriage.

Is this what it should have been like all along?

That thought alone is eye opening. This is the kind of relationship I want for the rest of my life. Easy, free, fun. I have no idea if Greg is going to be the one to give it to me, but at least I'm learning what to strive for. I'll call that a win.

Once everything is clean and put away, we move to the couch with our water and continue to enjoy each other's company.

"How long have you been divorced?" Greg's entire body is turned towards me, all his attention on me.

"I guess it's been official for about nine months."

"Isn't he already married though?" Leave it to Greg to be confused by how little integrity my ex has. That speaks volumes for his character that he can't even wrap his brain around it.

"Yeah, they got married a couple months after I said, 'I don't.'" I smile, because I think it's humorous. For as much as James wants people to think he's important, he seems to have no problem with people figuring out why he left his wife of fifteen years. Greg doesn't seem to think it's funny at all. "What?"

He shakes his head. "Sorry. Sometimes I forget that not every man thinks marriage means forever like I do."

"And yet, you're divorced."

"Touché," he says around his drink of water. "You make a good point, but that wasn't my decision. Libby left me."

This shocks me. I don't know Greg well, but from everything I know, he's practically perfect. Sure, he could be a total sociopath, but kids are usually pretty good judges of character and they gravitate towards him. That counts for something, right?

"Why in the world would she leave someone like you?"

"Someone like me, huh?" He grins like a stoner at 4:20 on April 20th.

"You know what I mean. Your house is clean. You can cook. You're kind and funny and fantastic with Peyton. Do you have a secret fetish or something?"

He chuckles and absentmindedly begins playing with a lock of my hair. "No, but I think she might. She's a little... high maintenance. One day she decided she hates my guts—I still don't know what that's about—and she left."

"That's terrible!"

He shrugs. "It is and it's not. I realized pretty quickly how relieved I was that she was gone. Don't get me wrong, it was awful losing Peyton that way. She was just a baby, and I had to fight like hell to get her a few hours a week. But besides that, it's like I could breathe when Libby left. She took all her crazy with her. I like not having to deal with that every day."

I can relate. I remember feeling that way when my divorce was finally complete. I was sad that it was over, but relieved as well.

Our eyes lock and he bites his lip. Suddenly, the vibe in the room changes. It becomes almost electric.

"I really like your hair," he whispers, as he begins to lean in closer, "I don't think I've ever seen it down before."

"That's because I got it done the other day," I whisper back.

Ohmygod what is happening? Is he going to kiss me? I hope he doesn't kiss me. Oh, but I hope he does. What do I do? All of these thoughts are scrambling my brain, but all I can focus on is his lips moving closer to mine.

"I really like it," he whispers one last time and his lips almost make it to his target, when I pull away and ruin it all.

"Why me?" I blurt out.

He stops and takes a breath. I'd be lying if I said I wasn't thrilled he was holding it in preparation for a little lip lock. But then he turns the tables on my question. "Why not you?"

"I…well…" He just said he didn't want any more crazy. That's all I seem to be these days. A hot mess of neuroses about every facet of my life. Deciding honesty is the best policy, I lay it all on the line. "Look at you. You're tall and handsome and have abs for days, and yes I caught a glimpse at the gym accidentally." I nudge his hand with my shoulder playfully making him blush a bit. "Women flock to you because you're kind and great with kids. Me? I have wrinkles and a leftover baby gut. When I drop the girls off at school and wave goodbye, the skin under my arm is still waving ten minutes later. I'm a terrible dresser and I'm slightly neurotic. We," I wave back and forth between us, "are not all that equally matched."

He thinks for a second and now I'm having second thoughts about my honesty. The whole point of a first date is to hide all your imperfections, not point them out for him to focus on. I'm gonna have to get a subscription to *Teen Magazine* to get some dating tips. They worked back in high school. Surely nothing has changed that much.

"Let me ask you a question," Greg finally says. "What are some of the things you *like* about yourself?"

"What?" This was not how I was expecting the conversation to turn.

"What do you like? For instance, you have some killer one-liners. I never know what you're going to say, and I like that."

"Really?"

"Really. Your turn."

I take a breath and think for a second. There have to be some things I like about myself. I never thought hard about them before. It takes me a few seconds to come up with something.

"Well, I kind of like how I parent." He nods encouragingly. "I watch too many moms become helicopter parents and I want my girls to experience life, and that's going to include disappointments and boo-boos. Sure, my job is to protect them from serious things, but I want them to be strong and independent and not be shocked when they don't always get what they want."

"I like that about you, too. What else?"

"That's not enough?"

"Humor me," he says with a smile.

"Ok." I clear my throat. "I like that I'm able to set aside my annoyance with my ex, enough to have family events with the girls so they can still have some sense of normalcy. Um… I like that I try really hard not to judge people, especially if I don't know them. I like my humor, I guess. I don't know. This is hard."

He shifts in his seat, grabs my hand, and starts playing with my fingers. "I wish you could see yourself the way I see you. You're fun and funny. You're kind and laid back. You love your friends and family fiercely and put them before yourself. I love the way you handle having a broken family. I wish Libby and I could get along that well. Those are the things I see. I don't see wrinkles or gray hairs or flab. I see *you*. And I like what I see."

"You do?" I whisper, totally and completely mesmerized by his words.

"I do."

"But I want you to think I'm pretty."

There. I said it. The crux of all my hesitation.

"I don't think you're pretty." My heart drops a bit. "I think you're stunningly beautiful. Even when you pull your hair up." Forget the drop. Now my heart soars as he leans in closer and this time, I lean back. "Can I kiss you now?"

"Please."

Instantly, his lips are on mine. They're soft and warm and feel so good as they move. He pulls back briefly, only to lock eyes with me, then to come right back. Only this time, his lips open and mine follow. His tongue is in my mouth, and he tastes like wine and pasta. And I love it.

I can't figure out where to put my hands. I want to run them through his hair and grab onto his shoulders and pull him to me, but I can't do it all at once, so I settle for wrapping them around his neck.

His kiss gets deeper and soon we're laying on the couch, him on top of me. Me enjoying the feel of him. We explore each other's lips and mouths and soon he's kissing down my neck and my body is ready to take this further. I want to feel his touch on my skin. I want my touch on his. I want to make this the start of something special.

Rubbing his hands up and down my back as we kiss, I know I'm going to feel it for days. There's no way I'll forget the feel of his touch.

His hands move up and over, grazing over part of my stomach…

And then I hit that visual wall. The one that makes me tense up and expect the worst.

I know where his hand is headed. "I'm not having sex with you," I blurt out right before he touches my boob.

He freezes. Slowly, he puts his hand back down and pulls us to a sitting position. I cringe. I blew it. The crazy he's not looking for just reared its ugly head and he's never going to want to see me again.

"I wasn't planning on having sex with you tonight."

"Oh." Well, now I feel foolish.

He pulls me forward and gives me a gentle peck on the lips. "It's not because I don't want to sleep with you. It's because I don't want to jump the gun. You're still skittish and I don't want to push you before you're ready. Before *I'm* ready."

My eyes widen in surprise. "Oh."

He cocks a half-grin. "And Elena, we may never get to that point. Who knows. We may be better as friends. But I hope you'll try this with me. I like you. I'd like to see where this can go."

I bite my lip, trying really hard not to smile like that girl whose picture turned into all those crazy stalker memes. "I'd like that, too."

"Good. Now, would you like to watch a movie?"

There's nothing I'd like more except.... "I think I need to head home. Kissing you is kind of, well, frankly it turns me on..."

He barks a laugh. One-liners for the win!

"... and if I don't leave, I may change my mind, which sounds great. But then, by tomorrow, you'll see how neurotic I can be, so I'm going to shut up now because I sound like a crazy woman."

Continuing to chuckle, he grabs my hand and pulls me to a stand. "You don't sound crazy. You make me feel good about myself." He kisses me again. I really could do this all night. "Let me walk you to your car."

We spend another several minutes making out against my car, until someone honks while driving by and reminds us we're outside. I feel smitten, which is something I haven't felt in a while.

The entire drive home is a blur. I lock every single moment of our date into my memory. Even if it doesn't work out, I'll have these memories. Memories of the way I feel. Memories of the way I should be treated. Memories of what I want. And I won't settle for less anymore.

My phone buzzes as I pull into my driveway. I know who it is right away.

Callie: *Well??? How was your date?*

Normally, I'd answer but this time, I ignore her. For the first time in a while, I'm going to be selfish and keep these memories all to myself.

CHAPTER
Twelve

"Let's begin our stretches everyone," the instructor says in a soothing, gentle voice. She is way too Zen for a toddler gymnastics class.

Nevertheless, all dozen or so parents guide their kids through various yoga-ish poses designed to give the child a good stretch, but also promote bonding with their parent. Or at least that's what it's supposed to do. Mostly it bores everyone involved to tears, and I mean real tears. Every week at least one kid has a meltdown because they can't go play. But what do we know? We're just paying to play with our kid in a safe environment.

"When are you going to tell me about your date?" Callie leans over to whisper-yell, as she wrangles Christopher into a downward dog pose while he makes fart noises.

"I'm not," I whisper-yell back, Max laying flat out like a star fish, unwilling to use any of her limbs.

Baby stretching is going well.

Once again, she tries to lean in so we won't be caught speaking during the quiet part of class, because that's how lame we are. "Why not?"

"Because I'm right behind you. She'll have to tell you later." Greg's head pops up in between us startling Callie and forcing me to stifle a laugh. He, on the other hand, has a huge ornery smile on his face.

"You jerk," she says and smacks his arm, eliciting a glare from the instructor. The three of us immediately straighten up and wipe the smiles off our faces. It's a good thing our kids are officially too old for a parent/child class and will be moving up to the kiddie class next semester. We get in more trouble than the kids do.

Now that the kids are officially warmed up, the instruction part of our class is set to begin. We all watch as Miss Hanaghan, which is what I lovingly refer to her behind her back, pulls out a box. The kids all fidget, anticipation thick in the air.

"We're going to work on our hand-eye coordination today," she says, and pulls out a purple plastic racket.

Uh oh.

I look at Callie, who looks from me to Greg, who looks from Callie to me, and we all have the same look on our face. The look that says *this isn't going to go well*.

The parents around us with their horror-stricken faces seem to agree. But being the good little paying customers we are, we take a gamble and soon every child has a racket in their hand. No adult, only the children.

Suddenly, I feel the overwhelming need to protect my shins from these weapon-wielding midgets.

"At this age, balls are too fast for these guys to hit with any accuracy, so we're going to use something they can take their time with." The instructor then dumps out a huge bag full of balloons, and the chaos begins.

For the most part, it's organized chaos. Some of the parents are standing behind their kids showing them how to hit the balloon like a tennis ball. Some parents are tossing it to their child to hit. Max has forgotten the racket completely and is enjoying tossing the balloon in the air and catching it. It's not exactly the point of the exercise, but she's learning how to catch, so whatever.

And then there's Christopher.

The three of us keep a close eye on him at first, knowing this could turn ugly at any moment, but he seems to be doing well. He won't let Callie help as he tosses the balloon up in the air and tries to hit it like a baseball. She looks at me, shrugs, and begins documenting this moment of calm with her camera.

He's surprisingly good with this hand-eye-coordination stuff, making contact with the balloon almost every time. The more he gets into it, the harder his swing. The harder his swing, the wider the berth the rest of us give him. And wider the berth, the more power he puts into it. It's a vicious cycle.

And then it finally happens. The moment we've all be waiting for, or at least those of us who spend any real amount of time with this child.

Christopher tosses the balloon up, pulls back, swings the racket forward, and loses his grip. The racket flies through the air across the room…

And nails the instructor in the face.

"Who in their right mind thinks it's a good idea to give plastic rackets to a bunch of two and three-year-olds?" Callie has been bitching about being kicked out of class since we got to our booth at McDonald's. Technically, she wasn't kicked out, but once the instructor's nose started bleeding all over the place, the room was deemed unsanitary and the rest of today's class was cancelled.

Greg quickly went into coach mode, assessing the injury. When he got within a few inches of the instructor's face to have a look, I thought she was going to pass out from swooning so hard. It made me roll my eyes, which Callie caught and promptly gave me shit for. Once Greg declared it was nothing more than a bloody nose, Callie was strongly advised to look into a different class, better able to keep up with Christopher's energy level. "If you ask me, she had it coming to her."

"I don't think she asked for it," Greg disputes, taking a bite out of his Big Mac, or whatever he got, and chewing until he can speak again. "But it wasn't her first class. She should have adjusted the class based on the kids. Especially since she's been teaching Christopher for several months."

"Exactly." She looks over her shoulder to peek at the kids. They've all got their mouths jammed up to the plastic window in one of the tubes, making blowfish faces.

I briefly wonder how much kids' slobber has been on that window, but then remind myself this is how mine have built up strong immune systems. "You think he should take a class at your gym, Greg?"

Greg immediately starts choking and shaking his head back and forth. "No…" he gurgles out in between coughs. "No way." He bangs his chest a few more times before getting under control again. "Christopher doesn't need gymnastics. He needs pee-wee football so he can tackle."

Callie deflates. "I looked into it already. They don't take kids until they're four."

"Oh, I bet if you took him to a practice, they'd make an exception."

Her face brightens. "You think?"

Greg nods slowly. "Oh yeah. It's every coach's dream to find a kid his age with natural abilities. Those are the kids you can't wait to work with and who you'll make extra effort to train."

"I have a question for you." I lick the ketchup off my finger and dip another fry. "Why do you bring Peyton to this class if you're the program director at another place? Wouldn't you get the class for free if you did it at your gym?"

"We don't have a class for her age that fits my schedule. But it works out better this way anyway." He takes a sip of his drink before continuing. "I don't want to bring my personal life into work. I wouldn't put it past my ex to show up on a Thursday simply to cause me problems at work. It's better that she not have any reason to go there."

"She sounds like a psycho," Callie states, sitting back in her chair and getting more comfortable. We may be here a while. The kids still have a lot of energy to burn since we left early.

"I don't really know for sure," he admits. "I just don't want to find out. I'd rather not lose my job because she gets a bee in her britches."

"A bee in her britches?" I giggle. "I've never heard that one before."

He looks at me and smiles, and I find myself smiling back at him. If no one was here, I'd lean over and kiss him. But they are, so I won't.

"Ick. Get a room," Callie says, screwing up her face and breaking the moment.

"We're not even touching each other," I respond with a roll of my eyes.

"Well you might as well be with all that googly-eye shit going on." She leans forward on her arms and looks back and forth at us. "Will you at least tell me if you had sex? I need a little excitement in my life."

Greg looks like a fish out of water trying to figure out how to respond. I shake my head and drop my napkin on the table, leaning in mimicking her pose.

"Ok, since you won't let it go, let's do this. What do you want to know?"

She begins rapid firing questions at me, and I rapid fire back.

"Did you kiss him?"

"He kissed me. Next."

"Did you kiss him back?"

"Yes. Next."

"Did you have sex with him?"

"No. Next."

"Are you going to?'"

I pause and slowly look over at Greg who has one eyebrow cocked. "Don't look at me," he mutters. "Answer the woman."

I purse my lips to suppress a smile and look back at Callie. "I'm invoking my right to my one free pass."

"You can't do that!" she complains.

"I sure as hell can. You made up the rules to this stupid game, two years ago when you didn't want to tell me where sand really ended up after your romp on the beach, remember?"

Her mouth drops open in indignation. "You promised we'd never speak of that again." She points her finger in my face. "No one should have to spend part of their honeymoon in the ER getting sand flushed out of their crack."

"You started it."

She stomps her foot under the table. "I wanna know if you're gonna get naked with the only hot guy we know," she whines.

"Then you should have been more patient and not asked in front of him." I gesture my head Greg's direction.

"Fine," she grumbles. "I'll wait until he's gone."

"How come I can't be a part of the conversation? I was there, too. Maybe I'll have extra information you can't get from Elena." Greg has a shit-eating grin on his face that makes me all gooey inside. I love how laidback he is and how he can have fun no matter where we are.

It also strikes me as interesting that we're all very nonchalant about this whole dating thing. In college and in my twenties, people didn't seem to be this matter of fact. There was more playing hard to get. Less openness. Maybe more mind games. It feels very freeing to be so open like this the day after a first date.

"Ok," Callie bites first. "How was your date, Greg?"

"Great." He leans back in his chair. "She ate all her dinner so I think she liked my cooking. And she's a really good kisser. I call that a success."

"Did you get some boob action, too?"

"Callie!" I throw my napkin at her and her lack of boundaries.

She throws it right back. "What? It's fair game until he invokes his own free pass." She turns back to him. "Well?"

"No boob action."

"Did you try?"

He looks at me, and I throw my hands up in the air. "Whatever. I'm sure it'll come up later anyway. Might as well tell her now."

Decision made, he turns back to her. "Yes, I tried. Yes, she shut me down. No, it didn't bother me. I'd rather wait until we're on the same page."

Callie whips her head around. "You shut him down? Why?"

I glare at her and this turn of questioning. I expected the third degree from her eventually, but I was hoping she'd miss it during his rapid-fire round and we wouldn't have to discuss it right now. Not in front of an audience.

"Elena. I'm serious."

She's not giving up, and it's starting to piss me off. This is my private struggle and she knows it. "I'm invoking a free pass," I say with a glare.

"You don't have another free pass." When I still don't answer, she huffs. "Please tell me it's not because of what he said?"

"Callie…" I warn.

"What who said?" Greg looks confused as he tries to follow our conversation. I sit quietly, not sure how to respond. I'm working on not letting James' words affect me anymore, but it's not always easy.

Callie continues to look at me, her eyes basically begging me to fill Greg in. Finally, I drop my head and nod. I guess he's going to find out how insecure I am eventually. It might as well be now so he can decide how much he wants to get involved with another hot mess and we can all move on with our lives.

"Her ex is a real dick," Callie starts, Greg nodding along. "Used to tell her all the time that if she wanted one, he'd find the money for her to get a boob job. Brought it up all the time and really put pressure on her to do it."

Greg gets a strange look on his face. "Besides being insulting, it's weird. Why was it important to him? Who cares?"

"That's what I said," Callie continues. "But it's worse than that. When he finally left her for Child Bride Barbie, he threw it in her face on his way out the door. Said if she'd had that boob job, he wouldn't have had to go out and find someone with a nice rack to turn him on. Oh, and that he couldn't spend the rest of his life pretending he enjoyed nuzzling a couple of stretched out socks."

I close my eyes and will away his stare, but I can feel it. I can feel Greg staring at me.

"Elena." I don't look at him. I'm embarrassed by my own embarrassment. I shouldn't still feel hurt over words that were said by a man who continues to prove that he's completely out of touch with what women really need... including his own daughters. I hate that I'm ashamed of my body. I should be proud of it and everything it's carried me through. But I'm not. And now Greg knows it's going to take a lot of effort to get in these pants. "Elena," he tries again, "you know he only said those things to try and alleviate his own guilt, right?"

I sigh and open my eyes, looking back and forth between my two friends. "I know. And I'm working on it, I really am. It's going to take time to retrain my brain, or whatever. It's no big deal." I take a sip of my drink and stand up, gathering trash. "Come on, Max. It's time to go."

"Elena, we don't have to leave now. We can talk about something else," Callie says, suddenly deciding the conversation I didn't want to have but was basically forced into was a bad idea. I can see the realization hit her that she went too far. Yes, we're three friends sitting around shooting the shit.

But we're not *just* three friends sitting around shooting the shit. This is one of those times when her mouth started talking before her brain caught up. I love her, but sometimes she forgets that even though it's not at all a hot-button issue for her, doesn't mean it's not one for me. And just because she's a complete open book with her private thoughts doesn't mean I am, too.

Looks like she's all caught up now.

"No, it's ok." And it is. Yes, I'm embarrassed, but seeing the regret on her face, I know she is, too. Of course she's forgiven without even asking for it. "I need to get her down for a nap anyway." Gathering all our stuff, I turn to leave the play area when a hand grabs me and turns me around.

"Everyone has something they don't like about themselves, Elena. Even me." Greg moves his hand from my arm to pull my body flush with his, his eyes locked with mine. He moves his mouth to my ear so no one can hear him speak except me. "I don't care if I never see or touch your boobs. I like spending time with you. And if we do end up having sex, remember one thing…" he moves his hand down and squeezes my butt cheek quickly. "… I'm an ass man."

He quickly grabs the wrappers out of my hands, walks around me and into the restaurant to throw our trash away. I, on the other hand, am completely stunned and am having a hard time breathing.

I look up at Callie who looks like the cat that ate the canary. She looks around quickly then lifts both hands, one of them making an "ok" sign, the other taking a finger and putting it into that hole. And then she winks, the perv.

All I can do is smile back as I try to stay upright, despite my swoon. She's right.

I'm absolutely going to have sex with him.

CHAPTER
Thirteen

I swing my front door open and immediately reach to catch the box that's falling in front of me.

"Sorry." It's Callie's muffled voice from behind another box. "I got them all the way to the front door, but knocking proved to be a real bitch."

We drop the boxes—that I now see are full of colorful clothes—on the couch with an "umph".

"What is all this?"

A bright smile crosses her face. "Congratulate me. I am officially a RowRow Apparel consultant!" She squeals and covers her mouth with her fingers. "Can you believe it?"

"I honestly can't believe it because I've never heard you talk about this before. What's going on?"

We pull bright dresses and skirts and tops out of the boxes and fold them absent-mindedly.

"Well, you know how Ben always thinks he gets to make the decisions around the house because he's the sole bread winner now?"

"Yep. And you know how I always call him a dick for it?" It's a continual argument with them. Because he makes the money, he gets to make the big decisions about what they do with that money. Sure, she can do whatever she wants within reason, but things like appliances and vacations… he always plays that card. "Well, I've decided we're going to be a two-income household again," she says with delight.

"How are you going to do that?" I'm really confused. "Christopher got kicked out of three different daycares and a church Mother's Day Out program. Where are you going to find someone to watch him?"

"That's the brilliance of RowRow Apparel." She has her finger held up like she's making an important point. "I do it out of my home on my own schedule. I can coordinate it around Ben being home."

"Oh, he's going to love that," I say sarcastically.

"That's part of what I love about it. I'm with Christopher while he works. He's with Christopher while I work. Sounds like an even split to me. He's got no room to complain."

She makes a valid point. But I'm still not convinced. "I don't know, Callie. You really want to spend all your free time doing this?"

"Think about it. I love to shop. I love to help other people shop. I love to tell them what to wear. This is the perfect job for me."

She's right. If anyone can be successful peddling clothing out of the back room of her house, it's Callie. Plus, these clothes are really nice. I already see a few things I might like to try on myself.

"You're right. This might be really good for you. But where are you going to keep everything." I make a mental note to try on a flowy sundress with daisies printed all over it. "Don't you have to keep several racks of inventory?"

She puts her hands on her hips, a strange look crosses her face and I swear there's an evil gleam in her eye.

"I'm keeping it all in the office."

"Wait. *The* office?"

She nods.

"The sanctuary no one goes into because it is a mecca of business and finances?" Ben's words. Not mine.

She nods again.

"Does your husband know this yet?"

"Oh yeah. And he's not happy." She smiles. "But what can he do? This is a business, right? That's the whole point of keeping an office. It keeps everything separate and out of Christopher's path. Hasn't that always been Ben's argument?"

"You're enjoying this a little too much." I'm such a hypocrite. I love it a little too much, too.

She shrugs. "Then he needs to stop being holier-than-thou when it comes to money. Once I'm making as much as him, he won't have an argument, and I'll finally get my new dishwasher."

"You planning on buying that dishwasher yourself? Because you know he's never going to pay for it."

"With my first paycheck. And..." she pauses for effect. "I'm going to pay the *retail* price."

I gasp and cover my heart, pretending to be shocked. Callie hates waiting for things to go on sale. She'd much rather get what she wants, when she wants it, and if that means paying full-price, so be it. Ben, on the other hand, refuses to buy anything until it's on sale. Yet another thing they argue about. I'm starting to wonder if they ever get along.

We continue pulling out clothes and sort it all by style and size. A few pieces get tossed my way to try on, which I comply with. It's purely for Callie's benefit. She needs to know how the clothes are going to look on all body shapes.

Of course, once the girls see what we're doing, they haul all their dresses into the living room and soon enough, we have a full-on fashion show happening. Complete with all my shoes, some up-do's and quite a few snapshots of the girls all dressed up and having fun. My mother is going to get a kick out of these later.

When it's my turn to walk the catwalk, the girls (with the help of Callie) choose that black flowy sundress with the daisies I'd been eyeing earlier. I don't usually wear dresses this form-fitting on top, for obvious post-baby reasons. But the girls are enjoying this, so what's the harm?

As I round the corner from our dressing room, also known as the downstairs bathroom, I strike a pose. The girls clap and cheer as I put a little extra strut in my steps and spin for effect.

If I had only been six inches taller and forty pounds lighter, I could have been a professional model. Obviously, I missed my calling.

"Elena that looks fantastic on you," Callie remarks. "You need to keep that."

"I might. I'll have to see how my budget looks." I plop down on the couch next to her and kick my feet up on the coffee table as the girls run off, more dresses in hand to try on. "I haven't balanced my checkbook yet. I keep putting it off. It's my least favorite chore."

"No, I don't want you to pay for it. I want you to have it."

I look over at her and see sincerity.

Wait.

Nope. That's not sincerity. She has something up her sleeve.

Cocking my eyebrow at her, I don't beat around the bush. "What do you want?"

"You know me so well." She turns her whole body so she's facing me. "I know people do a lot of these sales online and everything, but I want to do more parties. I want to give people a chance to try things on and feel the fabric. I want to be more like... like a personal shopper. I think that's where I really shine."

I nod my agreement. She's really good at eyeing a piece of clothing and knowing whether or not it will fit me before I even try it on. That is, when I let her drag me out shopping. Or when I'm desperate for something new.

"But it's a lot of work to drag all these clothes to someone's house, set it all up, do the party, tear it all down... I need help."

Sounds simple enough. "Ok. So you want me to come help you sometimes."

"Well yeah. I think it'll be fun. But instead of paying you in money, I propose you let me pick an outfit for you to wear out of my inventory. You'll be like my human mannequin."

"Oh yeah. That sounds amazing," I deadpan.

"Come on." She gently smacks my arm. "If we're both wearing the clothes, and wearing a completely different style, we'll be like walking advertisements. People will get to see what the clothes look like on real women, not just in pictures."

"Callie, I don't mind helping you. And I can pay for my own clothes. I just don't think you and I have the same style."

"But that's kind of the point. We have different styles. We have different builds. It'll really show how if you wear the right size and cut, they look fantastic on any woman. I bet I sell so much more because of that. And…" I knew there was an 'and'. "… it'll help beef up your wardrobe."

I groan.

"You've gotten a makeover. And a new hair style. Let me help you with your transformation. Please? You know I'm dying to get ahold of your closet."

"Ok, fine." I hold my hands up. "Fine! You can rebuild my wardrobe."

"Yay!" She begins bouncing up and down.

"Don't get excited yet." She stops bouncing up and down. "I have to approve every piece you pick out for me, and if I veto it, it's out, got it?" She nods. "And you don't get to step foot into my closet with a trash can like on that reality make over show. You only get to help me add to my wardrobe."

"I don't get to go into your closet *yet*." I start to interrupt but she talks faster. "Once you have a solid beginning with some really good pieces, we'll go through it together. If you still need it."

"Only if I need it."

She smiles and I know she wants to bounce again. "Thank you, Elena! I'm so excited. Our first party is this Friday."

"Callie, I can't get my mom to babysit that quickly."

"I already called her. She's in."

I roll my eyes to the ceiling. I should have seen it coming. Callie has spent way too much time living with Ben. She's a master manipulator now.

The girls come back in the room, Fiona holding Max's hand to help her walk in my high heels. Maura struts right past them both, pulling her best Cindy Crawford impression, right down to the small mole on her face.

I'm pretty sure it's actually a speck of marker from when they were coloring earlier, but it works on her.

We clap and cheer, and of course my phone rings right in the middle of all the fun. It's the doctor's office.

"Hey, I need to take this." I point at the phone and Callie nods, telling the girls how stunning they look and how good they are at walking.

If only she was with them every day, she'd see it's a rarity for them to all be upright at the same time.

"Hello?" I answer, as I close the front door behind me.

"May I speak with Elena Monroe, please?" a professional female voice says on the other side of the line.

"This is she."

"Hi, this is Brandy with Dr. Wassman's office. How are you today?"

My doctor is calling me at home. I'm assuming I could be better. But I decide to go the more traditional route with this conversation. "I'm fine, thanks."

"Good, good." Yep. I made the right decision. She's ready to give me some news and get back to it. "You had some bloodwork done a few weeks ago when you came in for your wellness visit, and I wanted to go over the results."

"That doesn't sound good."

"Oh, it's not terrible," she says, dismissing my concerns. "Everything looked pretty normal, no infections. The one thing the doctor is a little concerned about is your cholesterol."

This doesn't surprise me. "Yeah, it typically runs high in my family. Especially on my dad's side."

"Yes, but it was really high. Your LDLs are at 247."

Uh huh. And my dad's is consistently at 250. Has been for ten years. But I don't tell her that. "Ok, so I need to watch what I eat?"

"Well...." She pauses before dropping the bomb on me. "Dr. Wassman would like to start you on Crestor to try and get it under control."

"What?" I whine. I know I'm whining and I don't care. "Isn't there anything else we can do before trying medication? I eat terrible and I'm lazy. I admit it. Can't I do something with that instead."

"Well, um... hang on." She puts me on hold, as indicated by the fact that I'm now listening to the sweet sounds of "Never Gonna Give You Up" by Rick Astley, acoustic version. I hum along and of course as soon as we get to the good part, the nurse picks back up. "Mrs. Monroe?"

"Ms." I correct her. She ignores me. Whatever.

"Dr. Wassman says we can try controlling it with diet and exercise first. But you have to come back in six months to get it rechecked."

"Absolutely. I'll toss out my hot dogs and start eating salad tonight."

Yeah, I'm not doing either of those things. But she doesn't need to know that.

"Ok. Well if you need anything, or have any questions, give us a call."

"Thanks, Brandy. See you in six months."

We disconnect and I notice a text message.

Greg: *Hope you're having a great day with the girls. Can't wait to see you again.*

His sweet text makes me smile. It feels like he's wooing me. I've never been wooed before. James and I sort of fell into dating and never looked back. This is different. It's him pursing me. I like it.

Me: *Me, too. We're having an impromptu fashion show. I think I missed my calling.*

Pressing send, I meander my way back inside, plop myself down next to Callie and sigh.

She ignores me, too busy looking at all her new inventory.

"Where are the girls?" They're strangely quiet. It's freaking me out a little.

"They're in their rooms playing retail store."

"Retail store? How do you play that?"

Yet another gleam in her eye. "You fold all your clothes and hang your dresses nicely for your customers."

Leave it to Callie to come up with a way to get my girls to pick up their rooms.

My phone buzzes with another text.

Greg: *Supermodels are too skinny. You're perfect the way you are.*

If only he knew my doctor's opinion on that.

"I'll ignore the text message that just made you blush and smile since I'm assuming I already know who it's from." I shoot her an annoyed look, but as always it doesn't faze her. "But who called?"

"Doctor's office. My bloodwork came back."

She stops and looks at me—really looks at me—trying to see if it's bad news. "That took them way too long to get it back."

"It took them way too long to draw blood that day, too."

She keeps staring at me, waiting for me to give her the results. This is one of the things that sucks about getting older. A call from the doctor, any doctor, makes us all expect the worst while hoping for the best.

"My cholesterol is too high."

She immediately looks relieved and waves me off. "That's not a big deal. Everyone's cholesterol is high."

"No. Mine is really high." She still doesn't look at me. "Callie, I have to join a gym."

That finally gets her attention. She looks at me, face pale, hand over her mouth. "It's a fate worse than death," she whispers.

I snigger. "Ohmygod. Drama much?"

"Shut up. I hate the gym. I'd rather have a heart attack."

Me, too, I think to myself. Me, too.

CHAPTER *Fourteen*

When I was in my twenties, I loved working out. It made me feel strong and boosted my endorphins. I would run or do aerobics or swim at least five days a week.

Then I had children.

And having children meant being tired. That eventually morphed into being lazy.

Now the most exercise I get, besides carrying around small children, is running from my bedroom to the bathroom when Aunt Flo shows up unannounced.

But today is a new day. Today is the day I take back control of my body. Take back control of my heart health. And take back control from this damn treadmill that might as well be a rocket launching computer at NASA with all the buttons and functions it has on it. Seriously, how the hell do you turn this thing on?!

A quick, stealth glance at the woman running next to me does me no good. She's a tall, leggie blonde who has obviously been doing this for a while. And she isn't pressing any of the buttons. She's running like she's being chased by a bear and wants to make sure she's not last.

Don't worry, honey. Clearly, I would be the loser in that scenario.

Luckily for me, someone climbs onto the treadmill on my left and knows how to turn it on. Following her lead, I finally get mine going and soon enough, I'm working up a sweat.

Well, not really a sweat. It's more of a slight glisten, but I'm taking it slow. It's going to take some time to build up my endurance.

"You're gonna have to do more than meander to get your heart rate up."

What Greg doesn't know is my heart sped up the minute I heard his voice. We haven't seen each other since Christopher basically got us all kicked out of class. We've texted a lot, but not made eye contact. Supposedly, we're all going to keep meeting up on Thursday mornings for playdates, we just haven't quite figured out where, yet.

"Hey, you!" I put on my brightest smile, mentally berating myself for opting to wear my old, faded yoga pants to the gym so the new ones will stay clean to wear in public. "I didn't know you were a member here."

"Yeah, I'm here a few days a week. Gotta keep my strength up so I can spot all the kids at my job."

"That's why you do it? It has nothing to do with keeping that six-pack rock hard?"

He smirks and I realize I've said too much again. Crap. Now he knows I've been checking him out. I mean, he probably already assumes since we made out like a bunch of fifteen-year-olds the other day, but a lady isn't supposed to admit these things.

Fortunately, he's a gentleman and ignores the blush that crosses my face, although I can tell by the way his eyes crinkle slightly that he's at least amused. "That's definitely a nice benefit. But no. It's more about the job. Those gymnasts look tiny, but when a hundred pounds of flailing arms and legs comes barreling at you, you'd better be strong enough to catch them."

Leggy blonde on my right slows down her treadmill to a walk. Well, a fast walk. The bear would still catch me first. She has sexy sweat dripping down her barely covered torso and a tiny little butt with the right amount of cheek sticking out of her boy shorts. Ugh. She makes me want to reconsider ten years' worth of chocolate and macaroni and cheese.

"Hi Greg," she says with a breathy smile. I kind of hate her right now.

"Hey Heather." He raises his head in greeting and turns right back to me.

Take that, *Heather*, I think victoriously. Apparently, I don't do jealous well.

"Come to my spin class with me." He smiles encouragingly, which makes me want to jump right off this treadmill and follow him wherever he wants to go. But then I remember, he wants to go to spin.

"Uhh…" I hesitate. "I'm not sure I'm up to that level of endurance yet. This is day one for me."

"Come on." He persists and that smile... No way I'll be able to resist if he keeps looking at me that way.

"Fine," I huff and slap the stop button on my treadmill. *That* button is clearly marked. "But if I fall off the bike and hurt myself, you're going to have to explain to Callie why I can't be her walking billboard tomorrow night."

"Her what?"

"Long story. Where are the bikes anyway?"

"Up here." Grabbing my water bottle and towel, we head up the stairs, around the corner, through a room full of weights... frankly, I have no idea where we are or how I'll ever find this place again. But depending on how this turns out, that might not be a bad thing.

The room is darker than any other part of the gym. The lights are all turned off, I'm assuming to keep the temperature down a bit, and the only light comes from a few square windows.

"Welcome!" a female voice calls through the speakers. "Grab a bike and we'll be starting in a few minutes."

"That's Bianca," Greg informs me. "She's great."

Bianca smiles and greets everyone that walks in. She's a tiny, dark-haired woman of some sort of Latin decent. She has a slight accent, but I can't place where she's from. She's beautiful and has some kick ass legs. If that's what spin does for your backside, I'll be here every day.

Greg finds us two bikes, side by side, and adjusts his seat.

There are way more knobs and pully-things than any other bike I've ridden before. "Um, I don't have any idea what I'm doing," I admit.

"Here, let me help. Your seat should be about hip height when you're standing next to it, like this." He begins moving the knobs and adjusting things. "Your handlebars need to be a little higher than that. But for your height, you don't want them too far away or it'll get uncomfortable. Jump on and see how that feels."

Jump? Uh, no. Instead, I climb up on the bike and nod in agreement, pretending it's all correct. Really, I have no idea, and I have a hard time believing there's any way to make sitting on this thing comfortable. These are literally the world's smallest seats. Who's butt fits on these things? Well, besides *Heather* from the treadmill.

What I do know is the pedals have stir ups. Probably for people like me who have a legitimate concern about falling off a stationary bike.

"Ok everybody, let's get this party started!" Bianca yells, and the music begins pumping through the speakers. I can barely hear the *whir* of the bikes over the base. I'm not pedaling nearly as fast as everyone else, but this is kind of fun. I might be able to do this for an hour.

"Everybody up!" Bianca instructs and everyone around me stands up.

Wait, we have to stand up and pedal? I can barely stay on this thing when I'm sitting down.

But in the interest of not looking like the only schlump in the group, I go for it. And surprise! I can do it!

Look at me! I'm riding a bike while standing up on the pedals! Sure, the bike's not going anywhere, but I still get credit for standing, right?

"And back down!" Bianca yells again.

I try to follow along but sitting back down on that tiny little seat proves to be more difficult than I expect. I'm legitimately surprised it hasn't ended up in places no bike seat should go.

"And back up!"

Ohmygod, again?

I glance over at Greg who is following along just fine. He's barely even breaking a sweat. Me? It's been three minutes, and I'm ready to call it quits.

"Let's speed it up everybody!"

We stand up, sit down, speed up, slow down, and all the while I look more and more like I got in a fight with a garden hose and lost. Bianca tries to keep us motivated, which works for everyone. Everyone except me. I want to fall off this bike and die. Surely the hour is almost over.

"Relax everyone." Bianca finally sits back and grabs her water bottle. "Take a drink and get ready. That was a great warm up."

Warm up? Oh no. It's only been fifteen minutes?

Greg recognizes the look on my face and does what he does best... coach.

"You're doing good, Elena. The first time is hard for everyone. Just do as much as you can."

I'm breathing too heavy to speak, so I'm stuck with nodding my appreciation, as I wipe down my entire upper body. I hope this gym has enough towels. I'm gonna go through a lot of them.

I try really hard to keep up with the rest of the class, but eventually I give up and try to enjoy the fact that I'm still moving my legs. My heart is still beating. I'm sweating. My body is feeling stronger. For now, that's good enough.

The sounds of Ed Sheeran's "Shape of You" pumps through the speakers, getting me motivated again.

I love this song. What woman doesn't want a man to revere her body like she's a goddess, regardless of her shape? Someday I'll have that. Someday.

Plus, Ed Sheeran's voice makes me horny. But I'm trying not to remember that part while continually sitting up and down on the seat. One rub the wrong way and I'll never be allowed to come back.

Greg is sweaty and breathing hard. Yet somehow, he still looks amazing.

He catches my glance and smirks, then gives me a quick once over before his gaze lingers on my ass. My ass that's currently sticking out as I'm standing up on the pedals, bent over the handle bars. He looks back to my eyes, wiggles his eyebrows once, and mouths the words to the song right on cue… *I'm in love with your body.*

I gasp and lean to the left. Fortunately, I catch myself before I fall, but my heartrate never comes back down. I can't believe he did that, the little flirt.

Biting back a smile, I turn back to follow along with Bianca. Somehow, sticking my ass out no longer seems like such a bad idea.

By the end of class, I still feel like I'm dying, but I have to admit, I feel strong. I feel like I've released a lot of stress. I feel good.

Until I try to climb off the bike and nearly fall over. Thank goodness for those stir ups or I would have been flat out on the floor.

"Well? What do you think?" Greg hands me some wipes and we begin cleaning off our bikes.

"I think there are definitely more fun ways to get bruises on my bum," I joke. He half gasps, half chokes. "Oh, come on. You're still being shocked by some of the things I say?"

What is happening here? I'm the one flirting with him, not the other way around. When did I start doing that? I guess there's something to say for these endorphins. They make me a new woman.

"You know I like being shocked by the things you say. You always keep me on my toes."

Waddling my bruised butt to the door, I throw my trash away, grab a fresh towel, and wrap it around my neck.

"Do you have time to grab something to eat at the snack bar?"

"I wish I could." And I really, really do. "But I only have daycare for another, oh shit, forty-five minutes," I say, as I look at the clock.

He looks briefly disappointed but recovers quickly. "Oh is Max here?"

"Yeah. In the daycare. It's really nice that she gets to play with the other kids. But mostly it's nice that I can shower without her throwing the curtain back to tell me what color booger she blew out of her nose."

He laughs that deep chuckle and suddenly I wish I got the bruises in my nether regions the fun way. "You should try being a guy showering around a two-year-old girl. She's always pointing and asking, 'wat dat?'" I press my lips together to curb my laugh. "Yeah, you know what I'm implying. At least I've finally broken her of grabbing for it."

Laughter bubbles out of me at the thought of Peyton standing under him, looking up and grabbing for his manhood. I won't tell him how I realized I was getting lazy in my grooming habits when Max tried to pet me, post shower, like a kitten. I took clippers to that problem area real quick.

"Yeah, it's funny to you," Greg jokes.

"I'm sorry. You're right. It's not… ok, yeah it is." My laughter starts all over again, but this time he joins me. "Anyway," I say, pulling myself together, "James takes the kids this weekend. Can I have a rain check on lunch?"

His face immediately brightens. "Absolutely. I'll call you tonight to make plans."

"Ok."

"Now go take a shower. You've only got forty minutes left and you need to stand under that hot water for a while so your muscles don't hurt too bad tomorrow."

He leans in and in full view of everyone, including *Heather*, who I hope is catching all of this, kisses me. It's only a peck, but it's a leisurely one. A kiss that says, "She's mine." When he finally breaks away, I flash him one last smile, turn to the locker room and walk away, feeling confident and content.

I had a great workout, I've got another date, and my crush likes the shape of my body.

Now doesn't that put a little extra sway in my hips.

CHAPTER
Fifteen

Butt bruises don't lie.

Two days ago, I was sitting on a tiny little bicycle seat, feeling good about accomplishing some exercise. Today, I'm trying to sit gently on a bench while Fiona does gymnastics, but every time I move, it feels like that time I traded paddle licks with a two-hundred-pound college kid at a frat party on a dare.

I will neither confirm nor deny if I ever partook in such an exercise. But I will say, it took a month for those bruises to finally fade.

This is why I don't do Jaeger bombs. They give drunk college girls bad ideas.

Greg came out of the office a little while ago and started to come talk to me, but I was on an emergency call with my mom. Or what she considers a grandma emergency anyway. She wanted to verify that I had, in fact, said the girls have been so good today they could have ice cream instead of vegetables for dinner.

If that had been true, Maura blew it by trying to pull a fast one on her Mimi.

However, I give her credit for reminding me that we're out of mint chocolate chip, and I need to stop for some on my way home.

When I shifted in my seat to wave at Greg and subsequently winced, he laughed at me. The dirty look I shot his direction made him laugh even harder. If he wasn't such an amazing person and I didn't like him so much, I would have called him an asshole.

Ok, fine. I may have done that anyway.

Unfortunately, he's still on the clock and he didn't have time to stick around and wait for my mother to stop babbling.

And now here I sit... sucked into the reality show vortex with her again. I'm in Kardashian hell.

"He said he was going after the President if there wasn't more equality. Can you believe that?"

"She, ma."

"What?"

I glance at Fiona across the room, doing her best to swing on the bars. I'm thinking it's not her best event since she keeps falling off.

"Caitlyn Jenner wants to be referred to as *she*," I correct.

"She does?" For as much as my mother is obsessed with this family, I still can't get her to figure out the politically correct way to handle the drama that comes with it.

"Yes. It's part of the point of being transgender."

"Oh. Well I wouldn't know anything about that."

She continues to blather on about more recent Kardashian drama that she refuses to admit has been played up for publicity purposes, while I continue to watch Fiona. Fi is still struggling with her swing and I can see the frustration building.

Coach Zack is spotting another kiddo, so I don't think he realizes it's even happening.

"I worry about him, *her*," she quickly corrects herself. "Caitlyn couldn't even stand up to Kris Jenner when they were married. How is she going to stand up to a full-blown narcissist?"

"As good of a point as you have, ma," And she really does kind of have one, "I need to go. Fiona's having some trouble on the bar."

"Oh no. Did she hit a mental block like you always did?"

I hope not. I don't want her having the same struggles I do as an adult.

"Nah, she's having trouble with her re-grip. She's heading over to see me."

We disconnect as Fiona gets to me and jumps in my arms, tears streaming down her face.

"Hey, now," I soothe. "What's going on?"

She shakes her head, her little face still buried in my shoulder.

"You don't wanna tell me?"

Another shake. My little mini-me. When she's ready, she'll talk. But first she has to figure out how to explain it.

We sit and rock for a few minutes. Coach Zack quickly realizes she's gone, and begins looking around his stations, a panicked look on his face. I wave my hand until he sees me, point at her on my lap, and flash him a "thumbs up" so he knows everything is fine. I appreciate him as a coach anyway, but his look of relief when he sees Fi with me makes me feel confident he really cares about his kids.

"I can't do it, Mama." Her muffled voice is full of disappointment, and I wish I could do it for her. But I can't. As a parent, that's a tough pill to swallow. I can't make sure she'll always be successful because she is only human, just like me. But what I can do is guide her. Teach her. Give her the wisdom others have given me and hope it helps her become the best she can be.

I pull her out of the embrace and sit her back on my knees. "Ok, tell me what's happening."

"I'm supposed to do a big swing back and forth." She sniffles. "Three whole times. But after two times I fall down."

"Are you doing your re-grip?"

"I don't know what that is." She looks at me with inquisitive eyes. It's moments like these, when she's engaged in learning something, that I love the most. I love watching the light bulb go on in her head when she takes the information, processes it, and learns something new.

Using it as a pretend bar, I place her hand on my forearm and demonstrate. "When you're swinging out as far as you can, your fingers are kind of slipping. See how they moved?" She nods so I continue. "And when you swing back, as high as you can go, see how your fingers don't go all the way back?" She nods again. This is good. She's still with me. "When you get all the way back, as high as you can go, you let go of the bar and re-grip it as fast as you can. Like this." I pull her hand off of me and put it back quickly.

It's fast, but her eyes still widen. "I have to let go of the bar?"

"Not for long. It's more like a hop. See?" I move her hand back and forth and make hopping sounds every time she lets go for a fraction of a second. "You try it."

She continues with the motion I've shown her until I feel pretty confident she knows what to do. Now it's just a matter of going for it. "You ready to go try it on the bar?"

She hesitates, but finally agrees.

"That's my girl. I'll sit here and watch."

She walks slowly towards the bar, still nervous, but determined to get it right. I realize there is wisdom in the technique I taught her, and not only for athletics, but for life in general.

For the last year, I've just been swinging through life, trying to hold on but losing my grip. Sometimes I don't even realize how close I am to falling. But if I'm going to be successful, I have to let go of my insecurities and my fears so I can grab onto things differently.

Coach Zack says a few words to Fiona when she gets to the bars. I see her nodding in agreement and he stands back as she climbs up on the bar and gets in position to swing. Slowly, she begins to move back and forth, but then she starts to pick up speed. It takes three or four swings, but then I see it. A hop. It's a small one, but it's there.

My smile is so big, I know my cheeks are going to hurt later, but there's no stopping it as I watch her keep going. She's swinging, back and forth, her hops getting higher and her grip getting stronger as she gets more sure of herself.

Eventually, Coach Zack stops her and pulls her off the bar, giving her a high five in the process. My baby girl is beaming. She's so proud of her accomplishment, and why shouldn't she be? She took hold of her fear and conquered it.

She turns, gives me a giant thumbs up, and continues to smile when I return the gesture.

What an amazing moment for both of us. My first born learned how to re-grip the bar. And I learned how to re-grip my life.

CHAPTER
Sixteen

Once a year the carnival comes to town. When you live in the suburbs, this is huge news. Not that we don't have any form of entertainment around here. It's your standard things like bowling and movies. The choices aren't bad. They just tend to feel limited after a while. Talk about first world problems.

When the bright lights, impossible-to-beat games, and wildly expensive fried food shows up, we get way too excited. Well, most of us do anyway.

"How is it possible that you've lived here this long and never gone to the carnival?"

Greg pulls into a parking space and cuts the engine before answering, "I honestly don't know. I remember always thinking it looked like fun, but never got around to it."

"Well, you are in for a treat!" We climb out of the car and make our way to the entrance. Before we even get to the ticket booth, Greg is holding my hand. I like it. A lot.

Despite the fact that all the prices are clearly labeled, he still seems to be overwhelmed by what we should get. "How many tickets are we going to need?"

"That depends on how much we do. Usually each ride costs five tickets."

"How many rides are we going to do?"

"As many as you want," I say with a shrug. "Within reason, of course. There's a few I won't get on because they make me want to throw up."

"Weak stomach?"

"No. Age. I used to ride everything when I was a kid. There was nothing with too many twists and curves for me. Then I hit twenty-five, and that was the end of that."

"How about we start with five rides a piece?" he suggests, as we move to the front of the line. "If we decide to do more, we'll come back."

"Ok." I pull out my cash and sort through bills.

"Um, what do you think you're doing?" Greg gives me an amused, quizzical look.

"Paying for my tickets?"

"Hmm." Based on the look on his face, I guess that was the wrong answer. "I thought this was a date."

"Don't people go dutch on dates now?" Isn't this what independent women do these days? Obviously, I have no idea what I'm doing. "I thought this was one of the new rules of dating."

"I think we're both old enough that the new rules don't apply. Put your money away. It's no good when I take you out."

I bite back a smile and do as he says. As soon as we're through the gate and the gravity of all the possibilities are laid out in front of us, Greg's eyes light up.

"Look at that!" He points to the left, his other hand still firmly clasping mine. "We should go there first."

"I'm not sure that's a good idea."

He's pointing at a bungee system, where the riders are buckled into a harness so they can jump on giant trampolines. The ride starts, though, with being launched at least twenty feet in the air. Really, it's any athletic person's dream ride. Unless said athletic person has had babies and therefore has stretched out girly parts.

"Why not? It looks like fun."

I contemplate my answer and then realize, he's been married before. He has a daughter. None of this should be news to him. "I've given birth three times."

He gives me a blank stare. Ok, I need to be a little less subtle.

"You know when women have babies and things don't work right anymore…" I keep trying to lead him there, gesturing towards my nether regions with my hands, but we're not getting anywhere. I huff. "Greg, I don't have that much bladder control anymore."

He grimaces. "Ummmm… what?"

My face begins to heat. "You've never heard of that before?" Great. Now I've told the man whose leg I want to hump that if I jump too high I'll pee on myself.

Just when I think Greg is going to run away screaming, he does the opposite, putting his arm around my neck, pulling me close and kissing the top of my head. "I'm messing with you. I knew about that. I just wasn't thinking when I suggested that ride."

I smack his rock-hard abs with one hand, wrapping my other arm around his waist. "Asshole," I grumble, making a laugh rumble through him.

"I couldn't help myself. It was too easy." We continue our trek through the fun, dodging a distracted child here and there. We continue holding onto each other as we walk. I can't remember the last time any man had his arms around me in public. It feels so nice I almost don't want to go on any rides.

Almost.

"Well, since we didn't get you any Depends on the way here," Greg jests, "what do you want to do first?"

I look around at the carnival rides, all of them outfitted with bright lights and blaring music, designed to catch your eye. There are so many things to choose from, and frankly, most of them don't look very safe.

But then I see it. A ride worth waiting in line for. It's not so much a ride as a challenge, and I'm up for it.

"That one right there." I point at it and lead Greg that direction.

It's all yellow and black, and it's made of that blow-up material used for the giant kids' slides. This one, however, is a circle. There are six small pedestals for contestants to stand on, and when the operator turns it on, the middle spins swinging long, soft arms at us. Participants have to either jump over the low arm or duck under the high arm, depending on which one is coming at them. And they have to stay on their pedestal.

It's reminiscent of the TV show *Wipe Out*, which I used to love watching when I was pregnant with Fiona. I always wanted to be on that show. Now's my chance to see what I'm made of.

"The Meltdown, huh?" he responds, but he's not fooling me. He's feeling the same sense of excitement I am.

It doesn't take long for the line to move forward. Possibly because there's an age limit no one is paying attention to and kids keep getting turned away at the front of the line. It could also be because most of the adults here aren't willing to give it a go. That would mean putting their beer down, and who wants to risk the party foul?

As we step into the arena and get settled on our spots, I feel the anticipation as we wait. I wonder if this is how it feels to wait for the buzzer to sound before running over the Big Balls. Man, that was such a great show. I wish they'd bring it back.

In this case, though, there is no buzzer, which means Greg isn't ready when we start. As the arm starts moving, he underestimates the height of the high bar and even though he bends over, it whacks him in the head and knocks him down.

I, on the other hand, can see the low bar coming for me, but I'm laughing so hard about the look on Greg's face when he got hit that I can't jump high enough, and within seconds I'm right there next to him on the floor.

The operator stops the ride and gives us a few seconds to climb back in our spots, before getting back to business. Within seconds, everyone is laughing at everyone else falling over and the ride has to be stopped several times.

It's the most fun I've had in a very, very long time. One glance at Greg, and I know he feels the exact same way. That it's nice to leave the stress of everyday life at home and embrace the fun.

We spend the next couple of hours bouncing from ride to ride, a couple stops for more tickets in between. We scream as loud as we can when the gates of our cage fly open and we defy gravity on the Gravitron. We make out at the top of the Ferris Wheel. Greg even tries his hand at winning some carnival prizes. It doesn't go well. Well, it doesn't go well for him. The carnie in charge of the game seemed pleased with taking all of Greg's money.

Greg and I laugh and talk and break into song when Garth Brooks' "Friends in Low Places" blares through the speakers.

By far, it is the best date I've ever been on and the most I've felt like a person, not just a mom, in ages.

"You win." He shovels the rest of our fried treat into his mouth. I finally convinced him to take a break from the rides, long enough to inhale some junk food. "I wasn't really living until I ate a Fried Snickers Bar."

"Told ya," I say around a bite of my Fried Coke. Yes, Fried Coke, as in Coca-Cola. I have no idea who created it or how they make the liquid into a solid, but I don't care as long as they keep giving it to me. "I know my junk food. I didn't get this fantastic physique by eating salad all day long."

"Tell me about it." Tossing the napkin on his plate, he leans forward and grabs a bite of my treat. I try to snatch it back, but he's too quick for me. "Just know, someday when I'm too old to work out, I'll still embrace my love of food."

I wipe my mouth after taking the last bite. "Is that your way of saying I can expect you to become glutinous in your old age?"

"You better believe it. Food like this will be too hard to pass up." He pats his still flat stomach like he's making sure it hasn't grown in the last ten minutes of eating. "I'm glad I'm *not* too old at this point and we have spin tomorrow." He looks at me with a quirked eyebrow, as if he's challenging me. "You are going, right?"

"Yes, I'm going," I grumble. "As much as my butt won't like the bruises, I feel really strong when I leave."

"Good. I like it when Bianca makes you lean over the handle bars and stick your butt out."

I throw my napkin at him and he bats it away playfully. "You're such a pig."

"Mommy! Mommy! Mommy!"

My head whips over at the unexpected voices to see my girls running toward me. Max immediately jumps in my arms and lays her head on my shoulder. Maura and Fiona wrap their arms around my legs while I pat their backs.

"Hi girls! I didn't know you were coming to the carnival tonight."

The older two nod excitedly like little bobble head dolls. "We went on the Ferris Wheel and the Carousel and the bumper boats," Maura spouts off, gesturing her hands wildly.

"Mom," Fiona interrupts. "We went on those giant swings that go around in a circle. I thought I was going to fly off. I screamed so loud!"

"Did you do the Serpent yet?" Greg asks excitedly, ever the child at heart now that he's been introduced to the best thing to happen to our little town.

Fiona's eyes get wild. "No way. That looks too scary."

"Aw come on," he jokes. "I'll take you on it."

She shakes her head in protest but before she can say anything, a familiar voice jumps into the conversation. "We're actually getting ready to leave." Immediately, my mood declines when I see James and Carnie Barbie meander up to our group.

"Oh hey, James, Keri." I decide to play the civil card. It's not the kids' fault we all ended up here together. No use in making a scene.

I turn to Greg who is watching my ex and his current, clearly trying to assess them. I wonder what he could be thinking about them.

"Greg, this is James and his new wife Keri."

Keri, of course, immediately reaches out and shakes Greg's hand, whipping her hair over her shoulder, a flirty smile on her face. "It's nice to meet you. How do you two know each other?" She gestures back and forth between Greg and I, and I know this is a challenge on her part. She's not blind. She sees how attractive Greg is and is wondering how I ended up here with him. In her eyes, I'm nothing special. Why should anyone else see anything great about me?

Fortunately, Greg catches onto her game really quickly. "We *met* at the parent-child gymnastics class both our girls are in. We *know each other* because we continue to spend time together."

James's jaw clenches together. It doesn't happen for long, but I see it. Why in the world would he be mad because Greg and I spend time together? He's married. To his former mistress. That he was dating while we were married. Who I date now that we're divorced shouldn't concern him at all. Before I can even question what's happening, Greg sticks his hand out. "I've heard a lot about you, James."

The two men shake, a friendly enough gesture. I think. The tension really is palpable. I get that James isn't Greg's favorite person after some of the things I've shared. But I don't understand James' standoffish-ness. He enjoys making sure I know he's building a new family without me. Why does he care if I'm on a date?

"We'd love to hang out, but it's getting late and the girls need to go to bed," James announces, never taking his eyes off Greg.

The girls, of course, protest. Partially because they don't want to go to bed. Partially because they think if they stick around, they're going to get to eat my Fried Coke. They are mistaken. I work too hard in spin to give it up to them.

It takes a solid five minutes of hugs, kisses, and reassurances that they're coming home tomorrow for the girls to finally give up and go with their dad. The entire time, Keri is doing her best to flirt with Greg, Greg is glaring at James, and James is giving me a weird look that I can't decipher. Am I seriously the only one here who is interacting with the kids?

They finally walk away, and I immediately turn to Greg. "What the hell was that?"

"What?"

"You glared at James the whole time. Your entire demeanor changed when he came over."

He shrugs and gathers the trash off the table, and walks away from me. I'm quickly out of my seat, trying to catch up to him.

"Wait a minute, Greg." I grab him by the arm stopping him and standing in his path. "What is going on?"

"I don't like that guy."

"Really," I deadpan. "I couldn't tell."

He tosses the trash and crosses his arms over his chest. "He wants you back."

I'm not sure whether to laugh or smack him for making such a tasteless joke.

"He does not." My voice comes out softer than I intend. I'm stunned by how quickly this wonderful date has turned into a random fight. Over what? Jealousy? Surely that can't be right.

"Yes, he does." He leans in so close, I can smell the chocolate on his breath. "I'm a guy. I know the look he was giving you. You were watching the girls, but he was watching *you*. And I'm telling you, he regrets ever leaving you."

I blink several times as my brain tries to sort out what he's telling me. My ex-husband, the father of my children, the man I spent fifteen years building a life with, only to be discarded like those fruity-flavored Tootsie Rolls everyone hates at Halloween when a shiny new woman came along, is having second thoughts? This doesn't make sense.

"I just worry," Greg continues, this time his voice holds no malice, only doubt and concern, "that you want him back, too."

Any hostility I feel deflates as we get to the middle of what it all boils down to. Greg doesn't want to compete for me. He wants me to choose him, even if it's early and neither of us knows if we're going to end up being forever. Warmth runs through my body as I let his feelings wash over me.

He wants me. And he wants me to want him, too. It's like a dream come true.

Taking a step forward, I put my arms around his neck and tug him close. "Let me ask you a question. If Libby wanted you back, what would you tell her?"

He scoffs. "That she burned that bridge when she took my kid and left."

I pull his head down so our foreheads are touching and stroke his hair. "Exactly. I really think you're misinterpreting what you saw. James stopped looking *at* me and started looking *through* me years ago." He tries to interrupt, but I stop him. "Even if you're right, I wouldn't go back to him. He cheated on me. Betrayed me. I can't let that go, even if I'm civil."

One of his lips quirks up in a sad half smile. "He made a huge mistake when he left you, ya know?"

"I know," I say more confidently than I feel. I can fake it 'til I make it. "And his loss is your gain."

Greg gives me a quick peck on the lips and rubs my back a few times. With a deep breath in and out, he says, "Enough of this. Let's get back to our date. What do you want to do now?"

"Ooh! Let's do that Serpent you were talking about."

"Let's go." He grabs my hand to hold, which is quickly becoming a nice habit, and then leads me in the wrong direction.

"Where are we going? The Serpent is that way." I point behind us, thoroughly confused.

"I figured you needed a pit stop first so you don't accidentally pee on my leg," he says with a laugh and a smile.

I smack him gently, call him a name, and jog toward the ladies' room, because as much as I hate to admit it, he's right.

I hate when that happens.

CHAPTER
Seventeen

Dating Greg is amazing. Not because we do anything out of the ordinary. But because he is an amazing person. And he treats me like he thinks I'm amazing, too. That, in and of itself, is a wonderful feeling.

Some days we'll meet up in the mornings for spin class or so I can walk on the treadmill while he runs. He's taught me how to get the damn machine to work. That's been nice.

Some days we'll go out to breakfast once the girls are at school. Max doesn't mind as long as she gets pancakes. Every. Single. Time.

Some days we'll text until he goes to work and I get busy with the girls.

Weekends, though, those have been incredible.

He brings Peyton over for playdates. We take the girls to the movies. We go bowling. Sometimes Callie joins us. Sometimes she doesn't.

My childless weekends are extra fun. Besides trying different restaurants and even a wine bar, we've been known to spend a lot of time making out on my couch. Other than eating each other's faces off, we've taken things very slow physically. I know he's respecting me and giving me time to push through my own insecurities. But I feel like there's something else going on as well. Like he's taken a vow of celibacy, or he's trying to win a bet. I'm not sure. But whatever it is, it's giving us a chance to really get to know each other on a more personal level, and I like that.

Despite our shift in relationship status, we still keep our Thursday playdates with Callie. When Christopher was passive aggressively unenrolled in the little kids' gymnastics class we all sort of gave up on it. Max wasn't learning much anyway, and Greg said the instructor was about as effective as a cassette player in a music store. It took me a minute to figure out he meant the instructor's techniques were antiquated and unsafe.

I'd never even noticed there was an actual goal in that class beyond, "Don't let Christopher hurt himself." I was so busy trying to get Max to try things while laughing my ass off at Callie trying to *stop* Christopher from trying things. I admit, I deferred to Greg's expertise on the instruction.

Now we come to this amazing park about fifteen minutes south of our neighborhood. The playground is humongous. Two giant swing sets that connect with a narrow, yet fully-enclosed bridge are on prominent display. There are several different sized slides attached, as well as monkey bars for the big kids, built-in fine motor toys for the little kids, and swings for every kid.

I will never know why we ever spent money on a class when this was practically in our backyard.

"I like your shirt," Callie remarks, as we watch the kids play on the lime green wooden seesaw that coordinates with the rest of the bright-colored toys. It's a child's dream.

Greg and Peyton are running late. Something about his ex claiming Peyton was sick and an argument over her being outside. I don't know. He sounded miffed when I called. I decided it was best to let him stew on it himself.

"The lady at the grocery store liked it, too," I reply to Callie's comment about my shirt. When the woman approached me at HEB and asked where I got it, I was shocked. Callie's been claiming RowRow Apparel is the hottest trend right now, but I didn't really believe her. She tends to get excited about things no one else cares about. But when that woman squealed and asked who my dealer was—yes, like clothing is a drug or something, which I guess to Callie it is—I begrudgingly admitted Callie might be on to something.

She gives me a smug look, but I refuse to take my eyes off the kids. I'm not avoiding her, per se. I don't really care if she was right as much as I care that she gets flustered by my lack of care. What can I say? Sometimes I have to make my own entertainment.

Plus, I have a feeling this seesaw thing is about to go bad, and I need to be ready to spring into action.

Realizing she's gotten nowhere with getting a rise out of me, Callie tries again. "Did you at least give her my business card?"

"Of course I did. And I may have encouraged her to set up a party at her house."

"Oh yay!" she squeals and begins clapping, distracting Max from her play. Uh oh. "Did you get her name? Should I call her first?"

"No, she was in a rush." As Max's side of the seesaw lowers to the ground, she loses any remaining interest in the activity. "But whatever-her-name-is said she'd call you tonight. I guess she needs to place an order soon or something."

Before I can tell her to wait, Max scrambles off the seesaw and runs away. This, of course, causes Christopher to plummet to the ground, the force of the fall throwing him backward, where he rolls into the dirt and lets out a high-pitched wail for his mother. I've never heard him make a peep when he's fallen before. Either it's really bad, or he's changing up his M-O.

"Oh shit," Callie exclaims and jogs her way to him to do all her boo-boo inspections.

"I see this playdate is already going well." Greg comes up from behind me and plants a kiss right on my lips. "Hey, babe. Sorry we're late." Peyton runs by as fast as her little legs will go, heading straight for her favorite person… Christopher. She jumps onto him, tackling him back into the dirt again. Callie throws her hands in the air in defeat and reaches down to try again. As soon as he saw Peyton coming, Christopher's tears dried up anyway, so Callie's ministrations are no longer needed, whether she likes it or not.

Callie is going to be chopped liver when Christopher is old enough to have a girlfriend that meets all his needs. And the fall out is going to be epic, I know it.

I grab one of the bags from Greg as we walk to the nearest picnic table under the shade. It was his turn to bring lunch for everyone, which I've been looking forward to. He makes fantastic sandwiches. "Are you ok after your run in with Libby?"

He avoids eye contact with me, instead opting to sigh deeply and pull the food out to set up. "Yeah. Just frustrated.

I'm ok with Libby hating me, ya know? I don't understand it, but I'm ok with it. What I'm not ok with is her trying to keep Pey from me all the time. When did I become the bad guy in all this?"

My heart goes out to him. There are so many deadbeat dads out there who get away with never seeing their kids, never providing for them. But when a man like Greg comes along who wants more time with his daughter, he has to fight for it. I know there's more to the story, but he looks dejected so I don't push him.

Callie, on the other hand, has no filter.

"Why do you look like someone boiled your bunny?" She plops down on the bench, having given up on her son, and pops a chip in her mouth, oblivious to the severity of the situation.

"Callie," I warn, hoping she'll pick up on my cue to shut up.

She looks at me, confused. "What? Is something going on?"

"Yes," Greg snaps. "Something is going on. My fucking ex-wife wants to take my daughter on a weekend trip to San Antonio." We stare blankly until he gets to the punchline. "To visit some guy she met online."

Callie and I both gasp, but she recovers faster than I do, and the gloves come off. "Nuh uh. No. Nope. No fucking way. She's a fucking fruit loop if she thinks that's a good idea. Give me her phone number."

I put my hand on her arm to stop her rant, my eyes never leaving Greg. His hands are on his hips and he's looking at the ground. His breathing is heavy and his jaw is clenched. I've never seen him pissed off, but he's trying really hard to control himself. "What did she say when you told her no?"

He huffs a sad laugh. "That's when she started claiming Peyton was sick, and I had to fight to take her."

We remain silent, giving him a minute to collect himself. He must be doing breathing exercises and counting to ten or something, because he literally shakes his head, like he's shaking off all the stress. "Well, enough of that." He moves to continue unpacking the juice he brought. "We only have a couple hours and I'd rather spend it making good memories with my kid."

"So go." I grab the juice boxes out of his hand and gesture to Peyton. It's obvious he needs time with his daughter to help him get it all back into perspective again. Adult interaction can come later. "Go play with her."

He looks at me briefly, then smiles and runs off. I watch as he sneaks up on Peyton and grabs her from behind, swinging her into the air as she squeals in delight. His love for her is so transparent, it makes me sad Libby would try to take it away.

That's one of the sucky things about being divorced with kids. Even after the person breaks your trust, you're forced to still trust them with the well-being of the most precious things in your life—your kids. Regardless of how you feel, until the other person breaks the court's trust, it doesn't matter. And by the time a court sees it, the damage to the child has been done.

It's a no-win situation sometimes. And it sucks.

My best friend, being absolutely no help with setting up lunch, pops another chip in her mouth. "You need to give him a blow job," she says casually as she chews.

"Callie!" I exclaim.

"What?" She shrugs like she didn't just suggest fellatio in the middle of a playground as a way to fix a custody dispute. "He's stressed. You're horny." I gape at her, but all she does is roll her eyes and point a chip at me. "Don't even deny it. Making out only does so much for you. Go for it."

"I'm not even going to bother responding to your crazy. If it happens, and that's a big *if*," she begins to protest but I hold my hands up to stop her, "I'm not going to discuss it with you at the park."

She looks at me smugly. "What about at a dive bar during girls' night while your mom babysits."

I look over, pretending to think, and then back at her. "Ok maybe." She laughs because she knows I'm not stupid. She'll figure out when I have my first non-self-induced orgasm before I even have a chance to tell her. It's like she has a radar for these things.

Finally having everything ready to go, I look around the area to make sure the kids are ok. I know Greg's been right in the thick of it all, but I can't help when my mom instinct kicks in. And as it turns out, my instinct is dead on.

Christopher is sitting on top of a riding toy that's shaped like a giant duck. It used to be yellow, but now it's a faded shade of yellow-beige. Who knows how long the thing has been here. It's held upright by an industrial sized spring so, theoretically, it can rock back and forth. But in this case, the spring looks really, well, sprung. As Christopher rocks forward, the duck doesn't spring back into place. Instead, it keeps going forward. All the way, until the beak is touching the ground and Christopher rolls headfirst over the duck's head, landing in the dirt again.

"Good lord, can he not stay off the ground today?" Callie grumbles as she stalks off to make sure he doesn't have some sort of concussion.

My eyes search the playground for my child, and I find her. She and Greg and Peyton are all on the slides, side by side, getting ready to race. Max doesn't look like she's just having fun, she appears to be elated to have Greg's attention. Both girls do. And although lunch is ready to go, I don't call everyone over. This is one of those rare, beautiful moments that I want to observe, and lock into my memory.

For a split-second, I let myself wonder what life would have been like if I had met and married someone like Greg all those years ago instead of James.

But that train of thought isn't productive and only depresses me. I'd rather enjoy this precious moment and make a mental note of what I hope my future holds.

It's still too early to know if that future includes Greg. But he's a very good reminder of what I want. And I won't settle for anything less for me or my girls.

CHAPTER
Eighteen

Between Fiona, who is in second grade, and Maura, who is in kindergarten, we've been part of this elementary school for three years. That's three years of teacher meetings. Three years of class parties. And three years of music recitals.

While I typically don't mind school functions, I could really do without the recitals.

Mrs. Gray, who is aptly named, has to be the oldest woman in the entire world. Seriously. I'm pretty sure I saw a certificate about it on the wall in her classroom once.

She looks like an aging Chinese Shar-Pei—those dogs that have such wrinkly skin all over their face you have to wonder if their eyes are open and if they can actually see. That's Mrs. Gray. The wrinkles on her face are so deep, her eyes are barely visible. Her mop of hair is so white it's almost blue. And she slowly shuffles instead of walks.

Don't get me wrong, she's great with the kids and I've never seen her without a smile on her face. But it would be nice to come to one of these things and not have to hear the microphone squeal every time she turns it on. Seriously.

Every. Time.

Looking around at all the stragglers, I'm glad we got here early enough to get seats. Although if Greg doesn't get here soon, I may be forced into a bar brawl over this empty chair. If the daily chaos in the car rider line is any indication, these moms are willing to throw down at any given moment.

"Can you move down to the end?" Choirgirl Barbie yells over everyone in our row. "I need more room down here."

I don't bother making eye contact. I'm still searching the crowd for Greg. "I'm waiting for someone."

"Who?" James spits out.

The venom in his voice is a dead giveaway that he knows exactly who's coming and has a problem with it. I ignore him. I have more important things to do than engage in whatever pissing match he wants to start.

A sudden kiss on the cheek startles me, but quickly makes me smile as Greg takes a seat next to me.

"Sorry I'm late." He puts his arm around the back of my chair, a small bouquet of three carnations in his hand.

Max scrambles off her seat and climbs onto his lap. He doesn't miss a beat, just helps her up with the same ease he has with Peyton.

I snuggle into him and point at the flowers. "What are those for?"

"Isn't that what you do after a show? Give the performers flowers?"

"Pwetty Fwowers." Max reaches her chubby little finger out to touch one of them.

Greg looks down at her and smiles. "They are pretty. You think we should give them to Maura when she's done singing?"

Max nods and continues to gently pet one of the pedals. I know Greg would act the same way with her, even if we weren't dating, but it still makes my heart warm to know they feel comfortable with each other. Doesn't every mom feel that way when their child is loved for who they are, no strings attached?

"Max," James bellows. "Come sit over here with Daddy." She looks up, but doesn't make a move, except with that flower-petting finger. "Elena," he turns his demands to me as she ignores him. "Make her come over here."

I furrow my brows at him. "She's fine, James. Leave her alone."

"It is not appropriate for her to sit on some stranger's lap," he whisper-yells, glaring over my shoulder at the picture-perfect scene next to me.

"Are you for real?" Now I'm getting mad. And I'm mad that he's making me mad right before Maura's show. "He's my friend, my *boyfriend*, Max's friend's dad, and Fiona's gymnastics coach. You can't get any less stranger-danger than that, James."

He fumes, but won't let it go. "But what do you really know about him, Elena? Huh? You're just going to take his word for it that he's a good guy?"

"I'll give you that one," I deadpan. "Clearly, I'm not a very good judge of character, being that I married you," I whisper-yell back at him. People around us are starting to turn and look. I know I need to get this situation under control, but not only has James blindsided me in public, he's embarrassed and insulted me on top of it. "What is this really even about?"

"I don't think it's appropriate to bring him around the kids so much. You haven't even been dating that long. What if he's a pedophile or something?"

And now we've crossed the line from insulting to ridiculous.

"The gym does criminal background checks on every new employee. And all current employees are re-checked every five years," Greg throws in nonchalantly, still snuggling with Max. "You're welcome to call the office manager and have her read you the results of my most recent check if it'll make you feel better, James." While there's no challenge in his tone, I know Greg well enough to know he's putting James in his place. He's calling him on his bullshit. There's nothing to hide, and he can prove it.

James narrows his eyes. "How old are you anyway?" I throw my hands up in frustration.

"An interrogation?" I'm fuming now. Thank goodness Fiona is addicted to the Junie B. Jones books. I don't even think she's noticed all the arguing going on over her head. Greg doesn't seem phased at all.

"Thirty-eight."

I whip my head around to give Greg a seductive smile. "Really?"

"Really." He leans over and whispers in my ear, "Looks like I'm dating a cougar."

I giggle and rub my hand on his cheek.

But of course James clears his throat, determined to keep things awkward and uncomfortable.

Taking a deep breath, I decide to screw it. Might as well get this over now. Besides, we can't leave the other parents watching this soap opera without a resolution, now can we?

"What now, James?"

"He seems really old to have a two-year-old."

"You're four years older with a three-year-old," I reply. His questions aren't even making sense anymore. What is he up to?

"That's different," he argues back. "We have older children. How do you know he's not hiding more kids, like a secret teenager or something?"

My head drops as I give up on even trying to make a crazy man see reason. I can't even believe this line of accusations. They are outlandish, I don't even know how to respond anymore. Good thing Greg does.

"Nope. No other kids." He shifts Max to his other leg and she snuggles right in. I don't even want to look at James's reaction. I'm sure he's glaring again. "Got married when I was thirty-three, just a few years older than you were. Peyton was born when I was thirty-five, and I was divorced by thirty-seven. You can call my ex if you don't believe me, but be careful. She's a little on the flirty side. You don't want to fall victim to her charms."

That's when Keri finally stops primping in her portable mirror and jumps in, putting her hand on James's arm to stop him from going any further. No, she doesn't get involved when he's making a scene. Not when he's throwing wild accusations everywhere. But when the threat of another woman flirting with him is thrown into the conversation, she's on top of things.

Way to go, Self-Absorbed Barbie.

The ear-piercing screech of the microphone being turned on signals the end of this round of *Elementary School WWE*, and possibly the end of our ability to hear normal decibel-levels from now on.

"Good morning, everyone." Somehow Mrs. Gray missed the "PM" written on the clock, but she's still smiling, so all is forgiven.

"We are excited to bring you our kindergartners' very first musical performance." Her voice is shaky and slow, if I hadn't heard this spiel before, I'd be really struggling to understand her. "They have been working very hard on these selections."

"How is that woman not dead yet?" Keri blurts out, making several of us laugh. I have wondered that many times before.

But, as has been true for years, Mrs. Gray continues to defy the crypt-keeper and introduces a new generation of songbirds. "As our performers make their way to the stage, I have a few announcements."

Several kindergarten teachers come out from the wings and lead the kids onto the stage which is no easy feat. Most of the kids are staring at the audience with wide, overwhelmed eyes. Of course that leads to more than one collision. Several stop to wave, backing everyone up. And one little boy takes off running to the middle of the stage where he starts dancing.

Trying to get a hundred five-year-olds to walk in a single file line is like herding cats.

"We have been working on a special song with our fifth grade class," Mrs. Gray waves her hand towards the older students that are trying to get to their spot on the stage amongst all the distracted felines, I mean, children. "As a special treat, they will be accompanying us on the recorder."

A nervous laugh ripples through the audience and James reacts with an "Oh god." I haven't agreed with anything he's said for the last couple of years, but I definitely agree with that sentiment. Recorders should be banned. Surely there is some form of scientific evidence that shows massive hearing loss when an audience is exposed to the sound.

"Hey, I used to play the recorder as a kid."

I scoff at Greg's admission. "You just plummeted a few pegs on the hotness meter."

An amused smile graces his plump, soft lips as he grabs my hand and raises it to kiss my knuckles. I'd much rather have those lips on mine, but knuckles will have to do for now.

James grunts in disapproval, but I ignore it completely. He'll be taking the kids with him for the weekend as soon as the show is over, and I have big plans for Greg once we're alone.

Hopefully, very *big* plans. I guess I'll find out tonight.

It takes the teachers several minutes, but they finally have the kids situated on the risers. Well, as situated as they can get. They're all still either fidgety or frozen in fear. Maura is one of the odd men out. She's wearing her brand new pink poofy dress, her blond ringlets fixed in an up-do, the look complete with a tiara, which she *insisted* on wearing for her "debut on stage". I opted not to argue with that logic. Although I suspect Pageant Barbie down the row may have taught her that phrase since she likes the idea of parading my girls around like little Hollywood starlets.

I have a bad feeling those two will be bonding over their love of make up the older Maura gets.

Searching the crowd, she finally catches sight of me and throws her hand up in the air, waving and yelling, "Hi Mama!" We all laugh as I wave back.

Finally, after what seems like ages, Mrs. Gray has shuffled her way over to the podium and claps her hands to get the children's attention. Amazingly, they all stop fidgeting and keep their eyes trained on the old woman. A finger points at the fifth graders, a downbeat with her hand…

And I swear my ears start bleeding within seconds of the first note playing.

Max and Fiona place their hands over their ears while the rest of us pretend we're smiling, not grimacing. For twenty-five minutes, we're treated to songs like "Báte, Báte, Chocoláte", complete with dance moves, and a rousing rendition of "Row, Row, Row Your Boat", which includes an interesting array of nearly never-ending rounds. Finally, *finally*, Mrs. Gray begins shuffling back to the microphone, indicating the show is over. For the most part, it went off without a hitch. There were no major incidents, although it is possible one little girl peed her pants, and I think a little boy may have fallen off the top riser at some point. From this angle, it was hard to tell, but his head popped back up a few minutes later, so I'm assuming nothing is broken.

No one waits for Mrs. Gray and her snail pace to get to the microphone for dismissal. The crowd begins filing out of the room. It's pretty rude, but come on now. At some point the school needs to spring for an electric scooter.

As we follow along with the crowd surge, James snatches Max up from the floor, ripping her away from Greg who is holding her hand, and carries her away, calling for Fiona to follow closely behind him.

"Sorry," I mouth to Greg feeling oddly embarrassed by James's behavior. He's not my husband anymore. I'm not sure why I care, except I hate knowing what an idiot I was to ever see his charms.

Greg shrugs in response. "If it was Pey, I'd probably do the same thing," he yells in my ear, so I can hear him over the crowd. The noise is pretty deafening. But that's what happens when you cram four hundred people or more into one tiny corridor and make them wait in line to pick up their kid.

By the time we get to the music room, Maura is spinning in a circle showing off how her dress flairs.

"Maura," I call, making her stop mid spin.

Her eyes light up and she runs toward me, James and Keri following her movement only to glare our direction when she reaches us. "Mama, Mama! Did you see me?"

"I did!" I hug her tightly to me and congratulate her on a job well done. "You didn't look scared at all."

She puts her hands on her little hips and cocks her head like I should know better. "Mama, I am a singer. Of course I wasn't scay-ed."

I hold my hands up in apology. "I stand corrected. Of course you weren't. You did wonderful."

"I did, huh?!" She begins to spin again until Greg squats down in front of her, holding the carnations out in front of him.

"These are for you," he says with a smile.

Maura's mouth drops open and she breaks out into a smile. "You-a supposed to give flow-as to the singer after a show."

"I know," he agrees. "It's supposed to bring you good luck."

She smiles shyly at him and I know the final daughter has been won over by his charms. I'm not at all surprised, just a little bewildered as to why it took this long. But I guess he doesn't interact as much with her as he does with the others, only because of lack of opportunity.

Still, dating with kids in tow is a sticky situation. It's important for everyone to at least respect each other when trying to sort through the uncertainty of a new relationship.

Too bad not everyone subscribes to that belief. And by not everyone, I mean James. He stalks over to us and probably takes joy in ruining this sweet moment.

"Come on, Maura." He's trying to sound gentle and fatherly, but it comes across like he's a jack ass. "It's my weekend so we need to head home."

Several hugs and kisses later, even some for Greg which makes James look like his head is about to explode, they're out the door and my single-time begins.

"Told ya." Greg shoves his hands in his pockets. "He's jealous."

I shoot him a playful look. "I'd like to say you're wrong, but after all that, you might be right."

"Oh, I know I'm right."

I wrap a lock of hair around my finger and give him a flirty smile. "Is it wrong that after everything he put me through, it's really nice to see the tables have finally turned?"

He chuckles and grabs me by the hand. "Not at all. Come on. I have a dinner to make you."

I strut my way out the door. I have the hottest man in the school by my side, heading to his place for him to make me dinner, my cheating ex already forgotten.

Karma can be a bitch sometimes. But I love it when she's on my side.

CHAPTER
Nineteen

"Why don't you and your sister look alike?" I ask as I take a sip of my wine. It's a fruity Moscato I've never tried before. I really like it.

A smile plays on his lips, but he keeps up the quick pace of slicing mushrooms. "We're both adopted. But I'm assuming you already figured that out."

"I figured at least one of you was, but genetics are weird. I could have been wrong." Putting my wine glass down, I lean forward on the counter so I can see better as he cooks. "Did you see those twins that were born, one of them white, one of them black?"

He shakes his head. "No. They were really twins?"

"Yeah, it was really cool. Their parents are mixed race, half black/ half white. Somewhere in the development process, their little genes decided to pull one pigment or the other and they ended up with twins that have identical faces but look like they're of completely different races. In their baby pictures, they almost look like little dolls sitting next to each other."

Greg throws the mushrooms into a pan, creating a puff of steam and a loud sizzle as they sauté. "Sounds like someone is a little obsessed with that poor family."

"Their picture went viral so it was hard to miss. Plus, I've always been kind of fascinated with genetics and that was a really neat case. It's considered a rare phenomenon."

"And yet, you became a flight attendant." He grins at me while stirring the garlic into the pan.

"Touché. Although there is a big difference between being fascinated by genetics and having the desire to take a zillion science classes to get a degree in it."

"Good point." He wipes his hands on a towel and opens the oven to check on the steaks that are cooking in the broiler. The smell alone is making my mouth water and when my stomach rumbles, I realize I haven't eaten since the M&M's I had in the car right before school pick up. Being the gentleman he is, Greg pretends he didn't hear the rumble in my gut, but the look he shoots me says he's just being polite. "Don't worry. It's almost ready."

I love watching him work in the kitchen. Even if it's making macaroni and hot dogs, he always does it with such grace. Tonight, though, he's going all out. Steak with sautéed mushrooms, and asparagus with some sort of Hollandaise sauce. I have no idea if the two go together, but I don't care. It all smells good and I'm hoping it tastes even better.

Within minutes, we're sitting at his table enjoying generous portions of his cooking. The first bite makes me moan, eliciting a sultry gaze from my date. Oh yeah. I think we both may have high hopes for this evening's events.

"How old were you when you were adopted?" I feel like I need to slow down my bites. It's so good, I'm practically shoveling it in my pie hole.

He chews and swallows and grabs his wine glass. "You're back on that, huh?"

I shrug. "Curious is all. I like knowing things about you."

He wipes his mouth with his napkin, clears his throat, and leans forward, elbows on the table, like he's prepping to tell an interesting story. Now I'm really intrigued.

"My sister Joie was adopted out of CPS custody."

I stop mid-chew. "Foster care?"

"Yep. My parents tried for years to have kids but nothing ever happened, so they decided to become foster parents. Figured there was a child out there that needed them and they had an empty room."

"That's really admirable of them."

"I guess. It depends on if you look at it as a couple taking in a needy child, or a couple that can't have a child so they settle for adoption."

I gasp. "That's a terrible way to look at it! Do you really think that about your parents?"

"Not at all. But my sister did for a while. She was a horrific teenager. Used to throw it in their faces all the time."

"That's awful!"

"I know." He leans back and crosses his arms over his broad chest, resting his head back like his memories are taking him back in time. "Years of therapy confirmed that her insecurities are the same as lots of adopted kids... fears that you aren't really wanted, only tolerated because the parents can't get what they really want."

I blink once. Twice. My heart hurting for his very sad sister. "Is that what you think?"

He snaps out of this memory and looks me in the eye. "Not at all. But the circumstances around my adoption were different."

"How so?"

"One of the things my parents say they found out by going through the CPS process is that it can be really daunting. There's court hearings and case workers and interviews and no guarantees. Ever. At one point, they had already petitioned the court for adoption and some random relative showed up, wanting to take Joie away."

I gasp again.

"Exactly. She'd been with them a couple of years at that point. She was their child. And a distant relative who had no interest in her when she first came into care suddenly wants to shake her entire world up? Not cool."

"But they didn't get her?" I ask quietly, my hand covering my mouth in disbelief of the whole thing.

He shakes his head. "Nope. As soon as this aunt or whoever found out the state wasn't going to give her money, she disappeared."

"No wonder Joie felt like no one really wanted her."

"I know. The whole experience about put my mom in the looney bin. Once Joie was finally theirs forever, they got out of foster care for good. Said the process was too emotional and physically taxing, they only had it in them to do it once."

I run my finger around the rim of my glass, lost in my own thoughts. I always believed a child would feel lucky to be taken in by new parents. It never occurred to me that they would feel unlucky about the people who brought them into the world not caring for them, even if giving up that child was an act of loving sacrifice.

I guess it doesn't help that whenever the media talks about celebrities, they refer to their "adopted" kids, as if somehow the parent/child bond isn't as strong because of the legalities. Suddenly my way of thinking about adoption has shifted, and I know I'll make more of an effort to never categorize a child like that again, even unintentionally.

"Where'd you go?"

I look up at Greg through my lashes. "Sorry. Having a moment, I guess. Then where did you come from? The stork dropped you on their doorstep?"

He flashes the smile that dazzles me every time and I have to concentrate on what he's saying. "Nah. They never wanted to adopt out of CPS again, but when they found out some random family friend's daughter got pregnant in high school, they jumped at the chance to take in her baby."

"Her baby being you."

"Yep. I was the illegitimate child of a teenager."

"You don't sound broken up by it at all."

"I'm not." His demeanor shows no concern whatsoever. "I guess I'm not wired that way, emotionally or whatever. I'm grateful she gave me to my parents. I had a pretty normal, drama-free childhood until Joie hit puberty," he says with a chuckle.

"You've never tried to find her?"

"My birth mom? I'm Facebook friends with her."

A quick, disbelieving laugh escapes me. "What? That's kind of random."

He smiles in agreement. "I know. After Peyton was born, I think I could more appreciate the sacrifice she made and I kept thinking, as a parent, I'd want to know my child grew up happy and healthy. So I friend requested her and she accepted. We've never even talked, but she knows I know who she is.

And I hope it helps heal some of the hole her heart has for giving up her baby."

I blink back the tears I feel forming and cover his hand with mine. "You're a good man, Greg."

His thumb brushes over my knuckles and the vibe in the air changes. You can practically feel the electricity.

"You're a good woman, Elena," he responds softly.

This is it. This is the night we're going to take the plunge. I'm shaved all over. I'm wearing my favorite smelling lotion. I have a form fitting camisole on underneath that lifts and tucks my boobs. I don't have to take it off and I'll still look sexy. I'm ready.

Until someone knocks on the door.

Because isn't that just my luck.

"It's after ten," he grumbles absentmindedly, as he stands up to cross the room. "Who the hell goes door-to-door this late?"

Might as well make myself useful and work on the dishes.

Just as I step foot into the kitchen, I hear a woman's voice. "I didn't catch you at a bad time, did I?" My ears perk up. I'm not trying to eavesdrop—ok, fine, I am—but for some reason I don't want this person to know I'm here, so I place the dishes in the sink as quietly as I can.

"I didn't say you could come in." Wow. Greg sounds pissed. "What do you want?"

"We need to talk."

I can practically hear Greg's eye roll from here. Peeking around the corner, I see her. She's tall, probably pushing six feet in those hooker heels; long dark hair that would make a Pantene girl envious; hourglass figure accentuated by the design of her fitted dress; and her face—if she's not a model now, she definitely used to be. She's beautiful.

And she has the same eyes as Peyton.

Oh shit.

"There's nothing we need to talk about, Libby. You need to leave," Greg practically shouts. She ignores him and drops her purse on the couch.

He's got his arms crossed and he's blocking her way into the kitchen, which seems to irritate her.

"Um, can you move out of the way? I need a drink."

"No. Get out of my house."

I press myself as flat as I can to the wall, hoping she doesn't see me. This is Libby? Now I see why he married her. I don't think I've ever seen someone as stunning as her in real life before. I admit, Keri is beautiful, in her plastic Barbie way. But Libby is what wet dreams are made of.

Where are all these gorgeous women coming from and how did the model-esque genes skip me?

"It's about Peyton."

Greg's tone changes immediately to one of concern. "Is she ok? Where is she?"

"She's with my mom," Libby says dismissively. "And she's fine for now."

"Then what's the problem?"

"I need more money."

"Are you kidding me?" Greg practically yells. "You interrupt my evening to use our child to try and nickel-and-dime me some more?"

"You're such a fucking asshole, Greg!" She's yelling now, and I'm really glad I've kept myself hidden. "I can't provide everything she needs with what you give me!"

"You get a thousand dollars a month, plus you got half of our retirement, and half of our savings."

Shit. That's a lot of money for one kid. He either makes more than I realized or he got screwed in court.

"You're not hearing me, Greg," she yells. I chance another peek and her hands are clenched by her side. Hot tempered is not a good look on her. "The savings account is gone! I need more money!"

Greg's eyebrows raise and his voice gets super low, almost menacing sounding. "That's not my problem anymore. You live with your mother, so I know you don't have that many expenses. But if raising Peyton is costing you so much, I'm more than happy to take her off your hands."

Ouch. I really should remind him that I'm here and listening, but I'm kind of afraid of what will happen if Libby sees me. She is one scary woman when she wants to make it rain.

Her eyes narrow. "You just try it you little dick prick. No judge is going to give custody to a working father when she can be with her stay at home mom."

"The term 'stay at home mom' indicates you stay home with the child, which clearly, you aren't doing." He gestures to her club attire and her obvious plans to go out. "If money is tight, get a job like the rest of the single moms I know."

She straightens her spine and I must shift a little too much because she sees the movement and catches me watching. Her eyebrows immediately shoot up and the look on her face makes me uncomfortable.

"I see I've interrupted your evening," she says smugly. "Who's your friend?"

"None of your business," Greg spits out.

I could stay in the safety of the kitchen, but there's no reason to now. Besides, this is the woman who has tried time and time again to keep Greg's daughter away from him. It would be nice if I showed him some support, now that I've been outed.

Pretending I'm more confident than I am, I walk over to Greg and put my arm around his waist, holding my hand out to her. "I'm Elena. It's nice to meet you, Libby."

Greg relaxes into me a bit, although he's still more tense than normal, and kisses the top of my head in an obvious display of possession. That's fine. He can claim me in front of his ex if it makes him feel stronger.

The first thing I notice when she takes my hand is that she has a weak handshake. You know the kind where only the fingers touch. I hate that kind of handshake. I've always felt like it doesn't show sincerity at all. But I supposed she's not all that sincere in general.

The second thing I notice is her callouses. Either she's a former gymnast as well, although I doubt it because of her height, or she didn't always have money to spend. Her desperation for more suddenly makes sense.

She looks me up and down, obviously assessing me. It makes me uncomfortable because we both know I don't measure up to her standards. But somehow it feels important to stand my ground. Maybe because I already know how ugly she is on the inside.

Then she speaks. "I would think a woman your age would need more than a cocktail wienie to be satisfied."

I gasp. How dare she insult Greg! How dare she insult cocktail wienies! They're like little hot dogs in a can!

"Get out of my house!" Greg roars and grabs her by the arm to pull her that direction.

She rips her arm out of his grasp. "Get your hands off of me!" They glare at each other while she smooths out her dress and picks her purse up off the couch. Then she turns back to me. "Enjoy your pencil dick. Hope you have a dildo handy."

Greg's face is beet red and I know he's about to explode if I don't step in. So I unleash my inner Callie.

We're BFF's for a reason, after all.

"I don't know what you mean," I say as sweetly as I can. "Sex with Greg is the most satisfying of my life. If you're having problems, I have a friend who is a plastic surgeon. I'm sure there's something he could do to, you know… tighten you up."

She glares at me then stalks towards the door. As she passes Greg, she holds up her pinkie and mutters, "pencil dick."

The door slams shut, and I let out a breath I didn't even know I was holding. That sounds cliché, but geez. Standing up straight like that is hard on my weak back muscles. I guess I need to work with weights after all.

I lift my head up and see Greg staring at me. "What?"

"You stood up to Libby."

"Yes?"

He takes a step towards me.

"I've never seen anyone stand up to Libby before."

Another step.

"Is that good or bad," I practically squeak, him taking another step. Why is he walking so slowly?

"It was really hot." And then he's on me, kissing me, touching me, running his fingers through my hair.

I have *never* been kissed like this before and it's more amazing than I imagine.

"I hope the vibe I was getting earlier means you're ready because I have never, ever wanted anyone the way I want you," he growls. Literally growls and I almost have an orgasm on the spot.

"I've never been more ready," I whisper back, barely able to keep my eyes open as he kisses that sweet spot between my ear and my neck.

Needing no more confirmation, Greg sweeps me up in his arms and carries me down the hall.

The one advantage to him fighting with his ex… I'm gonna get all the make-up sex.

CHAPTER
Twenty

Within seconds, we're in his bedroom, clothing flying everywhere in our frenzy.

Before I can think twice, Greg is shirtless and I'm pantsless, and we're both out of breath. He moves away from me slowly and unbuttons his jeans.

I squeeze my eyes shut and try to get myself under control. This is the moment my body has craved for a long time. If I'm not careful, I'll either jump his bones and this will be over too soon. Or I'll jump his bones and scare him off.

When I finally feel confident enough to open my eyes, I know he's naked. Completely and utterly nude. I can see it in my peripheral vision. I want so bad to look and touch and kiss him everywhere. But I want to take this slow even more. Instead of letting my primal urges take over, I force myself to hold his gaze.

He seems strangely shy and it throws me off kilter for a second. Why would Greg be shy? He's like a god, personified.

My eyes peruse down his chiseled pecks, his rock-hard six-pack, his very nice hips, right down to his package.

His very… underwhelming package.

Holy shit. Libby was right.

I blink a few times, not believing what I'm seeing. He's perfect, so physically perfect, I wasn't expecting… well, I was expecting more. Much, much more.

"This is why I don't live up north," he chuckles nervously. "Could you imagine if it shriveled up?"

My eyes snap up to meet his. He's blushing and is clearly embarrassed. I've never seen Greg blush before. I've never seen him embarrassed before. It's disconcerting. This amazing, perfect, fantastic man—all six-foot-two, chiseled abs, face of a god—is ashamed because he's sporting what many would call a micro-peen.

Ok, it's not that small. But by today's cultural standards, this part of him is considered sub-par.

"Why would you joke about yourself like that?" I whisper.

"Defense mechanism?" he replies with a shrug. "Remember when I said everyone has some part of their body that they're ashamed of. Here's mine." His eyes dart around the room, looking everywhere except at me.

"Greg."

He refuses to look at me. Instead, keeping his eyes trained on the floor, waiting for me to make the next move. But I'm frozen in my own thoughts.

Does his size really matter to me? I know Callie and I have joked about things like this before. But when it really boils down to it, is this a deal breaker? I don't even have to think about it because I know the answer already.

No.

I don't care if he's hung like a horse or like a two-year-old. I don't care if he's sporting a six pack or a keg. I don't care if he has the face of an angel or the angel of death. I care about *him*.

What makes me pause is not this question. It's the sudden realization, that he thinks the same thing about *me*. What I perceive as physical flaws don't matter to him at all.

"Greg, please look at me," I plead.

Slowly, he brings his eyes up to mine and I can see the anxiety he's feeling. I recognize it, because it's the same anxiety I have.

Taking a deep breath, I make the decision to show him exactly how much this doesn't matter to me. Taking the hem of my camisole in my hands and never breaking his gaze, I pull it over my head and drop it to the floor, bearing my own physical insecurities to him.

"Funny how nursing children can make the balloons deflate and just... hang there. Unless I buy a strong underwire, of course," I laugh sadly.

He looks up at me and he's not amused. "Don't talk about yourself that way."

"I won't if you won't."

My point made, the anxiety in his eyes quickly slips away, desire taking its place. Insecure and nervous Greg disappears and confident, fun, lovable Greg is back.

"You know I'm really good at oral," he brags, a cocky grin forming on his face as we get more comfortable with each other's nudity.

"I have no doubt." I quirk my eyebrow. "And I'm looking forward to reciprocating. I've never done that before."

His head snaps back. "You've never given a blow job?"

"Well, I've started the process. But I have a weak gag reflex so I've never been able to finish it," I explain, as his hooded eyes continue to look me up and down. The look on his face makes me feel beautiful and desirable. I haven't felt this way in, well, maybe I've never felt this way. "I'm looking forward to you being my first completed BJ."

"Good god, it's hot when you talk about sucking me off," he practically growls, and in a micro-second, he's on me. His lips on mine. His hands exploring my body. His strong limbs picking me up and carrying me to the bed, something a weaker man wouldn't be able to do.

Wow. He is *strong*. This is such a turn on.

He lays me down, carefully laying on top of me and kisses down my neck. He rubs my nipple between his thumb and forefinger, and I'm so turned on, I don't even mind that he has to practically feel all the way down to my stomach to find my boob.

We both are imperfect. We both have our insecurities. And yet, neither of us care one rat's ass about those perceived flaws.

A realization hits me at the same time he tweaks my nipple, causing me to gasp.

"Oh my gosh, you can stick it in my butt!" I squeal.

Greg freezes, tongue on my neck, one hand still on my boob. He pulls back to look at me, a very confused look on his face. "Did you just say… What?"

"Do you know how long I've wanted to try exit-only stuff, but I've always been too scared to do it? But you won't hurt as bad," I blurt out. "And I bet it would even feel good. Do you think we can try that?"

He chuckles and leans on his elbows above me. "We can try anything you want after I get over the shock of you propositioning me for anal."

"I'm so excited now. There are so many things I've always wanted to try but with bigger-girthed men, forget it. I don't want to be ripped in half." I continue to ramble as my thoughts run away from me. "But with you, we can try all kinds of things. Like, like... a dildo and you at the same time!" He drops his head to my shoulder and I feel him shaking with laughter. But I'm not done with my rant. "We can be adventurous. I can't even tell you how happy this makes me!

"Don't you see, Greg? This..." He hisses as I wrap my hand around him and squeeze gently, rubbing my thumb across his tip. "... this is perfect for me. *You* are perfect for me."

I look up into his eyes and see an expression I've never had directed at me before... total and utter adoration.

He leans down and kisses me slowly, gently, passionately. "You are amazing, you know that?" he says when we come up for air.

I nod. "Only because you make me feel that way."

"It's more than that. It's just you. Thank you."

"For what?"

"For taking your shirt off." I smile and rub his cheek. He kisses my palm and then begins to shimmy his way down my body. "Now lay back."

"Why? What are you doing?" Suddenly, I feel a mixture of excited and like I've been caught off guard.

He pauses and looks up at me, a playful grin on his face. "You know that phrase, 'It's not the size of the wave, it's the motion of the ocean?'" I bite my lip and nod. "I'm about to show you why it's all true."

And that's what he does.

Four times.

He's lying on his back, gently rubbing my arm. I'm lying on his chest, absentmindedly rubbing his abs. We're still naked and all tangled up in each other. And I've finally found a reason to be happy I'm childless every other weekend.

I'd forgotten what it means to laze around in bed with a man and enjoy the feel of each other. I think I had that with James a few times before Fiona was born, but it was so long ago, I could very well be making up memories.

Regardless, this is my current reality, and I couldn't be more content.

"It really doesn't bother you?" Greg asks quietly. My hand freezes, mid stroke, as I try to figure out what he's talking about. It's such an open-ended question and my brain is still mush from all the orgasms that it takes a few seconds to figure out what he means.

Slowly, I push myself up until I'm leaning my head on my hand, my elbow on the bed next to him. "Are you talking about you're... um..." I wave my hand in the general direction, not sure what to call it.

He smirks. "My dick? Cock? Penis? Lots of words for you to choose from, Elena."

I roll my eyes at him, even though I can feel myself blushing. "We haven't talked about what you want me to call it, so I don't know."

He shifts until he's facing me. "How about you call it my Johnson?"

"What are you, a frat boy?"

He chuckles mildly, then his face turns serious. "I'm serious, Elena. If I'm not giving you what you need, I want you to tell me. I never want to not be good enough for you."

"Because of your penis size?"

He tries to smile because he knows the words sound ridiculous out loud, but he looks sad instead.

"Why does this bother you?" I ask, genuinely concerned about where this is coming from. We just had amazing non-sex. Why would he even question whether or not I'm satisfied?

He grabs a lock of my hair and begins to play with it absentmindedly. "Libby used to throw it in my face all the time. Whenever we would fight, that was her go-to argument. That I wasn't a real man because I couldn't satisfy her during intercourse. But she never wanted to try anything different to make it work, ya know?"

"Well that's stupid on her part. I've never had an orgasm during intercourse either, and James was probably on the above-average side. Didn't make a difference at all."

"Really?"

"Really. My body isn't equipped for that, and he wasn't interested in making the effort to try other things on my behalf."

"What a dick," Greg grumbles.

"I know. He really thought being well endowed automatically made him a good lover. He was so, so wrong."

"That's ridiculous. It's not about where you stick it. It's about paying attention to your partner's needs and likes. It's about noticing what makes them squirm and moan and get that look on their face."

"What look?"

"You know the look." He smirks. "The one where your eyes roll in the back of your head and your mouth falls open and your head falls back."

I feel flush as his words turn me on again. "Do I make that face?"

"Oh yeah." He smiles really big as I blush.

"Great." I drop my face onto his shoulder. "Now I'm self-conscious."

He chuckles and rubs my back. "Don't be embarrassed. It's a huge turn-on."

We lay silently for a few moments, him dropping kisses on my head every once in a while. Me, enjoying the quiet. But he can't let it go.

"Um, how much of this are you going to tell Callie?"

I pop my head up and look at him with confusion. "You mean besides the fact that I had the best sex of my life?"

"We didn't have sex." He wiggles his eyebrows up and down at me, making me smile.

"I know. That's the most amazing part of it all."

"I guess I'm wondering what else you're going to tell her."

And it hits me. He's worried I'm going to blather on to her about the thing he's most ashamed of. The thing he's most embarrassed about. I sit up quickly, situating myself cross-legged with the blanket over my legs. I don't care if it's made of actual gold, no woman needs to sit naked and cross-legged after having been diddled by her boyfriend. A relaxed vag isn't necessarily an attractive vag.

"You think I'm going tell Callie about... your size?"

He grimaces. "It's a micro-peen, Elena. Call it what it is."

"Stop that," I reprimand. "It's not that small, so I don't want to hear you say that about yourself again. I'm trying to get to the heart of the matter here." I shift closer to him. "Why would I tell Callie that? Why would I do that to you?"

He sighs and I know this has to do with Libby again. In this moment, I hate her more than I've ever hated anyone. "She used to make fun of me in front of our friends all the time," he grumbles, like he's ashamed to say it out loud. "We'd be out at a club or something, and we'd all be joking around and she'd make a snide comment like, 'Well if I got to hump more than a hot dog every night.' She'd say something like that almost every time we went out."

I crinkle my nose. Partially because that's insulting to him. Partially because that's insulting to my favorite barbeque food. She could do worse than a hot dog.

"I love hot dogs," I say under my breath.

"I know you do. Medium well. Don't burn it. At least two." He smiles for a second, but then continues. "At first, I thought it was her way of being funny with the crowd or whatever. But then I started noticing her girlfriends would look at me and laugh just a little too hard. Raise their pinkies at each other and stuff. At that point, I knew they were laughing *at* me. I got used to rolling my eyes and playing it off, but it still stung. It wasn't even because these other people were laughing at me, as much it was that my wife was purposely trying to humiliate me. And not privately. But in front of other people."

"Greg, if it wasn't that, it would have been something else," I remind him. "Libby is a back-stabbing whore who will use anything to hurt you as long as she gets what she wants."

"I know that." He rolls on his back and puts his arm over his eyes. "But you can understand why it makes me nervous that you tell Callie everything."

I stare at him while he lays there, his jaw clenching. His cheeks are still red from a blush that hasn't gone away. It occurs to me that this is something that really bothers him. Not in a "I hope we're on the same page" kind of way. He's been wounded by Libby as deeply as I was wounded by James.

The difference is, in today's culture, it's almost a given that women fight back. Social media explodes when women body-shame each other. There are articles written for women about loving your body and being proud of what you've got.

The same isn't true of men. Sure, there is some talk about not shaming either gender. But it's mostly about abs and receding hairlines. I can honestly say I have never once run across an article titled "Be proud of your penis, no matter what size it is!" But I have seen multiple articles talking about breast size. And while women may cry to their best friend about the pain they feel, the same can't also be said of men.

So this beautiful amazing man has suffered alone over his insecurities. He's been body-shamed for years by the person he was supposed to be able to trust with his secrets. It breaks my heart. All I want to do now is make him understand how much more he has to offer than that one little part of him.

No pun intended.

Slowly, I climb over and straddle him, my saggy breasts and lumpy belly on full display. "I've always been insecure about my body. Always." He swallows, but doesn't move. "When I was a gymnast, I had a tight little butt, but no boobs. And I hated that. Then I got older and the boobs never grew in. Instead, I had a big butt, cellulite, and still no boobs. Then I nursed three babies and ended up like this."

Greg swallows, but still doesn't move.

"When James told me he was having an affair and was leaving me, he said it was my fault. That if I had only had a boob job or had a flatter stomach or took better care of myself, maybe he wouldn't have had to go find someone else to turn him on."

"James is an idiot," Greg grumbles.

"And so is Libby." I grab Greg's arm and try to pull it off his face. It takes several tugs, but he finally gives up and moves his arm to the side. "Greg, I will never, ever disrespect you like that. I will never humiliate you like that. What we've shared, that's between you and me. No one else.

"Sure, I'm going to tell Callie that you gave me the best orgasms of my life…" He finally smirks. "And I'll probably tell her once we finally do have anal because she's as curious as I am…"

He grimaces. "Don't ever tell me if she tries it, too. I don't want that visual."

"Ben has a low-libido anyway. I think you're safe." He looks me in the eye as I run my hands across his beard. "But I'm making you a promise. I will never shame your body. Any part of it. Not even when you're old and wrinkly and you can't get it up anymore." That comment elicits a chuckle from him. "It goes against my entire character to use something intimate and personal as entertainment for others. I promise you. If you please promise that you won't make fun of me either."

He looks up at me, nothing but genuine care and, dare I say, love in his eyes.

"I hate that James made you feel less than because of something I think is beautiful," he whispers as he rubs his hands up and down my sides, his thumbs brushing over the spare tire around my waist.

"And I hate that Libby has such an aversion to hot dogs." He laughs and grabs me, rolling me over to my back, him on top. "Seriously, what is her deal? They are the ideal food. Not too big. Not small. Putting one in my mouth always puts me in a better mood..."

"Are you finished?" he growls, kissing all over my neck.

"...Especially if you put ketchup and relish on it. Ohh! We should bring condiments to bed! That could be fun."

"You're ridiculous. And I really want to be inside you."

"I'm not stopping you." My eyes roll in the back of my head like he said would happen. Then he pushes inside me for the first time, making me gasp in delight. "And you're amazing," I breathe.

That's no exaggeration. When Callie asks, because he and I both know she will, I can't wait to tell her his package comes with the biggest gift I've had in a long time—him. Because it's the truth.

CHAPTER
Twenty-One

"How was it? Is he amazing? Is he hung?"

Callie immediately begins asking the questions Greg feared as soon as I answer her call. I will never understand how she knew he and I had finally gotten down and dirty, but she claims she can hear it in my voice. Something about me sounding relaxed or whatever. Who knows. With Callie, sometimes it's better to smile and nod.

Yes, Callie and I have been best friends for a couple of years now and we share more with each other than with anyone else. But I meant what I said to Greg—intimate details about his manhood isn't her business. He didn't share that with her. He shared it with me. That's a trust I don't plan on breaking.

"You are a total perv, ya know that?" I shoot back at her, watching as Fiona warms up with the rest of her gymnastics class. I'm sitting on the same bench that I always use, and once again, butt bruises don't lie. But this time, it's a wonderful feeling because I got these bruises the fun way.

Oh geez. Next thing you know, I'm going to want my own red room of pain. I've officially crossed the line to insanity.

"Come on, Elena," Callie whines. "I'm living vicariously through you now. You know my sex life is practically nonexistent."

"Puh-leeze. You know you have no interest in being with Ben."

"You got me there. Neither one of us has a libido these days. It works for us. But that doesn't mean I don't want to hear about your love life."

"Not gonna happen, babe." The door next to me opens and I know instinctually that Greg came out of the office. I catch his eye as I answer Callie. "What happens between him and me stays between him and me."

He winks and mouths "Callie?"

I respond with a smile and a nod. He knows what we're talking about.

"He's standing right next to you, isn't he?"

I pull the phone back to look at it. "How do you know that? Do you have a camera planted on me somewhere?"

"Your voice gets all deep and sultry when he shows up," she claims. I'm not dismissing the idea that she's tagged me yet, though. She's a sneaky one. "Since you won't give me all the details, ask him if he'll take us to the beach so I can ogle him in a bathing suit."

I snort a laugh and cover the microphone with my hand. "She wants to know if we can go to the beach so she can ogle you from afar."

"Not afar," she yells in my ear, as Greg pushes his stomach out, rubbing a less than sexy pot belly. "I wanna ogle up close."

"Sorry, Callie. I'm not sure you want to see what I'm looking at up close and personal. It's, um... not quite what you think."

"He's mooning you, isn't he?"

"No, he's not mooning me." Greg laughs and walks away, heading over to greet his students.

"I don't wanna see a hairy ass, dammit! I want abs. And if you won't give me abs, I want details on your bump and grind."

"No."

Callie continues to whine in my ear about what a terrible friend I am for not giving her all the juicy details. I know she doesn't really expect me to tell her anything private, but ribbing each other is what we do best. Sarcasm and poking fun are our love language to each other.

I'm not hearing most of what she's saying anyway. I'm too busy watching my man work. He doesn't even realize how sexy he is, just by being him. As I watch him, memories of our night together come flooding back. It's crazy how he's awoken my libido and there's no shutting it down, whether he's trying to excite me or not.

For instance, when he crosses his arms, observing a student perform, it makes his biceps flex the same way as when he was holding my thighs apart, proving he is, in fact, a master at oral.

When he bends his knees and sticks his butt out, demonstrating how to stick a landing, it reminds me of the movement he made when he was thrusting in and out of me.

And when he wipes his brow with the hem of his shirt, which I have no doubt he does on purpose so I can see his abs in all their glory, all I can think of is how beautiful he is when he's naked and how much I love running my hands down his chest.

"Are you even listening to me?" Callie barks at me.

"No. Sorry. I was sidetracked." By my memories. But I don't say that.

"Uh huh. I know you're at gymnastics," she lectures. "And I know you're thinking all the dirty, dirty thoughts about how quickly he can get naked if you were to yank those athletic shorts down."

Busted.

"Seriously? Are you sure I'm not bugged? Fine. You caught me. But I really am trying to watch Fiona, too." Wherever she is. "I probably should let you go."

"What? No! You have to give me something! Let me live vicariously through you!"

I chuckle under my breath and I know I'm going to cave. But really, was there any question that I wouldn't eventually? "Ok fine."

"Yeah!" she squeals. "Was he amazing? Just tell me he's amazing."

"Yes, he's amazing."

"I knew it!" she shrieks. I'm pretty sure she's jumping up and down if the vibration of her voice is any indication. "And he's hung right? Tell me he's hung."

I knew we'd come back to this. But I've been thinking about how to answer this question for a couple days now, so I'm prepared.

"He's perfect. The most beautiful man I've ever seen."

She sighs and that's all I need to tell her. "I love that he's perfect for you."

He catches me watching him and winks. It makes my entire body feel warm and I realize... I'm falling in love with him.

Not lust-hazed, sex-fueled love. This is real, genuine, in it for the long-haul kind of love. Love that only desires to make him happy. The mature kind of love people who have been married for fifty years have.

And it doesn't scare me at all. I'm under no disillusions that we both feel the same way or that he's going to propose. But it certainly feels like what we're building is deeper than a passing fancy. What we're creating together could potentially last for the long haul. It feels right.

"I know, me, too," I admit to Callie, but I'm not in the mood to talk anymore. I need to process through these feelings for a bit. "Hey, I need to let you go. I need to concentrate on Fiona."

I'm lying, but it works.

We say our goodbyes, Callie still sighing like my life is her own personal chick flick. Me still in this new fog of emotion.

I finally spot Fiona working with Greg on the high bar. I guess Coach Zach is absent again. Shows you how much the blood hasn't gone back to my brain yet.

Fi swings back and forth, her re-grip practically perfect. Her legs are straight, her toes are pointed, her abs are tight. She stumbles every once in a while, but for the most part, she has this nailed. And then, when I least expect it, she swings out, lifts her legs up, and pulls herself over the bar until she's resting at the top, still in perfect form.

A pull over isn't a hard skill. But when you do it from a swing, it takes timing and strength and coordination... all things Fiona's been working hard on.

She's beaming, Greg is praising her, and I'm feeling an immense sense of pride. Look how far we've both come with a little encouragement from this man.

It's not because we were helpless. It's not because we wouldn't have figure it all out on our own eventually. But sometimes the people in our lives have more of an impact on us than we ever could have anticipated. That's what Greg has done for us… impacted us in ways he doesn't even realize.

It makes me smile. I'm not in love quite yet, but I'm getting there. And suddenly, all of our futures look incredibly bright.

CHAPTER
Twenty-Two

I'm convinced the only thing I ever do is plan or attend birthday parties.

Between my three kids, Callie's kid, and Greg's kid, there are five birthday parties this year. And that doesn't include classmates of my older two. Granted, Peyton won't turn three for a while, but her birthday falls right in line with the rest of them... two and a half months after Fiona's... two and a half months before Christopher's.

She may be the youngest of the bunch, but she seamlessly falls into the mix with the rest of the kids. Even where her birthday is concerned.

Today, though, we're celebrating Maura. My sassy, frilly, girly-girl is now six. And in sassy, frilly, girly-girl fashion, the house looks like it threw up pink decorations everywhere and all guests are required to wear a tiara. Everyone. Daddies included.

Of course, James balked at the idea because "Boys can't be princesses." That logic didn't go over well with the birthday girl. She may be a little princess, but she's the epitome of a Southern Belle—sweet and charming, and she'll kick your ass if you piss her off. Needless to say, James has fallen in line with the birthday girl's wishes.

Greg, on the other hand, slapped the tiara right on his head without a second thought. "Why can't I be a princess?" he'd said. "If Maura can slay a dragon, I can make sure the housework gets done."

He totally won brownie points with her for that.

He also won brownie points with me when he made sure my hot dogs were cooked to perfection and set to the side so no one would eat them.

He also made my ex look like an ass, which was fun for me.

Did I mention I'm totally falling in love with him?

"Do you need any help?" Greg wraps his arms around me and kisses the back of my neck while I put candles on the cake.

"Mmm." I lean back into him, enjoying the feel of being wrapped up in him. "I think everything is pretty much under control right now." Placing the last candle, I swivel in his arms to face him. "Are you ok? You've seemed distracted all day."

His smile doesn't quite reach his eyes and that has me worried. All day long he's been zoning out at the strangest times, and I keep catching him watching me. The expression he wears isn't something I can decipher. I feel like there's something he's not telling me, but I'm trying not to freak out. I trust him. I know he'll tell me when he's ready.

"Just Libby crap. But it's nothing to worry about." That's all he needs to say. The woman can't seem to play nice and I know it grates on him. He gives me a quick peck and pulls back, slapping me on the ass lightly. "You look really nice, by the way."

"That's because I'm wearing my latest skirt from Callie's collection." I pull away and turn back and forth, swinging the skirt around and posing for him. "You like?"

He growls quietly. "I always love skirts. They're easy to hike up over your hips…"

"Easy there, lover boy," Callie interrupts, as I bat his hand away from my thighs playfully. "Wouldn't want to traumatize the kids. And by kids, I mean James who is over there giving you the evil eye."

Sure enough, he's watching us from a distance, even though he should be paying attention to Birthday Girl Barbie, who's standing right next to him.

"Why do you always ruin my fun?" Greg turns to give her a mock glare, still holding me close to him.

She puts her hands on her hips and sighs. "This time I wasn't trying, I promise. I enjoy seeing smoke come out of James's ears as much as you do. I need your help getting the ladder out of the garage."

"Why do you need the ladder?" I ask. Even for Callie, that's kind of a strange request during a birthday party.

"Christopher's on the roof and can't get down."

We've had enough playdates together that situations other people would find to be an emergency, don't seem quite that catastrophic to us. We meander our way around the table, stepping out from under the porch and sure enough, there sits Christopher.

Greg shades his eyes with his hand as we watch the little terror dig for gold, seeming bored by all the attention he's getting. "How did he even get up there?"

"I knew that tree branch needed to be trimmed back," I grumble. "He climbed up my magnolia tree, didn't he?"

Callie shakes her head. "I knew he was a climber, but I had no idea he could shimmy up the trunk of a tree like a monkey. I tried to catch him, but apparently, he's been practicing. He's really fast."

"We should have taken him out of gymnastics sooner. He learned too much." Greg turns to me. "The ladder in the garage, does it extend?"

"Yeah, to fifteen feet or so, I guess."

"Alright, I'll be right back."

"You need me to stick around?" I ask Callie. She's surprisingly calm considering her child is on the roof of my house.

"Nah. Ben has his eyes glued on my devil child. I'm sure if something happens, Ben will catch him anyway." Sure enough, Super Dad is standing on the grass, eyes trained on Christopher, with his arms stretched out, saying things like "Don't be scared. We're going to get you down," and "Get your finger out of your nose and hold on to the shingles." It's kind of sweet except for the fact that every time he speaks, his voice sounds a little bit more hysterical.

"Maybe I should get a picnic blanket and we can all take a corner in case he falls." I've never had a child on my roof before. I have no idea what the protocol is with something like this.

"And make him think there's a make shift trampoline down here? That'll give him a reason to jump. No way." She brings up a good point. We aren't trying to encourage him to dismount, only trying to prevent him from breaking his neck when he finally does. "Besides, he usually bounces, not break, when he falls."

"You don't sound very concerned."

She shrugs. "Not my first rodeo with this kid. Besides, his dad can do the dirty work this time. I'm always the one who has to call 9-1-1."

Another valid point.

Greg comes around the corner of the house carrying the largest ladder I've ever seen in my life. I knew it was in the garage but I've never used it before. It looks really heavy and Greg looks really strong carrying it. I should be getting the cake and ice cream ready, but I'm distracted by his bicep muscles. They're flexed under the strain of carrying the ladder. His leg muscles are also tight. His face is showing a hint of strain, and the look reminds me of his "O" face. I get flushed thinking about how I know that.

"Damn." Callie pulls her sunglasses down her nose to watch Greg set up the ladder and lean it against the house. "I guess we don't have to go the beach after all. That man has muscles for days."

As soon as the ladder is situated, Ben scrambles to the top and tries to grab for Christopher who immediately moves away. This of course, makes Ben scream like a frightened little girl because he's worried Christopher is "going to fall off the edge". Never mind that he moved further away from said edge.

After several minutes of Christopher ignoring his father's pleas, Ben makes the final move off the ladder and ends up on the roof as well.

"Ben's afraid of heights, you know," Callie throws out there.

I look at her, my jaw dropped open. "Are you serious?"

"Yep. He hates them. I guess the love you feel for your child really does make you do crazy things."

Greg shakes his head and I know he's eavesdropping. It seems he's resigned himself to having to get involved in yet another Christopher calamity.

With a heavy sigh, he climbs the ladder to the top, making his shorts flex over his ass. Yum.

Ben is still inching towards Christopher who is still backing away from his dad. It's not going well until Coach Greg finally takes control.

"Christopher." He uses that commanding voice I've heard so many times when he's working. The voice that demands that children listen and comply. The voice that makes my insides melt. The voice that makes Callie suck in a breath and bite her lip, lust plainly drawn across her face.

I smack her arm and she has the wherewithal to look embarrassed about lusting over another man—*my* man. "Sorry," she grumbles.

"Christopher, you do not have permission to be up on the roof," Greg lectures. "Your father is trying to keep your safe. You need to go to him. Do you understand?"

Christopher nods.

"Now get your finger out of your nose and slowly scoot on your butt."

"No," Ben interjects, "Go to Greg, ok, buddy?"

Christopher looks at Greg like he's asking for permission. Greg nods.

"That's good. Don't go fast. Go really slow, but scoot over to me."

It takes a solid five minutes for Christopher to get to Greg, which is crazy because normally we can't get him to slow down. But I guess that's the magic of "Coach Greg".

As soon as they reach the bottom rung, the entire party breaks out in cheers. Greg hands Christopher to Callie, but he has no interest in being coddled after a near-death experience. Instead he wiggles down to the ground and runs to the swing set where he can climb up the rock wall to the fort at the top. Not sure why he didn't climb that to begin with.

"Well, now that this particular circus is over," I remark to Callie, "I'm going to go grab the rest of the stuff. Will you be ok by yourself out here?"

"I'm not by myself. I've got Coach Greg to do all the hard work." I barely catch a glimpse of him rolling his eyes at her comment.

I head into the house for silverware, plates, and ice cream. The air conditioning does little to cool my body. I'm feeling flushed from all the fantasies of Greg and I playing "gymnastics" I was having during the roof top rescue.

I wonder if we could practice my "flexibility".

Maybe he needs me to "stretch".

I wonder if doggie style works if he holds onto my hips while I'm in a handstand.

That's what his coach voice does to me. Makes me have inappropriate thoughts while I'm trying to host a children's birthday party. It's amazing how fast my libido picked up when I found the right person. I don't remember ever feeling this way with James.

Speak of the devil…

The door opens and I look over my shoulder to see James coming in. Whatever. Maybe he's here to lend a hand.

"Hey, can you grab the ice cream out of the freezer for me? It's in a big five-gallon bucket thing."

Before I even have a chance to register what's happening, James grabs me by the arm, whips me around, and presses his lips on mine.

His lips are strong and soft and familiar. And for a split second, I'm so stunned it's like muscle memory takes over and I don't do anything to stop him.

But very quickly, my wits come back to me and it feels wrong. *All* wrong.

The crack of my hand across his cheek echoes around the room.

"What the fuck was that?" I screech, pushing him away.

"I made a mistake, Elena."

"No kidding you made a mistake." Grabbing a birthday napkin, I wipe my mouth, trying to get his taste off me. "Your wife is in my backyard."

"No, I mean I made a mistake leaving you."

My eyes snap up to his. He looks… distraught? Regretful? Remorseful? All of those things I wanted a couple of years ago. Now that he finally has those emotions, it's insulting. "You've got to be kidding me. Leave me alone, James."

"No." He steps towards me and grabs my shoulders, looking me in the eye. "You don't understand. I miss you, Elena. I miss our friendship and the conversations we used to have. I miss the life we had."

Giving him a menacing look, I put as much venom in my voice as I can muster. "Take your hands off me."

Instantly, he does as I ask and puts some distance between us. I smooth down my skirt and straighten my blouse. "I don't know what the hell you think you're doing, but you made a choice two years ago when you decided to have a relationship with your secretary."

"That's what I'm saying, Elena. I made the wrong choice."

"Oh, I agree with you." I pull out more plastic silverware, arranging them on the tray, mostly to give myself something to fidget with. This is not a conversation I am prepared to have and it's taking everything in me not to stab his eyeball with this plastic butter knife. "But you don't miss me. You miss having someone your age to talk to so you don't feel old and out of touch."

"That's not true…"

I put my hand up to stop him. "You miss having someone who does your laundry and cooks your dinner and maintains your house, not like Homemaker Barbie out there who makes you pull your own weight.

"The only reason we're even having this conversation is because you don't want anyone else to have me. I'm like the toy you never played with but don't want anyone else to play with either. Well, sorry. It doesn't work that way."

"You don't get it," he tries again. "I've watched the transformation you've made over the last few months and I see the woman I fell in love with all those years ago is back. It's like you lost yourself when we had kids, and now, here you are. I miss my wife. I miss you."

What. The. Fuck.

"First of all, your *wife* is out back helping our six-year-old put press on nails on her fingers. As much as I don't like her, how dare you disrespect her like this?"

"But I don't love her like I love you," he whispers.

I snort an angry laugh and shake my head. It takes me a minute to gather my thoughts before I can even speak again.

"You don't know what love is, James." My hands are clenched into fists and I'm willing myself to stay somewhat calm. This is a child's birthday party after all, no matter what James has been smoking. "You don't even know what commitment is. All you see is a pretty outside package," I gesture to my clothes, "and that's what you want. But let me remind you that underneath, I'm the exact same person I always was. I wasn't good enough for you before. Your flattery isn't good enough for me now."

A throat clears and Greg is standing in the doorway, a strange expression on his face. "Am I interrupting something?"

I shake my head. "Nope. Nothing at all. I'm getting the last of the supplies while lecturing James on how doing drugs makes you a fucking idiot." I don't know why I lie to him, but this entire conversation has been such a buzzkill and I want to pretend it never happened. Rummaging around in my junk drawer for a second, I grab my favorite cherry flavored lip gloss. Ok, it's Fiona's lip gloss that I confiscated out of her laundry, but maybe this will help get rid of the lingering taste of James on my lips. "What's up? You have a weird look on your face."

Greg relaxes slightly, probably because of my nonchalant attitude. If he knew James had attacked my lips, he probably wouldn't be so carefree.

"Do you know if the screens in Maura's room are easy to pop in and out of the windows?"

I shrug. "I've never even thought about it. I have no idea. Why?"

"Ben's stuck now."

I bark a laugh. "He's still on the roof?"

Greg flashes that dazzling smile and those inappropriate fantasies are immediately back. We may have to unwrap our own presents later. And by presents, I mean each other.

"Yeah, Callie wasn't kidding about him being afraid of heights. He's literally frozen against the side. It's probably easier to reinstall the screen tomorrow than to try to drag a grown man down the ladder."

"Go for it."

He shuts the door and as he passes me, he stops. "You ok?" He gently intertwines our fingers as he looks in my eyes for any indication that I need his intervention.

Flashing a shy smile, I nod. "I'm fine. I promise. Go get Weathervane Ben off my roof."

"You and those nicknames," he remarks with a smile. He brushes his lips over mine quickly. "You taste like cherries."

"That's what I was going for."

I follow Greg with my eyes as he walks out of the room. The man makes my heart melt. When my gaze swings back to James, he looks sad. Like someone walked away with is favorite toy.

But that's the big difference between James and Greg. The former threw my heart in a box and forgot it was worth anything until someone else dusted it off. The latter recognizes my heart isn't a toy and he takes care of it.

"Let me make myself clear," I say to James, making sure he understands by my tone that I'm very, very serious. "The only reason you're here right now is because I'm mature enough to recognize that it's good for our children to spend special events with everyone they love, whether they're divorced or not." Snatching the ice cream bucket out of the freezer, I shove it into James's arms. "But if you ever pull that bullshit again, we'll go back to following the court order to the 't' and joint events will be a thing of the past. Got it?"

He nods sheepishly and opens the door, a loud thump coming from upstairs immediately followed by the sound of more cheers. I giggle at my own conjured up visual image of what the scene must have looked like when those two men came through the window.

I don't take much time to speculate. There's still a cake to cut and a birthday girl to celebrate after all.

A reassuring thought crosses my mind as I paste a smile on my face and rejoin the party. This is my circus. These are my monkeys. And as much as I'm not always in control of what happens, it feels good to know I'm getting a grip on my life again.

Only this time, I'm not relying on anyone else to make it feel complete. I'm making my own decisions. And that feels good.

CHAPTER
Twenty-Three

"You gonna tell me what really happened with James?"

I crinkle my nose like I'm concentrating on a particularly dirty spot of the dish I'm cleaning. Really what I'm doing is avoiding eye contact with Greg. We ended up having a really nice day and I don't want to messy it up with talk of my ex.

After the birthday cake was served, everyone stuck around for the kids to play for a while. The adult guests mingled and finished up most of the hors d'oeuvres, which makes my waist line and my refrigerator happy. Eventually it started getting dark, the kids all started getting cranky, and the house cleared out.

Only Greg stayed behind.

Between the two of us, we got all the girls bathed (me helping with the baths), hair and teeth brushed (Greg outfitting everyone in amazing fishtail braids), and tucked into their beds. They fell asleep almost instantly after such a busy day, and as much as I want to fall into my own bed with my boyfriend, clean up comes first.

I'm hopeful the booty call comes second.

But not if this conversation goes badly.

"Why do I get the feeling you're ignoring my question?" Crap. He's not going to let this go.

Taking a deep breath, I place the last of the dirty plates in the dishwasher and wipe my hands with a towel. Leaning back against the counter, I peek up at him through my eyelashes.

"He kissed me."

Greg's eyes practically bug out of his head. "He did what?" I can't tell if he's angry or in disbelief. "Is that why he had a hand print on his face?"

I cringe. "I didn't realize it was that noticeable."

"It was kind of hard to miss. I figured he'd said something that made you mad, but I thought he was just being a dick."

"He was being that, too. I mean, what kind of man kisses his ex with his current right outside the door?" I jump up on the counter and relax as I sit for the first time today. "I kind of feel bad for her. Don't get me wrong, I'll never trust her after what she did. But it's almost like I can see him starting the same patterns again, and she doesn't even realize what's coming. Is it weird that I feel this way?"

He moves forward and settles himself in between my legs, arms wrapped around my waist, my arms automatically moving around his neck. "I don't think it's weird." He kisses me in small pecks as he talks. "Even though she hurt you deeply, you still don't wish for her to be screwed over. That shows how much integrity you have."

"Mmm," is all I can say through the fog in my brain. His kisses always do this to me. "How much of the actual conversation did you hear, anyway?"

"Not much. Something about him not knowing what commitment is and you still being the same person you've always been."

"That was basically the tail end of it. He kept saying how he misses me and he wants me back." Something like anger briefly flashes through Greg's eyes. "I told him if he ever pulls that bullshit again, we'd go back to following the custody order as it's written, and nothing more."

Greg pulls back a bit. "You told him that?"

"Of course, I did. I'm not married to him anymore. I don't have to accept him, flaws and all. I'm civil for the sake of the girls, that's it. I don't have to be disrespected like that."

"But what if I wasn't here. Would you take him back then?"

"First of all, you are here," I say, as I run my fingers through his hair. "But even if you weren't, I've worked long and hard to know my worth. He still doesn't see beyond the physical. But that all fades. I don't want to be with someone who is always looking for the latest and greatest. That's not a real relationship. Besides, I'll never steal another woman's husband."

"Not even if she stole him from you first?"

"Not even then." I kiss him softly, melting into his embrace. "Plus, I have someone so much better, and I'm not giving him up."

Greg tenses, reminding me of his distance earlier. Something's been wrong all day. I can tell it's eating at him a lot.

"Now, your turn. Are you going to tell me what's really going on? You've been distant all day." He won't look me in the eye so I nudge him. "Hey. We're in this together, right? I want to help you if I can," I say quietly. "Tell me."

Taking a deep breath, he finally looks up at me. All I see is sadness. I've never seen Greg sad before. Frustrated. Angry. Irritated. Sure. But sad? Never.

"I'm just gonna say it, ok?" He swallows hard, his Adam's apple bobbing. I can't look away from it because something about this moment feels very serious, and suddenly I'm afraid of what he's about to say.

"I'm moving."

My body runs cold. I heard the words, but surely I'm misunderstanding the meaning.

"Did you, um… buy a house or something?" *Please say yes. Please say yes.*

"No." He shakes his head and strokes my hair. "I'm moving… to San Antonio."

My entire body freezes, except for my eyes that are blinking rapidly as I try not to let them fill with tears. This has to be a bad dream, right? A nightmare? James slipped something into to my mouth when he was trying to make out with me and I'm having hallucinations? This isn't happening.

But it is happening, as Greg continues to explain.

"Remember that guy Libby met online?" I feel myself nod, but it's more of a reflex than an actual response. This entire conversation doesn't seem real. "She's decided to move in with him. And she's taking Peyton with her."

"But… don't you have a morality clause or something written into your divorce decree? So she can't move in with some random guy?"

He continues to play with my hair like he can't stop touching me. Like he's running out of time. Which, I guess he is.

"No. I didn't even think to negotiate that during the proceedings. It was a stupid, stupid mistake. I should have known better because she's so irrational sometimes. But I didn't, and now I'm stuck. I can't be here with Pey in San Antonio, Elena. I can't." He's pleading with me to somehow make this ok. The selfish part of me wants to talk him out of it—to talk him into staying here. But I can't do that. I understand the sacrifice far too well.

Peyton is barely two. Seeing her once a month would be the kiss of death for their relationship. They'd never be able to have a strong bond if he didn't see her at least twice a week. And I'd never forgive myself if I put him through that.

"I know. I *know*." Stroking his beard, trying to keep my head on straight, I continue asking questions. "What about your job, though?"

"Dave has been working on opening a new facility in San Antonio for a couple years now, and they've asked me to go run it. The first time they offered I turned them down. I was going through the divorce process, and I couldn't up and leave them." He shrugs sadly. "But when Libby said they were moving, it sort of all fell together. They broke ground on the new gym a couple months ago and were looking for someone to get in there and facilitate the opening."

"Oh. Well that's good, I guess." I'm shell-shocked. This man, who is the best part of my life, besides my kids, is leaving me. Who knows if I'll ever see him again.

"Elena," he says gently, tears forming in his eyes. "I don't want to leave you behind."

I smile and try hard to blink my own tears away. "And I don't want you to leave me behind. But I can't uproot our entire lives. My whole support system is here."

"I know. And I'd never ask you to. As much as I hate him, I wouldn't want you to do to James what Libby is doing to me. But I just... I just found you."

He pulls me to him and hugs me tight. And that's when the tears begin to fall for both of us.

I don't know exactly why he's crying, but for me, it's the unfairness of it all. Here is this amazing man, a man who makes me laugh and builds me up, who loves my kids and is respectful to their father. He likes me for *me*... and we'll never have the chance to see if it could have been forever.

I feel like all the good that has happened to me over the last few months has been derailed.

"When do you leave?" I sniff, my voice sounding muffled against his shoulder.

"Next week."

A sob escapes me again. That's so soon. It's too soon.

"Libby told me yesterday that she's moving. I slept on it overnight. I was stunned and surprised by it all, I couldn't figure out what to do, ya know?" He sniffs. "But I realized I was avoiding what I had to do. I talked to Dave this morning before the party. As soon as we hashed out the details, I found some apartment online and rented it."

I nod as the information sinks in. My head is spinning. It's happening fast. Too fast. How am I supposed to say everything there is to say, to do everything there is to do, if there's only one week left to be together? It's so unfair.

"I know the girls are here," Greg says, still holding me tightly to him, "And I wouldn't normally ask because of that. But can I please spend the night? I just... I don't want to leave you yet. I need more time with you."

I nod through my tears, clinging to him as tightly as he's clinging to me. I keep my eyes shut, trying to memorize the feel of him, as he picks me up off the counter and carries me to my room.

This is, quite possibly, the last night we ever spend together. And I don't want to forget a moment of it.

CHAPTER Twenty-Four

We don't sleep much. We spend the night tangled up in each other.

Soft kisses, expressing our feelings.

Gentle touches, memorizing the feel of each other.

Passionate kisses, telling each other how angry we are about this forced separation.

And when he rocks inside me, whispering that he loves me for the very first time, my heart simultaneously swells and breaks.

He loves me.

He *loves* me.

And I know, I *know* I love him, too. We haven't had a chance to move to a deep, all-encompassing kind of love. But this is what love really is.

Respect. Care. Understanding.

Sacrifice.

Sacrificing our own happiness if it's what's best for the other.

Even as the waves of ecstasy overtake my body, I don't regret supporting his decision. Even as tears roll down my cheeks and he groans his own release, I know it's the right thing to do.

I love him.

I *love* him.

And this time, it means letting him go.

I wake when the sunlight peaks through my blinds. Thankfully, I'm up before the girls are. I'm all cried out and I need time to put my game face on.

I also need time to enjoy this moment. To feel the rise and fall of Greg's chest as he breathes. To hear his soft sighs. To smell his skin. To just be together.

Greg squeezes me tightly to him. It feels so right for us to be like this—intertwined, not really sure where one of us ends and the other begins.

"You ok?" he whispers, rubbing his hand down my hip.

I think how to respond before I say anything, but really, there's no good answer. "No," I finally admit. "But I will be. I don't have a choice, right?"

He rolls us until we're facing each other, and I sniff back tears for the umpteenth time since last night.

"I would never make you wait for me, Elena." I gaze into his tear-filled eyes and see nothing but love. "You're too dynamic of a person and you deserve to be loved. I would never ask you to do that. But I just…" He sucks in a sharp breath. "I can't believe that this is over already. And I'm going to pray every single day that somehow the circumstances change and that I can come back to you. But don't you dare wait for me while I pray, ok?"

A sob rips from my throat and I grab him to me, wrapping my arms and legs and heart around his. I guess I'm not as cried out as I thought. We cry in each other's arms for what seems like an eternity, before I can't take it anymore.

And I kiss him. I kiss him everywhere I can. His face, his shoulders, his arms and his chest. I kiss him as I cry and he cries as I kiss him. And we make love one final time through our tears, although I don't think either one of us actually finishes.

When we're done and we're emotionally depleted, we begin making plans.

"What day do you leave?" I feel emotionally drained, but at least I don't feel like I'm cracking in two. I'm sure I will again at some point, but for now, I'm at least functional.

"Friday. I want to get a little bit settled before I get Peyton on Saturday. She's already too far away, ya know?"

I nod because I do know. I can't even imagine how I would feel if my girls were five hours away from me. It must be a nightmare for Greg, knowing Libby isn't exactly forthcoming with information as it is. And knowing his daughter is living with some man he's never met, especially with her not even being fully verbal yet.

"I'm sad we didn't get to say good bye to her. Max, especially, is really going to miss her. I don't even wanna think about Christopher."

He chuckles. "At least I don't have to worry about getting that shotgun now. That kid was getting a little too flirty with my baby."

I smile, enjoying the deep rumble of his laugh.

"I have a lot to do this week, but I want to spend as much time with you as possible. Can we do that?" he asks.

"Of course. Want to come over for dinner tonight?"

"I'll be here. And call your mom today. Get her set up to babysit every night this week. I want to do all those things we said we were going to do."

"What things? I didn't realize we had plans." I love our easy banter. This might be the part I'm going to miss the most.

"Oh yeah," he confirms. "I want to take you bowling and dancing and to the food trucks downtown. I hear there is a fantastic hot dog truck that will probably give you an orgasm just by looking at the menu," he jokes, digging a ticklish finger into my rib making me squeal.

"I love hot dogs," I giggle, still squirming until I'm situated on him again.

"I know."

"You think we can cram it all in?" I smirk at his lofty expectations. "All the plans you never told me about?"

"We can try."

We get silent again, as the finality of this week hits us. I know from my divorce that grief will come in waves. But somehow, I feel like these waves may keep coming for the rest of my life. Maybe not huge waves. But there's no way I won't feel a pang of sadness whenever I think of Greg in years to come.

Licking my lips, I know I have to extend the same grace to him, as he gave to me. "Do me a favor, ok?"

He shifts so he can look at me better, putting one hand behind his head, and running his other fingers through my hair. "You told me not to wait for you. Don't wait for me either."

"Elena…" he whispers.

"I'm serious." I nudge him gently. "I hate this so, so much. But I don't want you to miss out on something good. We've both got a lot of years ahead of us, and I would hate to know you spent yours pining away for me."

His lips quirk like he wants to smile, but his heart won't let him. Gently, he licks his lips and pulls me to him, kissing me softly. Over and over and over again. When he finally rests our foreheads together, he gives me a quiet, "ok."

And then I hear Max yelling for me and I know our time is up. At least for now.

The five of us spend the next couple of hours enjoying the pancake breakfast Greg insists on making and putting together Maura's new toys. I could kill Callie for the *Create Your Own Make Up* set she gave my child. It's sticky, it's glittery, it gets everywhere.

I am *so* getting Christopher a puppy for Christmas.

Once all the toys have a new home and Greg gets the screen back on the window like he promised, he leaves to get a few errands done.

Grabbing my face, he kisses me gently once, twice, three times, and rests his forehead on mine again. "I'll be back for dinner in a few hours."

"Ok." My hands rub up and down his forearms. This is my favorite way he touches me.

"I'm serious, babe. We're going to make the most of this week."

"I know."

He nods once, my answer good enough for him. "I love you. I'll see you soon." And he walks out the door.

"I love you, too." Then I close the door behind him.

CHAPTER
Twenty-Five

L ike all of life's best made plans, the next week didn't work out like we expected.

A couple hours after Greg left, it began.

Me: *Fiona's throwing up. You sure you want to come back over?*

Greg: *I'll grab some Pepto on my way.*

An hour later, it got worse.

Me: *Maura just joined her sister. There's vomit everywhere.*

Greg: *Don't cook. I'll pick up food on the way over.*

And by dinner time, all three of them were in the throes of a full-blown stomach bug.

Me: *If there was any question about how much Max chews her food, the answer is she doesn't.*

Greg: *As gross as that information is, I guess full strawberries are easier to clean up than half-digested strawberries, right? Gag reflex notwithstanding.*

Me: *I hate to say this, but you need to stay away. You can't risk getting sick, too.*

Greg: *I hate that you're right. But I'm holding out hope this is a twenty-four-hour bug and we can pick back up tomorrow.*

Me: *You and me both.*

We were wrong. So, so wrong. Basically, the plague hit my house and it was all I could do to keep up with disinfecting, doing laundry, and praying I didn't get sick, too. Dates were out of the question.

Instead, we texted every day, while Greg packed up his apartment, finished up some minor projects at work, and avoided the sick ward of Casa de Influenza. It sucked, but what could we do?

Ironically, by Friday, the day Greg was leaving, the girls finally felt better. Not better enough to go to school or even go outside. But better enough that Callie could come by and take over for a bit so I could take a long enough shower to shave my legs.

It feels nice to not cut myself every time my calves rub together now.

"Hey, Elena!" Callie yells up the stairs as I pull my hair up into a messy bun. Hopefully I'll get back to doing my hair and wearing real clothes soon. But for now, I'm not wasting time on the effort in case someone relapses all over me. It happened twice this week. I'm not taking any more chances.

"Coming!" I yell back, pulling on my ugly sweats before making my way back down the stairs. As soon as I hit the bottom step, she's waiting for me. "Everything ok?"

She gestures her head towards the door, holding onto the end of the yarn while Fiona works on yet another friendship bracelet. Each of us is sporting at least five so far and the yarn never seems to run out, thanks to Callie's Christmas presents last year. "You have a visitor."

I knit my brows in confusion and look through the blinds to see what she's talking about. There, leaning against a U-Haul truck with his arms and legs crossed, is Greg. A smile crosses my face as I grab the door knob.

"You ok with the girls for a few more minutes?" I ask her.

She rolls her eyes at me and helps Fi untangle a knot. "Go. Go see your man."

So I do.

"Fancy seeing you here," I remark, as I make my way to the best man I've ever known. "If I had known you were coming by, I'd have dressed up a little."

A wide grin crosses his face. "You know I don't care about that."

He grabs my shirt collar and hauls me to him, kissing me quickly before wrapping his arms around me, mine immediately going around his neck.

"I thought you'd be on the road already."

"Did you really think I'd leave without saying goodbye?" he asks gently, as he kisses down my neck.

"If it meant staying away from World War Z inside, possibly yes."

He chuckles. "Why do you think I didn't get anywhere close to the front door."

He kisses me again, this time deeply. Our tongues exploring each other's mouths like our lives depend on it. Our lips melded together like we need each other to breathe.

"Wow," I breathe when we finally come up for air. "Now *that* was a kiss."

"It's always been my goal to leave you breathless."

"You left me breathless the first day you walked into that kids' gymnastics class."

His eyes soften and he kisses me again. This time slowly, like stopping isn't an option. I'm fine with it if it means he can't go. But he has to. A two-year-old we both love depends on it.

Pulling back, I scratch the wayward hairs on the back of his neck. "How long is your drive?" I already know the answer, but I'm not ready for him to leave quite yet. The last five days without him have been bad enough. I'm not sure how I'll make it through the rest of my life.

He pats the side of the dented-up truck. "Probably close to six hours in Big Bertha, here."

"You named your U-Haul?" I giggle.

"The guy at the rental place did," he clarifies. "But I don't wanna piss her off by calling her by the wrong name. You know how finicky women are. I don't need her to break down on me in the middle of nowhere."

I pinch him playfully for that remark making him chuckle. Then we pull each other close again, and stand there hugging silently for what seems like hours. There's nothing really left to say, and letting go means, well... letting go.

But it must be done. We have to do what's best for the children in our lives. Isn't that what being a good parent is?

Making sure they are taken care of first and foremost? Knowing he's got to be ready for Peyton's visit tomorrow, I pull back and prepare to say goodbye.

"You need to go," I whisper, blinking back tears.

He takes my face in his hands and tilts my head to look him in the eyes. It's my favorite way that he touches me. He knows that. And I love him all the more for giving it to me one last time. Grabbing onto his forearms for the last time, I give him the attention he is clearly asking for, a single tear rolling down my cheek.

"I love you, Elena," he says quietly, looking deeply into my eyes so there is no question about what he's expressing. "You are the second best thing to ever happen to me, right behind my daughter. No matter what, I will *always* love you."

"I will always love you, too."

He kisses me a final time. A slow peck before he sniffs and pulls away quickly, wiping his eyes with the back of his hand. It's like if he doesn't make a clean break, he'll never leave.

I watch as he turns to go.

I watch as he climbs into Big Bertha, lifting a hand in a goodbye.

I watch as he drives away.

An arm wraps around my shoulders, and that's when I allow the tears to fall. Callie just stands there, head on my shoulder, and does what best friends do—lets me cry while I watch until the street ends and the giant U-Haul becomes nothing more than a little dot in my blurred vision.

"You ok?"

I shake my head and wipe the tears from my cheeks. "No," I sniff. "But I will be. Eventually."

We continue standing on the quiet street. I'm not sure what for, but somehow moving will make it all the more final, I suppose.

Callie takes a deep breath, her head still on my shoulder. "Is it too early to tell you that that goodbye was totally reminiscent of the scene in *Dirty Dancing* when Johnny drove away, leaving Baby in the dust?"

A quick laugh escapes through the tears. "Yes. It's too early to tell me that. That movie was terrible."

"I meant the classic. Not the train wreck of a remake."

I sniffle and wipe my nose with the back of my arm. "Oh good. Comparing me to the new version would be insulting and I can't take it right now."

"I would never stoop that low. But I think you've forgotten that when Johnny leaves, it wasn't the end of the movie. He comes back for her."

We turn back to the house. In spite of my grief, there are still sick kids to care for and mom duty calls.

"And I think you're forgetting that this isn't a movie, and I certainly don't dance like Jennifer Grey."

"Well, yes. Your dancing leaves much to be desired." She links her arm through mine as we walk. "But you're missing my point. Call it a gut feeling, but somehow, I don't think your love story is over yet."

I appreciate her sentiment, but I know that's not the way life works. Life is messy and unpredictable. It can bring amazing happiness, but it can also bring sadness. I'm not fooling myself and pretending that this will "work itself out". It's up to me to take whatever life throws my direction and make the best of it.

Music is blaring when we walk through the door and my ratty looking girls, all still dressed in their pajamas, hair sticking up everywhere, are getting down to the sounds of some random Megan Trainor song. Who knows which one. They all sound the same to me.

"What's going on?" I shout over the music.

Callie jumps right into the mix and begins shaking her groove thang. Why am I not surprised?

"It's a dance party, Mama!" Maura yells and grabs me by the hands, forcing me into the middle of it all.

I don't feel like dancing today, but looking at the joy on my girls' faces, I do it anyway. I know I need to dance like there's no tomorrow. Because as the last couple of years have shown me, anything can happen. I have to embrace the joy whenever it's available.

Forcing myself to shake my booty, I spin and twirl until I'm dizzy. Smiling through my sadness, I laugh until more tears run down my face, pretending it's not my grief overflowing. I quite literally, fake it because I know I'll make it.

Yes, today, I'm allowed to feel sad, but I won't wallow in self-pity. I finally have a grip on my life. And no matter how badly it hurts right now, we're all going to be ok.

CHAPTER
Twenty-Six

Greg

"Come on, Big Bertha, you can do it." I smack the dashboard a few times, trying and failing to get rid of the rattling sound that started about an hour ago. I don't think it's serious, but you never know with a rental and I'm not paying double fees for a tow truck to get this monster to my new apartment and then back to her owner after I unload.

The drive has been easy, but it's been long. Lots of highway. Lots of flat terrain. Not a lot of distractions. And no distractions means hours of having your thoughts on a never-ending loop of all the things I should have said and done. It's its own kind of torture. It doesn't help that I'm worried about four little girls… one living in a strange place that I'm driving towards and three sick ones that I'm leaving behind.

It's weird how I'm sad over the loss of someone else's kids, almost as much as I am about losing the actual someone.

It's not really helping that my mood calls for country music. Reba McIntyre is currently serenading me with words about her broken heart after a painful split from the one she loves. Talk about depressing. I could change the station, but that would require taking my hands off a wheel that doesn't have power steering just as the traffic increases, so I'm gonna go with it for now.

"We're almost there, Bertha," I say, but I'm not sure if I'm really talking to the truck or myself.

I haven't stopped thinking about Elena and her girls since I cranked the engine and put the truck into drive. Memories have flooded my mind and if I'm being truthful, I'm not trying really hard to push them out. I don't want to forget a second of our time together so I keep hoping the more I think about her, the more locked into my memory the last few months will be.

I want to remember how I felt the first time I saw her. She was relaxed and carefree with her messy bun and yoga pants, not freaking out when Christopher tackled Max to the ground yelling "Mine!". Thinking about it still makes me smile. Elena went with the flow of it all. She never judged Callie for Christopher's crazy antics like a lot of people would have. She just loves them for who they are.

I remember the playdates at McDonald's where Elena would always spit out an unexpected one-liner, making me choke. She had an uncanny ability to say the exact right thing as I took a drink. And by the look on her face when I coughed, like her goal all along was to shock me, she was pleased to accomplish that.

I remember her standing up to Libby. Her pulling together the inner strength I always knew was there, and she had forgotten about, to show my ex that we were in it together. The fire in her eyes as proof that it doesn't matter what anyone says, we're a team. End of story.

I remember the first night we spent together, getting to know each other's bodies and what gave each of us the most pleasure. She was worried about what I would think of how she looks, she never stopped to think there could be anything less than perfect about me. In her eyes, even after I bared my biggest insecurities to her, she was still right. I was perfect to her. And slowly but surely, she realized, in my eyes, I was right, too. She's the most beautiful woman in the world to me. Not because she's shaped like a modern-day supermodel, but because she's shaped like a woman who has lived a full and satisfying life. You don't get stretchmarks and less than perky breasts from maintaining a teenage figure. You get them from really *living*. And that is so much more attractive than boobs you can bounce quarters off.

Mostly, though, I remember watching her come into her own. I was lucky enough to see her transformation as it happened. She claims it was because of me that she found herself again. But that's not true. She found herself because she was never really gone. She was being covered up by a narcissistic asshole who made a point of treating her like she wasn't worth anything. As much as I hate how he left her, once she was free of him, she was free to shine again. And shine she does.

As the flat terrain begins to make more shape and the city of San Antonio begins to come into view, I know nothing I ever do will be as hard as leaving her today. It comes second only to letting Peyton get in that car with Libby and drive away last week. But that pain was short-lived when I made the decision to follow them. I will live with the pain of leaving Elena for the rest of my life. I will also live with the regrets of not being a stronger man, because this entire situation has proven I'm not nearly as strong as I should be.

While I watched Elena get a grip on her life, I was sitting around being a pussy with my own. I've let Libby run the show, because it's been easier to play nice. I've been so afraid of losing what little time I have with Peyton, that I lost sight of how much my ex controls things. And this time it cost me the woman I know could be the love of my life.

That's not ok.

I meant it when I said I've already started praying circumstances will change. Knowing how unpredictable Libby is, it's only a matter of time. But until all the answers on how to change things become clear, I'm going to focus on getting my own grip.

As I veer off to the right, taking the exit that will lead me to my new home, I make a vow to myself… things will not continue the way they have been. I will find a better balance.

For the girls.
For Elena.
For myself.
I'm going to make sure of it.

THE *End*

BALANCE check

a
#MyNewLife
romantic comedy

M.E. CARTER

CHAPTER One

Elena

"Ooof!" I drop the world's heaviest box next to my feet, which happens to be next to the world's largest industrial shredder. Ok, not really. But holy crap that box is heavy.

I really should get rid of my paperwork more often, but sometimes I get so caught up in my work that I procrastinate until it overflows.

Fine, that's a lie. I'm not getting caught up in my work. I'm getting caught up in the gossip at work. It can be juicy behind the scenes at an elementary school.

I've only worked here for a couple of months, but so far, I like it. I'm at the same school as my girls, so I get to have lunch with them sometimes. And I'm interacting with actual adults throughout the day. Not that Callie isn't an adult, even if she acts like a twelve-year-old boy half the time. But I'm expanding my horizons. Or so I tell everyone.

Going back to work was a hard decision to make. It was another life change to push through, but a necessary one. When Greg moved away nine months ago—and yes, I'm still keeping track—we made it a point to text and call almost daily. Eventually, he got busy with his new job and, frankly, the distance got too hard on me emotionally. I wondered constantly when I would get the text that he'd moved on and was dating again. It threw my anxiety into overdrive.

A couple of months after he left, I realized I was backpeddling. So I cut it off completely. It was one of the hardest things I've ever done. But my insecurities and doubts about my own worth were rearing their ugly heads, and I couldn't go back to where I had been. I just couldn't. Greg said he understood and we had, yet another, emotional moment full of tears. But he stayed true to his word and let me go.

This, of course, led to a lot of soul searching. First thing on the agenda was licking my wounds. Once Callie and I realized licking the ice cream spoon that went along with those wounds was bad for the waistline, I pulled myself together and began looking for ways to improve me. Finding a job was priority. If I was going to move forward, I needed to stop isolating myself. And while it was nice staying home with the girls, realistically, the bank accounts would run dry at some point if I didn't go back to work. And so would my sense of well-being.

Obviously, being a flight attendant again was off the table because... kids... but I'm still pretty good at customer service. So dozens of applications later, here I am, the front desk receptionist at Woodman Elementary School.

Mostly, my job entails answering phones, signing kids in and out, delivering gluten-free, GMO-free, flavor-free birthday cupcakes to various classrooms. But occasionally our principal, Betty Windham, gives me a project or two, and that's when my shred pile stacks up.

That, and when this same principal begins bitching to me about interoffice politics.

"Why, *why* did they think this wouldn't get out?" she huffs as she pours her third cup of coffee for the day.

Yes, my industrial-sized shredder, that is actually really fun to operate, is in the breakroom. It's annoying for those on break. But for me, it comes in handy. When I have a huge pile to shred, I will see and hear way more than on an average day. Do I spread the gossip? Hell no. I don't want to be *in* the drama. I just like knowing all about it. Sue me.

I hand Betty two creamers and a sugar. I was given a head's up by the previous receptionist how Betty likes her java, and how much easier things would be if I made sure we always had supplies handy.

She was right. The one day the regular sugar ran out and we only had Splenda, I thought for sure Betty's head was going to explode. She's not a bad person to work for... just an addict. No judgement from me. That mint chocolate chip ice cream is sitting in my freezer for a reason.

"Thanks." She snatches the packets out of my hand and begins doctoring her cup. "First of all, interoffice dating never works out. We all know this. We all *should* know this. But do my mid-life crisis teachers ever remember that? No. They begin humping like bunnies, and then I have to field phone calls from the scorned spouses."

Jerry Camperly and Maggie Ray. It's common knowledge they began a torrid affair last year after Jerry's wife had her implants removed. Somehow that tidbit plays into the story, but I haven't quite figured out how, and I'm not asking. Jerry's a great fifth grade teacher. Very good with science and math. Not a great husband.

Maggie, on the other hand, is a total nitwit. Don't get me wrong, she rocks the skinny jeans and three-inch heels she wears every day, never even so much as twisted an ankle while chasing those second graders—but she's not the sharpest knife in the drawer. Thinking this affair would stay under wraps is proof of evidence number one. Especially when the principal sees and hears all, and is the biggest gossip of them all. Even if she doesn't mean to be.

"Who called this time?"

"Maggie's husband. Wants to have a meeting or something to hash it all out." She waves her hand around as she gets riled up. "I told him, 'I am not a marriage counselor. What happens off these school grounds is not my business, and you will not drag me into this.'"

"Good for you. How'd he take it?"

She sighs. "He cried." She takes a long sip of her cup of joe and moans before getting back to it. "I'm sympathetic and all…"

No, she's not.

"… But this isn't my first go-round with Maggie. I've been at this school for fifteen years and this is the third affair of hers that I know of."

"How is that even possible? We don't have that many male teachers."

She shrugs. "Who says it's always a teacher?"

I grimace. Surely she's not talking about old Mr. Northman, the janitor who's been here since the dinosaur age. He's nice and all, but with his bug eyes and bad teeth, I don't even want to visualize someone kissing him. A shudder runs through me as I shake off the thoughts.

"At some point, Maggie's husband needs to get a backbone." Betty pivots and walks away, grumbling about missing her calling as an author because "you can't make this shit up."

Turning back to my shredder, I gather some files and let the paper massacre commence. There is something satisfying about shoving these papers through a row of razor blades, determined to chop it all up into unidentifiable pieces, never to be put together again.

It's possible I may still be harboring some anger from the last couple of years' events.

The door opens as I enjoy the tiny little screams of tree fibers and Tripp Mackey walks in.

Our school seems to be an anomaly when it comes to the number of male teachers we have. We have four. FOUR. Jerry the cheater, Coach Thompson who teaches P.E., Mr. Reed who runs the science lab for all of the grade levels and Tripp Mackey.

I barely have enough time to look away before I blush. Tripp Mackey is very, very pretty. And by that, I mean he is panty-dropping hot. Tall, dark, handsome. With the right amount of scruff and a smolder he must have perfected in college, he has been the star of many a teachers' fantasies.

Setting his looks aside, the fact that he teaches third grade reading, writing, and social studies makes him truly swoon-worthy. It's no wonder almost every woman in the building has a crush on him. Probably most of the men, too. He's practically perfect.

He's also very, very young. He graduated with his teaching degree only a couple of years ago.

That's why most of us look but don't touch. No one wants to be tagged as the dirty old woman of the school. Ok, maybe some of us wouldn't mind it so much.

"Hey Elena." Tripp flashes me a perfect smile full of perfect teeth and a perfectly wicked twinkle in his eye. I may be a tad dazzled by him. Just a tad. "I see the office gossip has you backed up on your shredding again."

If I wasn't blushing before, I am now. It's no secret that I hear a lot on the job. I suspect we all do. And I suspect we all hear it from the same person, too.

"I wish that was true," I lie because I will never confirm the things I've heard. "But this is my own procrastination. A little too much Candy Crush, I suppose."

"Sure, sure. So I was thinking…" He leans against the counter and crosses his arms. I try not to watch how the movement makes his biceps flex, because if I don't pay attention to what I'm doing, I'm likely to cut off a finger. There's nothing sexy about spewing blood all over the breakroom floor from an accident with the office supplies. "Would you like to go to dinner with me sometime?"

I freeze, still holding onto the paper that's being gobbled up by the machine, until it makes a nasty groaning sound.

"Oh, shit!" I exclaim when I realize I almost forced the gears to go in reverse. That wouldn't have been good. "Um… I… I'm sorry, did you just ask me out?"

I'm so flustered that I grab too much scrap paper, shoving it into the machine and immediately jam it. Shit.

Tripp chuckles and scoots me out of the way, popping open the top, and unclogging the jam. "Sorry. That was my fault. I should have had a better lead in." A slam of the top once the paper is cleared and we're back in business.

Turning to look at me, he is apparently going to give me a lead in this time.

"So I think you're really nice. And you're really funny. And I know I'm a bit on the young side, but I'm hoping my life experience makes up for my age." Gotta love Tripp, he actually looks kind of shy and vulnerable in the moment, not his normal bravado. "And I'd really love to take you out on a date."

I blink once. Twice. Three times, as my brain swirls with way too many thoughts to process at once.

Am I ready to date? That's the big question. It's been nine months since Greg left. I like my life. I like where I'm at. Am I ready to open up my heart again? And maybe even the bigger question is...

Do I want to open up my heart to a teeny bopper?

Physically, the answer is yes, of course. Good lord it's been way too long since I've had Greg's mouth on mine, his body on mine, his hands on me...

And right there is my answer. If the first thing that pops into my head while one man asks me out is thoughts of another man, clearly I'm not ready.

Taking a deep breath, I open my mouth to respond, but Tripp cuts me off with a hand to my forearm.

"Think about it. You don't have to answer me today. Or even next week. Just think about it. I'm not going anywhere." Then he turns and swaggers out the door. Literally swaggers. Puts his hands in his pockets to make sure the seat of his pants pulls tight as I watch him walk away.

Damn that kid. He just used his best *ass*et to make sure I didn't say no.

He's good. He's real good.

CHAPTER Two

Greg

The house is coming together pretty nicely, considering I bought it "sight unseen."

I guess that's not totally accurate. I'd seen the outside of it before and the floor plan is pretty standard for the area. I'd just never stepped foot inside this particular house until I backed the U-Haul into the driveway this morning.

It hasn't taken long to get everything unpacked. Joie, my sister, came with me to help and she's the most organized person I know. Almost obsessively so. When we were kids, it used to annoy me, but every time I've moved, her color-coded boxes have come in handy for getting things where they need to go.

There are more boxes with purple labels than anything else. That was Peyton's color. She's going through a phase and everything has to be some form of lavender. Sheets, pillows, stuffed animals, clothing, even her toothbrush. I don't mind. Peyton probably has the most stuff, but being that she's not yet three, everything is fun-sized anyway. Even her furniture.

The hardest part of it just being the two of us was maneuvering my sofa through the front door. I had no idea those little block legs on the bottom of the couch would make it so hard to get through a standard doorway. Thankfully, Joie had the exact right tool we needed in her giant bag. She calls it her purse. I call it a "Mary Poppins bag." There is no telling what kinds of shit she carries around all day long. Seriously. I noticed a loose heel in one of my loafers while we were packing up the other day. Joie pulled a portable shoe repair kit out of that bag. Who the hell carries around a portable shoe repair kit?

My big sister, that's who.

"I have to admit, this place is way nicer than I thought it would be," she calls out while breaking down another cardboard box with a giant yellow label. She said yellow was the color of sunshine and a kitchen should always be bright and airy, hence, why all the kitchen boxes have a yellow sticker on them. I don't understand the logic, but I don't ask. She has been a godsend during this move. The first thing she started unpacking was the eating area, which we both know is the most important room to me. I, on the other hand, tackled the re-assembling of furniture. Between the two of us, it's taken a few hours, but it's starting to look like a home in here. "When you told me you were going to buy it without seeing it first, I thought for sure you'd end up with a money pit."

I grab two beers out of the fridge and hand her one. "You don't have a lot of faith in me."

We clink bottles and both take a drink before she speaks again. "Wrong. I don't have faith in almost everyone except you. I still think the seller is hiding something. But I guess it's too late to worry about that now."

"Relax, Sis. There's nothing wrong with this place. The old guy who used to live here kept the lawn meticulous. It's reasonable to assume he kept the inside meticulous, too. Did you see how clean the hot water heater is? And look at this place." I open my arms wide and gesture around me. "So far, I'm right, right?"

Sure, the three-bedroom, two-bath brick house needs some updating. All the counters and cabinetry are original, but the big things have been updated and painstakingly cared for over the years—A/C, flooring, appliances. Even the pergola in the back yard was updated a couple of years ago.

"Yeah, but the price..." she maintains.

"Joie..." She looks at me and sighs, knowing what I'm going to say before the words even come out of my mouth. "If you inherited your grandfather's house, a house that was totally paid off, would you want to waste time bartering for a better deal, or want to unload it before you had to pay all the taxes on it?"

"I know, I know. It's just so hard to believe. Especially for this neighborhood."

"It was a once in a lifetime deal," I admit, walking to the window and pulling down the blinds to see out.

Joie comes to stand next to me and we look out on the quiet street. My new neighbor across the street is mowing the lawn. Someone from down the way is pushing a stroller. She waves at a jogger and her dog as they pass by. There hasn't been much traffic since we've been here, which will be great when Peyton spends the weekend. And I'm sure she'll want to play with the girls that live next door. We've missed them.

After three long years of waiting, Peyton's weekend visits will start up next month, the weekend after her birthday. Because of our divorce decree, she hasn't been able to spend the night up to this point. I understood the decision when it was made. She was only a baby when Libby and I got divorced and was really young to be separated from her mother. But knowing her mother isn't the one that's normally cared for her for the last few years, it's been her grandmother, it makes me even more excited to share all the moments I've been denied until now. I can't wait to spend four days or so a month making her breakfast and reading her bedtime stories. We've done all those things before. But it feels different now.

"It's like things are starting to fall into place, ya know?" I say out loud, even though I'm really talking to myself. "The house, the job, Libby... I prayed every day for the circumstances to change and now, here we are."

We watch as a car drives up next door. I haven't seen this car before. It's a smaller four-door. Briefly, I wonder what it's doing when the driver's side opens and a familiar face steps out.

"Oh shit!" I yell and drop to the floor so she won't see me. Joie stands above me, looking like I've lost my damn mind. "What are you doing?" I practically screech. "She's going to see you!"

"She can't see me through the blinds, Greg," she argues and turns back to the window.

"You don't know that!"

"Yes I do. She can see my eyes, that's it."

"Joie come on..." I plead. She sighs like I'm a nuisance.

"You moved into the house next door to her, but you don't want her to see you? That makes no sense."

"Not yet," I hiss, grabbing at her shirt, trying to pull her down to the floor. She ignores me and keeps spying on my new neighbor.

"Ooh, you never told me what a looker Elena is. She's pretty."

"Would you fucking hit the deck?"

"Where are the kids?" she asks, still ignoring my hysteria. "I wanna see what my future nieces look like."

"You're killing me, Joie," I groan. "I need some time to figure out a game plan."

The blinds snap shut and Joie puts her hands on her hips, looking at me like I'm even more nuts than she already thought. "You mean you plan to keep this a secret? For how long?"

"I don't know."

"Greg, you moved back here for her."

"No, I moved back for Peyton."

She waves her hand, cutting me off. "And then you bought the house next door to Elena so you could be close to her. You keep saying things are finally falling together, but you're gonna wuss out when it's finally go-time? That's not the brother I know." She turns back to the window and looks back out.

She's right. I can't hide from Elena. But I don't know anything about her life anymore. It's been six months since I've talked to her. She could be dating, or engaged. Hell, she could be married. I don't know.

"Oh she's looking this way. I should wave. Hi, Elena!" Sure enough, my asshole sibling begins waving which causes me to panic. I grab the hem of her shirt one last time and yank as hard as I can. She doesn't see it coming so she immediately falls off balance and lands on top of me with a thud.

"Ahh!" she yells. "What is the matter with you?"

"Can you give me a minute to get my bearings straight before you start forcing the issue?" Quickly, I reach up and grab the drawstrings, closing the blinds. "I don't want to assume she's going to run back into my arms and make a fool out of myself if she's already moved on."

Joie looks at me as she resituates her now disheveled ponytail, understanding dawning on her face. "You're really nervous, aren't you?"

I purse my lips. I hate admitting weakness to my older sister. But I still need her help getting this place set up, so I don't have much of a choice. "Yes."

"I've never seen you nervous around a woman before. Not even Libby."

"I know."

"You really do love her."

I nod.

She breaks out into laugher and starts singing. "Greg and Elena sitting in a tree…"

"Ohmygod, would you stop?" She doesn't.

"K-i-s-s-i-n-g!"

"Joie!" I snap my hand over her mouth, cutting her off. "This is not funny. I got Peyton moved, got my old job back, got a house. I still have to think the rest of it through, ok?"

She raises one eyebrow at me. That either means she thinks it's a given that this is going to work out, or it means she's about to punch my lights out. Either way, I remove my hand from her face.

She pushes a strand of dark hair out of her face and clears her throat, sitting criss-cross in front of me. "I'm here for a few more days. And I'll do my best not to race over there and introduce myself, ok?" She interrupts me when I start to respond.

"But, we can't do this every time she opens her front door. Have you ever seen a forty-one-year old woman hit the deck? It's worse than if I tried to drop it like it's hot. And the last time I did *that*, my pants ripped straight down the middle."

A laugh escapes me. "Seriously?"

"Ask Isaac. He was there. It sounded like an explosion in the back of my pants."

I smile and shake my head. "I know I'm being ridiculous. I'm just not sure how to break the news to her. How do you say to someone, 'I know we broke it off completely six months ago because it was too painful, but surprise! I'm your new neighbor now!'?"

"You really don't think she'll be happy to see you? From everything you've said, it sounds like she loves you." Joie taps her fist on my knee gently a couple of times. I put my hand over hers. Even though she's obnoxious, she's still my anchor when things get rough. She's a good sister that way.

"I don't know. Just give me a couple of days to sort it out, ok?" I give her a stern look. "No going over there and making BFFs yet. Promise?"

She huffs, but nods. "Fine. But I will meet her at least once before I go home, no matter what. Back at you promise?"

I roll my eyes. "Fine. Like I could stop you anyway."

She responds with an evil, big-sister grin.

I'm so screwed.

CHAPTER
Three

Elena

"You're gonna go, right?"

I knew that would be Callie's response when I told her about Tripp. She's been supportive of my feelings since Greg left, but it was inevitable that she would pounce the second there was even a possibility that I would get laid again. It's exhausting having someone live vicariously through you.

"I don't know, Callie." I check my hair in the rearview mirror while I wait for the light to turn green. Jordan, my hair dresser slash Callie's husband's sister's niece, added a bunch of lowlights to my highlights the other day. I still can't decide if I like it or if I look like a zebra. "He's nice and all. He's just so *young*."

"Listen." I can practically hear her waving her hand around, getting ready to make a point. "Once you're old enough to drink, age doesn't matter anymore."

I roll my eyes and take my foot off the brake, moving along with the rest of the shmucks trying to make our way away from the office to home for the weekend. "I'm going to respectfully disagree based on the fact that I've been to my fair share of frat parties, and legal drinking at twenty-one is way different than legal drinking at forty-one. Ask the porcelain gods."

"Who said I want you to drink with the guy? I'd just like you to get laid."

See? Pouncing like the horny lioness she is.

"I'm not going to say the thought hasn't crossed my mind," I admit, as I turn into my neighborhood. "He sure did flash me his, um, *ass*ets today when he walked out of the room."

"Mmmm.... Put his hands in his pockets so his pants would pull tight, did he?"

"How did you know that?"

"I love that move. It's like a mating call for millennials."

"And therein lies the big problem. I'm not even close to being a millennial."

She sighs in the overly theatrical way that says she's frustrated I'm not seeing her point. Oh, I see it alright. I just don't know if I want that point in my bed quite yet.

"Look, I know how to make you feel better about this whole thing," she tries again. This ought to be good. "The cougar range."

"The what?"

"The cougar range," she says again. I wait for a few seconds, humoring her and letting her have a weird dramatic build up before I finally bite.

"And what is the cougar range?"

"I'm glad you asked." I shake my head and look to the heavens, also known as the ceiling of my car, silently praying for patience with my exasperating best friend. "Cougar range is a mathematical equation to determine if someone is in the right dating age range for you."

"And what, pray tell, is the equation?"

"Ok first, you need to stop working at a school. You've used the words 'therein' and 'pray tell' in the course of this one conversation and it's freaking me out."

I look up again, this time being silently thankful my new car has Bluetooth technology so I don't get frustrated and throw my phone.

"Oh hey look, I'm home." I'm not. But if she thinks I am, she'll hurry up and get to the point. It's been a long day. I need to stop peopling for a while.

"Fine! I'll hurry. The cougar range is half your age plus seven."

"Wait… so you mean it's socially appropriate to date anyone who is at least twenty-seven?"

"Exactly."

"Tripp is twenty-five," I remind her. "He's still too young."

"Close enough."

"Well, that's up for debate still, but I really am pulling into my driveway." Lies. I'm pulling onto my street. "I need to go relieve my mom from babysitting duty."

"What's the rush? She only has Max. Max is easy."

"She had everyone this afternoon. The girls had early release for teacher in-service day, so they went home at noon."

"Oooh. Now it makes sense why you're openly talking about having sex with some whipper snapper."

I gape at her, even though she can't see it. "I am not! You're the one who brought it up."

"Pfft. Semantics. Anyway…"

Seriously. I'm too tired for this. Especially now that I see a U-Haul in the driveway next to mine. Well, this is unexpected.

"… are we still on for the park tomorrow?"

Even with me going back to work, we still try to do playdates every other week. Instead, we go on the Saturdays I have the girls, and I bring all three with me now. The park is a little more crowded than it used to be on Thursdays, but extra kids means more friends for Fiona and Maura to play with.

"Yeah, I was planning on it." As I pull into my driveway, I look for a car, or something. Anything that will give me an insight into who these new neighbors are. The sweet old man who used to live there died in his sleep about three months ago. We didn't see him often, but Mr. Blitman was always smiling when we did cross paths. He lived alone, but he decorated for every single holiday. Christmas was his favorite. And his house was really popular on Halloween, too. Probably because he gave out the full-sized candy bars.

I've been wondering who bought the house since the "sold" sign went up last week. Whoever it is, they must have paid cash for them to be moving in less than two weeks after it went on the market.

"Do you mind if I invite my friend Deborah?"

"Who? What?" I check out the house through my car window but don't see anyone going in and out. Hmm. I wonder if they're done already. That was pretty fast.

"Deborah. My new RowRow Apparel teammate? You're not even listening to me are you?"

I snap back into the conversation. "Sorry, no. I'm eyeing the house next door. Someone's moving in, and I'm trying to figure out who."

"Mr. Blitman's house?"

"Yeah."

"Wow. That was fast. I hope mandatory distribution of full-sized candy bars was written into their sales contract or there are going to be some very angry children on Halloween."

Climbing out of my car, I stretch my arms and legs. "Leave your eggs at home, lady. I'm not bailing you out of jail for egging his house if they don't give in to your chocolate cravings."

Glancing again at the house, I barely register Callie talking about me being a buzzkill. I'm too busy noticing someone peeking through the blinds. Hmm.

"But, yeah, that's totally cool if Deborah comes. As long as she doesn't think we're too crazy, I'm good."

"Don't even worry about that. She's as crazy as we are."

"Maybe we should warn the people at the park."

She laughs. "Maybe so. Ok, go take care of those sweet girls. I'll see you in the morning."

"Bye." I shut my phone off and grab my purse and bag off the passenger seat before locking all my car doors and heading toward my front door. As I glance at the house next door again, the person peeking out suddenly disappears. That was odd.

Seconds later, the blinds snap closed.

I just shake my head. I can pretty much guarantee Callie won't be getting her beloved candy bar this coming October. Looks like weird neighbors moved in.

Fantastic.

CHAPTER Four

Elena

No one would ever say that I'm very spatially aware. I'm the person that either tries to shove way too much food into a small Tupperware container, or the container only ends up half full and the food rots because of all the extra air. My mother gives me grief about it all the time.

So I should have known better than to try and fit a cooler into the back of my new car. The trunk is a lot smaller than the SUV I had, but did I bother to notice that before trying to shove the Igloo in? Nope. And now it's stuck.

"Come on, Mom!" Fiona yells from her seat as the car bounces up and down every time I tug. "We're going to be late."

I grunt out a response. "I'm… going… as fast… as I can."

She sighs so loudly I can hear her back here, and I'm positive she rolled her eyes. I'm not sure when my sweet girl turned into a bossy pants, but I could have sworn puberty isn't supposed to start at eight years old.

"Oh my goodness, do you need help?" A woman, who I assume is the new neighbor, comes racing across the grass. The first thing I notice is that she has a beautiful smile. Her bright white teeth are accentuated by her light brown skin and her dark hair is held back by a tie-dyed bandana. I haven't even spoken to her yet and she already seems to exude happiness.

This is completely contrary to the weirdness that happened in that house yesterday. Maybe she has a special needs child living with her. Or maybe a drunk uncle. Or a Norman Bates. I shiver thinking about how creepy the house is going to be at Halloween. Those big candy bars may not be worth it this year.

I realize I'm completely bonkers with this line of thought, but hey, you can never be too careful.

"Are you trying to get it in or out?" she asks when she reaches my driveway.

"Out. I misjudged the size of the hatch."

She giggles and I immediately like her. Especially when she says, "I do that all the time." It's nice to know someone understands me since my own mother would laugh at me for this.

I also realize she looks strangely familiar. But before I can inquire as to if we've met before, she grabs hold of the cooler. "Ready?" I nod and grab the other end. "Pull on three. One…two…three…"

We pull and jiggle and pull some more, but in less than a minute, the cooler is back on the driveway, us huffing from the exertion. "Thanks," I puff out.

"Oh it's no problem. I'm Joie, by the way." She reaches her hand out to shake mine.

"Elena. Nice to meet you."

"You, too." She leans over and peeks in the window of the car. "And these are your girls?"

The way she says it gives me that creep factor again. I can't tell for sure, but it almost seems like she already knew I had girls.

"Um… yes," I say slowly.

She looks at me, realization dawning on her face, but then she smiles. "The realtor mentioned you had little girls when I said my niece would be staying over sometimes. I asked when I saw the swing set."

"Oh, of course." I feel like a fool because her explanation makes complete sense. I would be curious about children in the neighborhood if I moved, too. "Do you not have children?"

"I have a son, Isaac, but he's off at college now."

"Wow, you don't look old enough to have a college kid." I wouldn't have pegged her to be older than thirty-five, and even that's pushing it.

She giggles again and her infectious laugh puts me at ease. How does she do that? One minute I'm thinking I live next to a serial killer, the next I want to be invited to her house for tea. *This is how they do it*, I think to myself. *This is how they draw you in and make you trust them.*

I really need to stop watching the Investigation Channel before bed.

"I was really young when I had him," she explains. "But he turned out great. Plays football for Flinton State now."

"That's not too far away." I grab the handle of the cooler and drag it over to the passenger side. Once I move the front seat back, I know it'll fit. Max won't have any leg room, but she's short. She'll be fine.

"Far enough away for him to have a life, but not so far that I never see him. It works." She helps me heave the container into the car and what do you know? There's too much room and I have to move the seat forward again.

There's either too little room in the trunk or too much in the front. Just like with the Tupperware. I should never be in charge of packing a moving van.

"Anyway," she says as I shut the car, "I'm sure you have a busy day. I wanted to introduce myself."

"Yeah, I'm glad you did. Welcome to the neighborhood."

Watching her walk away as I climb into my car, I still can't get a good read on her, but I can't shake the feeling that I know her from somewhere. The entire ride to the playground, in between answering eighty bazillion "why" questions and breaking up a few fights over leg room, I think about where I've seen her before.

By the time we get to the park, I'm no closer to the answer. But I am closer to lunch time and I'm getting hungry. Coffee for breakfast doesn't seem to cut it anymore.

The girls take off running with excited shouts while I heave the cooler out of the front seat and drag it to the picnic table Callie has commandeered. It doesn't surprise me she showed up early. Keeping Christopher contained at home for too long always results in something breaking… a knickknack, a favorite toy, spindles of the staircase when his head gets stuck.

"Hey," she greets me, clicking off her phone and putting it down to help me unload. "What did you bring?"

It was my week to bring lunch for everyone but after working all week, I didn't put in much effort. "Peanut butter and jelly."

She crinkles her nose in disgust. "Ew."

"I made us ham and cheese," I clarify.

The look on her face immediately changes. "Yay!"

"Please. You think I'm going to eat P-B-and-J? I practically have a gag reflex smearing the peanut butter on the bread."

"Then why do you make your kids eat it?" she asks through the bite she just took. "Mmmm," she moans, eyes closed as she enjoys.

"It's a rite of passage," I respond, tossing the rest of the sandwiches on the table along with apple slices and a giant bag of barbeque chips. "My mom tortured me with it when I was a child, so I'm torturing my own kids with it."

She shrugs one shoulder. "Plus it's cheap."

"Exactly."

She swallows and takes a drink before speaking again. "Did you meet the new neighbors yet?"

My turn to crinkle my nose. "Yes."

"What? You say that weird. What's wrong?"

"She seems nice, but…" I trail off, trying to figure out how to explain myself.

Callie looks at me for a few seconds, finally shaking her head slightly with impatience. "But what? She's drunk? She's loud? She's got a glass eye?"

"What does having a glass eye have to do with anything?"

"It doesn't. I just thought you were trying to be politically correct or something."

I roll my own non-glass eyes. "No. No glass eyes. I just can't get a read on her. She knew about the girls, which was really weird. And yesterday I saw her peeking out the window, but as soon as she saw me looking, she disappeared and the blinds snapped shut."

Callie stares at me without blinking before finally speaking. "You've been watching the Investigation Channel again, haven't you?"

"Shut up," I laugh and toss a package of napkins at her, which she easily deflects.

"Give her a chance. She probably saw the girls outside yesterday. Your kids aren't exactly quiet."

"I know. And she did say the realtor had told her about the girls. But I swear I know her from somewhere."

"Maybe. You do work at a school. You see a lot of people."

I shake my head. "Her son is in college."

She shrugs. "I don't know. Maybe she came with a friend to pick up the friend's kid. Maybe she's a stalker. Or maybe you're completely off your rocker."

I stick my tongue out at her. "What's your problem? You're ultra snarky today."

She sighs and leans her arms on the table. "Ben and I are fighting again."

I groan. "What is it this time? Wait…" I hold up my hand so she doesn't speak. "Let me guess." I tap my finger to my chin as if I'm actually serious about my guesses. Because lord knows, Ben argues over the most ridiculous things. "You used vegetable oil instead of olive oil in last night's dinner, so obviously you're trying to give him a heart attack from cholesterol."

"Nope," she says with a shake of her head. "He threw out the vegetable oil last week."

"He did?" I ask, getting sidetracked momentarily.

"Yep."

Shaking it off, I get back to my guessing game. "You only vacuumed under the couch, but not the underside of the couch."

"That was last month's fight."

"Ah. Well then, I'm out of guesses."

She takes a deep breath. They've been married for seven years and I know the constant fighting wears on her sometimes. No matter what she does, it's never good enough for him. "I'm spending too much money on my inventory."

"For RowRow? This doesn't make any sense. You pay for the inventory and then turn right around and sell it for a profit."

"Yep."

"Didn't you make like ten thousand dollars last month alone?"

"Yep."

"So what's the problem."

She snorts. "No idea. Something about me needing to completely sell out before buying more."

"Wait, wait, wait… he wants you to sell out completely? Has he never been to a department store? That's not the way it works."

"I know. But you know Ben. He always has to be right. Even when he's not right."

"Man, that sucks. Sometimes I wish I could give him a piece…."

"Oh, hey there's Deborah!" Callie exclaims, cutting me off.

That was weird. She's never been distracted when we're having a serious conversation before. But I roll with it. It's not often we have other people joining us for playdates. Not since Greg and Peyton started coming with us.

A pang hits my chest when I think about them, but I push it aside and paste a smile on my face. It's been nine months. I'm moving on.

I'll just keep telling myself that.

Callie stands up to greet Deborah with a hug, a towheaded boy standing next to her. He looks about Christopher and Max's age. Maybe a little older.

Speaking of, where are Christopher and Max? I quickly scan the playground, counting heads. Fiona's hanging upside down on the monkey bars, Maura is belting out the lyrics to the latest Disney flic while swinging, and Christopher is sliding down the tallest slide in the park, Max right behind him.

As he gets to the bottom, Christopher can't slow himself down and flies off the slide, landing on his back in the dirt. Max has the same problem and lands right on top of him with an "oof." They immediately begin wrestling.

Eh. They're fine.

Turning my attention back to Callie's new friend, I introduce myself.

"Hi, I'm Elena." I reach out to shake her hand. "I think we met at one of Callie's sizing parties a couple months ago."

"Yes, I remember." She takes my hand to shake it. "It's nice to see you again."

She has one of those weak handshakes where I only get to hold her fingers. Ew. I hate that kind of handshake. But her smile makes up for it, so I let it go quickly.

Literally. I couldn't hold her fingers for one more second. No wonder Callie greeted her with a hug.

"Thanks for inviting us," she says kindly, putting her hands on the little boy's shoulders. "Trevor doesn't have many friends, so it's always fun to bring him on playdates."

"Oh, did you guys just move to the area?" I feel bad for the boy. It's never easy being the new kid.

"Oh, no. I've lived here my entire life." She smiles. "But you know how hard it is to make friends these days."

I look over at the playground to see Fiona playing a hand slapping game with another little girl while Maura, who is apparently done with her practice for Broadway, plays tag with a group of kids. Max and Christopher—yep, still wrestling.

But I shouldn't judge. Some kids have a harder time than others. Maybe getting to know our kids will help him.

"How old are you, Trevor?"

"He's five," Deborah answers for him.

I bend down so I can make eye contact with him. "See that little girl over there in the yellow dress?" He nods. "That's my little girl Maura. She's six. Would you like to play with her and the other kids?" He nods again, making me smile. He must be terribly shy.

After calling Maura over and introducing them, they run off to play leaving the adults behind. Callie and I turn right back to our lunch, but Deborah has a strange look on her face. I can't figure out what it means, but I realize she probably didn't realize we were having lunch.

"Deborah, it was my turn to bring lunch today so I made an extra ham and cheese for you and and p-b-and-j for Trevor if you're interested."

"That's so nice of you, thank you. But Trevor's allergic to peanuts." She smiles sweetly and plunks a giant purse on the table.

"Oh I'm sorry." I begin gathering sandwiches to put them back in the cooler, not knowing how severe his allergy is. "Do the kids need to wait to eat? They can survive on apples and chips for a while."

"Oh no, it's fine!" Deborah begins pulling out coordinating Tupperware containers that snap together and have compartments and fancy lids. And all of them have the exact right amount of food in them. "His allergy isn't airborne. Just ingested. Well, I mean, he only had an allergic reaction once and it totally could have been teething, not peanut butter. But who wants to take the chance, right?"

Ooookkkkkkk, I think to myself. I'm gonna pretend that wasn't weird.

"I wish I had brought enough food to share with the other kids," she continues.

She pops the top of the largest container open revealing celery sticks, hummus, and is that kale? No way my kids will want any of that.

"I think we'll be good," I say, Callie quirking her lips as she tries not to giggle. No way Christopher will touch that stuff either.

We continue setting out drinks… our regular juice boxes to Deborah's homemade, organic grape juice… and chit chat as we get to know each other. She has one child. Been married for six years to some guy who is a big wig in an oil company downtown. Was a kindergarten teacher for a couple of years before having Trevor and becoming a stay at home mom. Deborah's a little quirky, but she seems nice enough.

When we're finally set up and Max has complained one too many times about being hungry, we call them over for lunch.

Fiona and Maura trot over. Christopher and Trevor… that's a different story. They're on opposite sides of the swings and as they come around, racing to the table, they run right smack into each other… knocking heads and falling to the ground.

"It's ok!" Callie yells automatically. "Rub some dirt on it! You'll be fine!"

Before her words are all the way out of her mouth, Deborah is running full-speed, scooping Trevor up in her arms as he's rubbing his head, screaming like he's got a nail shoved through his foot.

I glance at the shoes he's wearing. Nope. No nails. Just a bump on his head.

We watch as Deborah kisses all over Trevor's face, rocking him and cooing at him, like he's on his death bed.

I look over at Callie who has the same look I'm probably sporting. One that says, "I'm trying really hard not to be judgy right now, but I can practically hear the helicopter blades from her parenting style."

"Are you thinking the same thing I am?" Callie finally says.

"I'm trying not to. Especially since our parenting style looks like that." I point at Christopher who is still sitting where he fell, only now Max has joined him and is doing exactly what Callie said… picking up dirt off the ground and rubbing it on his forehead. "You really think we have room to judge someone?"

"You're such a better person than me."

"Yep," I agree.

"And she's such a better mom than us."

"Yep," I agree again. But really, the jury's still out for me.

THE GETTING A GRIP DUET

You can never trust someone who gets the Tupperware portion sizes right every time.

CHAPTER Five

Elena

"Run, baby. We're late."

Fiona and I race in the door to the gym; her sprinting through the gate and joining her class for the tail end of the warm up, me heading for my regular bench. Recently, we've been a little behind schedule. Mostly it's because working has put a kink in my ability to get anywhere on time. Funny how taking ten hours out of your day leaves very little time for anything else. Go figure.

But it's also because of my mother's newest obsession... Real Housewives. She ran out of Kardashian episodes a few weeks ago, so she moved on to New Jersey and it's been nonstop ever since. As soon as she showed up to babysit the other two kids, she began babbling on about how much she loves Teresa's spunk, even if she is a horrible person.

I wish I had a picture of her face when I told her Teresa went to prison. She had no idea. For a woman completely obsessed with reality TV, my mother stays remarkably far away from the tabloids. She says it's because you can't believe a thing you read in them.

Yet she considers reality shows actual reality. There are no words for that woman sometimes.

I will admit, bringing Fiona to her class was hard when Greg first moved away. Being in the building brought up so many memories. Plus, any time one of the kids would mention him, my heart would sink. And when the new director introduced himself to me for the first time, I thought I was going to burst into tears.

It felt like everything was still exactly the same and everyone was going on with their lives like Greg had never even been there. But to me, the most important part was just... missing. It left what felt like a gaping hole in my chest.

Over time, that gaping hole became smaller and smaller until it became a tiny pinprick that pokes me every once in a while. Ok, it's a big pinprick. But I don't feel like I could cry everyday anymore.

Strangely, moving Fiona to a different class on different days helped me with the hurt. Fi worked really hard and moved up to the more advanced level, so she has Coach Pete now. He's a nice guy, always has a smile on his face. And I never saw him with Greg, so that's been nice for me. I know it's selfish, but not having any memories of the two of them interacting gives me a little bit of peace.

Which is good because I don't have time to feel depressed while we're here. It's two hours every week where I have uninterrupted time to catch up on emails, calls, and texts. I need to take advantage of it.

Settling myself on the bench, I grab my phone and open it, beginning the tedious task of going through everything I may have missed throughout the day. But of course the first text I see is from my mother and it came in seven minutes ago.

Mom: *Are you sure Teresa went to prison? She's a terrible person, but she's not a criminal.*

I shake my head in amusement. I am never going to hear the end of this until she gets to that episode.

Me: *Yes, Mom. It was all over the news. Google it if you don't believe me.*

Mom: *That'll ruin the surprise of that episode.*

Me: *Didn't I already ruin the surprise by telling you?*

Mom: *Yes, but you didn't tell me what all happened. That's still a secret.*

Me: *It's not a secret. I don't even watch the show and I know she was only in the slammer for six months or something.*

Mom: *ELENA JOANN MONROE!*

Oh shit. I just got shouty capitaled.

Mom: *You stop ruining things for me or I'm dumping out all your wine bottles and filling them with water.*

Me: *Thank you, Jesus.*

Mom: *Jesus turned water into wine, not wine into water. Where did I go wrong with you?*

Me: *You stopped making me go to church when I was sixteen and I lost my moral compass?*

Mom: *I have regrets now. Don't rush home. I'm baking chicken for dinner. And don't say a word about it. I felt like cooking today. Also, Maura swears you said it was ok for her to wear your lipstick. Yes or no?*

Me: *No! And thanks for dinner, Mom. I'll text you on our way out.*

Maura and her obsession with all things girly are going to kill me, I just know it.

I close my eyes and sigh, re-centering myself and taking a breather. My body relaxes so much now that the obnoxious chore of cooking has been taken off my plate, I barely hear the *snick* of the office door closing next to me.

This is my first time being a single, working mom. And it. Is. Tough. Granted, I don't do as much cleaning anymore because no one is home to mess up the house. But staying home meant having momentum. I got things done because I was already up and moving and accomplishing other goals.

Somehow, leaving a job and driving home kills that momentum. So any time my mom decides to cook dinner for us, I won't argue. I just thank her profusely and am grateful it's one less thing I have to do.

Opening my eyes, I search the room for Fiona and find her practicing her back handsprings with Coach Pete. Not bad. She's still jumping up instead of back a little too much. Recognizing the technique problem is the curse of being a former gymnast.

Regardless, it's so impressive watching how far she's come. Seeing her smile every time we're here makes me smile, too. She loves being at the gym. I'm pretty sure Coach Pete plans to bump her up to team and start her on several hours a week by winter.

And so the life of an athlete, and the athlete's chauffer (a.k.a. Mother) begins.

I watch as Fiona gets herself back into position—standing straight, arms high above her head—but just as she squats down to put some power into her jump, she gets distracted, her eyes widen, and she squeals as she takes off running.

"COACH GREG!" she's yelling as she runs across the floor and flings her arms around a man's waist.

Greg? *My* Greg? What is she talking about?

As the kids begin to crowd around him, the man slowly turns my direction. When our eyes lock, I suck in a breath.

Ohmygod. It's Greg. He's missing his beard, which is really weird since I've never seen him without facial hair, but it's definitely him. His baby blues are a dead giveaway. And right now, they are staring right into me.

What is he doing here? Is he visiting? Why didn't he call me?

All these thoughts run through my brain as I strain to listen to what's he saying to the kids, but they're too far away. Instead, I have to focus on another coach answering one of the parent's questions.

"Today is his first day back," the coach says, completely oblivious to how hard my heart is pounding, even though I'm sure it can be heard if you get close enough. "The San Antonio gym is up and running now, so we snatched him right back from them."

He's back? And he didn't tell me? He let me find out when it became gym gossip?

Different emotions course through me. I'm sad he didn't think to contact me. I'm shocked he's back. I'm excited to see him. But more than anything, I think, I *think* I'm pissed. Pissed that he wasn't more sensitive to the fact that I'd be here. Pissed that he sprung this on Fiona, who knows him better than the average gym rat. Pissed that he didn't give us a head's up so we could be mentally prepared for his arrival. Not a phone call. Even a text message would be nice. Hell, he could have texted Callie so *she* could've given me a warning.

Maybe he didn't think about it because he's moved on. Maybe he's dating someone else and I never cross his mind. Why would he think to tell me he'd be here if he's got a girlfriend he's with all the time? That would make sense. He's a wonderful guy. I'm sure the women in San Antonio were as enthralled with him as the women here.

Still, I wish I had known. More than anything, I needed time to prepare my heart. Instead, I'm sitting on this damn wooden bench, shell-shocked.

For the remaining time in the hour-long class, I force myself to watch Fiona. I won't look at Greg, even though I can feel him gazing at me. That first glance, the one that felt like he was seeing right into me, I couldn't get a read on his emotions. He almost stared at me blankly. I don't know what that means, but I don't want to find out. The possibilities are too scary.

So I focus on my daughter and the happiness she exudes as she perfects her skills. I smile when she smiles. I clap when she looks at me. I flash her a thumbs up when she flashes it at me first. Basically, I pretend I have any idea what's going on around me, when really all I'm doing is avoiding seeing the love of my life make his entrance back into our lives, without so much as a Facebook message.

The hour can't end soon enough, and by the time Fiona has her cover up and shoes on, I'm ready to bolt. A warm, strong hand stops me, though, as we push through the crowd to get out the door.

"Elena," he says, and I squeeze my eyes tight to center my thoughts. Just the sound of his voice makes my whole body tingle, never mind the warmth of his hand on my arm. Glancing up to make sure Fiona is still by the water fountain, I finally turn around.

"Hi Greg." I stare at him, this beautiful man I love, this man I've grieved over. I try desperately to hold my emotions in check because I *refuse* to cry in front of him or anyone else. "How are you?"

"I'm back," he says with a hopeful smile.

I nod. "I see that."

He clears his throat and tries to put his hands in his pockets, but there are none in his athletic shorts, so he drops his hands to his sides. "Listen, um, can we talk?"

I think about it for a second. I want to, I really do, but if I stop to talk now, I'll break down into a blubbering mess of tears and now is not the time or the place. Plus, I'm still pissed and I need a minute to sort out my feelings. So I respond the only way I can.

"No," I say, and turn around, grabbing Fiona by the hand as we walk out of the gym and away from the love of my life.

CHAPTER Six

Greg

I screwed up.

Badly.

I knew I needed to call her to tell her I was back, but I wanted to woo her with no thoughts about the past, only looking forward to our future. I thought I had more time to come up with a good, solid plan on how to do that.

But I didn't. I waited until the last minute, and it bit me in the ass. So now, instead of being in her arms, catching up and making plans, I'm standing in my small foyer, staring at my front door, and trying to pull together enough balls to walk over to her house and beg for forgiveness.

But will she forgive me or kick my *cojones* when I finally pull it together? I don't know. The look on her face when she told me she didn't want to talk was pretty telling in itself. She was pissed.

Underneath that anger, though, she was hurt. I could see it plain as day. If she hadn't left immediately, she would have lost it. Hell, I was having a hard enough time holding myself together and I knew what was coming.

Remembering that look of pain is what cements my decision. I grab the knob and turn, exiting my house before I change my mind. As I tromp through the grass, determination running through me, I make a mental note to throw some insect killer on the giant ant hill in between our yards. Wouldn't want any of the girls stepping in that.

A couple of knocks on the door and I stand there, rubbing my sweaty palms on my pants, while I wait for her to answer. I think I have the timing right. The girls should be in bed right now. Unless their bedtimes changed, too. Now that I think about it, I don't know anything about their nighttime routine anymore.

Feeling dejected and a little more than frustrated over my consistent fails, I begin to turn around and make the quick walk home. The click of an unlocking deadbolt stops me.

"Greg?" Elena says, swinging the door wide open. Her hair is pulled up in one of those messy buns and she's wearing her favorite yoga pants—the one with the tiny hole in the butt and the bleach stain down the thigh. She's so beautiful. "What are you doing here?"

I clear my throat, which seems to be a habit lately, and clench my hands, silently praying she'll give me the time of day. "I was hoping this would be a better time to talk. Now that this isn't all being sprung on you."

She blinks once and stares at me, like she's trying to decide. "You caught that, did you?"

"Yeah, I knew you needed some time to get your thoughts in order." I give her a small smile. "I'm really sorry, Elena. I thought I had another day to figure out how to tell you I was back."

She looks at me quizzically, but doesn't move out of the doorway to let me in. That's fine. We can do this on the front porch.

"What do you mean you had another day? You didn't even plan on telling me until tomorrow?"

"No. I mean…" I sigh, trying to piece the words together. "I was trying to find the right way to tell you, and I thought Fiona was still taking a Thursday class."

"The right way to tell me would have been to call. Or text. Email. Hell, send a carrier pigeon." The anger is returning and I can't say I blame her. I could have done any one of those things. Except the pigeon. "Instead, I found out in a room full of children when they all started shrieking about Coach Greg being back and hugging this man I don't even recognize because his beard is gone."

I furrow my brows. "What does my beard have to do with anything?"

"Nothing. I'm mad and your face looks weird now, so I'm going to be mad about that, too."

With that statement, I feel like we've overcome a major roadblock. Admitting to being angry and slightly irrational means she's still processing her emotions. It's one of the things I love about her and I can't help but smile, now that I get to see it as it happens. "I'll grow it back."

"Thank you," she huffs and crosses her arms. "But really. Why didn't you at least warn me?"

The dejected look on her face tugs at my heart. I put that look there. I made her feel like an afterthought with my inadvertent lack of respect and my general ability to act like a pussy when I get scared. I only hope I can get that look off her face and make her feel like the amazing, cherished woman I know she is.

Taking a deep breath, I start from the beginning. "Remember when I said I would pray every day for the circumstances to change so that we could be together?"

She nods once but doesn't uncross her arms, so I continue.

"I did. Every day. You were the first thing I prayed for in the morning and the last thing I prayed for at night. You and the girls."

She looks down and bites her lip. I know I have her attention, even though it's hard for her to hear.

"I found out last week, Libby decided to move home with her mom. She and Navi broke up for some reason. I don't know. I didn't ask. I didn't really care. First thing I did after Libby told me was call Dave and talk to him about coming back. He needed me here more than he needed me in San Antonio. So I started packing immediately, broke my lease on my apartment, and bought a house. Fortunately, Joie had some time off before her classes start so she could come help me. I couldn't have done it all without her."

Elena's eyes snap up to mine. "Joie?"

"My sister?"

Elena glances to my house and back to me. "You moved into Mr. Blitman's house next door?"

I shrug sheepishly. "It was a really good price and the best location I could have asked for."

I can't tell if knowing I'm her new neighbor makes her angry or not, but her arms aren't crossed anymore and she's looking at me incredulously.

Ok, so still angry it is.

"I *knew* I knew her from somewhere," she finally says. "Joie was a little too interested in the girls."

A single laugh barks out of me. "Yeah, Joie is kind of a busybody. She couldn't wait to meet you."

"Why?"

"She wanted to see who her brother is in love with."

And there it is. I just laid it all on the line. She's either going to take it or leave it, but at least she knows now.

She looks stunned by my admission. I'm actually kind of stunned myself.

"I thought she was a stalker," she responds quietly.

I guess we're going to leave my admission alone for now. That's fine. At least we're talking.

"Watching Investigation Channel before bed again?"

She quirks an eyebrow at me.

"Sorry," I mumble. I guess she's not quite ready to joke around with me yet.

Instead, we stand there staring at each other. I can practically hear the wheels turning in her brain as she tries to decide how she feels about all this. I wait patiently. I don't want to put too much pressure on her or push her too fast.

Finally, she sighs. "What do you want me to say, Greg?"

"I want you to come to my place for dinner," I admit.

She shakes her head. "I don't know if I can do that. Things have changed, you know?"

My eyes widen. "You're dating someone." I was afraid of that. Shit. I've been a fool to think she would still be single. She's too much of a catch.

"No."

I close my eyes in relief that I may still have a shot, and then open them back up to look at her beautiful face. "So then what's changed, Elena?" I plead. "I want to be with you."

She looks a little bit like she feels the same way, but she's too stubborn to admit it yet. It's another one of those things I love about her. "Well, for starters, I have a job now."

"Ok, I can work with that. What else?"

"I... um... I don't know. It's just different." If her sole reason for not dating me again is because of a new job, I might not be in as much hot water as I thought. "Greg, the circumstances you prayed for didn't change. You dropped everything when Libby moved. Again. The motivation is different. I'm glad you're back, and it'll be nice having Peyton next door to play, but Libby isn't exactly stable. How can I trust that you won't follow her the next time she meets someone online and wants to move across the country?"

And there it is. The heart of her hurt, confusion, and the reason she doesn't want to get close. She doesn't trust that I won't break her heart again.

I could stand here and argue with her. Try to convince her that she's wrong. But it would be a waste of my breath and would only piss her off more. Instead, I silently agree to acquiesce. For now.

"I understand," I say with a nod and tuck my hands in my pockets. "The offer for dinner is still on the table. Just so we can talk and enjoy each other's company again."

She doesn't respond. Just looks at me like she's not quite sure what to say.

I begin backing away from her porch, into the grass. "If you need me, you know where to find me." I gesture over my shoulder to my house. "Oh, and there's an ant pile at the property line, so keep the girls off the grass for a couple days until I can fix it."

She nods once and I turn to go.

"Greg?" Her voice stops me and I look over my shoulder at her. "I'm glad you're back."

Four words. Four simple words are all she says before closing the door on me. But those words give me hope that I have a chance.

A smile stretches across my face as I make the short walk home, barely missing the ants I warned her about just a few seconds ago. My thoughts are too excited about the possibility of winning her back to even care.

CHAPTER
Seven

Elena

Deborah's house reflects the personality she displayed on our playdate last weekend. It's bright and cheery. All the furniture is inviting. There are toys stacked in brightly colored bins.

And the entire place smells like lemon cleaner and Lysol. Seriously. There is not a speck of dirt in the place, and I'm afraid to drink anything for fear I put the glass down without a coaster and mess up something.

It's a very conflicting vibe. Like she wants people to feel welcome in her home, but not so welcome that they mess it up.

Considering how much inventory Callie and I lugged in tonight, it's too late to worry about clutter. She's just going to have to deal. Judging by the tight smile on her face, she's barely holding it together. Especially since we've been here for a couple of hours and clothes are pretty much strewn everywhere.

Most of Callie's RowRow Apparel parties have had a really good turn-out. The company as a whole is the hottest thing out there, and when you add Callie's personality and fashion knowledge, people get excited.

Tonight, has been no different. Right now, there are no less than a dozen women looking through racks of clothing, commenting on patterns and material. It's a really relaxed atmosphere, affording us lots of time to interact with people on a more personal level. I admit, I was leery about it when Callie started this venture last year, but she really has made it work. I'm proud of her for it.

"So," she begins, plopping down next to me on the couch for the first time all night. I've been lucky that she's been distracted all night since I know what she wants to talk about. I'm not ready, though.

So I do my best to deflect. "I think that one woman, with the dark hair, I can't remember her name…"

"Kathy."

"Yes!" I say, snapping my fingers as the name rings a bell. "She's trying on a couple of dresses, but I want you to look at the style. I think she might look better in the longer version."

"Ok. But hey, yeah, I don't care. Let's talk about Greg."

Dropping my head back on the couch, I know I'm not getting out of this one. "I don't want to."

"Why not?" She nudges my leg with hers. "You've been missing him for nine long months, and now he's back. And he lives next door. Why haven't you jumped his bones yet?"

Deborah happens by right as Callie says that and her eyes widen slightly, but she never loses that tight smile. I'm starting to get a really weird vibe from Callie's new friend.

"Because I'm not going to run right back to him the second he knocks on my door."

"Oooh!" An evil grin crosses her face. "You're playing hard to get. This I can get on board with."

I'm not having this conversation now, I think to myself.

"I'm not having this conversation now." I jump up from the couch and pretend to sort through the discarded clothing, putting them on hangers. "And I'm not playing hard to get, so please let it go."

Thankfully, Kathy walks around the corner and asks for help deciding if the dress she's wearing is the right size. Callie immediately goes into Project Runway mode, which gives me a breather from her incessant badgering. She's done a decent job of letting me stew for a few days as I get my bearings straight. But now that there is wine and clothing, she's letting her guard down, which means I have to talk to her about it, whether I want to or not.

"Elena?" I turn from the rack and see another one of the party goers standing in front of me. Once again, her name escapes me, so I refer to her as "snack girl" because she has refilled her plate no less than six times since we've been.

Seriously. I can barely remember my own kids' names. It's unreasonable to think I can remember the people at these parties, too.

"What kind of skirt are you wearing? I've been eyeing it all night and I think I need to try one on."

"You definitely do," I exclaim, switching into salesperson mode.

Callie was right about that, too. People ask me about the outfits she puts me in all the time, and then they buy them. Usually, though, I'm not the one to help them decide what size works for their body. Tonight, I make an exception, just to keep my bestie off my back. "They're right over here. What size do you normally wear?"

As I work with "snack girl", I notice Callie glaring at me out of the corner of my eye. She knows this is my least favorite part of these parties and the only reason I'm being overly helpful is to avoid Greg talk.

Unfortunately for me, I'm better at this stuff than I thought. Before I know it, Snack Girl is loaded down with different options to try and is headed for the bedroom, also known as tonight's dressing room.

Callie takes advantage of the vacant spot by my side and immediately sidles up next to me. "You can't avoid me."

"I can try," I shoot back, hanging up more discarded clothes.

"Elena, stop." She puts her hand on my forearm, so I do as she says. I'm not getting out of this. With a look of concern, she lays it all on the line. "Did you at least agree to be friends with benefits?"

"Ohmygod," I groan, which really, is the only appropriate answer to this line of questioning. I should have known better than to think Callie would have any sympathy to my concerns. She's way too excited that Greg is back, which I should have anticipated, and thinks she's going to live vicariously through me again.

She follows me around the rack, doing exactly what I knew she was going to do… pester me. "Maybe you two should start dating again. You love him, you know you do. Are you afraid you can't separate your emotions? Come on. You can be fuck buddies for a while first."

We hear a gasp and look over. Once again, Deborah chooses this opportune moment to walk by. We stare at her and she stares at us. We're all staring until I finally break the silence.

"The short dress with leggings combo looks really good on you, Deborah."

She blinks once and turns away from us, shaking her head as she walks into the kitchen, probably to gather more organic pâté. Pâté by itself is pretty gross. Rest assured, the organic kind is a zillion times worse.

"Maybe we shouldn't talk about this right now," I suggest, partially for poor Deborah's benefit, but mostly for my own.

"You're right." She claps her hands together, which is never a good sign for me. "Let's talk about Tripp."

I groan. "Let's not."

"Oh come on, Elena. He's hot and he's young." She sighs dreamily like what I need in my life is another kid. "This is your one shot at being a cougar! Take it!"

"Oooh," another random shopper, this one I refer to as "the drunk" stumbles up to us, yet doesn't spill a drop of her wine. Impressive. "Who is a cougar?"

Callie doesn't miss a beat. "Elena is hopefully."

The Drunk's eyes widen and mouth opens in delight. "You haven't gone for it yet? Younger men are *the best*. They have this," she sucks in a horny-sounding breath, "stamina that men our age don't seem to have any more."

Callie quirks an eye at me. "Did you hear that Elena? I bet Tripp has stamina."

"His name is Tripp?" The Drunk slurs. "That even sounds sexy. Tell me he's sexy."

"Oh he is," Callie answers for me, even though she's never seen him. "He likes to put his hands in his pockets when he walks away from her."

The Drunk gasps. "I love it when they pull their pants tight across their ass. It's my favorite move."

Callie looks at me and gestures to The Drunk like she just proved her point. I roll my eyes and continue with my sorting. "I'm not going to go out with a twenty-five-year old because he has a nice rear."

"You're going out with a twenty-five-year old?" Snack Girl says, popping out from nowhere to enter this very humiliating conversation.

"No!" I shout at the same time Callie yells, "Hopefully!"

The Drunk is fingering all the clothing while mumbling, "Hate to see him go, but love to watch him leave."

"I'm twenty-five and I date older men," Snack Girl shrugs. "What's the difference?"

"Stamina," The Drunk answers. Someone really needs to take the booze away from her. And maybe hide all their teenage boys.

"I'm just saying, those gender and age roles are so antiquated," Snack Girl continues. "If you have common interests and are attracted to each other, why not?"

Callie tilts her head, eyeing me as if to say *Yeah. Why not?*

I sigh in defeat. "Ok fine. You win. If he asks me out again, I will say yes." Cheers erupt around the room and I'm finally aware that this conversation has been more public than I first realized. Holding my finger up in the air, I make it a point to add, "But there will be no finding out about his stamina!"

The women all laugh and side conversations about former dating escapades pop up all around us. As much as I didn't want to discuss my own dating life, at least it made everyone around us relax and is giving them something fun to talk about amongst each other. Even The Drunk and Snack Girl are trading stories.

The only one who doesn't seem amused is Deborah. Her teeth are clenched together, and I'm afraid she's going to shatter that tray of celery and almond butter if she squeezes it any tighter. Seconds later, she stomps over to Callie and me, fire in her eyes. But it's venom that comes out of her mouth.

"I love how easygoing you guys are when we're hanging out, but can we *please* stay professional during this party? I am getting ready to launch a RowRow business. I don't want to be known as the woman who has raunchy parties!" And she turns and stomps away.

I look over at Callie who has a stunned look on her face. She finally looks over at me, still seeming very unsure about how to respond. "I think… I think I would normally tell someone to buzz off after that. But I know she has been nervous about this party all week, so if being more professional will help her feel less anxious, we should do that."

I shrug and reply with, "She's your friend. You do what you think is right."

Thankfully, another customer, who I call "Shorty" due to her lack of height, interrupts us to ask a question about getting her items hemmed. The distraction throws Callie right back into sales mode, but doesn't do quite the same with me.

I'm just as much of a hot mess as the next gal, but yelling at me for acting the exact same way I always do irks me. What you see is what you get with me. If that's not enough, there's nothing I can do about it, and I'm not going to try.

But Callie is my best friend and if defaulting to professional me for the rest of the night makes her feel better about the situation, I'll do it.

Deborah, however, doesn't get as much grace from me. I still have my eye on that one.

CHAPTER *Eight*

Elena

If you had told me a year ago that spin would end up being my favorite class, I would've said you're insane. My gosh, the class is *hard*. It is non-stop cardio for an hour, and my instructor somehow makes it a muscle work out as well. Some days I leave with my shoulders aching. It takes some serious teaching talent for your students to have aching shoulders from riding a stationary bike.

Despite the pain I feel during the class, the strength I feel after it's over is addicting. I haven't actually lost any weight. That would require me to change my eating habits and let's face it… I like my food a little too much to care. For now, feeling empowered and strong is enough.

I wave at Bianca as I walk into the dark room and head to my favorite bike. Bike #12 is my normal stop. It's on the second row, off to the side, next to the tiny window so there's the perfect amount of light. Plus, the fan blows directly on me. After half an hour of exercise, this is an important thing.

Standing next to my favorite method of torture, I adjust all the knobs. Raise the seat until it's hip height. Move the handle bars forward because my arms are short. Situate my water bottle on the right side for easy reach during our rest periods. Step up on my peddles and…

"Good morning, Elena."

I stare in disbelief as Greg adjusts the bike next to mine. *What is he doing here?*

"What are you doing here?"

He smirks at me and continues with his set up. "Taking a spin class. What are you doing here?"

So he's got jokes this morning. "I know you're taking a spin class, funny guy. Why are you taking the same class I'm taking? It's a Saturday morning. Don't you have a meet or something to be at?"

"I came back mid-season, so we're keeping things like they are until next year." Like always, his movements are fluid and graceful as he mounts the bike and begins peddling. I look more like a baby panda bear rolling around as I climb up.

Finally situating myself on my seat, I say, "But that doesn't explain how you ended up in my class. Did you know I'd be here…" I trail off as it hits me.

Callie.

"You asked Callie when my class was, didn't you?"

His conspiratorial smile is the only answer I need. What a traitor. She and I will be having words the next time I talk to her.

Suddenly, the music begins pumping through the speakers and any further conversation is put on the back burner.

"Good morning, everyone," Bianca yells in her chipper, slightly accented voice. "I'm glad to see you guys here on a Saturday morning. Are we ready to get started? Get those legs moving."

For some reason, this class helps my brain clear out. I don't know if it's working off all the stress, or what, but I always feel better emotionally after it's over. That's one of the reasons I do it three times a week. We're only in the warm up, but I can already tell I'm gonna need more than one class to push through the irritation I feel.

Ok, that's not exactly true. I know I *should* be irritated. Greg broke my heart when he left. I don't fault him for it. He had to do what was right by his daughter. But finding out he came back the way I did makes me assume I'm an afterthought. I don't like feeling that way. I want to be a forethought.

Maybe I'm not irritated as much as I'm hurt. I thought the connection we had ran deeper than that. Now I'm questioning all the memories I have from before. Everything feels slightly tainted. But is that a valid feeling or me being irrational? I honestly don't know.

While we stand up and sit down and go faster and slower, I take the time to sort through all my thoughts. I love Greg. I never stopped loving Greg. But I'm afraid. For as much progress as I've made this last year with my feelings of insecurity and self-doubt, I still struggle with my fear of getting hurt again. Is that holding me back from experiencing something wonderful? And is wonderful even worth it if I end up hurting again?

"Let's add more resistance," Bianca shouts and I grab the knob, cranking it to the right, as The Weeknd begins serenading me with lyrics about how much I'm worth it. *Yeah, I am*, I think to myself as I get into my groove.

"Earned It," the remix version, has become one of my favorite songs in spin. We go slower, but add lots of resistance, working out our quads and glutes until they burn. I probably won't be able to sit down later because of the amount of effort I'm putting in today, but I refuse to stop. I have too much stress to work out.

Shooting a glance at Greg causes me surprise. The man is dripping sweat and his newly grown stubble is glistening where droplets have gotten stuck. He's breathing heavy and it's obvious, he never took a spin class in San Antonio because he can't seem to keep up. This revelation makes me smile.

Turning back to Bianca, I follow along for the remainder of the hour, sorting through my emotions, working out my stress, and feeling more and more like myself with every passing minute.

"Holy shit," Greg breathes, as we wipe down our bikes at the end of class. "I forgot how intense this class is."

It's my turn to smirk at him. "Looks like you didn't keep up with your workouts while you were away."

He laughs. "I did, just not my cardio, apparently." He tosses his disinfecting wipes into the trash and turns back to me. "Have you thought any more about my dinner offer?"

Avoiding answering, I walk out of the room, him hot on my heels. I wasn't expecting him to just let me walk away. I knew he'd follow. But I'm still unsure what to do and I'm waiting for some clarity.

"It doesn't have to be dinner, ya know," he continues, increasing his pace to catch up and walk next to me. "We could do coffee or just stand in our yards and talk. I'll bring the Dos Equis."

I snort a laugh. "I'm sure the neighbors would love to see us standing around in the front yard drinking beer. Should we bring lawn chairs, too, and make it even classier?"

"We'll pretend it's a meet-your-new-neighbor thing. Who knows, maybe I'll finally meet the guy who lives across the street. The one with the ratty car parked on the street?"

"You know he leaves that car there on purpose so no one parks in front of his house, right?"

Greg looks at me incredulously. "Really? He hates his neighbors that much?"

"He hates people in general," I explain. "I've lived there for how many years, and I've met him once. And only because he was upset that my trash can didn't get put away fast enough after garbage pick-up."

"See? It'll be good for us to hang out. It'll show solidarity against the neighborhood bully."

We stop in front of the treadmills so I can face him. "You're really determined, aren't you?" I ask, a flirty smile on my face. I don't know why I'm suddenly feeling self-assured. I guess having a hot guy tailing you through the gym begging for a date is a confidence booster.

"I really, really am," he replies, flashing me that dazzling smile.

"Greg! You're back!" We both whirl around when we hear her voice.

"Hi, Heather," he says, and immediately shifts his attention back to me.

Heather. I've seen the leggy blond burning up the treadmill almost every time I've been here for the last year. For the most part, I've ignored her. There's been no reason to feel any ill will. But hearing her flirty voice directed at Greg while he's in the middle of a conversation with me grates on my nerves.

"We've missed you around here," she tries again.

He, however, doesn't even glance her direction, keeping his eyes trained on me, when he says, "I've missed being here."

That moment, combined with what can only be described as jealousy, works in his favor.

"The girls are with James this weekend, so I'm free tonight." I turn and saunter toward the locker room. "Don't forget the wine," I call over my shoulder.

With that, I put a little extra sway in my hips, knowing he's loving watching me leave.

CHAPTER Nine

Greg

When Elena finally accepted my invitation to dinner tonight, I wanted to jump for joy right there. But I figured I needed to keep at least a little of my dignity intact, being that I had followed her around the gym like a puppy dog. Not that I really minded. There are worse views.

That little extra swing in her hips as she walked away didn't go unnoticed by me, but I know she's still reluctant. I'm not sure if she's more hurt about how I handled coming back, or afraid I'll leave again. Either way, I'm hoping tonight will help reassure her that I strongly believe my prayers were answered. I don't care if Libby is ultimately the one who made the decision that changed everything; it's what I had wanted all along.

Next time my ex pulls that shit, and I'm not dumb enough to think there won't be a next time, I will be stronger and will fight more. I promised myself that months ago. Now I have to convince Elena that I won't break my promise.

Puttering around the kitchen, I do a last-minute check of my food prep. The pasta doesn't need to be put on until the chicken is almost done cooking. I've already flattened the chicken breasts to one-quarter inch thick. Fresh green beans are soaking in cold water. And the wine is already chilled. There's nothing left to do except season the meat and pop them in the oven.

A knock at the door stops my preparations and makes my heart speed up. Racing to the door, I have to stop myself from answering too quickly. Yes, I'm desperate. No, I don't want to seem that way. She likes calm, cool, collected Greg. I can introduce her to neurotic, overly-excited Greg later.

A quick sniff of my pits and my breath, and I'm good to go. Until I pull the door open.

That's when I see her and I swear I stop breathing.

Her dark blond hair is sleek and shiny. Her plump lips painted a dark pink color that I want to kiss off. Those twinkling hazel eyes smile at me, even though they look like they're still unsure. And of course, she's wearing one of those skirts Callie must have given her. I hear her business is thriving. Not that I really care about what Callie's been up to right now. The skirt is too distracting. It flares from Elena's hips, making her look curvy and accentuating that ass I love.

She's so fucking beautiful.

"Are you going to let me in?" She gestures inside the house.

"Sorry!" I blurt, realizing I've been standing there looking like an idiot. Pulling the door wide, I wave her in. "Yes, please. Come in. You look beautiful."

"Thank you," she says, as she steps over the threshold and I feel like I can finally breathe again. Elena is in my home. She's willing to have me in her life again. What that will ultimately look like remains to be seen. But this is a good start.

"I bet it looks different than the last time you were in here, huh?" She drops her purse on the couch, although I'm not sure why she brought it since she lives next door and can run home if she needs something. "Mr. Blitman's kids redid the floors and Joie made me do some painting."

"I've actually never been in here before." She looks around at all my pictures and knickknacks. There aren't many, but most of the ones of Peyton are up. "Oh! Look at Pey! She's so big now."

She runs a finger over the latest shot I have of my baby girl. It was taken a couple of weeks ago at my parents' house. We're in the backyard during a pool party they had and I'm holding Peyton. I'm smiling at her, and she's looking at the camera with the biggest, cheesiest grin on her face. I can't remember what was making her smile, but it's such a good candid shot, I had to print it out.

"She turns three on Wednesday."

Elena's eyes whip over to mine. "Already?"

"I know. I can't believe it. Next weekend will be my first full weekend with her. I'm having a birthday party for her on Saturday if you want to bring the girls."

"Ok," she says softly.

"Oh!" I exclaim. "Let me show you what we did to her room. I can't wait for her to see it. She hasn't been over yet, so it's a surprise."

Guiding her around the corner and down a small hallway, I open the door to the bedroom. Elena gasps.

"Ohmygod, Greg, it's so beautiful."

I can't disagree. The walls are painted a very soft, pastel purple. Her small bed has a white canopy over it, draped from the ceiling. White bookshelves and storage cubes line one wall, all her toys put in their proper places. And a long white dresser is on the far side of the room. All the knobs are either purple or pink and have various princess paraphernalia painted on them.

It's perfect for my princess.

"You did this all by yourself?"

I chuckle. "Uh, no. I suggested purple since it's the favorite color right now." Elena sniggers. She's got three girls. She knows the phases. "But Joie really helped me put it all together. She's really creative."

"I'll say." She runs her finger tips over the dresser as she looks around. "I may have to hire her if I ever get around to decorating my girls' rooms."

We stand there for a few minutes, me looking at her as she looks around the room. After being away for so long, it feels surreal to have her right next to me. I could spend the night just watching her and be perfectly content.

And then her stomach lets out an angry growl. It's a good thing, too. My creepy, stalkerish thoughts were starting to freak me out.

"I guess you're hungry," I laugh, as she covers her face in embarrassment.

"I can't believe that just happened."

"Your stomach always gives you away. Come on." I grab her by the hand, intertwining our fingers and lead her out of the room. She lets me, which makes me smile even bigger, if that's possible. "Let's go finish cooking so we can get you fed."

We make our way into the kitchen to finally get dinner going. I wish I had started baking the chicken earlier. It may have been her stomach that growled, but mine isn't far behind.

Handing her a glass of her favorite wine, Elena tells me all about her new job at the elementary school, and all the drama that happens outside of the classroom. Homeschooling looks like a viable option for Peyton's future if this is what teachers are really like. Who knew there was so much scandal behind the scenes?

"Having a day job looks good on you," I remark as I rub more seasoning on our dinner. And it does. She looks happy. Settled. Content.

Licking her lips after taking another sip, she sets her wine glass on the counter. "I think I just like being useful. Not that I wasn't before. But now that the kids are a little older, they aren't as dependent on me for everything. I guess I got a little bored being home all day and not having adult interaction at night. This seems to balance me out a bit."

"Does Max go to daycare?"

She shakes her head. "My mom and Callie switch off days keeping her."

"Callie keeps her?"

Quirking an eyebrow at me, she says, "Have you met Christopher? Having Max over keeps him entertained for a few hours so she can get things done."

"I'm surprised those two don't destroy her house when they're together."

"Oh they do," she jokes. "But no more than if he was by himself."

"What about Fiona and Maura?"

She shifts on the stool and watches as the chicken finally goes in the oven. Just thirty more minutes until dinner. I hope we can hold out that long. "Usually they come home with me. I got so lucky getting a job at their school."

"Sounds like it." Setting the oven timer, I thoroughly wash my hands, because salmonella would be just my dumb luck, and dry them on the new hand towel Joie insisted on getting me as a house warming gift. Cheapskate. "I don't have to start the pasta for about fifteen minutes. You want to hang out in the living room while we wait?"

She nods and slides off the stool, making her way to the couch and sinking down on the cushions.

She practically purrs, "I love this couch. I missed this couch. It's so comfortable."

I missed her on the couch. Mostly because of all the memories I have of her laying on it with me on top of her. But I'm not going to go there tonight.

Pushing the memories aside, I situate myself next to her. I can't help myself when I grab a lock of her hair from off the head rest and twirl it around my finger absent-mindedly. She turns her head to look at me, but doesn't pull away. That's a good sign.

"How was San Antonio? Was Peyton ok? I worried about her the whole time she was living with that guy."

I smile. This is another thing I love about Elena. There was no "out of sight, out of mind." She loves my child enough to worry about her safety and well-being. I'm glad I get to reassure her.

"Aputi was a huge surprise," I admit. "I thought for sure Libby had gotten herself involved with some crazy dude. But he was great."

"Aputi? That's an unusual name."

I chuckle. "He's an unusual guy. He's this huge Samoan dude. Played football in college and liked San Antonio so much he stayed. He's really interesting."

Elena smiles evilly. "You got to know him? I bet that pissed Libby off."

"I didn't know him well. Just a little chitchat here and there when we would pass Pey back and forth. The first time I went to go pick up Peyton, though, ohmygod, I had no idea what he'd be like."

"He's the one that answered the door?"

I snort. "Libby didn't even look up from her phone when I got there. She sat on the couch while we sized each other up. Here Aputi was, all tatted out with this menacing look on his face. He stood there staring at me, his arms crossed. I thought for sure he was going to try to kick my ass."

"I take it he didn't."

I shake my head. "Not even close. We stood there for a second, but I never backed down. Finally, he said, 'I've got a daughter. Her mom moved and took her away.' What do you say to that, ya know?"

Elena nods. She gets it. There was no good way to respond to him.

"But then he said, 'I respect a man that uproots his whole life so he can still be with his kid'."

Elena gasps.

"I know," I respond. "That wasn't what I expected either. Anyway, Pey came running up behind him and wrapped her arms around his legs, peeking around him. As soon as I saw the way he stroked her hair to reassure her, I knew she was in good hands."

"Wait," Elena interrupts. "Why was she afraid of you?"

"She wasn't. As soon as she realized it was me, she came running out the door and jumped in my arms. But knowing she felt comfortable enough that he would protect her, that made me feel comfortable, too. Aputi and I got along great after that."

"I don't get it." She turns to face me, making the lock of hair fall away. "If he was such a great guy, why did Libby leave him?"

I shrug. "That's the million-dollar question. Before I left, I made it a point to go back over and thank Aputi for being so good to Pey. He was really tight-lipped about what happened, but I could tell the break up wasn't his choice."

"Aw. That's kind of sad."

"Yes and no. I hope he finds someone wonderful someday, but I know from experience, Libby is probably not it."

We sit and stare at each other, not really sure what else to say, but knowing we'll never have enough time to say it all.

"I really missed you, you know?" I finally whisper.

"I really missed you, too."

Stroking her silky hair again, my gaze wanders to her lips. I've missed those lips so much and I can't stop myself from wanting to taste them. A quick glance in her eyes find her looking at my lips, too. Knowing we're on the same page, I lean in, anticipating the moment when I finally get to kiss her again. My mouth is just centimeters from hers...

And the smoke alarm goes off. And not one smoke alarm... *all* of the smoke alarms begin screaming at the same time.

The home inspector wasn't kidding when he documented that they all work.

Jumping up off the couch, I race to the kitchen and throw the oven door open, waving away the thick black smoke as it billows out. Once I can see a little better, I grab the pan of chicken with a hot pad and drop it on the stovetop, while still flapping the hot pad to move the smoke out. Everything on the pan is all charred and black.

"I opened the front door." Elena walks into the room, her hand moving to and fro in front of her face and grimacing. She immediately opens the back door, too, and the breeze blows through almost instantly, making it easier to breathe. "What happened?"

I look down at the oven again. "What the…? How did I turn it up to six-hundred degrees?"

"I didn't know ovens go up that high." She looks over my shoulder and points to the knobs. "Probably because the timer is right next to the dial. I bet you bumped it."

I shake my head. This could only happen to me, just when I'm about to make-out with the woman of my dreams.

It takes a few minutes to disable all of the blaring smoke alarms—pretty sure every single one in the house went off—and get most of the smoke cleared out.

Looking at our ruined dinner, I realize this is worse than I thought. "I think I might need to go oven shopping." Not to mention, not only do we not have much to eat now, but the moment of seduction is gone. Damn cockblocking oven.

Then Elena giggles and nothing else matters. I haven't heard that carefree, happy sound in so long. As cheesy as it sounds, it's almost makes me feel like I've finally come home. It's wonderful.

"How in the world did you burn it all so badly?" She glances over my shoulder at the charred remains, still giggling.

"I have no idea. Most of the appliances were replaced so I assumed this one worked, too." She quirks her eyebrow at me.

"Yeah, I know. I made an ass out of you and me and all that crap."

She laughs even harder, which makes me smile, and suddenly I want to keep this oven if burning things will make her smile. But we still have the problem of dinner.

"So I haven't had time to go full-on grocery shopping yet," I admit. "Which means the only thing left for dinner is pasta and green beans."

Rounding the corner, she grabs her purse of the couch and gestures for me to follow. "Then it's a good thing you know your next-door neighbor. I know for a fact she's stocked with all kinds of things to eat."

Racing to catch up to her, I grab my keys and lock the front door behind us. The back door can stay open for a while. With a privacy fence backing up to more neighbors, I doubt anyone will even notice.

"Oh yeah? What does she have that we can make quickly for dinner?"

She flashes a flirty grin over her shoulder as she answers. "Hot dogs."

And I just fell in love all over again.

CHAPTER Ten

Elena

We never did get that moment back. But we had a good time hanging out. Once I got over the initial irritation at how it all came about, I realized I can enjoy having Greg in my life again. Dating or not, he's funny and sincere, and he's still my friend. He's *always* been my friend. Even when we were dating, the friendship came first. If that's the only thing we ever salvage, it'll be enough.

Maybe.

Ok, who am I kidding? It'll suck because I love him. Yes, I admit it. I *love* him.

I just hope I can get a handle on my fear.

"Girls, don't step in that ant pile," I yell, as they run through the yard to Greg's house and the birthday party in the backyard. From what I gather, he's tried several ways to kill the colony that's trying to take over, but so far, the buggers won't die.

I'm pretty sure I heard Greg let out a battle cry the other day when he realized he'd lost yet another round, but I didn't ask about it. The war over control of the yard makes him twitchy.

Before I can catch them, the girls have followed the balloon trail through the open gate to the rear of Greg's house. And yes, it's a balloon *trail*. He strategically tied purple balloons to some sort of stakes and made a path to party central. It's genius. It keeps dirt from being tracked through the house to a party that's outside anyway. Why didn't I think of that?

Making my way around the side of the house, I see a giant inflatable slide shaped like a castle. I look up just in time to see Christopher lose his balance at the top and tumble all the way to the bottom, bouncing at the end and landing in the grass. I stop and watch what he does before reacting, but he sits up, shakes it off, and runs to the beginning again.

He's fine.

"They just gave you your old job?" I hear Callie inquire as I walk up to them both. Greg puts his arm around me and kisses the top of my head. Callie quirks a questioning eyebrow at me quickly so Greg doesn't see, but I do. I quirk mine right back in a silent *I'll tell you later*.

"It actually worked out really well," Greg explains, keeping his arm draped over me. "Dave, my boss, couldn't find the right person to run the gym here, but he had a great candidate in San Antonio that they were about to hire when I decided to move."

He tenses slightly, but I reach up and pat his arm, letting him know we don't have to pretend he wasn't gone. Him leaving has never been the issue. It was sad, but understandable.

"When everything changed, that guy still hadn't found a job, so Dave snatched him up as soon as I called him."

Callie sucks the straw of her Capri Sun and glances up as Christopher does that tumbling thing again. She doesn't even flinch as he tumbles a good fifteen feet to the ground. I guess his new acrobats started long before we showed up. "That doesn't really sound good for the other guy though. To be unemployed for that long?"

"It's not like managing gymnastics operations is a huge field," Greg banters. "Especially ones that specialize in, and are successful with, competitive teams."

"Then I would have thought it would have been easier to find someone to run the facility here," I throw in. "They went through what, two managers while you were gone?"

"Three," he counters.

"See? I lost track. It was nuts," I say. "You could tell the instructors were starting to get really frustrated. You've only been back a couple weeks and the atmosphere is already so much better."

Greg smiles down at me. "Thank you. That means a lot." I smile back up at him and we stare at each other, lost in a moment. I know he wants to kiss me. I kind of want him to kiss me, too. But before we can make any sort of move, Callie clears her throat, breaking the moment.

"Ok, seriously. You guys need to hurry up and either shit or get off this pot."

"Callie!" I exclaim as Greg chuckles.

"No really," she continues, handing her drink to her son when he races up to her side. "You used to do this back and forth flirty stuff all the time, and here we go again. It's obnoxious and is not entertaining at all. I've seen musicals with less tap dancing than you two do around each other."

"Booze is in the house, Callie," Greg mentions. "First cabinet on the right, right above the stove."

"Thank god," she grumbles, stomping off in the direction of the door.

I step out of Greg's embrace and turn to him, eyes still wide from her outburst. "What the hell was that?"

He runs his hands up and down my arms, giving me chill bumps that I'll never admit to. "Ben is giving her more shit."

I groan. "What is it this time?"

"I didn't get all the details but it has something to do with taking their vacation money and using it to turn one of the bedrooms into a media room instead."

If I wasn't wearing makeup, I'd rub my hand down my face in exasperation. Callie's not even a TV watcher and Ben spends all his time online. How is this a necessity over a week on a cruise ship with twenty-four-hour child care?

"Let her drink it off. Between the two of us, there are plenty of beds for her to pass out on."

"It's not her passing out that I'm worried about," I mumble, watching Christopher tumble down the slide, yet again, this time getting tangled up with Max and taking her down with him.

Greg looks over at me, trying not to laugh. He's doing a crappy job of it. "I've got extra Benadryl in the cabinet just in case."

"Good man." Handing him Peyton's gift, I add, "Here. Take this." He puts the present up to his ear and shakes it, grimacing when it rattles. I roll my eyes and make it a point to reassure him. "What do you take me for? A monster? It's not beads, paints, or a drum set. Just some pink and purple Legos that make all kinds of princess shapes."

He begins to smile, and then it drops and his eyes narrow at me. "They're the tiny Legos with instructions in Spanish that I'm going to have to try and interpret while I make the damn things myself, aren't they?"

Patting his shoulder, I try hard not to smile too big. "Be glad it's not a puppy. That was Maura's suggestion for a gift."

"You're a family full of evil people, you know that?"

Flashing a grin, I spread my arms wide and yell, "Welcome home!"

He kisses me on the cheeks, making me flush, and shakes his head as he walks under the pergola to place the box with all the rest of the presents.

Looking around, I notice quite a few people I don't know. None of them look even remotely familiar, except for Libby. She's sitting in a lawn chair, nursing a beer next to a woman that looks a lot like her, except older and more worn out. The years seem to have been really kind to the woman, but she looks tired. I guess when you're practically raising a three-year-old because her mother is too busy gallivanting around town to stay home, it can get daunting.

As I move toward the slide to better monitor the children, Peyton comes racing around the corner and crashes into my legs. Instinctually, I grab her to make sure she's not hurt.

"Are you ok, Peyton?" She looks up at me and cocks her head, like she's trying to place me. And then the lightbulb goes off.

"Lena!" she squeals and jumps up in my arms, pointing at all the kids and naming everyone she can remember. "Look, it's Cwistopha! And, and Max! And, and… I don't know that gul."

I can't help but laugh. "That big girl is Fiona. She's Max's sister, remember?"

"Yeah!" she yells as her arm wraps around my neck, clinging to me. "Fiona and Mawa!"

"That's right. Fiona and Maura. You're very smart."

Pey grabs my face with her chubby little hands and looks right into my eyes. "I miss you, Lena. I wuv you," and then she hugs me tight. Tears prick my eyes, even though they're closed, and I hug her back. I knew I missed this girl while she was gone, but I think part of me refused to admit how much. It's strange loving someone else's child sometimes. Briefly, I wonder if this is what my teachers feel like when their former students visit them.

The moment is sweet, but short-lived when a venomous voice starts speaking next to me.

"Well, well, well. You just can't stay away from the teeny weeny, can you?"

Taking a deep breath, steeling myself for the inevitable pissing match, I look over at Libby.

"Nice to see you again, Libby. I'm sorry it didn't work out with Aputi. I hear he was a nice guy."

Her eyes narrow at me as Peyton looks up. "'Puti here?" she asks.

"No, baby," I say gently. "He's at his house."

"Oh." She lays her head down on my shoulder, completely ignoring her mother. Sadly, Libby doesn't even seem to notice. Either she's had a whole lot more beer than I know, or she's really pulled away from Peyton emotionally in the last year. The thought makes me sad. This precious girl deserves to be snuggled and loved and cherished. Now, more than ever, I'm grateful Greg sacrificed everything to be with his daughter. Between him and Aputi, it seems they were the only stable forces in this child's life.

Well, except Joie, of course. If she's as much of a busybody as Greg makes her out to be, she probably spoils her niece rotten.

"Yeah, it's funny how my boyfriend and my ex got all chummy behind my back," Libby spits out. "It doesn't make for a very solid relationship with your man when he and your ex like each other better than they like you."

Whoa. I think she just answered my question. She is *way* more drunk than I realized. The last time I met her, she was all about lobbing personal digs, not giving away personal feelings. No wonder Peyton would rather find comfort in me than go to her own mother.

"But it doesn't matter," she slurs. "It's not like I want either of them anyway. Aputi was shit at oral. And you can have Greg's teeny tiny pecker."

Callie gasps next to me. I didn't even hear her walk up. Her eyes catch mine, jaw wide open, and I know what she's thinking… this bitch be crazy.

Trying to deflect, I do the only thing I can think.

"Libby, this is my best friend Callie. Callie, this is Libby. Peyton's mom." I widen my eyes slightly, shooting her a look that says she needs to be careful with her words around this one. Callie's heard all the stories. She knows how unstable Libby is. I'm just not sure she expected personal insults to be flung in front of a three-year-old.

"Oh good," Libby responds, "Another one of Greg's whores. Are you banging him, too?"

It's almost funny how insulting she's trying to be, and failing at it. Especially because going up against Callie's wit isn't a smart idea when you're sober.

"Nah. Elena gets all the banging," she says, Libby following the wave of her hand. If she's not careful, she's going to fall over. "I use Greg for his handyman and parenting skills."

Libby snorts and wavers a bit. Yeah, she's going down soon if she doesn't switch to water. I can only hope Peyton doesn't see it when it happens.

"Handyman skills," she spits out with a laugh. "Yeah, he's good at nailing things. And I mean with something the size of a nail." She raises her pinky, insulting Greg's manhood once again, but before we can respond, the man in question shouts "Hey" from across the lawn.

He looks angry as he comes stalking up, and I take a step back when he stops right in front of Libby. "You were invited here as a courtesy only, not so you could start shit with my friends. So, you have two choices… you're going to take your drunk ass back over there and park it next to your mother. Or you're going to leave. What's it going to be?"

"Pffft," she spits out. "You can't kick me out of my daughter's birthday party."

"Not if I don't have to. But you are a guest in *my* home and if you can't get it together, I will escort you out. So have a cup of coffee and sober up. You're a mess."

"Okkkaaaaay," I singsong and turn to Callie, shifting Peyton into her arms. "Pey, why don't you go with Callie. I bet she knows where Christopher is."

"You do?" Peyton's eyes are wide, as she latches right onto Callie like she never moved away and we've been here with her all along.

"I do," I hear Callie coo when they walk away. "He's having fun over here…"

Once they are safely out of ear shot, I turn back to see Greg and Libby still staring each other down. Libby is swaying again, but Greg isn't backing down.

"Listen here, Pencil Dick." She lets out a small burp before continuing. "No matter what you do, that is my daughter right there." She waves in the exact opposite direction of where Callie took the tot. "How would it look if you kicked her mother out of her birthday party, hmm? You would look like the asshole that you are, so stop with the threats, ok? Now I'm gonna go hang out with my mom and our friends, and I would appreciate it if you don't bother me again." She turns, flipping her hair our direction and stumbles back over to the pop-up tent she was sitting under, dropping into the chair and toppling backwards to the ground.

Greg looks over at me, but I'm at a loss for words. The last thing I expected today was a drunk Libby pulling her passive aggressive bullshit in front of the entire neighborhood. Not only is it bad for the kids to see, it makes her look trashy. But it does clarify one thing for me.

This is why I'm afraid. This situation right here. As long as Libby is around and Greg can't follow through with his threats, she stays in control.

And as long as she's in control, it's only a matter of time before Greg leaves and breaks my heart again.

CHAPTER Eleven

Elena

Another week goes by faster than I can blink. I don't remember time moving this quickly before I had a job. I don't know if it's because I'm so busy, or because the clock speeds up the closer I get to death. Either way, I swear time keeps moving faster.

Peyton's party turned out to be relatively drama free after Libby sat back down. I guess she wasted her last bit of energy on that ugly scene, because she didn't move from her chair the rest of the afternoon. Not to get another beer. Not to help Peyton open presents. Not to sing Happy Birthday. It was… weird.

As eye-opening as the party was in some ways, it helped others shift back to normal. It's like Greg was reassured Callie and I have his back, which blew the lines of communication wide open. Now he and I text all day. We stop and chat in the yard. He came over to talk to me at the gym while Fiona was in her class. We laugh, and we give advice about parenting, and we have serious discussions. No topic is off limits. It's like he never left.

Except the kissing part.

That still isn't back to normal, and while my emotions are still hesitant to hand over that part of me to him again, my body is raring to go. It makes it hard to concentrate when he shows up in my spin class. Which he did again today. The bastard sat right behind me, knowing I was going to have to bend over the handle bars at some point. I strategically flipped him the bird during that part, making him laugh out loud, when he could barely breathe, which of course meant he lost his stride.

Serves him right.

Pulling into the parking space of our favorite park, the girls begin fighting over whose shoes are on the floor. Never mind that only one person has bare feet. Surely, that doesn't mean those are *Max's* shoes.

Yes, actually it does. But have you ever tried arguing logic with an almost four-year-old? It's pointless. Instead, I keep her fully strapped down, while I put her shoes back on, the other two kids already off to the playground.

Finally getting her situated and putting her down, Max takes off running, yelling at the others to wait up. Until she sees Christopher. Then she purposely races past him, just inches away from running into him. As soon as he realizes it's her, off they go together.

I wipe my brow like I've been in a wrestling match. Which I kind of have been. But it's also just hot out here. I never thought I'd miss the days when we took that mommy and me class. A/C sounds good right about now.

I find Callie at our normal picnic table. With *Deborah*. I knew she was going to be here today. As rude as she was last week, the more I thought about it, the more I realized Callie was probably right.

Deborah is at the very beginning stages of her new business. She admits to not having a lot of friends and like Callie said, she's anxious about doing a good job. So if she wants us to tone it down a little during work hours and be a little more professional, I can do that without being a judgy bitch.

I mean, I won't forget that it happened. But I can be the bigger person. In several ways. The skinny bitch.

Pasting a smile on my face, I greet them both. "Hey ladies."

"Hi, Elena," Deborah says with a smile. Callie waves a carrot stick at me while she chews. I never thought I'd see Callie eat a carrot, but it looks like her options are a bit limited.

The table is covered with brightly colored Tupperware containers, each filled with the exact right amount of different finger foods. There are carrots sitting next to some sort of dressing. No doubt it's organic. Bite-sized cheeses. Black olives. Yet Deborah keeps bringing out more.

"Wow." My eyes keep going back and forth across the table, noticing something new at every pass. *Are those kale chips?* "Did you really put in this much effort for us, Deborah?"

"It's my turn to bring lunch, right?"

I half nod, half shrug. "Yeah, but you didn't have to spend so much time. My kids would have been happy with peanut butter and jelly."

She makes a face. "Do you know how many preservatives are in regular peanut butter? And how much refined sugar is in jelly? This is much more healthy."

"Well, I'm impressed. Thank you."

She smiles brightly at me again, only this time she looks a little embarrassed as well. "I know it looks crazy, but Trevor is my only child, ya know? I just want to do it right."

"And you don't think chicken nuggets are doing it right?" I inquire, leaning forward on the table, Callie still munching away.

Deborah gathers all the lids and stacks them neatly in the bottom of her matching tote bag. "It's not that. I feel like there are so many toxins we're exposed to—pollution and chemicals and medications. If I can remove some of that by eating organic, it makes me feel better about giving him medication."

"When you phrase it that way, it doesn't sound crazy at all," I admit. "It actually sounds really smart."

She's beaming now and I get the strange feeling she doesn't get praised very often. Maybe I was right to give her the benefit of the doubt. Maybe.

"I didn't know Trevor was on meds," Callie finally pipes up, snatching a few purple grapes from a different container.

"Oh, he's not." She pulls out some brightly colored cloth napkins, placing them in a neat pile on the table. "But it's inevitable that he will be someday. I guess I'm being proactive."

A mass of dark, springy curls runs by at that moment yelling, "Hi, Lena! Bye, Lena!" as, who I assume is Peyton, sprints to the playground, making me laugh. I look around and see Greg meandering toward us, hands in his pockets.

"What's Peyton doing here?" He sits down next to me on the bench and kisses me on the top of the head. "Isn't this Libby's weekend?"

Keeping his hand locked on my neck, he gently massaging the sides. Despite the heat, I don't mind it at all.

"Supposedly she had to go to work and her mother was busy, so I've got her today."

"Oh, that's nice."

"Yep." That's all he says, which is weird, but if I know Greg, he's biting down his irritation at his ex.

Reaching over, I grab his hand, smiling at him. "Well for what it's worth, I'm glad you guys are here."

He smiles back, rubbing his thumb over my knuckles and, once again, we're locked into each other, having one of those moments where the rest of the world fades away.

Until Callie interrupts.

"Would you two boink already?"

"Callie!" Deborah chides loudly. I don't know if I'm rolling my eyes at Callie or Deborah, but either way they're both ridiculous. Greg laughs while I pull away, putting a little distance between us. My hormones can't take much more of these staring contests.

"What?" Callie responds. "Give me that knife." She grabs a plastic utensil off the table and begins slashing it through the air. "Can you see that? I'm literally cutting their sexual tension with a knife."

"Would you stop that?" Deborah hisses, snatching the knife out of Callie's hand, making her pout. "This is a family park."

Callie shrugs. "That means everyone here knows what sex is."

Deborah gasps in horror. "Except the children!"

"Greg, this is Deborah," I say, looking at him with wild eyes, hoping he understands my exaggerated facial expressions for what they are... my unspoken way of saying she drives me crazy. "She's a little uptight."

She squeaks in annoyance. An actual squeak.

"I can see that," Greg laughs. "It's nice to meet you, Deborah."

She closes her lips tightly, trying to get herself under control before speaking. "It's nice to meet you, too." Straightening her spine, she says, "I'm going to get the children for lunch. I hope we'll have a more appropriate conversation while they are here," and she turns to stomp away.

I turn my glare to Callie. "That is *your* friend," my finger pointing in the lunatic's direction.

She waves me off. "Whatever. We only have a few minutes. I have rapid fire questions."

I groan, but Greg gets a grin on his face. "It's my turn to play." He sits forward and leans in towards Callie. "Hit me."

She leans right back, narrowing her eyes. And then it begins.

"Did you have sex with her?"

"Not since I've been back."

"Do you want to?"

"Yes."

I feel like sitting up a little taller. Greg still wants me. *Boom.*

"Did you kiss her?"

"No."

"Why not?"

"I almost burned the house down instead."

"Why'd you do that?"

"The oven was broken."

"Did you get a new one?"

"Yes."

"What kind?"

"LG700, double oven with gas stove top."

Wait, what? What is happening here?"

"Four burners or five?"

"Five, but the middle can change out to be a skillet."

"Was it expensive?"

"Very."

"When I save enough paychecks, will you take me to buy one just like it?"

"Of course."

"Done!" Callie yells and slams her hand on the table. Greg sits back victoriously like she landed on *No Whammies*. And I'm still sitting here trying to figure out what the hell just happened.

Looking back and forth at them, they each sit there like nothing weird is going on. Finally, I can't take it anymore. "What was that?"

Callie snatches a kale chip out of a container and sniffs it, grimacing and throwing it under the table. "What? I need a new stove," she says like that explains it all. Suddenly, Christopher pops out from underneath the table, making her screech. He climbs up on the bench next to her, discarded kale chip in his mouth.

The other kids aren't far behind, and before I know it, six sets of grubby little hands are reaching for finger foods. With the way they're acting, you'd think they've been starving for weeks, but I know for a fact they ate stepped-on vanilla wafers off the floor less than two hours ago.

"Wait, kids!" Deborah says sternly. "We need to sanitize our hands before we eat."

Callie freezes, cheese cube halfway to her mouth, and drops it on the plate. "Yes. We need clean hands." She puts her hands out, like she even knows what hand sanitizer is.

I furrow my brow. "Why? It's just dirt." I continue loading food on a plate for Max, knowing full well I don't have any baby wipes on me.

To my surprise, Deborah pulls a giant bottle of industrial sized hand sanitizer out of her bag and begins squirting all the kids', and Callie's, hands. You can tell who has used this stuff before. Trevor is rubbing his hands together nicely. Maura is sniffing it. And Christopher is licking it off his palm. Maybe the alcohol in it will slow him down a bit.

"You always have to wash your hands, Elena," Deborah says condescendingly. "Way too many cases of botulism come from places like the park."

I turn to Greg who mouths *botulism?* at me and shakes his head in amusement.

We finally get all the hands washed, some of them twice, and are preparing to dig in when Deborah announces, "Ok, let's fold our hands and close our eyes."

Even Callie has a strange look on her face this time, and I swear Christopher is about to come unglued from how long he's been denied the goodies in front of him.

Now, I'm not one to poo-poo on people blessing their food. I was raised that way. But when you are in the middle of the park with a bunch of pint-sized heathens about to go ballistic if they don't get nourishment, I think God already understands how grateful you are.

But that's just me.

Surprise of all surprises, Trevor says the blessing. A long, drawn out prayer that thanks God for every single item of food, every single friend he's ever had, every animal he can think of, and several people who apparently live in a heavenly zip code. By the time he's done, I'm sure ants have carried all the food away.

"Mama, I'm *hungry*," Max wails just as Trevor says, "Amen."

Deborah shoots me a look and addresses Max with a smile on her face. "It's good to say the blessing before you eat, Maxine." *Maxine? Since when did we start using her legal name?* "You need to learn patience somehow."

Ok, now I'm starting to get pissed. I understand we don't parent the same way and she's all into organic foods and is anti-germ. But that sounded a whole lot like a passive aggressive dig my direction.

The way Greg is watching this all go down quietly, one eyebrow raised as he slowly nibbles a celery stalk, I'm betting he thinks the same thing.

"Mom," Fiona's nose is scrunched as she picks up a strawberry off her plate, "do I have to eat this?"

I open my mouth to tell her no, because strawberries always make her stomach hurt, but before any words can come out, Deborah responds for me. "You need to eat everything on your plate. It's healthy, which I know you're not used to, but we don't waste food. We're grateful for everything we get. Especially when it's free."

And now I'm done. Asking me to be professional is one thing. Criticizing my parenting is another thing. But this passive aggressive bullshit, especially when it's directed at my kid, doesn't fly with me.

Standing up, I wipe my mouth with my cloth napkin and toss it on the table. I can feel Callie and Greg staring at me, waiting to see how I'm going to react.

"Thank you for an... interesting lunch, Deborah," I spit out with as much false kindness as I can muster, "but we've gotta go."

She blinks a few times and looks stunned at my sudden decision to leave. "But we just started lunch."

"Don't worry about us." I gather up the few belongings we have—my keys, my phone, Fiona's fidget spinner that doesn't do anything except distract her. "We're going to McDonald's on the way home. Come on, girls."

"Yay!" they yell and scramble to their feet, following right behind me as I stomp my way to the car. My jaw is clenched and I'm trying hard to keep from muttering obscenities, but I'm done with this crap.

Behind me I hear Peyton's little voice say, "I want McDono's." It makes me feel a little guilty that we ditched everyone so dramatically.

Until I hear Trevor say, "Mommy, what's McDonald's?"

CHAPTER Twelve

Greg

Watching Elena walk away, I realize I have two choices:

I can sit here and finish lunch, which actually isn't half bad for rabbit food, or I can follow her and figure out what's really going on. Because even for Elena, that exit was a little over the top.

Yes, this Deborah lady was being a bitch, but normally Elena would either brush it off or have some witty comeback. I'm not sure if I'm missing something, or if Elena's hurt runs deeper than what happened here, but there's really no choice… I have to follow her home.

Popping one last olive in my mouth, I wipe invisible crumbs off my hands as I stand up. "Well, ladies, it's been an interesting experience, but we need to go, too."

I grab Peyton and climb over the bench while Callie tries to convince me to stay. "Come on, Greg. You just got here. You don't have to leave."

Something about the fact that Callie isn't at all concerned about Elena's feelings really rubs me the wrong way. Far be it for me to not say anything. Even if I don't like how Callie is treating this particular situation, I have respect for the fact that we can be brutally honest with each other. So that's what I give her.

"But I do have to go. The woman I love, your best friend, just took off like a bat out of hell because something is wrong. And I'm a little disappointed that it's not at all concerning to you."

Callie has the wherewithal to look guilty, so I nod at her once in acknowledgement and turn to leave.

Before we make it halfway to the car, Elena peels out of the parking lot and turns onto the main road. Shit. She is really pissed. I can't wait until we get home to talk to her. I need to calm her down now.

As quickly as possible, I strap Peyton into her chair and then strap me to my own seat. Once we're safely on the road, I grab my phone off the passenger seat and hit the short cut to her number.

"What." She doesn't answer with a question. Nope. That was a basic "Why the fuck are you calling me" statement, designed to intimidate someone into leaving her alone. Good thing I don't intimidate easily.

"Talk," I demand.

She huffs. "What do you want me to say, Greg? And why do you care so much?"

Ouch. That stings a bit. But I try not to take it personally.

"Elena, first and foremost, I am your friend. Something is going on here and whatever it is, you need to talk about it."

"You're making something out of nothing, Greg," she insists. "Let it go."

"No way," I say, her eerily calm tone ensuring I can't let it go until I get to the bottom of it. "So spill."

I realize there's a squawking voice in the background and she may not even be listening.

"Are you paying attention?"

"No," she says and then her voice sounds different, like she moved the phone away. "Yes, I need two 6-piece happy meals with juice, and, hold on… Does Peyton still like nuggets?"

She moved the phone back to her mouth so fast, it takes a second to register that her question is directed toward me. "What?"

She huffs, but makes sure to annunciate more. "I said, does Peyton still eat chicken nuggets?"

"Oh. Yes."

I hear the phone move away again. "And two 4-piece happy meals with juice."

Waiting for her to finalize the order, I can't help but smile. Even when she's telling me to leave her alone, she's planning on at least feeding the girls together. As soon as I know I've got her full attention, I try again.

"Elena, what's really going on here?"

"Look, Greg," she snaps, the sound of giggling girls in the background, "I need a minute, ok? Let me get home first." And the phone goes dead.

It takes another ten minutes to get across the neighborhood and onto our street. Yet, somehow, when I drive up in my driveway, Elena is already home and unloading the girls out of her car, handing each of them a paper bag and juice box. How fast was she driving to be able to make a McDonald's run and still beat me home?

Peyton runs straight to Elena as soon as I get her out of her carseat, and reaches out for her own paper bag. The tender way she treats my daughter, even in the middle of an emotional breakdown, or whatever you'd call this, makes my heart swell. I find myself grateful once again that Libby is an unstable mess and ran home when things got tough.

Following her inside, Elena continues to ignore me, but at least she hasn't kicked me out. I'm still waiting to see how this all shakes out. But despite our silence, we work together to get the girls settled. I learn quickly that each of them needs an open ketchup packet, but I have to make sure to hand it over quickly so *they* can do the squirting on their own. Apparently, that's a very big deal. I learned that lesson the hard way on my first attempt at helping Max. It might be a few days to get full hearing back in my right ear.

When they finally dig in, chattering amongst themselves, I lean against the counter… watching. Elena continues to ignore me, instead pulling a package of hot dogs out of the refrigerator.

"Elena."

She pulls a pot out of the cabinet but doesn't respond.

"Elena," I try again.

Still nothing. Instead she walks to the sink and fills the pot with water.

"Elena," I say a little more forcefully.

She slams the handle, turning the water off and whips around to face me. "What?"

"Talk to me."

She shakes her head and turns back to the sink. "There's nothing to say."

"Sure there is," I disagree. "You made quite a show back there, but you don't want to talk about what's going on."

"Do you think I was wrong to leave like that?"

"No. Deborah was being a real bitch." The girls all giggle at my language, and a small smile quickly crosses her lips in response. They are cute when they think something is funny. "But people are bitchy all the time and you don't ever have that reaction, so I feel like something else is going on."

Closing her eyes tight and squeezing the bridge of her nose between her thumb and forefinger, I can practically see her trying to get her thoughts in order. "I don't like her. I'm sure she's generally a nice person, but I just don't like her."

"She didn't seem like a nice person today," I respond, as she carries the pot to the stove and turns on the burner.

"The first time I met her, she was an overbearing, all organic, no GMO, gluten free, dye free, fun free, helicopter parent. Which was fine. But every time since then, she has to *put me in my place*," she says with air quotes. "Like I'm not good enough for her or something. I'm so tired of not being good enough."

"Elena," I whisper, her overly-dramatic behavior suddenly making sense with just those few key words.

"It took me so long to stop hearing James's voice in my head of never being enough, you know? Never being pretty enough, or a good enough housekeeper," she lowers her voice just slightly, looking over her shoulder at the kids who aren't paying much attention. "Or good enough in bed. You were there. You know how hard that was on me." She shakes her head and blinks back tears. "And now this, this person Callie wants to be friends with." Her shoulders slump and her head drops. "I'm so tired of not being enough for anyone."

In a flash, I'm standing right in front of her, hands cupping her checks so she has to look up at me. "You are more than enough to me, Elena. So much more."

She blinks rapidly, a few stray tears sliding down her cheeks. "Not enough for you to not leave me," she says quietly.

"But I came back," I whisper in response.

She looks so defeated, it breaks my heart, and I know what she's about to say. "Not for me, you didn't."

I pull her to me and wrap my arms tightly around her. I feel like such an ass, not recognizing how scared she is about my involvement back in her life. She's terrified that she's an afterthought in every decision I've made recently. She has no idea every choice, when to come back, where to live, hell, growing my beard back, has been as much about her as it has been about my daughter.

Hugging her tight, I look at and see the girls staring at us silently, eyes wide. I can't tell if they're unsure about seeing their mother cry, or if they're confused by seeing the way non-crazy adults act with each other. Either way, Elena's breakdown is not something they need to witness. And what I'm about to tell her is not something they need to hear.

"Hey Fiona," she looks over at me, "since you girls did so good eating your lunches…" which is a bald-faced lie as most of them haven't even touched their nuggets yet, "… why don't you get some popsicles out of the garage freezer and take them in the backyard to eat them."

"Can we use the hose to spray each other off if we get dirty?" she asks, eyes shining with excitement at the prospect.

A small giggle erupts against my chest, and I know Elena is going to be ok if the kids can still amuse her.

"Just make sure the water isn't hot before you spray it at each other."

A chorus of "Yay!" and "Let's go!" come from the table as the girls scramble out of their chairs and run away.

Rubbing my hands up and down her back, and waiting until the girls are out of earshot, I let Elena in on a secret I haven't told anyone until now. "I need you to listen to me. Yes, I moved back when I did because Peyton was already here, but that's not the only thing that happened."

She pulls back, but not away, so I adjust our bodies until she can look at me. "What do you mean?"

"For a few weeks before they broke up, I got this vibe that something was off with Libby and Aputi. I've seen this from her before, so I knew it was a matter of time before she took off again. I was already documenting every little thing. If I saw Libby ignore Pey, I documented. If she was drunk when Pey was around, I documented. If she caused trouble when I picked her up or wasn't home when I dropped her back off, I documented." Pushing a stray piece of hair out of her face, I take a second to appreciate being this close to her. I've missed being able to put my arms around her and touch her like this. "I was waiting patiently for her to cut and run again, and when she did, I was filing for full custody and moving back here."

Elena gasps. "What?"

"It doesn't feel right anymore," I reply with a shake of my head. "You saw Libby at Peyton's birthday. She's partying more and more and seems to be pulling away from Peyton. That's not good for her, so I'm watching really closely anyway. I was so excited when they came back home instead. It bought me some time to get back to you before I deal with Libby."

Elena blinks back tears again, only the look on her face is completely different. These aren't tears of sadness and insecurity. They're tears of joy. "Really? You were already going to come back and bring Peyton with you?"

"Baby, I was coming back to you one way or the other. That was never up for debate. Libby just made it happen sooner than I expected."

"I've never liked Libby so much," she jokes, making me smile. "She's kind of a bitchy drunk."

"She's kind of a bitchy sober, too," I say with a smile. "But listen, I don't know anything about this Deborah chick. And you and Callie have some things to work out. But don't let anyone convince you you're less than anything again. You are more than enough. For me. For the girls. Don't you ever doubt that."

She smiles and tugs gently on the front of my shirt, my arms still wrapped tightly around her. "Thank you."

"You're welcome. I love you."

Then she says the words I've been dying to hear for nine long months. "I love you, too."

When her lips touch mine for the first time since I moved away, I finally know for certain, we're going to be fine.

CHAPTER Thirteen

Elena

As every gymnast will tell you, skill level seems to come in waves. First, you find yourself doing pretty good on one particular apparatus. You're learning skills. You're sticking landings. You're feeling confident.

And then there comes a shift. You hit a plateau. Sometimes it happens because of a growth spurt. Sometimes it's a mental block. If you can push through it, eventually it will get better. But until it does, you suffer through a lot of falls, and a lot of self-doubt.

That's where Fiona is right now with the balance beam.

For quite a while, she seemed to have spot-on balance. She could turn, leap, even cartwheel and her skills were always solid. But something has changed over the last couple of weeks, and now she's suffering through one of the most discouraging parts of gymnastics.

Huffing, she plops down next to me on the bench during her two-minute water break.

Handing her the squirt bottle, she takes a swig, the scowl never leaving her face.

"You're doing fine," I try to encourage. I get a no-nonsense glare in return.

"I keep falling."

"Everyone falls. You just have to get yourself back up."

"I didn't fall two practices ago."

She's got me there. Two practices ago, she was still riding the top of the skill wave, which was fun to watch. But let's face it, you can't ride high forever. That's not reality. Slumps happen. Falls happen. Waves peter out. The key is knowing how to see it coming so you can prepare yourself for the inevitable.

Kind of like I've been doing with my two best friends lately.

"Has Coach Pete talked to you about balance checks?" Turning my body so I'm facing her, she opts not to move, just shakes her head while she takes another drink. "A balance check is a way of taking a pause in the middle of your routine so you can readjust so you don't fall."

She looks over at me. "So I just stop?"

"Sort of. But you don't stop all the way. It's more like pausing yourself right after a skill. Let's say you do a leap. When your foot lands on the beam, you stop for a tiny second."

"Why?"

"In that second, you concentrate on feeling where your foot is. Is it in the middle of the beam or do you need to move it a little? Feel where your body is. Is it tight or are you loosey goosey? Are you standing up straight, or are you leaning to the side? Once you check those things, you know how you need to adjust your body so you can move to the next skill."

The crinkles her little eight-year-old brow while she thinks. Then she says, "But what if I'm doing all those things wrong?"

I smile at her, knowing this is more than just gymnastics tips. This is a life lesson she's going to need someday. "If something's wrong, you fix it before you keep going. If you don't, your routine is either going to be really messy, or eventually you'll fall." Just like in life.

Damn, I'm good at this parenting thing sometimes.

She nods quietly, still thinking about what I've said. But I see that quiet determination behind those precious eyes. Slowly, she stands up and walks back onto the floor, passing everyone until she gets to the high beam.

Biting my lip, I feel a strange amount of anticipation as I watch this moment which could very well be pivotal for her. She, however, seems cool as a cucumber.

I watch her climb back on the beam and get into position. She runs through the poses and turns of her routine, and then she goes for the leap that has been giving her trouble.

As soon as she lands, I see it. Her foot is slightly too far to the left and her body is leaning. But then she pauses. It's a split second, and most people wouldn't even notice it unless they're trained to see it, but it's there. And what do you know… she adjusts accordingly, doesn't fall, and continues on with her routine. Only now there is a huge smile on her face.

"Is your balance check with me finally over?"

I didn't hear Greg come out of his office, but it doesn't surprise me that he overheard our conversation and knew part of it was about him.

"You caught that, did you?"

His lips twitch into a small smile as he leans against the door jam, arms and legs crossed. Pushing off, he comes to me and kisses me on the top of the head, something he's never, ever done at his work place before. I kind of like it. "I did. I hope you're done feeling me out and are ready to move forward."

I nod. "Yeah. I am. I needed a minute to get my bearings straight and make sure I wasn't going to fall again."

"Don't be afraid of falling, Elena. I'll always be here to catch you."

My phone rings in my purse, breaking our moment. He squeezes my shoulder and says, "Maybe it's time to move forward with Callie too."

Glancing at my phone, sure enough, that's who is calling. "How did you know it was her?"

"Lucky guess," he shrugs. "Plus, she's been texting me non-stop since Saturday because you haven't been taking her calls. She's really upset over this."

"She is, or you are because you've had to put up with her crazy?"

He laughs. "She is."

"She should be." I say it like an unfeeling bad ass, but I'm not fooling either of us. I miss my best friend as much as she misses me. Now that I've licked my wounds and worked things out with Greg, it's time to let Callie make amends.

Ok, ok. I should probably make some, too.

One last squeeze of my shoulder and he walks away, leaving me to have this conversation privately. Well, as privately as you can get in the middle of an open gym.

"Hello?" I answer.

"Oh, thank God," she bursts out. "I thought you were never going to talk to me again."

I bite back a giggle. And Greg says *I'm* overdramatic.

"Obviously I was going to talk to you again, you goof. I just needed a balance check."

"A what?"

"Never mind." I wave her off like she can see me even though she's on the phone. What can I say... I'm a hand talker. "I had to sort a few things out."

"Oooh! Did you sort them out with Greg?"

Her comment makes this giggle come out. I'm not at all surprised her main concern would be whether or not Greg and I are back together. Which we are. I think.

"Yeah, we sorted things out. For the most part. Now that you say that, I may need to clarify this with him because we never got that far in our conversations."

Huh. The last few days we've shared a lot of "I love you's" and a lot of kisses. But we've never actually said, "So we're back together again." Looks like we'll be having another serious conversation soon.

"Pfft." I can almost hear Callie's hand waving around this time. "That man is so head over heels. You don't even need to talk about it. It's obvious."

"Maybe to you."

"Of course to me. You should have seen him when you left the park." I get a twinge in my gut at her reminder of the fall out. "He jumped up so fast to chase you, I thought his butt was on fire."

"Yeah, he was pretty great that day," I admit, picking an invisible piece of lint off the pants Callie gave me at the last party. I like them. They're fitted in all the right places, but don't look overly sexy. Just my style.

The silence on the other end of the line tells me she's trying to figure out exactly what to say, which is funny since she's had days to decide. But I know she'll comment when she's ready, so I don't push it. I've got nowhere else to be.

Finally, she speaks. "I'm sorry, Elena. I should have said something to Deborah. I should have stood up for you and I didn't."

This right here is why she's my best friend. She's not perfect, none of us are. But when she's wrong, when she knows she hurt me, even inadvertently, she's the first to own up to it. It kills her when she hurts people. That's how big her heart is. And her heart is what I love most about her.

"You should have," I respond. "But I get it. RowRow isn't a hobby for you. You are running a legitimate business and you're in a precarious situation, you know?"

"Yeah. I know. It's why I'm not really sure what to do in this situation. She's already so close that if I cut her out, I'm afraid of the backlash."

I take a deep breath, because I have to make this easy on her. Well, easier than it could be. So I bite my tongue from what the vindictive part of me wants, and say what the adult part of me knows is right.

"Look, you have to work with her. I get that. But I don't." Looking up, I see Greg watching me. He winks, giving me the support I didn't even realize I needed to have this conversation. "I'm not asking you to choose. I'm really not. But I'm asking you not to share any part of my life with her. I'm sure she's a nice person, but you know how long it's taken me to feel good about myself again. I'm not going to let someone take that away from me again. Not even for your business."

"I would never ask that of you," she responds. "I thought Deborah was one thing, but once I really went over the scene in my head, I realized she's not at all who I thought she was."

"Most people aren't. Why do you think my only friend is you?"

We both laugh, knowing that statement is more than a joke. People really do suck half the time.

"I love you, Callie," I say, feeling overly sentimental like I always do after fighting with someone I love. "That isn't going to change because you have shitty colleagues."

We laugh again, because humor is what we do.

"Well, I won't make you hang out with those colleagues again."

"Thank you."

"Anything for you. No matter who else comes along, you'll always be my BFF."

I smile at the endearment. "Promise?"

"I promise."

I feel really light and free in this moment. I took the balance check I needed, made the adjustment necessary, and moved on. It feels good. And it's nice knowing this time, I'm not going to fall.

CHAPTER
Fourteen

Greg

Elena is not one to jump into the important things without really thinking them through. Not disciplining the girls. Not big purchases. Not relationships.

Maybe she was more impulsive before I met her. But years of getting screwed over has made her leery and less trusting. I don't fault her for that. In a weird way, I kind of like that she didn't even trust me until I really proved myself. What can I say, I'm a man. I enjoy the chase sometimes.

Although, lately there's been less chase and more leaning on each other for support. It started when Elena's mom got the flu and couldn't watch Max for a couple of weeks. Callie offered to take over, but it didn't make much sense to force Max out of bed that early every morning, so I started coming over before Elena went to work. I enjoyed the bonding time with Max and it gave me a chance to get a few things done around her house—like oiling the squeaky closet door and patching the hole in Maura's room that was left over from when she had a raging fit and threw a tiara across the room. The girl may be a princess, but she's got an amazing pitching arm.

As if that wasn't big enough, James decided their custody agreement wasn't working for them. Something about being locked into certain weekends every month with his kids. So, because Elena is kind like that, they switched to him seeing the girls every other weekend. At first, we didn't think much about it. But then Elena sat down and did the math and we realized the change means he spends even less time with the girls.

We still can't figure out if he knew that when he made the switch, but it seems awfully coincidental the request came on the heels of two weekend visits, back to back. The girls aren't rambunctious, but they're constant energy. If James's new wife Keri likes sleeping in on weekends and sipping coffee while reading the newspaper, she had parenting all wrong.

After we realized the time frames, Callie, Elena and I wagered on what his next move will be. Yes, actual wagers with money and our John Hancock's on the betting page. Inappropriate? Maybe. But making light of the situation seems to be a better tactic than letting it cause everyone distress. So we just go with it. I'm now hoping to win a Ben Franklin from Callie when something "comes up at work" and James starts picking them up on Saturdays mornings instead of Friday night. That's always the way it goes, right?

On the one hand, it's sad that James is seeing the girls less and less. What kind of father does that? On the other, at least he's phasing out gradually instead of disappearing suddenly.

The only advantage to all the changes is our weekends overlap sometimes. Instead of me having Peyton when the girls are with James, they're either all with us or all gone.

This is one of the "all gone" weekends. And I'm taking advantage of it.

"Where are you taking me?" Elena asks with a smile. We've been driving for close to an hour, but I haven't said a word about where we're headed.

"On a date."

She punches my arm lightly. "You're still not going to tell me? It's getting more and more rural out there. How do I know you're not taking me somewhere to get rid of me?"

"First of all, if I got rid of you, who would take care of the girls during the week while I'm at work? That's too much coordinating with your mother. Second," I turn and quirk an eyebrow at her, "I swear if you don't stop watching the Investigation Channel, I'm going to disable your cable."

She gapes at me playfully. "You wouldn't dare."

"We're turning onto a country road now." I ease the car into the turn lane and take a right. "Swear to me you didn't just have a passing thought about duct tape and a shovel being in the truck and I'll let it go."

She doesn't respond and avoids my gaze.

"Uh huh. That's what I thought."

"Just drive, funny man," she grumbles. She's so damn cute when she's being paranoid. I can't help myself when I reach over and grab her hand, bringing her knuckles to my lips.

"I've only been back a few weeks. You haven't driven me to murder quite yet."

She snorts a laugh but doesn't pull away from me, instead watching the scenery out the window as it changes.

The road in front of us gradually gets less paved and turns more into a gravel road, and eventually a dirt trail emerges as we get closer to our destination. The trees are so dense, we can't see the sky and the automatic lights on the dash turn on so I can see all the indicators.

Suddenly, there is a break in the trees and the sky opens up. Elena gasps as the scene unfolds in front of her.

"Greg," she breathes, stunned by the view. A small lake is before us, the sun glistening off the water in reds, purples, oranges and yellows, as dusk moves in.

There's nowhere to park, just the end of the road, so I stop the car when we get close enough to the water.

"What is this place?" she asks reverently, her eyes never leaving the landscape as we climb out of the car.

I smile at her reaction. I was hoping she'd be happy about my surprise. Looks like it's mission accomplished. "Welcome to Heisner Lake."

"It's beautiful."

Grabbing a picnic basket and thick quilt out of the trunk, I take a few minutes to get everything set up while she gazes out at the view. Watching her take in the scene as it unfolds in front of her takes my breath away and it hits me… she's it for me. She's the last person I'll kiss and touch and love. She's the one who will help me raise my daughter and I'll take care of her daughters like they are my own. It's "game over" for me.

The thought should bring me to my knees, but it doesn't. It makes my chest swell. It's not the right time yet. We've got lots of things to sort out first, but knowing my future is going to include this woman gives me a sense of peace like I haven't experienced before.

Not able to be away from her for one second more, I wrap my arms around her waist and rest my chin on her shoulder. "Come sit with me," I say quietly in her ear. "I brought wine."

She chuckles lightly. "Trying to get me drunk and take advantage of me?"

"I thought you were a sure thing," I joke, eliciting a light smack on my arm.

"Only for you."

I take her hand and lead her over to the quilt, pulling out the wine.

"Food comes later." I hand her a glass of her favorite Moscato and pour another for myself. "Right now, I want to enjoy the sunset with you."

We settle into each other, her back snuggled into my front and watch as the sun continues to throw rays of all different colors across the sky.

"I think this is the most romantic date we've ever been on. What's the occasion?"

I kiss the top of her head. "No occasion. We've been so busy lately, I wanted to get out in the peace and quiet for a little while."

"How'd you find out about this place anyway?"

Taking a large gulp of my wine, I place the glass on the ground next to us. "A buddy of mine, a coach at a different gym, had a bonfire out here a couple years ago. He owns the property and lets his friends use it to camp or whatever."

"I'm surprised he hasn't built a house on this land."

"Too far from town, I think. Plus, he likes the idea of owning some property in a secluded area that developers can't do anything with. Like he can protect a small piece of nature."

"That's really nice."

We lapse into a content silence again as the last of the light fades away. Fortunately, I had the foresight to set up an electric lantern, so all I have to do is click it on. It gives us just enough light to make it seem like we're in our own little glowing bubble.

Suddenly overwhelmed with desire for this woman, my hand cups the back of her neck, bringing her to me. As I lean in to take her lips with mine…

Her stomach growls. Loudly.

"Ohmygod," she groans.

"What is it about me that makes you hungry?"

She giggles, leaning her forehead on mine. "I think it's knowing how much energy I'm going to expend later."

"So I *can* get you drunk and take advantage of you tonight." I kiss her lips lightly and begin to pull away.

But she pulls me back to her, kissing me deeply. I'm lost in the moment, lost in her lips and her tongue and her taste. She breaks away, breathing heavily. "Who says I have to be drunk for you to get laid?"

A low growl comes from deep within me and I attack her again, laying her on the ground underneath me as I plunder her mouth with mine. Somewhere in the back of my mind, I recognize her wine glass spilling somewhere, but I don't care. We're too busy dry humping like teenagers at the end of a dirt road to care.

"I love you, Greg," she whispers, as I kiss behind her ear, down her neck, across her collarbone. "I love you so much."

"Love doesn't even describe what I feel for you." Nuzzling her breasts, I take one nipple in my mouth through her clothes, biting lightly. I love it when she moans in pleasure.

But when her stomach expresses other desires, my salacious plans are thwarted and I can't help but laugh.

"Why does that always happen at the good part?" she complains as I laugh.

Patting her hip, I grab her hand and sit us both up. "Come on. Let's get my woman fed."

"I hope you brought hot dogs." She runs her fingers through her hair, trying to smooth down the wayward strands. It doesn't work, which I love. Reminds me that I'm the one who messed it up in the first place.

Flipping the basket open, I figure out quickly where the spilled wine ended up. "Oh shit. Everything is sticky." She leans over to see what I'm complaining about as I start pulling dinner out.

Dinner that's covered in ants.

"Oh shit. Babe, don't touch that."

She snatches her hand back to her chest like she's been burned. "Why? What's wrong."

Using the lantern to see inside the basket, I curse. "Son of a bitch. There are ants everywhere."

"Are you serious?" She sticks her head so far over, I can't see into the basket anymore. "How does this shit always happen to us? We haven't been here that long?"

"I guess the ants like your favorite wine as much as you do. They followed it straight to the goods." I make a face as I find most of our dinner devoured. "Hop up. Let's shake everything out."

Instead of spending the next ten minutes eating or making out, both equally enticing ideas at this point, we beat out the quilt and empty the basket of all the ruined food. Now I understand why Elena springs for the zip baggies instead of the cheapy fold over ones I use. Maybe dinner would have been saved if I wasn't such a cheapskate.

And I still can't figure out how those bastards got into the Tupperware container of strawberries.

Once it's all cleaned out and most of the colony has moved on—thanks to us throwing their meal out in the forest where they can eat without being disturbed—we're left with half a bottle of wine, one turkey and cheese sandwich, and a whole lot of trash.

"That didn't work out as planned," I say with my hands on my hips, trying to decide if it's worth making myself comfortable on our blanket again or if we should call it a night. "Remind me never to take you camping."

She shrugs, settling herself on the ground. I guess we're staying. "I'm more of a glamper anyway."

"Glamping, huh?" I settle down next to her again and hand her the sandwich. "Like a suped-up RV set up in the woods?"

"Uh, no." She takes half the sandwich and hands it back to me. "Like a fully-loaded cabin with bathrooms and A/C on the outskirts of a town that has real restaurants for nourishment."

I chuckle and take a bite of my half of dinner. "Noted."

We eat in silence for the twelve seconds it takes to get through our remaining food, but we never take our eyes off each other.

"What?" I finally ask. "Why are you looking at me that way?"

"You're a good man, Greg."

I smile sheepishly and my face feels hot like I'm blushing. It's not uncommon for her to compliment me, but somehow being all alone like this makes it feel more personal. And she's not done.

"Tonight solidified it for me."

I laugh. "Our picnic basket is empty, our dinner has been ransacked, and I barely got to second base. Tonight is bordering on tragic."

She throws her head back, letting out a hearty laugh. "But when tragedy strikes, you give up your sandwich for me. I'd say that makes you a keeper."

I smile as I inhale the last tiny bite. If a crappy turkey and cheese sandwich makes me a hero in her book, my future is looking secure.

CHAPTER Fifteen

Elena

"What do you mean he uses the fold-over baggies instead of Ziploc? What kind of a monster is he?"

I shoot her a dubious look implying she is being way overdramatic about how Greg stores his food.

"Focus on the important part, Callie," I scold. "He spilled. The. Wine."

"I was trying to forget that part. Party fouls are too traumatic to think about." She snatches a box of Twinkies from one of the bags and breaks open the package. Junk food is much more our speed on Saturday playdates. "What's with all the plastic grocery bags full of food, anyway? Are you making us eat all the leftover crap that's about to rot in your fridge?"

I wish I could be offended at the comment, but she pretty much has me nailed. "I haven't had time to go to the store. Be glad for what we have. Here," I hand her a knife and a bunch of half rotten bananas. "Cut these up and throw the good parts in this bowl. Maybe we can trick the kids into thinking it's part of a fruit salad."

"It's only bananas."

"Have you met our kids?" We look over and see Fiona pushing Max, Christopher, and Peyton on an old-school metal merry-go-round, circa 1979. Not sure why the city hasn't taken it out yet, since I'm sure it gives anyone who uses it during the summer first degree burns, but at least it keeps the kids happy.

Until Christopher loses his grip and goes flying off it, landing in the dirt. The girls all giggle as he shakes it off, and runs to jump back on.

I glance back at Callie who shrugs in response. "Point made. We don't have the brightest bulbs in the bunch."

"Is it any surprise? Look at who we mated with."

We both laugh at my quick wit as we finish setting things up.

"Seriously, Elena?" She holds up the stack of red Solo cups and half a 2-liter of Diet Sprite. "Tell me this isn't left over from the last birthday party at your place."

I screw up my face, trying to come up with some sort of witty explanation. Eh. Who cares. It is what it is.

"It's what I had. Between my mom getting sick, Greg watching Max, work, and everything else going on, I haven't had the time. Besides, it's so much more cost effective to get rid of what I have instead of letting it go bad."

She takes a sip of the drink she just poured and makes a wry face. "Too late. This stuff is totally flat."

"They won't care. All they'll know is its sugar water."

"I hope you brought something different for us."

Holding up two 16-ounce bottles of Dr. Pepper, our favorite unhealthy beverage, I flash her a triumphant smile. "I had to get gas on the way here, so I grabbed some adult beverages."

"I'd hardly call these adult beverages," she quips as she snatches one out of my hand and twists off the top. "But I'm not complaining." Taking a big gulp and following it up with a contented sigh, she adds, "The only way this would be better is if it was a fountain drink from Buc-ee's. They have the best carbonated water to syrup ratio."

"Mmmm...." I respond, getting excited over the thought of visiting our favorite truck stop. "One of these days, we're making a road trip to Madisonville to buy some Beaver Nuggets."

"We really should do our Christmas shopping there this year."

To anyone outside of Texas, the idea of grocery shopping at a truck stop would sound foreign. But Buc-ee's is like no other place out there. It's like the Neimann Marcus of truck stops. Not only do they have the largest and cleanest restrooms you have ever seen in your life, they have a huge deli that specializes in everything from sandwiches and grill items, to fudge and pastries. And their gift section rivals any boutique store in the country. I have bought more than one baby gift in the children's section of that place.

And yes, I said children's section. As in, there is more than one section of gifts and goods to choose from. It really is a one-stop-shop of unique and quirky present ideas.

"Sounds good to me. When we get home, we can look at our calendars and block out a day when James has the girls and you don't have any parties."

Callie throws all the discarded banana peels in one of the now empty plastic bags. There is probably more rotten banana being tossed than there is good banana to eat, but at least they didn't totally go to waste. I'm tired of spending a hundred bucks a year so I can watch the ripening process as it happens on my counter.

"Why don't you see if Greg can watch them that day?" She makes a face as one of the rotten parts squishes on her finger. "Seems like you guys have been trading off a lot lately." She gestures toward Peyton who is happily picking flowers next to a wrestling Max and Christopher.

"Yeah, Libby decided she had to work all weekend, so she dumped Pey off with him."

Callie holds up her hand, looking confused. "She has a job?"

"Supposedly. She won't give Greg a straight answer about where she's working, and I'm not sure he really cares beyond curiosity anyway."

"Maybe she's a stripper," Callie spouts off as she combines the remnants of three different bags of chips into another bowl. That's three more things I won't have to bring home to my pantry.

"I thought of that. But knowing Libby, she thinks she's too good to be a stripper." I shrug. "Maybe she's a high-priced escort."

Callie munches on a chip and thinks for a second. "I wonder how much escorts really make. And if they really do have to put out."

I laugh. "I'll be sure to ask her next time I run into her."

"I triple dog dare you."

Dropping the handful of leftover ketchup packets that have been saved up over the years onto the picnic table, I gape at her. "You can't just skip to triple dog dare! You have to start with a regular dare!"

"No way, man. I know you too well. I'll have to challenge up every time you see her and it could be months before I get my answer."

"Selfish, selfish woman," I grumble.

"No, smart, smart BFF," she brags. "Speaking of Peyton's parental units, where is Greg anyway? How come you have Peyton?"

Things are finally set up enough that I can pull out the main entrée... hot dogs. Of course, even when I don't have time to go grocery shopping, I always have extra hot dogs on hand. Based on Callie's non-reaction, this is not surprising to anyone.

"He had to coach a meet today. I don't know if another coach got sick or what, but he had to leave at six-thirty this morning to get there on time."

Callie waggles her eyebrows. "So I guess you had a slumber party last night?"

I raise one eyebrow in return. "I never kiss and tell."

"Liar."

"I know."

"I wanna know about this slumber party."

"And I want you to call the kids for lunch."

She climbs off the bench with a groan. "You're such a slave driver." But she does it anyway.

Just like I had planned, ok, fine, like I had *hoped*, the kids are perfectly content with hot dogs, mixed chips, half rotten bananas, and flat Diet Sprite. We call it a "mish-mosh" lunch and they are so entertained by the word "mish-mosh", they keep giggling while they eat, which is making Callie and I giggle, too.

Until a familiar voice shows up.

"Hi Callie. Elena," Deborah says in greeting, a tight look on her face.

This is the first time we have run into each other since the incident I call "Doomsday Playdate." She looks nervous, which is not something I've ever seen on her face. The only thing I've ever seen on her face is a smile, or a scowl. And possible a speck of Brie during the RowRow party at her house, after she "dropped" the plate full of cheese on the counter.

But this anxiety is different and, dare I say, the most honest I've ever seen her be. Trevor must feel her nerves, as he's hiding behind her legs.

It makes me kind of sad that her poor son, who had such a hard time making friends with my girls, has already lost his nerve with our kids. And dammit, if that doesn't make me feel guilty about cutting off that relationship so abruptly.

"Hi, Deborah."

"Deborah," Callie and I address her simultaneously.

Deborah clears her throat. "I didn't expect to see you guys here."

"We come every Saturday," Callie explains, and I watch Deborah's face fall as she realizes she's been uninvited to our playdates.

And the guilt piles on.

Well, hell.

"Oh," Deborah utters sadly, nodding her head like she understands why we wouldn't want her around.

The kids keep munching away, staying unusually quiet. They're either picking up on the tension surrounding them, or they're really enjoying their mish-mash. It must be the food. I made it with love.

#sarcasm

"So, um, I wanted to apologize," Deborah utters, shocking Callie and I both.

We look at each other, Callie's drink bottle frozen halfway to her mouth.

She clears her throat and puts the bottle down on the table. "What exactly are you apologizing for?"

Deborah nervously bites her lip before responding. "For the way I treated you, Elena."

I have to give her credit. I never expected for Deborah to speak to me again, let alone apologize. I admit, my respect for her has shot up several notches because she had the guts to approach us.

"What do you mean?" I question. I know what she means, but I want to hear her explanation. Maybe there's something I'm missing and some reason I need to forgive and forget.

She sniffs and glances around the park, avoiding eye contact. "My husband says I'm really judgmental and…" she glances at the kids and lowers her voice before saying, "…witchy."

My lips quirk to the side. The only little ears she's protecting are Trevor's. And maybe her own.

"He points it out all the time. I really don't mean to be, it's just…" She shifts on her feet, biting her lip again and wringing her hands in front of her. Now half the kids are watching the awkward display in front of them like it's their own personal dinner theater. "My mom was really, really strict with public impressions. I couldn't do anything, go anywhere without an outfit, full make-up, and my hair done. Not even the doctor's office when I was sick. She always used to say the way you present yourself is the most important thing."

"Your first impression isn't the problem, Deborah," I point out.

She nods. "I know. But sometimes when we're with other people, especially people I don't know, it makes me really anxious to think about who is going to overhear a lewd comment or think I'm not classy enough because of who I'm with."

"So I'm not classy enough for you," I challenge, and she winces.

"That's not what I mean," she quavers. "It's not that you're not classy enough. It's that you don't care what people think of you. I admire that so, so much. I wish I could be like that. But the anxiety I feel sometimes about being perfect is almost crippling."

Glancing over at Callie, I see her sitting back, letting Deborah say her piece and letting me decide how to handle the situation. Not that I have any idea what to do. But knowing Deborah feels that bad about herself makes me sad.

"I didn't mean to make you think I was judging you, Elena." Tears glisten in her eyes and I realize how hard this conversation is for her. "In my mind, I was reminding you to be the best version of yourself while we were here."

"But that's not what it felt like."

"I know." Her voice is so quiet I have to lean in to hear her. "And I'm sorry. I really like you guys and wish we could be friends, but I understand why you wouldn't want to be around me. I hope if we see you out here again, you'll let Trevor play with your kids. I want him to grow up to be more like them than like me."

Well, hell. If a mother's plea for friends for her child isn't enough to warrant letting this go, I don't know what is.

I take a breath and look at Callie who is smiling. She knows my heart and knows what I need to forgive people boils down to one word... remorse. And damn it all, if Deborah didn't take full responsibility for her own actions.

Leaning forward on my elbows, I look her straight in the eye. She looks sad, remorseful, and a little bit scared.

"What I like about you, Deborah, is your smile. You bring this joy into the room wherever you go."

She blinks back her tears, shock evident on her face.

"But then you ruin it by worrying what people are thinking about you. You completely miss that you make such an amazing first impression."

"Really?" she murmurs. "You really think that about me?"

I nod. "I absolutely do. So, here's what's going to happen."

Callie chuckles but we ignore her as we work out the boundaries of our own friendship.

"You and Trevor are going to join us for lunch, and then we're going to let the kids play together while we sit here and enjoy the adult interaction."

"Ok," she agrees quickly, wiping a lone tear off her cheek.

"And every time you start that judgmental crap again, I'm going to call you out. I spent a lot of time learning how to be ok with myself and who I am, I'm not going to let you unravel it."

"And I don't want to," she practically pleads. "I like you the way you are."

"And you're going to learn to like yourself the way you are, too. Got it?"

The tears are flowing freely now as she sits down in an empty spot, Trevor sitting down next to her. Callie and I hand them each a hot dog and pass over the bowls of chips and browning bananas.

As she fixes a plate for herself and her son, the smile she normally wears, the genuine one that expresses her happiness, crosses her face. Trevor even seems lighter as the children begin to chatter again, seemingly aware that the show is over.

Well, almost.

"I assume you guys said the blessing before we sat down?" Deborah challenges.

I give her a hard glare and she winces.

"I did it again, didn't I?"

"You did."

"Sorry."

"It's ok." And just to prove that I can accept her for her flaws if she can accept mine, I hand her the olive branch I never thought I'd ever give…

"Can I borrow your hand sanitizer?"

Her responding grin practically lights up the playground.

Yep. Forgiving her was definitely the right thing to do.

And just like that, our weekly playdates expand by two.

CHAPTER Sixteen

Elena

"Good morning, Elena."

The deep timber of his voice startles me out of my focused thoughts causing me to whack my foot on the overflowing recycle box under my desk.

"Ouch!" I call out, immediately reaching to rub my stubbed toe.

Tripp's eyes widen. "Oh my gosh, Elena, I'm so sorry. I didn't mean to make you jump."

Examining my throbbing appendage, I curse myself under my breath for wearing sandals today instead of something with a covered toe. At least I have an excuse to go shoe shopping. Obviously, these aren't "work appropriate." Yay!

"It's ok," I finally respond, still wincing a bit. "I'm behind on my shredding again." I gesture to the overflowing box. "It's like having a giant brick down here. It's great as an ottoman. Not so good when I kick it."

His handsome face changes from a guilty expression to a panty-dropping smile.

Damn. He really is an attractive man. If only I was fifteen years younger.

Ummm, nope. I think I'd still want Greg.

"You were concentrating really hard." He leans his hard body against my desk, crossing his feet. "What does Principal Windham have you working on today?"

I pull my arms across my chest, stretching my back muscles. Hunching over a computer for long periods of time makes me ache. Yet more proof that I'm not young anymore. "I'm updating everything on the website. Now that the district is changing our email portal, I'm trying to make sure all the teacher's email addresses are current."

"I thought the rollover wasn't happening for another couple of months."

"It's not," I agree. "But I need to get the new information set up while both email addresses still funnel to the same place. Less confusion for the parents that way."

"Ah." He crosses his arms and gets more comfortable. "So you're planning ahead."

"Clearly not since all my paperwork is getting backed up under here," I state, tapping the box again with my uninjured foot.

"You know, if you need help, I'm always willing to stay a little late so we can get it all done." He throws me a smoldering pout. A couple months ago, that look might have made me swoon. But now it doesn't do anything except make me flattered that he thinks I'm fun to flirt with.

As much as I want to bat my eyes at him, even if it's just to keep the fun banter going, I can't seem to do much more than give him a smile that resembles a mother humoring her son.

"As much as I appreciate the offer, you know the shredder is where I get all my inner-office gossip. And I can't miss out on that."

He belts out a sexy, throaty laugh, that does absolutely nothing to turn me on. Seriously. Greg has ruined me.

"And how are the office lovebirds doing anyway?" he inquires, even though he knows I don't usually divulge anyone else's information. This time, however, I'll humor him a bit.

Looking around making sure no one is approaching, I reveal, "Not so loving anymore."

His eyebrows shoot up. "Really. I was wondering if that ass grab was really an accident."

My jaw drops. "She did not!"

"Oh, yes she did," he assures, his body language indicating he's not nearly as traumatized as he pretends to be. "Last week when we were on that field trip. She claims she accidentally brushed up against me while we were getting on the bus, but it felt an awful lot like a full-palmed caress."

I laugh so hard I'm grateful to already be sitting down. "Like she... she..." I can't catch my breath. "... like she caressed your bum?"

"Cupped my behind, complete with a squeeze."

Tears leak out of my eyes, and I can hardly breathe, but I can see him laughing right along with me. Like I said... totally traumatized.

It takes a few seconds to pull myself back together. "I'm so sorry." Waving my hands in front of my eyes, I try to dry up the tears and pull my breathing together. "I can't wait for the rumor mill to start spinning about this."

He groans. "I was doing so good staying out of that web."

"No you weren't." He looks at me quizzically. "Oh please. You can't convince me you haven't noticed the way all the single women around here ogle you."

He twists his lips to the side playfully. "Not all of them."

"Pfft. Name one woman in this building that doesn't start drooling when you do that whole hands-in-your-pockets-pulling-your-pants-tight-over-your-ass move."

His eyebrows shoot up in surprise. "How did you know that was a move?"

"Who doesn't know that's a move?"

Lies, lies and more lies. I had no idea that was a move until Callie told me. But he doesn't need to know that. Interested in him or not, I don't want him to think I'm a complete tool.

"Hmm," he hums in answer, the guttural sound practically vibrating through me. And still... my hormones don't seem to notice. "I thought I was smoother than that."

"Oh, you're smooth," I jest, leaning back in my chair. "Some of us have just been around a while. We know all the moves. We were there when they were invented."

He looks me dead in the eye and lays it on the line. "Is that why you won't go out with me?"

My breath catches. It's been so long since the last time we talked about it, I thought he'd given up on the idea of taking me out.

"Tripp," I interject quietly.

"No, it's ok." He looks down and shrugs. "I know my age is a deterrent."

Placing my hand on his forearm, I set him straight. "It's not your age, Tripp. It's not even mine. I mean, originally I hesitated because I've never been a cougar before." His lips curl up in partial amusement. "But that has nothing to do with it now."

He peers up at me. "Then what is it?"

The door suddenly opens up and a throat clears behind me. Without even turning around, I know who it is. "I already found the love of my life."

Tripp takes stock of Greg standing in front of my desk and then winks my direction. "At least I know it's not about me."

Shooting him a delighted expression, I finish putting him at ease. "Nope. Not at all. My destiny just involves a really hot, scruffy gymnastics coach. But don't give up yet. You'll find her. You have at least fifteen years."

He blows out an exasperated breath. "That's a long time to wait."

"It's worth it. I promise."

Tripp pats my hand and pushes off my desk. "I guess I should head back to my class. My conference period will be over soon and I better be ready for the hooligans to show up."

He turns to walk away, but I stop him. "Hey Tripp, can I give you some advice?"

Looking over his shoulder, he waits for my words of wisdom.

"Don't try to find her in this school. I hear everything and just..." I shake my head and crinkle my nose. "... just trust me."

He chuckles. "Noted." And then he's gone.

Swiveling my chair around, I stand, and I lean over my desk to give my sexy boyfriend a quick peck, loving that his newly grown beard is long enough now to tickle my lips.

"What was that about?" Greg pries, watching through the glass wall as Tripp ventures down the hallway.

"I think I broke my first heart."

Greg chuckles. "Really? How does it feel to be such a vixen?"

I snigger. "Honestly, a little like taking candy from a baby."

"You're not that old."

"No, but he is that young."

"It goes to show how wonderful you are, that even men in their twenties want you."

Chortling, I poke fun at him. "That was really, really cheesy."

His responding grin makes my heart flutter. "But did it earn me brownie points?"

"Always," I tease and lean back in my chair, exaggerating my movements as I cross my legs, making it a point for my skirt to ride up a bit. If the lust in his eyes proves anything, he knows I'm toying with him.

Interesting how a hot twenty-something can try to flirt with me and I don't respond at all. But the second Greg ventures into the room, my inner-siren comes out.

"So, what brings you to my neck of the woods, anyway? Just wanted to see my smiling face, I assume?"

"Of course. But I also thought you might be hungry." He holds up a paper sack I didn't notice before.

"Coney's Island!" I squeal in delight. "How did you know?"

"Don't get too excited," he backtracks as I snatch the bag out of his hand and begin digging through it for the goods. "I got plain foot-long hot dogs."

"That's the best kind," I say, still digging around for more goodies, like ketchup packets. "Never ruin a perfectly good weiner with things like chili and cheese."

He barks a laugh. "Do you even hear yourself talking sometimes?"

Moaning my approval as I take a huge bite, I talk around my lunch. "Not when you've distracted me with presents, I don't." Looking down, I realize how rude I'm being. "Um… you don't want any, do you?"

"No baby," he chuckles. "I would never come between you and your hot dogs."

Winking at him, I continue to devour my food as the principal approaches. "How's it going with the web… Oh! I'm sorry," she declares when she notices Greg. "Are you eating lunch in front of a visitor?"

I wave his direction and take another bite of my hot dog. Not even my boss will distract me from this nitrate-filled goodness. "Ms. Windham, this is my boyfriend Greg."

Her eyes widen and her head cocks in surprise, no doubt wondering how she missed this bit of information that can be shared. Greg takes her reaction in stride and puts his hand out to her.

"It's nice to meet you, Ms. Windham. I've heard great things about you."

She eyes me sardonically. Clearly, she doesn't think I've actually said great things about her. I shrug and say the first thing that comes to mind. "What? I like working with you."

My answer seems to delight her and she turns back to Greg. "Well, I've heard nothing about you, but I guess the grapevine runs swiftly around here. Elena has been wise to keep you to herself." She leans in as if she's telling him a secret. "Some of my teachers aren't known for keeping their hands to themselves."

I gasp. "You heard about the ass-grabbing?"

"From what our bus driver says, dear, it was a full on fondle."

Greg's eyes bounce back and forth between us as we discuss how Tripp's "ego" was stroked last week. When his phone rings, he excuses himself and steps away, mouthing *Libby* my direction.

I nod in understanding and continue listening to my boss as she spouts off about how many times she's had to talk to Maggie Ray's husband on the phone and how I may have to start fielding all her calls. We both know she secretly enjoys it and gets more pleasure out of bitching about it than she ever would if he left her alone. But I humor her and nod in agreement.

All the while, I'm trying to eavesdrop on Greg's conversation when his body language suddenly gets tense.

"Since when?" he demands from across the room, pacing as he listens to her on the other end of the line, Ms. Windham still babbling on.

"Over my dead body," he suddenly bellows, making me still. Even my boss looks over, knowing something is wrong.

"You stay put. I'm coming over and we're gonna talk about this." He presses the end button so hard, I'm grateful he doesn't have an old-school flip-phone or he would have crushed it. As it is, he still might do some serious damage to this one.

"Greg?" I say, not wanting to sound as scared as I suddenly feel, but somehow knowing the rug is about to be pulled out from underneath me. "Wha... what's going on?"

Placing his hands on his hips, he turns to face me, a murderous expression covering his normally jovial face. Then he spits out the words I've been dreading since that first day I found out he had come back.

"Libby. She's moving to Austin."

My whole body runs cold as he turns and hightails it out of the room, and out of the school. For the umpteenth time, I feel like I can't breathe.

Here we go again.

CHAPTER Seventeen

Greg

I am not doing this again.

That's the only thing I can think as I drive to Libby's house, hands gripping the steering wheel so tightly, my knuckles are turning white. The anger is coursing through me and it's taking everything in me to get my breathing under control.

All of this is a game to her, and that infuriates me. My life is not a game. Our child's life is not a game. And I'm tired of her making us the unwitting players just so she can feel like she has some sort of power. She isn't going to uproot my life again. Fuck that. It's not good for me, it's not good for Elena, and it damn well isn't good for my three-year-old daughter.

Screeching to a halt in front of her house, I slam the car door and stalk my way to the door. Before I reach the door, I stop, close my eyes, and take a few deep breaths.

Libby wants me to fly off the handle. She gets some sort of pleasure out of making me crazy with emotion. But if I'm going to get through to her, if I'm going to make a very strong point, I need to calm down.

She will *not* control all our lives anymore.

Pounding on the door, I wait for her to answer, running through all her different excuses in my head while I stand there. She's going to surprise me, no matter what I do, but at least it makes me feel somewhat prepared.

The door finally flies open and Libby stands there, clearly annoyed that I've come over. Her lips are pursed, her hand is on her hip, and her head is cocked like she has better things to do than discuss uprooting our daughter again. So much beauty on the outside. So much ugly on the inside.

"What do you want, Greg?" As she stands in the doorway, I know she's trying to block me from going in, but this conversation isn't happening through the door. Pushing my way past her, she shrieks, "Hey! I didn't invite you in."

"And I didn't ask," I spout off. "Where's Peyton?"

Crossing her arms, she throws me for the first loop. "She's at daycare."

What? "Since when does she go to daycare?"

She rolls her eyes like this is common knowledge and I'm an idiot for not keeping up. "Since always."

"Bullshit. I've been watching her in the mornings when your mother goes to work and she can't find you because you haven't gotten home from partying yet. Where. Is. *My. Daughter*?"

She drops her arms and walks through the open-concept room to the fridge, grabbing a bottle of water. At least it's not a beer. I'll at least give her credit for not normally being a day-drinker.

Taking a swig, her eyes never leave mine. She's drawing this out, not ready to give in to me yet. It's a battle of wills, but I'm not going anywhere until we hash this out. I've got nowhere to be. Except work in a little while, but they can start without me. This is too important.

Finally, she caves. "I told you. She's at daycare. They have a drop-in program, but it doesn't always have availability and I don't always have the money to take her." Her hands go back on her hips. "If you would give me more in child support, I might be able to actually take her regularly so she could get on a routine."

"And if you dropped her off with me in the mornings, since you know full well I don't work until the afternoons, you could save yourself a whole bunch of money."

Daggers shoot out of her eyes. She was expecting me to be emotional and possibly irrational, not lob rational ideas back at her today. And the last thing she wants is for me to spend more time with Peyton. My daughter is my weakness. Keep me from my child, and I'm crippled. Libby knows that and loves to exploit it.

It's all more games. How did I not see all this crap before now?

There is nothing I won't do for Peyton. But I won't follow along behind Libby blindly anymore. Peyton needs to see what a strong man is like. What putting your child's needs above your own means. What loving your child more than you love yourself is all about.

Crossing my arms over my chest, I brace for the showdown that's about to begin. "Now, what in the hell is this crap about you moving to Austin."

"I got a job."

"Where," I demand. I'm through with asking her things. From now on, we shoot straight or not at all.

"At Dell."

"Doing what."

She slams the water bottle down on the counter. "It's not your fucking business, asshole."

"It *is* my fucking business," I yell, taking one step toward her. "You don't have a degree in anything that has to do with computers so my guess is you got an entry level job in the call center. Yet here we are, in a town ripe with call centers that don't require you to take my daughter away from me!" I roar, and she actually takes a step back.

Briefly, very briefly, I think we might be making some headway, but she pulls herself together quickly.

"I don't have to justify anything to you, Pencil Dick." And here we go. She's lowered herself to the name calling, so I know this is about to get nasty. "The mileage limitations in our divorce decree became null-and-void the minute we all moved to San Antonio. And I have physical custody of Peyton so you can't stop me."

She thinks she's got me, but I've been anticipating this move and planning for it for over a year now.

"You gave me a week's notice that you were moving to San Antonio, so you could live with a man you met online."

She rolls her eyes again. "What does that have to do with anything?"

"Whenever I would pick Pey up or drop her off, Aputi would do the hand-off with me because you were too busy playing on your phone, and he can verify this."

She huffs and begins to speak, but I keep going before she can get a word in edgewise.

"Less than a year later, you up and moved back home because things got too 'hard'." I throw up the air quotes, to add insult to injury.

She blanches as I continue pointing out her flaws.

"You were falling-down drunk at Peyton's birthday party."

Another step towards her. This time, she steps back.

"Your mother drops the child off with me most mornings on her way to work because you aren't home yet from a job you supposedly have, but no one can verify. A job that causes you to work overnights which severely limits your career choices and makes a lot of people have a lot of questions about what kind of business you're actually in."

"What are you implying?" she whispers.

"What I'm telling you is that you. Are. Not. Moving." A strange sense of calm comes over me, knowing I've got her right where I want her.

"I have a job there, Greg."

"Decline the offer. I guarantee you haven't even begun the search for employment in this area. But let me make this clear."

She swallows hard, waiting for me to drop the ax.

"I'm not playing this game with you anymore. You're not going to uproot Peyton on a whim and mess with all of our lives."

"It's my life, too."

"No!" I bellow. "If you even pack one box, I will file for full physical custody so fast your head will spin."

She gapes at me, but I'm not done.

"I've been documenting for two years, and I will sue under the grounds that your home is an unstable environment for a child. Don't. Push. Me."

"No judge would remove a child from her mother!" she screams at me. But I call bullshit.

"No judge would hesitate with the amount of evidence I have against you and all the character witnesses I can call. And I *will* call them."

It's clear she knows I'm serious. So she switches tactics. Tears begin to flow down her cheeks. "You would take a child way from her mother? How could you do something like that to her?"

"I will do anything to make sure she is healthy, happy, and has both parents in her life. Even if it means forcing your hand. And let me remind you of something," one more step forward, strictly for emphasis purposes, "if I win custody, *when* I win custody, not only will your child support cut off, but *you'll* have to pay *me*."

The truth of my words runs across her face momentarily making her pale, but in true Libby fashion, she recovers quickly. Steeling her spine, she pulls up to her full height and glares at me.

"Get out of my house."

With a menacing smirk, I step back. "I'm glad we understand each other. See you tomorrow for the hand-off."

I turn and stalk out the door, closing it gently behind me.

I got her. She knows it. I know it. And it's done. The ball is in her court, but if she pushes me there will be a fight. And it feels good.

Smiling, I climb in my car, turning the ignition and put it into drive.

Now to head back to Elena and begin my future.

CHAPTER Eighteen

Elena

"Angie knew she wo... would... wouldn't feel better," Maura sounds out the words as she reads her newest easy reader book, *Green, Green, Go Away*, all about a little girl that hates the color green.

It's like the author wrote about Max and new her aversion to yellow. I have no idea why she suddenly decided "it's yucky", but I've given up making macaroni and cheese for lunch now.

"She was so mad. She *hated* green and would *nev...* never like it. Angie kept think...ing... thinking, 'Green, green, go away. Don't come back another day.'"

Stroking Maura's blond curls, I try to concentrate on the story and help her when she gets stuck, but my mind is on other things.

It's been almost eight hours since Libby dropped the bomb via cell phone, and I've gotten one text from Greg. *One.* And all it said was "It's under control. We'll talk soon."

Obviously, we have different definitions of the word soon.

"What's that word, Mama?" Maura points her little finger at the colorful page.

"Occurred," I answer, trying to re-engage my brain to the task at hand. "It suddenly occurred…"

"It suddenly occurred to her that green might be lis… listen… listening," she reads. For a six-year-old, Maura is really advancing with her reading skills. I have to give it to her teacher, Mrs. Robinson. She's done an amazing job taking my child, the one who prefers to play dress up and doing hair to any form of learning, and finding the kinds of books that catch her interest. No wonder she's the most requested first grade teacher in our school.

With her eyes beginning to droop, Maura finishes her chapter and I gently pull the book out of her hands. "It's time for sleep, my princess." She snuggles down into the covers, and falls asleep right in the middle of her nighttime prayers.

Sneaking out of her room, I take a quick peek at Max, who is out like a light on her tummy, butt up in the air like she's still a baby. And then I pull my phone out of my pocket.

Still nothing.

I have to keep reminding myself that I trust Greg. I really do. But Libby is a loose cannon and it's her I don't trust. She has no interest in doing what's best for anyone but herself, and even that's debatable. What if he can't convince her to stay? What if she takes Peyton again? Will he follow her this time? And can I possibly survive losing him again?

Sighing in resignation, I walk into Fiona's room. She's powering through her first Harry Potter novel and loving it, so it's been a struggle getting the book out of her hands at night for the last couple of weeks.

"Ok, baby cakes. It's time to shut it down."

In an uncharacteristic move, she immediately obeys, marking her spot with a bookmark and closes the book. Then she reaches her arms up for a hug. "Why are you sad, Mommy?" she whispers into my neck.

Her words surprise me. I thought I was pretty good at hiding my distress from my kids. I guess not.

"What makes you think I'm sad?" Pulling her tighter, I inhale the scent of her kids' shampoo. It reminds me that the most important part of the equation isn't the adults. It's the kids. I need that reminder.

"Your eyes look sad. Like they did when Greg moved away. Is he moving away again?"

Wow. My very astute daughter put that together easily, didn't she?

Pulling back, I begin the process of tucking her in for the night, being very careful with my words. "I don't think we have to worry about that, baby," I say, straddling the line between lying and protecting her from a reality I'm unsure of at this point. "He just moved in next door. It takes a long time to sell a house, so he can't really go anywhere, right?"

She nods, but doesn't look convinced. Yeah, me neither, kid. Me neither.

"Why don't you say your prayers, ok?"

"Ok, Mommy." She folds her hands and closes her eyes. "Dear God, thank you for the day. And thank you for Mommy and Daddy and Maura and Max. And I guess thank you for Keri because I have to say that."

I stifle a giggle. Maura may think their step-mom is the best thing since sliced bread, but Fiona still isn't convinced.

"And please, please don't make Greg move again. I love him and I love Peyton and I miss them when they're gone. Amen."

It breaks my heart that my sweet sensitive girl is worried about something I can neither confirm nor deny. I wish I could do something to make her feel better, but until I have information, there's nothing I can say. We're all stuck in limbo. So I do what I can do—I kiss her on the head, my lips lingering for longer than normal as I silently request that her prayers are answered.

A final tuck of the blanket, some "I love you's," and a flip of the light switch, and I'm alone with my thoughts, no longer using the kids as a distraction from my own personal fears.

Keeping myself busy seems like the best course of action. Not only because things like a final load of laundry needs to be put way and last-minute dishes need to be clean. No, I'm trying to keep my thoughts from going out of control. But, try as I might, it doesn't work.

I keep thinking about how it felt when Greg moved away last time. I understood, then. I really did. It was so, so painful, but he'd made the right decision for Peyton. She needed her father and going with her was the only way to do that.

This time feels different, though. This time, he's setting a precedent for the future. Will he continue to follow Libby every time she moves on a whim? Will he face his own fears and fight her back? Will he figure out a way to stay? Is it important enough for him to stay with me?

Am I that important to him?

Rationally, I know none of these decisions have anything to do with me. We aren't married. We aren't even engaged.

Until he proposes, we have separate lives that overlap, they don't intertwine. But I trusted that he wouldn't hurt me again. I trusted that he was done with Libby's games. Now I'm questioning all of that. And it all boils down to one issue.

I just don't think I'm strong enough to lose Greg again.

Sure, I can function for my kids. I can even function for myself. But my heart would be closed off for good. There's no way I could open myself up to that kind of heartache again. Ever.

Not even if Greg came back.

Finally, *finally*, my phone dings with an incoming text, right as I'm closing the dishwasher and drying off my hands. It's him.

Are you up?

Trying to sound calmer than I am, I respond.

Me: *It's 9:30. Of course I'm up, goofball.*

Greg: *I don't want to knock and wake up the girls. Let me in? Please?*

Approaching the door, I take one last deep breath and remind myself there is nothing to worry about until there is. I need to have an update before I jump to any conclusions.

But then the door opens, revealing the man I love more than life itself. Suddenly, the anxiety I've fought all day long combined with him looking tired and disheveled are overwhelming, and I dissolve into a puddle of tears.

He reaches for me, pulling me into his safe embrace and holds me while I cry, murmuring words of reassurance and stroking my hair. I barely hear what he's saying, focusing on my breathing and his scent.

When the tears finally stop, he pulls back, cupping my face in his hands, gently wiping the tears away with his thumbs. "Why are you crying, baby?"

"Why didn't you call me?"

His shoulders drop. "It's been a really, really long day. Two of my coaches called in sick, so I had to cover every single class."

"You weren't avoiding me?" It comes out like a question because I'm still reeling from all the pent-up emotion. It makes sense that he wouldn't have time to contact me if people called in sick, but I'm still in that stage where I need lots of clarification.

His eyes widen. "Oh god, no! That's why I sent that text. I didn't want you to worry. I think I had a total of ten minutes at my desk today, and that's only because the office manager forced a pen in my hand to sign paychecks. I still haven't even opened my emails."

"Oh." My eyes are downcast, but my hands are clinging to the front of his shirt, his arms still wrapped around me. I want so badly to ask what happened with Libby, but I'm still so afraid, the words won't come out. Thankfully, he knows the wait is killing me.

"Before I say anything else, I need you to hear me. Elena, look at me." He tilts my chin up with the tip of his finger, looking me in the eye. "No one is moving." My breath hitches. "You hear me? We are *not* moving."

My entire body sags and I feel like I can breathe again. "Really?"

"Really," he confirms again. "Even if Libby goes, I'm staying."

"But Peyton—"

He cuts me off. "I threatened to file for custody."

Well doesn't that make my eyes blink fast as I wrap my brain around what he just said.

"After I got that phone call, I went straight to her house to confront her. Told her I was done playing her games and if she even thinks about moving, I'll file for full custody, citing an unstable home environment."

"You did?"

He nods. "Sure did. I told you I've been jotting down notes when things didn't sit right for the last couple of years. But since we went to San Antonio, I've been documenting everything. And I called Aputi today."

I look around, wracking my brain, trying to remember the name. Then it hits me. "The ex-boyfriend from San Antonio."

"Yep." He clasps his arms tighter around me, forcing my hands up and over his shoulders. "Do you remember how he told me about his daughter moving away from him?"

"Vaguely."

"It hurt him really, really deeply. And as much as he really liked Libby, he always recognized she wasn't exactly doing right by Peyton. I think it may have brought up a lot of old hurts for him or something. Maybe that's why he was so good to Peyton. I don't know." He shakes his head like he's refocusing his thoughts. "Anyway, he's usually a pretty chill guy. But when I talked to him today, he said the one thing he hates more than anything is a mother using the child to get back at the father. And that he'd testify on my behalf if it comes down to it. Even if it makes Libby hate him."

I gape at him. Documenting behavior is one thing. Having an ex-boyfriend testify against you changes everything.

"And she knows that? Libby knows Aputi would testify?"

"She knows. I think that's what finally made her realize how serious I am. But just to make sure, as soon as I left, I put in a call to my attorney."

"What did he say?"

He smirks in victory. "Let's just say Libby will be receiving a strongly worded letter regarding my intensions, should she push me. In case she doesn't believe me."

I am floored. Like, lay me out, step over me, I am not moving, floored. I knew he had it in him to stand up to her, but I never realized he would shut her down so easily and efficiently. Assuming Libby knows he's serious and doesn't keep pushing the issue. But even then, there is no longer any doubt in my mind that he would immediately sue for custody if it came down to it. There's also no doubt in my mind he would win.

My thoughts go into overdrive, thinking about how that would work in the future. Obviously, that would mean babysitting her every night while he finishes up at the gym, but I love Peyton like she's one of my own. There wouldn't be any complaints from me. Greg and I are a team.

He kisses me sweetly on the eyes, distracting my revelry, as if he's kissing the last of my doubts away. "Are you alright? I know it's a lot to process."

I smile, eyes still closed, enjoying the peace that comes with knowing everything is going to be ok. No... that's not right. It already *is* ok.

Pulling him down to me, I kiss him gently on the lips, hoping to convey my relief and my love and my acceptance of his situation. His big hands go back to my cheeks, holding me in place as the kiss goes deeper.

"I love you, Elena," he maintains, never taking his lips off mine. "Just know, someday, I'm going to marry you."

My face breaks out into a joyful grin and I don't bother putting a filter on my words. "I would love nothing more than to marry you. But before you decide that, you need to know one thing."

"What's that?" he asks in between kisses.

"I'm not having another baby." Indicating toward my belly, I continue with, "This shop is closed."

"No way," he agrees with a chuckle. "I already have four weddings to pay for. We're not having another and risking walking down the aisle a fifth time. That would be my luck."

"Wait… you're planning to pay for my girls' weddings, too?" I can't help the wide smile now. He's not only charming. I know he's being truthful, so of course I'm swooning again.

He shrugs like it's no big deal. "I love them. They're my girls. All four of you are. I want to take care of all of you and make you happy."

"You already do," I say, kissing him again. "You already do."

Epilogue

Five years later

Greg was right when he said he was going to marry me. Less than a year after he bought the house next door, we gave up trying to do things on the society-approved timeline and went for it. We knew we were going to be together forever and raise our girls as one big happy family anyway. What was the point in delaying the inevitable?

Best decision we ever made.

Planning a wedding while working and raising children seemed like such a daunting task, we opted to celebrate the way we do it best… with a backyard barbeque. It was basically all the same people who come to all the birthday parties anyway. They just all dressed in their Sunday best and a florist set up white flowers everywhere.

The one hitch we ran into wasn't much of a surprise. Greg warned us that Christopher would be a loose cannon as a ring bearer and it was probably a better idea to keep the rings in his pocket than actually put that child in charge of the jewelry.

He was right.

I guess Christopher got bored as he was waiting to walk down our makeshift aisle. As soon as his foot hit the back patio, he took off running, threw the pillow right at Greg's face, and then climbed to the top of the play scape. I mean, all the way to the top. At the peak of the fort, one foot on each side of the roof.

My matron of honor spent my wedding standing underneath the structure so she could break her son's fall if needed. No judgement here. We all agree, broken necks and mini-tuxedos don't go well together. There's no way to get your money back if a penguin suit has to be cut off in the ER and those deposits aren't cheap.

A caterer put the final touches on the party, providing an amazing hot dog bar, complete with all the fixings you could ever imagine, and weiners cooked to perfection. Greg fed me the first one, wedding-cake style, and didn't even smash it on my face.

He's so romantic.

I became Mrs. Greg Brady that day, a fact Callie never seems to let go of. And honestly, with as many kids as run around here, the last name seems perfectly fitting.

In the shock of all shocks, and I say that sarcastically, James and Keri broke up shortly after Greg and I got married when she found out he was cheating on her. Part of me wanted to roll my eyes that she was so shocked a man who got engaged to her while he was married to someone else could suddenly fall out of love with her. The other part of me cheered when she took him for half of everything he had. Which was half of what he started with when *we* got divorced. So now he has a quarter of everything he started with.

You'd think he would learn his lesson. Nope. He's already married to someone else. That's wife number three. So far. Good luck, dude.

We actually don't hear from James very often. He stopped picking up the girls on his scheduled weekends a couple years ago and only shows up every once in a while. Like when he's showing off what a good dad he is for his new wife. At first, it was hard on all the girls. Especially on Fiona. She has the most memories of him so I know, at a minimum, she's disappointed in who he turned out to be. I do, however, suspect Maura is more affected than she usually lets on, but the girls have an amazing therapist who reassures me that everything they're feeling is appropriate and they're open with her about their feelings and are incorporating healthy ways of coping with their grief. It also helps that Greg does an amazing job as a stand-in father. But they've always loved him, so it doesn't surprise me at all. It also helps that we got custody of Peyton.

Yep. She lives with us full time now. Libby started dropping Peyton off more and more because she was "busy" or "had to work." We didn't mind at all. In fact, we encouraged it. Our home was the most stable environment Peyton had and the more she could be surrounded by normalcy, the better off she was. Eventually we had enough documentation that we went ahead and filed for full physical custody. Libby fought it at first, but when her own mother agreed it was best for Peyton, she went ahead and signed off on the change. She also raised holy hell about losing her child support, but we never once heard her complain about losing her daughter. It was a huge sign that we did the right thing, even though it was stressful and expensive.

Many, many times over the years, Greg and I have laid in bed, discussing how we found these losers and how the hell they fooled us into marrying them. Clearly, they are terrible people. So we're either really stupid or they are very good at showing different sides of themselves depending on the situation. Welcome to the age of entitlement and narcissistic behaviors. Ain't it grand?

"Mo-OOOOOM!!"

Greg winces as Fiona's shrieking voice bounces around the room. I slap his hand away from the bowl of chips I just poured, but he's determined.

"Those are for the party," I remind him as he finally gets one and pops it in his mouth.

"If I have to put up with a dozen teenagers tonight, I get to snack on their food. Even trade."

We look over when Fiona comes storming in the room, stopping to put her hands on her hips and shoot us a glare. "Why are there nine-year-olds at my party?" she demands in that tone all thirteen-year-olds have. "This is a boy/girl party for teenagers only. So why are they here?"

"Because they live here," I respond. "And you can't kick them out of their house."

She huffs. "Can you at least kick them out of the garage? They don't need to be at my party." She looks down at our hands, Greg's still clasped in mine, his arms still wrapped around my waist. Crinkling her nose, she adds, "And can you stop, like, doing that?"

"Doing what?" Greg asks innocently and begins kissing his way down my neck. "Kissing your mother? No can do. Her kisses are too sweet."

Fiona turns and tramps away mumbling, "You guys are disgusting," under her breath. The whole thing makes me laugh. He loves embarrassing her.

"You do realize she's the least-dramatic of the bunch," I say, as I pull away to grab the hot pads and pull the pigs-in-a-blanket out of the oven. "Once the others start going through puberty, we are totally screwed."

"And I will have fun embarrassing them with our acts of love. Ow, that's hot," he blurts out, dropping the croissant and shaking out his fingers. Serves him right for grabbing food straight off the cookie sheet before it has a chance to cool.

Before I can reprimand him for stealing more party food, a booming voice calls from the front door. "Is that dinner I smell?"

Aputi rounds the corner and kisses me on the cheek, handing me a platter of freshly made taquitos.

Yes, Aputi. He's been the most surprising addition to our fold.

Right before we got married, as we were trying to figure out what to do with Greg's house, he got a call from Aputi. Turns out, his daughter lived in the area and didn't want to stay with her mother anymore. In her full-blown teenage years, the two of them weren't getting along and she wanted to get to know her dad better. Of course, Aputi jumped at the chance to raise Amber for the few remaining years of her childhood and decided the best course of action was to move here so his daughter could still be close to her mom.

In that moment, we became rental property owners and it's turned out great having them live next door. Not only is his daughter, Amber, our favorite babysitter, the love of Aputi's life was practically around the corner. Her name is Deborah.

Yes, *that* Deborah. As it turns out, the uptight, high strung, half-crazy woman who ended up divorced when her husband decided she was too OCD for his taste, is the perfect match to this quiet, huge, intimidating Samoan dude. He calms her crazy. She takes care of him. They *adore* each other and it's ridiculously cute to watch.

"Thanks," I remark, putting the platter next to the rest of the food. "Where's Deborah?"

"She's cooking the rest of the taquitos and trying to get Trevor off the Xbox." He snatches a handful of chips out of a bowl, eliciting a glare from me that he completely ignores. "She'll be here in about ten."

"You didn't want to wait for her?"

An ornery smile crosses his face. "I'd rather be here to see the fireworks when Christopher shows up."

"Christopher is coming?!?" Fiona screeches again.

Greg immediate rubs his ear with his finger, a grimace across his face. "Weren't you just in the other room? I need to attach some bells to your shoes. You're getting too sneaky as you age."

Fiona completely ignores Greg, too busy staring me down. I look back at her like she's being ridiculous. "Of course, Christopher is coming. This may be your first girl/boy party," I chide as a shove the bowl of chips in her hand to take out to the garage, "but this is our family."

She stomps her feet, some sort of garbled half yell/half scream coming out of her mouth before she turns on her heel, flipping her hair over her shoulder in a huff as she leaves.

Aputi looks over at Greg. "This is gonna be a fun few years."

"At least she's not dating yet," he responds, patting Aputi on the shoulder. "Hope you're enjoying that."

Aputi groans. "Don't remind me. It took everything in me not to pound the shit out of the loser Amber brought home for dinner the other day."

"Who brought home a loser?" Callie asks, walking in with a giant cake box.

"Amber," Aputi responds.

Callie carefully slides the box onto the counter. "You say that every time she's dating someone new."

"It's true every time she's dating someone new."

The cake box is opened, revealing a two-teared, black and white cake with Fiona's name written in beautiful calligraphy icing, a giant 13 candle at the top. It's beautiful. And over the top. Some things never change.

"Well," she responds, as she steps back and inspects the cake for any flaws that need to be fixed. "Get used to it because she'll probably marry a loser the first time around. Look at all of us."

We all look at each other and kind of shrug like "She's not wrong."

Despite her dig, Callie and Ben are still married and spend most of their time arguing. I'm convinced she gets some sort of sick pleasure out of thinking up creative ways to get him back when he pisses her off. For instance, the time she gradually weaned him off caffeinated coffee all the way to decaf. He kept increasing the number of cups of joe he would drink to make it through the day. Then one day, she added back the full-strength version without telling him. He was strung out and jittery as hell. I'm still not sure how many hours he stayed awake before he finally crashed.

That's when I realized it's all some weird form of foreplay they enjoy, so I stopped even asking about it. Now, when she bitches, I just laugh at the ridiculousness of it all. If it works for them, who am I to judge?

Suddenly, Christopher and Trevor go racing by, Max and Peyton hot on their heels. No telling what they're up to, but judging by Fiona's scream, it's not good. Yet, we're all so used to it, none of the adults even make a move to go investigate.

Christopher is still a death trap waiting to happen. We can't figure out how he hasn't broken any bones yet, but there are wagers floating around our group of friends about concussions and teeth being knocked out. At nine years old, Christopher has been playing pee-wee football for a while and he loves it. I'm convinced he'll play through college and maybe even beyond. Aputi practically foams at the mouth when anyone mentions Christopher's potential.

I look around the room as Deborah walks in and realize, it's all done. We're ready for tonight. All we need now are a dozen teenagers to walk through that door and the party will officially begin.

Suddenly it hits me… I have a teenager. The memories of my own teenage years are so vivid, and that's the stage my daughter is now in.

Wow. It's like her life is just beginning. What a strange revelation.

Greg puts his arm around my shoulder and kisses the top of my head. Whispering in my ear, so as to not interrupt the conversations around us, he asks, "You ok?"

I squeeze my arms around him and nod. "Yeah. Having a moment, I guess." He holds me tighter and we enjoy watching our friends and family laugh and be together.

It's been fun building this big group of friends. I've always had only one or two close-knit people to lean on, so having an entire tribe that helps take care of each other has been an unexpected joy in my life. Five years ago, I wouldn't have expected this.

Rubbing my hands down his stomach, I look up at Greg. He looks back, a contented smile on his face. "I love you, you know?"

His grin only gets bigger. "I know. And I love you, too."

Kissing me, I realize how happy I am in the moment. In my life.

I've still got flab. He's still got abs. I still make him laugh. He's still great at oral.

I had a second chance to find my one great love, and here it is.

And it's a Perfect 10.

THE End

LITTLE MISS *perfect*

HOW DEBORAH AND APUTI CAME TO BE

M.E. CARTER

CHAPTER
One

Deborah

"I... I don't understand."

Rick grabs an armful of socks and underwear from the drawer of our heavy oak dresser that has been passed down through five generations of Miller women. It's been sanded and re-stained a time or two, making it impossible to tell that it's over a hundred years old. The solidity of the wood is obvious when Rick slams the door shut, making a bang that echoes through the room.

"What's not to understand?" Tossing the clothes into a suitcase, he refuses to make eye contact with me. It's been that way since he started packing. I'm not really sure if the lack of eye contact is indicative of guilt or because he's revolted by me. "Our marriage is over. I'm leaving you. The end."

He keeps saying those words, but none of it makes sense. "But why? Is it something I did?"

He snorts an unattractive laugh, which is unlike my very proper husband. A deep chuckle or even a chortle is more his personality. Maybe a haughty laugh. But nothing about this situation even remotely resembles normal behavior for the quiet, placid man I married. "Something you did?" He sounds condescending, but I'm still not clear why. "It's a lot of things you did. And a lot of things you didn't do. I can't take living with your neuroses anymore."

I actually know what he's talking about. He wouldn't be the first person to call me neurotic. Tight-wad. Uppity. OCD. I've been called all of them. None of which is true, at least in the clinical sense. I just like order and lists that can be checked off. Things run like a well-oiled machine when there is a plan that can be adhered to.

Speaking of well-oiled machine, I need to take the SUV in for its three-thousand-mile maintenance.

That can wait. The situation at hand is more important, and figuring out what my husband is so angry about is priority because I'm very confused right now. Rick has never complained about how organized I am before. I thought he appreciated how smoothly our home runs. I'm very quickly finding out I'm wrong, but he's not giving me the answers I need.

"What are you talking about?"

He looks up at the ceiling, seemingly exhausted by my lack of understanding. But really, does he blame me? Up until ten minutes ago, I thought we had the perfect life. The perfect marriage.

Rick is a junior partner at Watson and Sons law firm. He's not a "son" but had an impressive internship, and he was hired over a dozen other final applicants eight years ago. He's on track to become a senior partner at some point, but a few Watsons probably need to retire before that happens.

His generous salary has allowed me to stay home with our son, Trevor, who is arguably the most perfect six-year-old in the world. He's sweet, kind to others, smart, and loves to read. He's every mother's dream for a child and has given me another purpose in my life beyond taking care of my husband.

The three of us live in a wonderful four-bedroom home in one of the more affluent neighborhoods in town. We eat healthy, attend church weekly, and make sure Christmas cards are sent out by December tenth every year. We donate to the ASPCA as well as various local programs for children.

Together, we make a picture-perfect family that the Jones's would be proud of. Which is why this news is so hard to understand.

Finally making eye contact, Rick gives me a look I've never seen before. It's... exasperation. Or maybe frustration. I can't tell. But for the first time since he started packing, I'm starting to think this isn't a bluff. "I can't live in a house that is as spotless as a museum, Deborah. You know how stressful it is to be afraid to track dirt into my own home?"

Blinking rapidly, I try to wrap my thoughts around what he's saying, hoping to figure out a way to fix this. "So, you want more dirt in the house?"

He huffs. "It's not about the amount of dirt, Deb. It's about the amount of effort. There is no relaxing around here. No being real. You know I haven't seen your face without makeup on ever? Not once. Not even since we've been married."

My hand comes to my face. Of course he's never seen me without makeup. Uncovered, he'd see the blemishes I painstakingly conceal every day. Thick, full hair was gifted to me by my mother's genes. Flawless skin was not.

"So you're leaving because of my makeup?"

"You're not understanding me." He slams another drawer after emptying all the crisp, white T-shirts and dumping them into another suitcase. His lack of care means they're going to be wrinkled, and I'm beginning to think he deserves it. "It's the rules and guidelines and regulations. We can't have sex with the lights on, or God forbid I see you naked. I can't use the bathroom if you're in there painting on your, whatever this is," he says in an ugly tone, gesturing to his face. "I didn't want a plastic Barbie doll for a wife."

I skip over the nonsense he's spouting at me. Rules, regulations, and order are what keep this house flowing smoothly, but he clearly isn't understanding that. Maybe he'll understand more direct logic and consequences of a situation like this. "But what about the house? We have a lot of equity built up. It would be unwise to sell it in a buyer's market."

"Keep it." He zips up the small suitcase, places it on the floor, and pulls the handle. "My girlfriend and I already signed a lease on a beachfront property."

I gasp. "Girlfriend? You have a *girlfriend*? Have you been sleeping with her and me at the same time? Do you know how many diseases we could all be at risk for now?"

He rolls his eyes, clearly not caring about the horrific position he's put me in. "I'm not discussing this with you. I'll draw up the divorce paperwork tomorrow and have you served within the week so we can get this process started. In the meantime, I'll pick Trevor up on Thursday night for dinner. I'm sure you'll never let him visit my house since it'll probably have sand on the floor sometimes."

I watch him stalk out of the room, sure he's going to turn around and say he's changed his mind.

Any minute now.

The door slams and still, I wait.

And wait.

And wait.

And then it hits me—Rick is gone. He's really left me, left our family, left our life for some other woman who probably doesn't even know she needs to be checked for diseases now. I'd feel bad for her, but instead I find myself wondering what I should do.

What does this mean? I never planned on being a divorcée. I don't know what all that involves. Do I need to stock up on box wine and guacamole? Do I need to find a Bunco night?

Elena would know. Her husband left her because she wasn't good enough for him too. But then she ended up getting a job and meeting Greg, her daughter's gymnastics coach. Now they're married and have a happy life, so she knows how to handle things like a husband leaving unexpectedly. She'll be able to tell me what to do.

Checking the clock, I calculate the amount of time I have until I need to pick Trevor up from school. Thankfully, Rick decided to leave me in the middle of the day which doesn't throw off our schedule too much.

Two hours and four minutes until school pickup. Good. That gives me enough time to sort some of this out. Although I'll have to push off vacuuming the wooden blinds until tomorrow…

No matter. This is more important.

Climbing into my clean white Subaru that was detailed at Pirate's Booty Car Wash yesterday, I check the air freshener to make sure it's still working to its maximum capabilities. Then I drive exactly four miles over the speed limit to Elena's house. Fast enough to get me there quicker, but not fast enough that the ticket would be worth a police officer's time to pull me over.

It just takes a few minutes to get to her neighborhood. Turn onto the main road and cross the railroad tracks by looking left, then right, then left again, all while ignoring the honks behind me.

Pulling up in front of her house, I realize there are no cars in the driveway. That's weird. Elena doesn't work outside the home either. I'm not sure what exactly she does all day since her baseboards could use a good wipe down. But that's neither here nor there. Maybe her car is in the shop.

Oh please, let her car be in the shop. I've stayed very calm and collected for the last however long, but I have under two hours to come up with a plan for my new single life, and we'll need every minute to get it all straightened out.

Carefully walking up the sidewalk, I knock on the door and wait.

When no one answers, I knock again and wait.

Still no answer so I knock again and wait.

Panic begins to set in. She's not home. Elena's the only one who will know what to do, and she's not home. Turning to lean against the door that could use a good power wash, I realize how shattered my life really is.

For the first time since I can remember, I have no husband, no plan for the foreseeable future, and no idea how dirty the back of my shirt is getting.

What am I going to do?

CHAPTER Two

Aputi

With my hands on my hips, I look around the room and nod at my progress.

"Not bad," I say to myself. Especially since I've only lived here for just over twenty-four hours. There are only a few boxes left to be unpacked and the house has been deep-cleaned. I have to give Greg and Elena credit for that, though. There wasn't much dirt left after he moved out. It was just the icing on the proverbial cake that was this house.

Grabbing the empty boxes, I drag them out to the garage and begin breaking them down for recycling pickup tomorrow. Yet another perk of the move. I've never lived in an environmentally conscious neighborhood before.

Just a month ago, when my daughter's mother told me they were relocating here, I panicked. No, my daughter doesn't live with me full-time and no, San Antonio isn't that far away. But I'm hardly a part-time dad. I'm the guy who has coached all the pee-wee sports. The dad that shows up at every school orientation. The man that coordinates doctor's appointments. Sure, Chrissy and I were way too young when we had Abigail, but that didn't stop either of us from making her a priority, even when we realized we would never make it as a couple. The reality hit us about a hot minute after I dropped out of college to provide for them.

No shock there, right? That was sixteen years ago, and Chrissy and I still work together to give Abigail the best life we can, and that meant uprooting when Chrissy's job transferred her here. It's not like anything was really tying me to San Antonio anyway.

Even before Abigail was born, I've never been one to live to work. It's always been about experiencing life to the fullest. That's probably why quitting college at twenty-one years old didn't really bother me. Sure, it meant the end of my football career and frat parties. But in my mind, there was no other choice. Regardless if their parents are college graduates or not, a baby needs diapers and food. It was hardly a sacrifice.

So, I ditched my scholarship, got forklift certified, and went to work for a distribution warehouse. The work pays relatively well, being that I've continued to get certified on various machines. And I've been promoted several times because of my work ethic and ability to be a team player. It works for me, and I'm happy with my life.

Plus, it meant finding a decent job here before even putting in my two-week notice in San Antonio. Finding a place to live, however, was a much more stressful process. Well, until I called Greg.

Carrying the official red recycling container down to the curb while balancing several broken-down boxes on top, is no easy feat. But I'll gladly do it, grateful I'm not having to haul all my trash across a parking lot to a dumpster. Easy access to my own trash cans is yet another benefit of living in an actual house.

Greg's house. It should be weird, but it's not.

Greg and I knew each other when I lived with his ex-wife and daughter for a short period of time. I really liked Libby and was hoping things would work out, but almost immediately upon them moving in with me, I realized it wasn't going to last for long. Libby was nice at first, but she was more interested in having someone provide for her than being in an actual relationship. Plus, she was a bit of a drunk. I'm all about drinking a beer or two while watching a football game or going to a barbecue, but I draw the line at being smashed daily.

The only reason I didn't cut things off sooner was because of their daughter Peyton. That little girl was just a baby, and Libby barely paid attention to her. It didn't bother me that I was doing most of the care for someone else's kid. I'd already raised one, so it was almost like second nature. Libby never noticed I was suddenly the parent, but Greg did. The last time I saw him before they all moved away, he shook my hand and thanked me for taking care of his daughter when he couldn't be there.

That spoke a lot to me about the kind of man Greg is. I have a lot of respect for him being able to recognize I was part of the village surrounding that child, even if it was only for a short time. So, when I found out where my little family and I were moving to, Greg was the first person I called. Not knowing anything about the area, I wanted an opinion I trusted to help me figure out the safest places for me to live. I'll have a sixteen-year-old over on a regular basis. Need to make sure she'll be safe here.

As fate would have it, Greg was just back from his honeymoon, and they were trying to decide what to do with his house. Now, here I am, moved into the nicest home I've lived in since I left my mother's house almost twenty years ago, and I'm leasing to own it within the next year or two.

As an added benefit, I've seen Peyton a couple times as well. It took her a second to remember me, but once she did, the hugs began. Man, I love that little girl. It seems like everything is finally falling into place.

Catching my second wind, I turn back to my house, determined to get the last of the boxes unpacked. Movement on the front stoop of the house next door catches my attention.

Sauntering over to check it out, I realize it's Deborah, Elena's oddball friend. I've only met her once briefly when they had a barbecue shortly after I moved in, but it was a memorable meeting. She brought veggie hot dogs and gluten-free ketchup or something for her kid. When her back was turned, Greg gave him a real hot dog. I've never seen a child sneak behind a bush to eat a hot dog with real ketchup before.

The scene in front of me is almost as odd. Deborah is half standing, half crouching in front of Greg and Elena's door, sliding slowly to the ground. And I mean slooooooowly. It'll probably be another hour before she makes it all the way down. I'm surprised her legs haven't given out yet.

"Deborah?" I ask gently, trying not to poke the proverbial bear. She looks surprised when she notices me standing in front of her. "Deborah? I don't know if you remember me. I'm Aputi, Greg's neighbor. Are you okay?"

The words are barely out of my mouth when her face crunches up in a very odd-looking grimace and a long-winded shriek comes out of her. It's like a cross between a deflating balloon and that sound your car makes when the fan belt is getting ready to go out. A single tear slides down her cheek.

And then, just as quickly as she crumbles, she pulls herself right back together.

Pushing off the door, Deborah stands up, straightens her clothes, and wipes away the wetness from her face. "Sorry for that emotional display. It's been a hard day."

That was an emotional display?

"It's okay."

"No. No it's not okay," she commands, nodding once for effect. I'm not sure if she's trying to convince me or herself of, well, whatever she's adamant about. "It's highly inappropriate for me to bring people into all my drama. Except Elena. She's been divorced before, so she'll know what to do. Plus, she's my elder, so she's wise or something."

Shaking my head, I'm struggling to keep up with whatever she's talking about. "Hold on. Are you getting a divorce?"

Her face contorts again and yet another long-winded noise comes out of her mouth. I'm still not quite sure what's happening, but I think this might be her version of going into hysterics.

Once again, it lasts just a few short seconds before it's over. "I'm so sorry. I can't seem to keep myself pulled together. Yes. It appears I am about to be a divorced woman, and I'm not sure how to navigate this."

Somehow, the fact that she's very clearly trying to remain rational during what is obviously a very trying time, is kind of endearing. Strange, yes, but I learned years ago we all deal with life differently. Unless I'm reading this all wrong, I think Deborah just needs a supportive friend.

"Wanna talk about it?"

"Nothing to talk about." She smooths the front of her pants again of invisible wrinkles. "I was looking for Elena. She's been divorced before, and she revamped her entire self, and now look at her. I thought she'd know what to do. I have exactly," she pauses to look at her wristwatch, "one hour and forty-three minutes to put together a solid plan on how to live as a single mother."

I chuckle and her eyes snap up to mine, obviously unhappy at my outburst. "Sorry. I'm not laughing at you. It's going to take longer than an hour and forty-three minutes to figure this out. Maybe you need to talk some of this out first. Are you sure you wouldn't like to come in for a bit? I know I'm not Elena, but I have a teenage daughter, so I'm not completely inept at dealing with female emotions."

I say that last part with a smile, hoping it warms Deborah up to me, but she remains stoic as she takes me in, probably trying to figure out if this is a "stranger danger" situation. At six four and two eighty, I'm a pretty big guy. I know my size can be intimidating, especially to women. But Deborah doesn't seem afraid. More annoyed that I'm trying to make her smile.

This isn't going well so far.

"Okay," she finally says with a shrug, shocking the shit out of me.

I falter and blink a couple times, before pulling myself back together. "Okay? You'll come inside and talk for a bit?"

"You already saw me cry. Twice. Maybe you can help me put those emotions aside and forge ahead."

Huh. I did not see that coming.

"Well, okay then." Pointing toward my new house, I add, "I just moved into Greg's old place." Then I lead her across the lawn and through the front door, heading straight for the kitchen while she takes in the details of the front living area.

"Would you like something to drink?" I call over the half-wall that separates the two rooms. "I don't have much—some bottled water and Gatorade. But it's all cold."

Still looking around the room, she sits on the couch. "No, thank you. Did you just move in? It smells like bleach and Lysol."

Smiling as I twist the top off my favorite Blue Ice Gatorade and making my way back to the living room, I'll take that as a win. It wasn't what I was going for, but I suppose that's better than the house smelling like dirty socks and man stink. "Yeah, I officially moved in yesterday."

She nods. "I can tell. You really should skip the bleach and look into non-toxic cleaning product options. They are much better for your respiration. I have a lot of recipes that use vinegar as a cleaning agent. It works magic on your windows, and don't get me started on the benefits of using it on your kitchen counters..." Suddenly, she stops and closes her eyes, taking a breath. "I'm so sorry. I'm not trying to sound critical."

Her apology strikes me as odd, and I have the overwhelming need to reassure her. Furrowing my brow, I try to put her mind to rest. "Why are you always apologizing? You haven't done anything wrong."

"I think I do more things wrong than I realize," she grumbles.

I don't think we're talking about cleaning products anymore.

Leaning forward, I put my bottle down and clasp my hands together. "I take it you didn't know the divorce was coming?"

She looks dejectedly at her hands on her lap. "I don't really want to talk about that part. It's over and done with. Rick has made his decision and moved in with his girlfriend. But I always have a plan and right now, that's what I need to come up with. A plan on how to move forward."

My heart breaks when she looks up at me, the pain so very evident in her eyes. Her entire world has been upended sometime recently, and she's doing her very best not to crack under the weight of her grief. I'm not sure she realizes she's doing it. But she's very aware of what she needs to get to the next step.

Order and control.

I don't fully understand that, but I can respect it, and I think I know how to help.

Crossing the room to the small desk that houses my laptop and important papers, I snatch a notepad out of the drawer and turn back to her.

Checking the time on my phone, I give my best guestimate and say, "We've got one hour and thirty-nine minutes until school pickup. Let's get this plan written out."

The look of relief that radiates from her just about knocks me over, and I can't help but wonder how many times her soon-to-be ex made her feel this way.

With a smile like that, I'm willing to bet it won't take long for his loss to become someone else's gain.

CHAPTER Three

Deborah

I turn onto the main road and cross the railroad tracks by looking left, then right, then left again, all while ignoring the honks behind me. A few more minutes and a couple of turns later and I'm making a U-turn at the end of the cul-de-sac to park on the correct side of the road in front of Aputi's house.

It's rude to turn up unannounced. I know that. But in my emotional state the other day, I didn't think to get his phone number. I probably could have asked Elena for it, but that seems unnecessary. Plus, she has a tendency to distract easily, and I don't want to be responsible for her vacuuming going on the wayside or something.

Still, I need to properly thank Aputi. He was a wonderful help as my life crumbled around me. It took exactly one hour and twenty-seven minutes to write out the top ten things I need to focus on as my life shifts into new territory.

Hire an attorney and file an emergency petition to ensure all money is deposited into the joint accounts as normal. It never even occurred to me that Rick would cut us off. He's much too straight-laced to be *that* man. But it never occurred to me he would move to the beach with his new girlfriend either. I know the ocean is fun to visit, but hurricane prep and cleanup is the kind of stuff my nightmares are made of.

Schedule an appointment with my doctor to check for any disease exposure.

Vacuum the blinds. I never got to that the other day, and I can't seem to focus on anything else until it's done.

Tell my girlfriends, Callie and Elena, about the divorce so they can be supportive. I still don't quite understand what that means they'll do, but Aputi assured me I was going to need a tribe around me. Again, I don't quite understand what he means, but I can try it.

Figure out a budget. This is going to be a little trickier. Rick has always been the one to pay our bills, so I honestly don't remember how much they are. I'm sure I'll have to cut back on a few things. Making my own bento boxes instead of purchasing ready-made ones will help with living on a budget.

Explain to Trevor why his daddy isn't living with us anymore.

This is the one that broke my heart the most. For all his flaws, Rick is a good dad and is deeply loved by his son. Yet, I'm the one who has to tell him his daddy isn't coming back. The thought brings tears to my eyes. At this point, I've told Trevor that Rick is on a business trip, but I know I have to tell him the truth soon.

The other four items were all Aputi's ideas. They focused on things like having a "girl's night" and "finding a hobby". All things he described as self-care. Does he not realize eating healthy and keeping my house nice is also a form of self-care? Apparently not.

Regardless, the entire conversation helped organize the situation in my brain. I walked away feeling stronger. Like I can do this. And for that, I owe him so much more than the gluten-free, low-carb, non-dairy enchiladas I'm bringing to him.

Carefully stepping over the crack in the sidewalk, I gingerly make my way to the front door. It needs a good painting and the landscaping could use some weed eating. But considering he's only lived here a short time, I'm impressed to see the front stoop has been recently swept and the welcome mat looks free of mud. Not very many people have that much attention to detail.

Knocking twice, I suddenly realize the blood is draining from my face as my anxieties kick in. What if he's taking a nap? What if he has company? I should have called first. Darn it. I know better, but with all the kerfuffle happening around me, I forgot all the reasons why you always call before showing up.

Turning quickly back to my car, I make it only a couple of steps before I hear the door open behind me.

"Deborah?"

I freeze and take in the sound of his voice. His tone doesn't indicate he's irritated or upset with me. More curious about my surprise visit. Turning slowly, I straighten my spine and brush the invisible lint off my neatly-pressed pants.

Decision made, I take two quick steps toward him and shove the dish his direction. "I brought you this."

He takes it in his hands, confusion written all over his face. Great. I'm already messing this up.

"As a thank you for the other day."

He cocks his head and looks down at my gift, still not speaking. I should have presented it better. Maybe if I'd put it in a gift bag or attached a thank you note to the top. Shoot. My brain is all swirly. I'm usually so much better at this kind of thing.

"You brought me food?" Aputi finally asks, still inspecting the bowl.

"As a thank you," I interject quickly so there's no question.

Aputi's mouth stretches into an amused smile. "You said that already."

Flustered at yet another faux pas, I thank my lucky stars my makeup covers a multitude of sins, including blushing when I'm embarrassed. Taking a deep breath, I try to center myself because it might not seem like much to everyone, but a healthy meal is the sign of true appreciation, and Aputi needs to know how much I appreciate him.

"It's my award-winning chicken enchiladas, famous for their hand-rolled corn tortillas and creamy secret sauce. The chicken comes from a free-range farm where the hens are fed only high quality, GMO-free corn, and all the rest of the ingredients are local and truly organic. Not like the federal requirements, which is only thirty-three percent organic to use the label legally. These are well and truly artificial ingredient and pesticide free."

Aputi peels open the lid and sniffs the food. If I'm not mistaken, he looks excited to eat them. That's exactly what I was going for, which makes me happy.

"They don't have onions, do they?"

Lifting my chin with pride at a job well done, I give him the answer most people love to hear. "Chopped to the finest size possible so as to add flavor, but not an overwhelming crunch."

"I'm allergic."

Throwing my hands over my mouth, my eyes widen. "Oh, I'm so sorry. That was so stupid of me. I shouldn't have made them without asking you first." I snatch the dish away from him and hug it close to my chest. "I'll make more for you right now and bring them right back over. Well, it's going to be a couple hours because I need to deep clean the kitchen to rid it of any onion residue, but if I shift around my cleaning schedule and maybe read through Trevor's teacher reports while he's doing jujitsu, I can have them over by dinner time."

"No Deborah. Please don't go out of your way."

Aputi steps toward me, his hand out, but I instinctively take a step back, making sure to keep the food far out of his reach or breathing space. I'm just know he's about to go into anaphylaxis shock. It's a good thing I have an EpiPen in my purse, for times like these, but I might have to go pick up another one at the pharmacy if I need to use it now.

"No, really. I want to. It's the least I can do for almost killing you."

"You didn't almost kill me."

"I did. I handed you onions and practically made your throat close up myself."

Aputi does the last thing I expect him to do. He laughs. Well now I'm not only embarrassed, I'm annoyed as well.

"Why are you laughing? This isn't funny. This is life and death."

"I'm laughing because you're cute."

"I beg your... what?"

Did he just say I'm cute? I've been called a lot of things, but *cute* has never been one of them. But looking at him leaning against the door jamb, arms crossed over his *very* wide chest that I never noticed until just this moment and…WOW is he a large man. And not in a bad way. In a I've-had-many-lovers-because-I'm-so-virile kind of way. That's saying a lot because I don't ever read books that have the word "virile" in them, so you know he must have that look about him if I notice it.

"I said, I think you're cute."

I furrow my brow, still not sure how to take his statement. Is this a compliment or condescending? "I don't understand what you mean."

He shrugs one shoulder. One very massive, very muscular shoulder. How odd to be thinking about his shoulders at a time like this. I'm almost a divorcée and just tried to kill Aputi with onions. Yet, I'm ogling his shoulders. Am I turning into a floozy? Is this what they mean by "emotional upheaval"? I may have to ask Elena about this as well.

"What other interpretation can there be?" Aputi asks me. "Bringing me dinner as a thank you is one of the nicest things anyone has ever done for me. And then to be so concerned about my food allergy that you practically run away with my meal… it's really sweet. Nice. Cute."

"Oh." I find my eyes blinking quite a few times as I process what he says. Usually people find me overbearing, not endearing. This is a new reaction. I'm still unclear on how to proceed. I think I need to leave and go clean my bathroom. Nothing clears my thoughts more than making my mirrors shine. "Well, um, I'll see you later."

Turning on my heel, I make quick work of walking back to my SUV and climbing inside, laying the enchiladas inside my travel warming bag so they stay fresh and ready to eat. Still feeling frazzled by the entire exchange, I don't notice the vehicle coming up behind me until it honks.

Slamming on my brakes, my body jars forward as I barely avoid the collision. The dirty red Jeep in great need of a paint job speeds around me, the driver probably making a lewd gesture my direction. I barely notice. I'm too busy trying to figure out these weird emotions.

Aputi thinks I'm cute? As in, endearing? How is that possible, and why does it delight me so much?

CHAPTER
Four

Aputi

As wary as I was about moving here, the last couple of weeks have actually turned out to be pretty great. My new job is about thirty minutes away, but the drive isn't terrible. I'm up early for the morning shift, but I'm home by mid-afternoon. It works perfectly because Abigail already tried out for and was added to the junior varsity softball team at her new high school. Working early means I can be at all the games as soon as the season officially starts.

Turning into my neighborhood, though, all I can think about is how beautiful of a day it is. Perfect for starting the yardwork I've been wanting to get to. I've spent the last however many years enjoying the perks of apartment living. And by "perks", I mean sharing walls with loud neighbors, scrambling for parking, and generally living at the mercy of when maintenance can make it out to fix whatever breaks. The freedom to do things on my time is the only explanation I have for being excited to mow my lawn.

As I pull into my driveway, the to-do list running through my head comes to a halt. What is Deborah doing hanging out at Elena's door again? And this time with the hot dog kid.

I could pull right into the garage and pretend I don't see her, but I'm not that kind of guy. Plus, I like Deborah. Just with the small amount of interaction I've had with her, I can understand why other people can find her overwhelming at times. But that's not how I feel around her at all. I suspect she has high standards for herself and puts one hundred percent into everything she does. I'm not sure I personally could maintain those kind of expectations all the time, but I admire her for always putting in that much effort herself.

Climbing out of my Ford F-150, I shout her direction. "Hey!"

She startles, and as I walk toward them, I put a smile on my face to try and put her son at ease. The closer I get, the wider his eyes and mouth both get. If I hadn't pegged her for being flustered by something and trying to keep her emotions on an even keel, I'd probably be laughing at his reaction to my size. I'm used to it, but it always gives me a good chuckle when it happens.

"Trying to ding-dong ditch Elena again?"

Deborah's eyes look back and forth like she's listening but not exactly hearing me, her mind on other things. "What?"

I chuckle to myself. "Nothing. Are you okay?"

"Yes," Deborah answers a little too quickly. "I mean, no. I mean…" She takes a breath and I'm starting to realize she does that when she's agitated. Probably to slow her heart rate and thoughts. "Elena was supposed to watch Trevor so I could go to the gyn…uh… dentist."

"The what?"

"The dentist." Her neck flushes because she's lying. Interesting.

"You mean the gynecologist."

Her eyes widen, and she throws her hands over the boy's ears. "Aputi! A lady never speaks of such things."

I really should have known better than to call her out like that, especially in front of her son. Next time, I'll have to filter my responses a little more if I want to stay friends with her. Still, I can't help but rib her just a little. She's cute when she's flustered. "I have a daughter. I know where babies come from."

"Be that as it may," she says sternly, leaving no question where she stands, "just pretend it's the dentist."

"Yes, ma'am."

She opens her mouth, then closes it. Then opens it again. "Are you making fun of me?"

"Maybe a little," I say with a smile. "Did it get your mind off whatever crisis you're having?"

I can't be sure, but I think her eyes soften and her whole body relaxes. She even removes her hands from the child's ears. It's as if she understands my intensions are not to be mean, but to help her refocus, and that changes her entire perception of me. Also, she's surprised it worked. "Oddly, yes."

Mission accomplished. "Well good. And since Elena's not here, why don't you leave him with me? What's your name?" I ask the boy, who seems to have gotten over my size already. Bummer. It's always a bit of an ego boost when little boys look up to me.

"Trevor," a very timid voice responds. "My name is Trevor, and Maura is my friend."

It takes me a second to remember Maura is Elena's middle daughter. She's a couple years older than Peyton, but these kids are still growing faster than I can keep up with. And man, they have a full house. I don't know how I'm going to keep track of everyone. I may need to pass out name tags at the next gathering.

"Why would you want to watch him for me?" Deborah is eyeing me skeptically. Not that I expect her to jump at the chance to have me babysit. She's less of a "dive right in" kind of person and more like a "first dip your toes. Then get used to it. Then dip your foot. Then get used to it. And continue," type person.

"Because I'm off for the rest of the day, and Greg gives me a good deal on rent. I might as well help them out by helping you out."

"But... what experience do you have with kids?"

"Well, I have a sixteen-year-old daughter, and I haven't killed her yet."

Deborah's eyes widen. "You do?"

"Why is that so surprising?"

She blinks several times, probably trying to figure out the answer herself. "I don't know. I guess because you never mentioned her before."

"Yes, I did."

"You did?"

"Yep. But we weren't exactly talking about me last week when you were here. Unless you count finding out about my onion allergy."

Her neck flushes prettily again, and I realize the color stops as soon as it reaches her face. Wow. That's some thick makeup for a blush to not come through at all. I can't help but wonder why she wears so much. She has such pretty eyes and nice full lips; it's a shame they're covered up so heavily.

"I'm just kidding with you, Deborah. Seriously. Trevor will have a great time. And I'll text Elena to let her know he's with me. He can go play with her kids at their house when they get back."

Worrying her lip, I can tell she really needs me to help her out but is battling her own anxieties about leaving her child with a strange man. Understandable, I suppose.

"I don't want to impose on you," she finally says quietly. "I seem to be doing that enough as it is."

I wave her off, hoping she begins to understand that helping her is really not a hardship for me. "It's no imposition at all. I was only going to do some yardwork. I'm dying to get my hands on my new lawn mower.

Her eyes flash over to look at my garage, as if the machine is going to come out by itself and attack us all. The visual image of people running through the neighborhood streets screaming like in a 1950s black and white horror flick almost make me laugh. Almost.

"Are you sure?"

"I'm positive. You don't have to worry. Like I said, I have a daughter, and I haven't killed her yet."

My attempt at joking falls painfully flat. But does that stop me from continuing? No. No it does not.

"And remember Greg's daughter used to live with me. She's not dead either."

Deborah sighs, which I take as her coming to a decision. Either way, it makes me finally stop word vomiting everywhere.

"Okay. That would be very helpful. I'll just put SPF 70 on him before I go. I have his hat in the car. And rubber boots. You don't have any children-sized work gloves he can borrow, do you?"

Man, this woman is always prepared for anything. I like it.

"I'll see what I can do."

I am hot. I am sweaty. I am proud of a job well done.

Trevor and I have spent a couple hours doing yardwork and it looks great. Especially when you consider the fact that Trevor is six years old, less than four feet tall, and insisted on learning how to push the lawn mower. I followed closely behind and guided him but let him do all the pushing. Consequently, the lack of symmetry of the lines are going to make some people crazy when they drive by, but it was worth it. The look on his little face when he saw his accomplishment was nothing more than well-deserved male pride.

We celebrated with turkey and salami sandwiches and Gatorade. I've never seen a kid down his lunch so fast. His comment about never having eaten processed meat before may have tipped me off as to why he was so excited over that extra piece of salami I put on his sandwich. Oops. I probably should have asked about food allergies before Deborah left. I assume he's fine, though, since he hasn't broken out in hives.

As Trevor holds the black plastic garbage bag that is three times his size, I attempt to dump the grass trimmings inside. It's slow going, only because I'm making sure not to dump it all over him. He's really enjoying doing manual labor, so there's no reason to rush. What in the world has this kid been doing all his life to be having so much fun doing yardwork?

Does he not play outside? Regardless, taking my time is a small price to pay for how much he's enjoyed today.

I pour the last of the trimming into the bag as Deborah's stark white SUV comes to a complete stop in front of the house. As I help Trevor learn how to tie the tops of the bag together and push all the air out, I simultaneously watch Deborah carefully make her way toward us. She's always so put together, part of me is praying her black pants and matching flats won't get dirty by walking through the yard.

"Trevor," she singsongs to her son.

He jerks his head up and when his eyes find her, a toothless grin immediately breaks out across his face. "I mowed the lawn, Mama!" He sounds so proud of himself, it's hard not to smile along with him.

I pluck the floppy garden hat Deborah insisted he wear off his head and ruffle his hair before dropping it right back on him. "He sure did. See what a great job he did?"

Deborah looks around, clearly concerned as to the safety of Trevor using a blade-wielding machine and probably more than a little wigged out by the lack of pattern in the yard. But she's also trying not to burst his bubble.

"Don't worry," I quickly interject to calm her fears. "I walked right behind him and kept my hands on the handlebar. Trevor did all the work, but I was his safety net."

My words seem to help her relax just a bit.

"You did a wonderful job," she says with delight, then her eyes go wide as she takes in his appearance. "My goodness, you are filthy."

"A little dirt will put some hair on your chest, right my man?"

Trevor nods his head, hat flopping as he moves. "I'm gonna have hair on my chest and be big like Aputi, Mommy."

As if he's trying to prove his point, Trevor uses all his might to try and move the bag, which is now about four times as heavy as he his. Neither of them is going anywhere despite how much he groans with effort.

"I'm sure you will be. Just don't grow up too fast on me." Deborah beams lovingly at him while he continues to grunt and strain.

Turning back to her, I ask, "Did Elena ever text you?"

Her eyes widen a bit. "I can't believe Greg got his front tooth knocked out at work! I knew gymnastics was a dangerous sport, but it never occurred to me it would be dangerous for the coaches."

I chuckle lightly, thinking about the picture of toothless Greg that Elena sent me. It was one of the funniest things I've seen lately. Partly because there was the giant hole in Greg's mouth. Partly because Elena made sure he was good and drugged before she snapped the pic.

"I don't think he's normally in harm's way. Maybe they were working on a new trick."

"Maybe. I'm just glad this happened before I ever considered enrolling Trevor." Speaking of, he finally gives up and drops the bag which hasn't moved at all. As he turns toward his mother, panting heavily, Deborah's eyes go wide again. "Oh no! I put you in dirty pants?"

Confused, I furrow my brow. "I think he got dirty doing yardwork. I'm sorry. I didn't realize he was supposed to stay clean."

"No, that's not it. I never did get that grass stain out of his pants." She leans down to inspect the spot on his pants I didn't even notice as if it's a terrible travesty. "Maybe if I mix bleach and spot remover and let it sit. Darn it." Suddenly her hands go over her eyes. "And on the same day I didn't leave a healthy bento box. I am falling down on the job as a mom."

"Deborah, it's okay. We had lunch after we mowed."

She gasps. "You did?"

I shrug. "Sure. A man's gotta eat. Feeding him was no big deal."

"It's a big deal to me. The only job I have is being a mom, and if I can't do it to the best of my ability…" Her face changes to an unreadable expression, but she takes a deep breath and nods her head once. "Well, I guess I have to try harder next time."

Suddenly, it hits me. Whether she recognizes it or not, Deborah doesn't need to try harder. She's probably the best mom I know. A real Pinterest mom. What she *does* need is validation for all her hard work. Just like Trevor felt pride in mowing the lawn, she needs to feel pride in the fact that she tries so hard in the first place. She needs to know people see what a good mom she is.

"You're right. I'm sorry."

She opens her mouth but pauses before responding until her brain catches up to my attitude shift. "Wh-what?"

"I said I'm sorry. Just because I didn't think it was a big deal to make him an extra sandwich doesn't mean I can dismiss the importance to you."

Deborah blinks a few times, clearly stunned at my words. I seem to do that to her a lot. "Oh. Well, thank you for that. No one has ever said that to me before." It makes me wonder what kind of people she's been hanging out with for, oh, her entire life, if no one has ever recognized her need for validation. That's about to change.

"I think maybe no one has ever understood why you do it before."

"What do you mean?" she asks so quietly, it almost comes out as a whisper.

"I don't think you're striving for perfection."

"You don't?"

"No. I think when you decide you care about someone, you put your all into it. You want them to know how important they are to you, and this is your way of showing them. Packing Trevor lunch isn't about being the perfect mom. It's about him knowing you love him and haven't forgotten to meet his needs. Am I onto something?"

A blush creeps up her neck, only this time it's so strong I can actually see a bit of it through her makeup. Or maybe I just know it's there because I'm beginning to know what makes her tick, and I'll be damned, but I really like it.

"No one has ever figured that out before."

"I think maybe," I take a deep breath before going for the gusto, "no one was looking at you before the same way I do now."

Her jaw drops. "How do you look at me?"

"Like your beauty comes from inside you. Not from what your outsides look like."

If it was possible, I swear her jaw drops even more. I know she isn't divorced yet. Hell, her husband left last week. She's probably still counting it as hours since his departure. Like parents who tell their kid's age in months. But for as uptight as Deborah is, she intrigues me. She excites me. In a way, she reminds me of my mother, which could signal an underlying Oedipus Complex. But more than likely, it's just the similarity of both their deep love for their children and a desire to put others first, no matter the cost.

"Mom." Trevor begins pulling on Deborah's pant leg, breaking us out of the moment. She and I both shift on our feet, grateful for the reprieve. She didn't need to respond to my words. She just needed to know I felt them.

Pulling the garden hat off his head, she begins stroking her fingers through his sweaty hair. "Yes, my love."

"I wanna go watch PBS Kids. Can we go home?"

I resist sniggering in humor and appreciation. Even Trevor's TV watching is nothing less than the best in educational television. Such a Deborah thing to do. There can never be any doubt that her love for her son runs deep.

"Of course. I'm sure you're tired now." Turning toward me, she digs through her purse until she finds a small packet of hand sanitizing wipes. "Well. Thank you again for helping me with Trevor. Especially at the last minute," she says while wiping the sweat and grime off her hand.

"It really was no problem."

"I know. But it meant a lot to me." She smiles shyly and places her hand on Trevor's shoulder to guide him to the car. "Anyway. Bye."

"Bye."

"Bye, Aputi!" Trevor yells, tripping on his own feet as he walks. Thankfully, Deborah steadies him before he faceplants in the middle of the yard.

"See ya, Trevor." As they walk away, I realize I never asked how her appointment went. But I know she won't appreciate me yelling across the neighborhood about the gynecologist, so instead I call out, "I hope everything went well at the dentist, Deborah."

She turns back around, eyes wider than they were, seeming like she's considering her words. "I...I don't know yet. We'll see what all the test results say."

I nod in understanding. "I'm sure everything is just fine," I reassure. "And if not, I'm still here. To help. Whatever you need."

She smiles a little bigger, still very much unsure of how to respond. Which is okay. I don't need her to say anything, just know that I'm here. For her. And I'm not leaving.

Not even when she finally gets Trevor loaded up and drives away.

CHAPTER
Five

Deborah

Writing out the numbers as carefully as I can, I'm sure to dot every "I" and cross every "T" of the curly script words I'm putting down on the small paper. I was surprised when the attorney's office said they'd take a personal check, but I suppose if it bounces, they won't take me on as a client, so they don't have much to lose. Except an hour's worth of work and three hundred fifty dollars.

I was also surprised how much this consultation was going to cost me, but Elena assured me this practice is one of the best in the area. She made out well during her divorce, so I have all my fingers crossed they'll do the same for me. Not that I want to get a divorce, but it's not about what I want. It's about making sure Trevor has what he needs. Essential oils and organic produce aren't cheap.

Carefully pulling the check out by its perforation, I hand it over to the receptionist behind the glass window. It never occurred to me an attorney's office would need those extra security measures, but they are oddly reassuring. If they're worried about a disgruntled spouse coming after them, that must mean they get the job done.

"Okay, Ms. Dickson. Have a seat and Ms. Hartley will be with you shortly."

"Thank you so much."

Ms. Hartley. Kendall Hartley is my attorney's name. Or at least, I hope she'll be my attorney. I looked her up on the internet after Elena gave me her name, and she looks very kind in her picture. Right now, that's what I need. Someone who is no nonsense and tough when working for my benefit, but who can also be kind to me as I navigate it all. There's so much more to sort through than I realized. Not only do we have to divvy up all our household goods, I don't even know what Rick has in the way of assets. Does he have a retirement account? A 401K? Do we have savings? I've just always used the credit card and let him do all the finances. I'm quickly learning that was a mistake on my part. But the alternative seemed so overwhelming at the time. I'm so glad I have Elena and Callie to help me figure it all out. They won't let me forget anything.

And Aputi. He's already been a huge help.

My mind drifts as I think about his kind eyes and genuine smile. He's this huge teddy bear of a man. How is he still single at his age? Actually, I don't know how old he is, but he's well into his adult years which means he's either a menace once you get to know him better, or he hasn't found the right woman yet.

Somehow, I don't think it's him. From what I understand, he was living with Greg's ex-wife for a while. I've accidentally interacted with Libby a time or two, and I can't figure out how she always ends up in relationships with the good guys.

Also, I suppose there's my answer. Aputi is still single because he gravitates toward the crazy women. Is that why he likes me? Is it because I have a little crazy in me as well? Most people call it neurotic, but that's just a more clinical term for the same thing…

"Deborah?"

My name being called brings me back to the moment at hand. Like a moment of truth, to be honest.

Standing, I run my hands down my pants, flattening out the creases. Then I meet her hand in the middle to shake.

"I'm Kendall Hartley. Won't you join me in the conference room?"

I like her immediately. She's got a very calming presence, which is exactly what I need when anxieties kick in. Oh, I so hope she takes me on as a client!

Once the door is closed, we're seated around a small round table. Kendall offers me a drink, which I decline due to the brand. It's not known for being the most purified. Plus, my hands are shaking enough, I'm afraid I'll spill it.

Flipping over a page of her legal pad, Kendall immediately gets down to business. "So, you need representation for your divorce. Have the papers been filed yet?"

"I don't know. Rick was going to handle that, but I haven't received anything yet."

She looks up through her lashes as she jots down notes. "But you know you're getting divorced."

"Yes. My husband moved out three weeks ago to live with his girlfriend."

She nods once, slowly. "Ah. Infidelity. I'm sorry to hear that."

"I am too. Fingers crossed my pap smear and blood tests come back normal." My eyes widen and I throw my hands over my mouth. "Oh my gosh! I can't believe I just said that! I'm so sorry; that was so inappropriate to say. You're just so calming to be around, the filter in my brain didn't work. Rest assured, it won't happen again."

Kendall stops writing and looks at me. "It's okay, Deborah. That was actually the next thing I was going to suggest. Any time there is a history of infidelity, it's a good idea to go see the gynecologist. Your health is the most important thing."

"Well, my son is the most important thing."

She smiles in understanding. "I agree. But you can't take care of him if you aren't healthy, so I'm glad you've already taken such a big step. That means you're already on the right track in a relatively short amount of time."

Relieved that she and I are on the same page in just a few minutes, I'm a little more confident we are going to work well together. "Thank you for that. My friend Aputi helped me put together a list of things I need to get done and that was on it. Now that I say it, it's a little weird he thought of it since he's a man. I didn't realize at the time, but I suppose nothing makes me happier than being able to cross something off a to-do list, so it's irrelevant."

"A to-do list is great during times like this. In fact, that's what I'm making right now. So let me get a bit of information. You only have the one child?"

"Yes."

"And he's your husband's child?"

A bit of an odd question considering Rick's the only man I've ever slept with, but I suppose it's not unrealistic. "Yes."

"And does your son live with you?" She's writing faster than anyone I've ever seen. It's quite impressive, and yet the chicken scratch is a little much for my organizational tendencies. No matter. She has a job to do and this is just the beginning.

"Yes. Rick, my husband, um… soon to be ex-husband I suppose, moved into a beach house somewhere. He said I could have the residential house because of Trevor."

"We're gonna need him to sign off on that asap, then," she says more to herself than me. "Okay. Got it. And is he paying child support or is his income still going in the joint accounts?"

"Um… I…" Wracking my brain for the answers, I find myself stumbling over my words. "I… uh…" Suddenly, out of nowhere I realize I have no idea if he's putting money in our account. I never thought to ask. I was so determined to continue on with life as we know it, I never thought to clarify such a massive detail that will make a huge impact on our lives. Swallowing back the lump in my throat, I whisper, "I don't know. I don't know anything about our money."

Kendall stops writing and looks up at me. "Deborah?" Glancing up, I fight the urge to bite my bottom lip. I always battle feelings of inadequacy, but right now is the worst it's been in a long time. Rick promised to take care of me. To take care of us. And in this moment, I realize I'm not sure he's paid the mortgage. He could have handed me the house because he knew it was about go into foreclosure. I don't know how much he makes, so I don't know how much child support I should be getting. I know nothing because I blindly trusted him. All of a sudden, I realize what a huge, terrible mistake that was. And I feel so stupid I can barely breathe.

Laying her pen down, Kendall pushes the box of tissues closer to me, while I dig out the package of aloe infused tissues I have in my purse. I prefer them because of their softness. Much better for the tender under-eye skin when I cry. Not that I'm going to cry now.

I think.

Maybe.

"Deborah." I refuse to look up at her as I dab underneath my eye with the soft cloth and sniff softly. "You aren't the first woman to be in this position, and you won't be the last. That's why you're here. I can help you. I *want* to help you. It's going to be hard, but you have to trust that I know what I'm doing and I'm very good at my job."

I nod but still refuse to look up. I don't want her to see how deep my humiliation runs.

"The first thing we need to do is file a motion for all income to continue being deposited into the joint accounts and all bills to continue to be paid from those accounts. That will ensure nothing else changes until we can get to mediation and decide everything else. If you agree to that, we can get started on it today and have it filed no later than tomorrow morning."

I nod again. "Yes, let's do that please."

"Since you haven't been served with divorce papers yet, we can wait on him to do it, or we can take that step first. It's up to you."

Do I want to take that step? Do I want to be the one to put the final nail in the coffin of my marriage? I'm not sure what the right answer is, but I don't like this sense of helplessness. I have a check list of items that need to be done in order for us to continue on with our lives and getting over the hurt of him having a girlfriend behind my back is not on that list. Maybe it should be.

And that's when I'm hit with yet another realization—I'm not sad. I don't miss Rick or the way he leaves his wet towels on the bathroom floor every morning. I don't miss the way he treats his allergies with over-the-counter meds and refuses to try eating local honey to inoculate himself. I don't miss how he turns off my essential oils diffuser the minute he walks in from work or how he adds salt to all my cooking or how he has a very strange obsession with Dr. Dre.

I don't miss him at all.

And yes, I'm sad my life is in upheaval. I'm sad Trevor's dad is gone. I'm scared of the changes. But I'm also very, very angry that we have been put in this position to begin with. Never once did Rick try to talk to me about his concerns. He never asked for marriage counseling. He never asked to see me without makeup. He never talked about any of it until he gave up.

He. Gave. Up.

And I never do. I work tirelessly until things are as perfect as I can get them. Had I known we were having issues, I would have put in the same effort.

Something Aputi said suddenly runs through my mind. He said, "When you decide you care about someone, you put your all into it." He's right. It's exactly what I do. But I wasn't given that option with Rick. He kept me at a distance by never telling me how he felt, which meant I wasn't the best wife I could be. He didn't allow me to even try. Our marriage never had a chance, and I never knew it until this moment because I was never part of the equation. My thoughts, my hopes, my desires were never important enough to take into consideration.

Well. That makes this decision easy.

"If he hasn't filed already," I say, feeling resolved, "let's do it. I'd like to move on from this time of my life. I don't do limbo well."

Kendall smiles at me, a real smile. Probably female solidarity, which is fine with me. Until my two girlfriends, I didn't have much of that, so I'll take Kendall's support. Even though I'm technically paying for it.

"Sounds great. We'll file the Petition for Divorce and Emergency Motion for Support to include exclusive possession of the home and custody of your son immediately. If you have a current address for your husband, we can serve him at home or at work. It's up to you."

I can't explain my next thought, because it's so very out of character for me. But it hits me out of nowhere. Maybe it's natural to want revenge on someone who has hurt you, but that's never been me. Or maybe I've always been so focused on staying, well, focused that I never stopped to be vengeful. But why not poke the bear? Rick didn't seem to mind poking me on his way out the door.

"Can we serve him at home? I know it sounds horrible and very improper, but if he's served divorce papers at home, his new girlfriend will know he never filed. I don't know why it's important for me that she knows he hasn't gone through with it yet, but it is."

Kendall's lips quirk to the side, and I know she's fighting a laugh. "Because you're taking back the control they took from you."

My eyes widen. She's right. Whoever this girlfriend is, she and Rick made decisions about the course of my life without me. They took the organized, controlled life I live and threw a wrench in the works, as if it's not important or has no value. But it does. And I'm back in control of it. And I want them both to know without a doubt they won't be calling the shots on the direction my life is going anymore.

Three weeks after he left and I'm already getting back on track. Wow. I'm pretty good at this divorce thing.

"Not anymore, they're not," I finally respond, and Kendall goes back to her chicken scratch. Now there are arrows and circles around certain things. If I wasn't so busy and the office wasn't so far from my house, I'd offer my services to type up her notes. There is no way she can remember what all that means if she were to look at it in a year.

"Okay. So one child. We need to get all your husband's financials. I'd highly advise going through his desk or any drawers or cabinets. Likely all his financial information is online, but he might have hidden passwords somewhere and you have a right to see those accounts. Any random statements he has forgotten about will help move us in the right direction. He'll be ordered to hand it over anyway, but it'll give us a better idea of what you can expect as far as assets. How long have you been married?"

"Nine years."

One of Kendall's eyebrows quirk up and suddenly I'm nervous that it's not a good sign. "I assume you've been a stay-at-home mom during most of that time?"

I shrug a shoulder and give her a slight nod. "I worked at a hospital in administration for a couple years after college, but once we got married, I quit."

Kendall takes a deep breath, and now I'm even more on edge. "You need to be prepared. Child support will only be a portion of his salary and is meant to provide for the child. But he has no legal obligation to take care of you."

"But..." I blink a few times, processing what she's just said. "But I thought I would get alimony. I haven't worked in over a decade."

"You have to be married for ten years to qualify for it. And even then, you have to show you have no skills and no ability to provide because you've been taking care of him."

"But I have been. Taking care of him, I mean."

"I don't doubt you at all. I can tell just by the way you're prepared with a fresh note pad and three different colors of gel pen that you took very good care of him. Probably more than he deserved. But a judge isn't going to order alimony under the circumstances. Not in this state."

My breathing gets shallow and my chest tightens. No alimony means no ability to pay bills. No ability to pay bills means getting a job. Which means Trevor will have to go to daycare where he'll be exposed to germs and processed foods and cable cartoons.

"You don't need to panic." Kendall hands me a bottle of the not-triple-filtered water I already declined. "Getting this motion filed for him to continue providing will buy you at least several months, maybe longer. If he has a million dollars in assets, you may be entitled to fifty percent of that in the divorce. We'll get you taken care of. You just have to be ready."

I want to believe her. I mean, logically I do. But the rest of me can't stop thinking about what a bad position I'm in.

I have to get a job. I have almost no skills. I've been out of the work force for a decade, and I certainly can't get a job that will give us the kind of life we have now.

A crushing weight settles on my chest, and it takes everything in me to focus on breathing and listening to everything Kendall tells me. I'm frightened and stressed, and I kind of want to throw up.

I guess I'm not as good at this divorce thing as I thought.

CHAPTER Six

Aputi

I knock on the door and take a good look around as I wait. Coming to Deborah's house uninvited and unannounced is a gamble. She's so very set in her ways, there is a good possibility she'll turn me away. Or, more likely, she'll get flustered and slam the door in my face.

Extreme panic seems to be the way it goes when I surprise Deborah, so my money is on the door slam. But it's a chance I'm willing to take. When Elena answered her phone, and I heard the hysteria in Deborah's voice, I knew she needed a friend. Anyone who can panic so loudly it can be heard across the room by someone who isn't even holding the phone, shouldn't be left alone. In spite of the strange looks the newlyweds gave me, I offered Elena a reprieve from coming over to be with Deborah and offered to do it instead.

Her house is exactly as I expected. A custom two-story with a red brick exterior, large windows, and a two-car garage. The lawn looks meticulously maintained but doesn't have the same charm as the uneven lines on my yard. Then again, a yard service probably mowed this baby, not a child.

While it's only a few minutes from my house, the neighborhood is much more hoity-toity. Not in the actual houses, but in social status. Or so I've been told by my next-door neighbors. It kind of reminds me of that time I took Abigail to Florida for vacation and we stayed in a hotel in Orlando. Everyone knows that damn mouse actually lives in Kissimmee, but the prices are so much less expensive when you stay one mile away from the border of the town.

The door slowly opens, and I turn to smile at my newest friend.

"Aputi?" She doesn't look angry or upset. Just confused as to why I'm here. "Is something wrong?"

The door hasn't slammed yet, so I'm pleased to see we're making progress on the friendship front. Encouraged to continue, I reach my hand out and give her a Tupperware in offering.

Continuing to look perplexed, Deborah takes it from me, inspecting it carefully. "What is this?"

"It's my world-famous Thai noodles."

"Thai noodles?" She furrows her brow.

"Yep." I shove my hands in my pockets and watch as she continues to inspect the bowl, like she's not sure what to do with it. Has no one ever brought her food before? Actually, probably not. She's so busy trying to take care of others, I doubt anyone stops to realize she needs a little TLC sometimes too. "They're not like I normally make them. I had you in mind when I pulled the recipe, so I made sure to get all organic ingredients because I know that's important to you. And I tried making the noodles with zucchini instead of pasta. It's not really my favorite, but it's not bad. The flavor is all about the sauce anyway."

She blinks a few times, and I can't tell what's running through her mind. It's sweet that she's kind of stunned, her mouth open just slightly like her jaw hasn't started working again after the initial shock of my visit.

"You did this for me?"

My heart beats a little faster and also falls just a bit. I want to show this woman how she deserves to be treated. I want her to know she has value and importance. It's so obvious no one has ever taken the time to do that before. As much as I like Elena, I don't think she realizes Deborah is always the one who is blown off. She's always treated as a stereotype. But that's not who she is. She's so much more than people give her credit for.

"Of course I did. I knew you were having a bad day and figured you could use some healthy comfort food."

Her eyes close slowly and she takes a deep breath. I know that move. It means she's overwhelmed and needs to take a moment to center herself.

I also know she wouldn't appreciate me knowing that. Deborah doesn't like people seeing beneath what she presents, too afraid what's on the inside won't be good enough. But she also needs to know I see *her*. And I'm here to support her.

"You were with Elena when I called, weren't you?"

I shrug, because what else can I say that will make her any less nervous? Nothing. She'll either accept my friendship or she won't. It's completely up to her. But I really do hope she accepts it.

I also don't tell her that calling Elena her "wise elder" gave Greg a huge laugh and consequently started them bickering when the call was over. It was all in good fun, but considering Elena is a couple years older than Greg, I think a new nickname may have stuck.

"Well, I appreciate you thinking about me. That doesn't happen very often." A look of resolve crosses her face and she smiles. "Would you like to come in? Looks like there's enough for two in here." She gently waves the bowl in her hand.

"There was actually enough for four when I made it." I pat my stomach indicating how full I am. "That's how I know it's good. I don't think I could eat another bite of it."

Opening the door wider and stepping aside, Deborah gestures for me to enter. "I'm glad you said that. I actually just finished cleaning up after dinner, but I didn't want to be rude and not sample your cooking."

"Save it for tomorrow. That way you don't have to cook."

"I might do that. Thank you."

Stepping over the threshold, two things immediately cross my mind. First, I can't help feeling somewhat victorious that Deborah invited me inside. I honestly figured this would be a drop-and-run kind of deal, but I'm not unhappy about this turn of events. We've spent a bit of time getting to know each other on my turf. I'd like to get to know Deborah on hers too.

And second, what a turf it is. The house is just as beautiful and cared for on the inside as it is on the outside. Yet, it doesn't come across like my grandmother's house used to—with that museum quality that made me afraid to touch anything for fear I would break something important. No, the plush couches have obviously been vacuumed and fluffed recently, but they also look comfy and inviting. The decorations are mostly pictures of family and friends scattered around the walls and sitting on tops of tables.

And she wasn't kidding when she said organic, non-toxic cleaners are the way to go. This house is spotless but doesn't smell like chemicals at all. It smells almost fruity. Interesting. It's like I'm getting a peek inside who she really is already.

Following her to the immaculate kitchen, which is so clean there is no indication they ate already, we make small talk.

"Where's Trevor?"

"He's in the shower."

"By himself?"

I'm not being critical. I just expected she would be in there with him. She strikes me as the kind of person who would be terrified of her child drowning during bath time.

She sighs, and it appears to out of resignation. "It's his latest thing. He claims to be a big boy and wants to do it himself. So, I let him, as long as I get to wash his hair and his back."

"Wow. I guess you suddenly blink, and they're grown up, huh?"

"It seems that way. Fortunately, though, he likes to talk about everything and nothing in the shower. So I can keep an ear on him with the monitor."

Sure enough, she holds up a white walkie-talkie looking device that was sitting next to the refrigerator. As she turns up the volume just a bit, I hear a child's voice singing about thigh bones being connected to knee bones, an oddly appropriate shower song.

"So your Thai noodles are world famous?" she asks as she puts the monitor down, opens the fridge and stashes the bowl away for tomorrow.

"Well, maybe just family famous."

She hands me a bottle of water she just pulled off the door panel. It's not the normal store brand of H_2O I always buy. This seems like some fancy stuff. She either has some really expensive tastes or there is a specific reason she spends more than double what I do. My guess is the brand I'm using is going to kill me at some point, and I just don't know it yet.

"I'm kind of surprised," she continues as she grabs two clear glasses out of the cabinets and fills them with ice. "With a name like Aputi, I assumed you were Hawaiian."

"I am. Born and raised on Oahu. We're just a family of foodies so we cook anything that's tasty."

Her eyes widen and I can see the fluster beginning. "Oh! I didn't mean that you can't eat other foods because you're Hawaiian. I mean, I don't think you only eat pineapple and coconuts. I mean... oh my gosh, that sounds so ignorant of me. I can't believe I said that. It's like I open my mouth sometimes and words just fall out. I'm so sorry to stereotype you, Aputi."

I chuckle at how quickly she can take a normal conversation and get so thrown off balance by it. Plus, I'm not offended at all. "You didn't. I can see why you'd think that. And for the record, I like pineapple. Pineapples from my home island are the best."

"But I didn't have to mention them. That was so inappropriate of me." How it's possible, I don't know, but suddenly her eyes widen even more as another thought crosses her mind. "And then I didn't even ask what you wanted to drink. I just assumed you would drink water." She throws her hands over her eyes. "I don't know what's happening to me today."

Taking two steps towards her, I pull her hands from over her eyes, hoping my touch will calm her anxiety. I know it makes me rest easier, knowing she's not dealing with this alone. There's no reason for her to spiral like this. Not around me. "Deborah, stop. You didn't offend me or hurt my feelings. You didn't say anything wrong. It's like when you brought me chicken enchiladas. We're in Texas, so any pre-judgements weren't stereotypes, they were just thoughts."

She groans. "Don't remind me of the time I accidentally almost killed you."

Apparently, I'm not making this any better, so I try a different tactic. "You didn't almost kill me. And you were right about drinking water. I work in a warehouse all day. I'm always thirsty."

She looks up at me and takes yet another breath. "Water is a natural cleanser too. It keeps your skin looking younger and more vibrant."

"See?" I smile at her because no one but Deborah would tell a big, burly man like myself how to keep his skin vibrant. "You're treating me like a king, and I just got here."

Nodding a few times, her whole body relaxes until finally she pulls away and turns back to the task at hand. "Thank you, Aputi. I appreciate how you always know the right thing to say. I don't really have a lot of friends, so it's helpful."

I already figured that much, but knowing she trusts me enough to admit it is a good start to this new relationship. I hope I can get her to trust that I like her for who she is, and she doesn't try to front with me as much as she does everyone else.

Still, I lean against the counter to give her some distance, knowing our friendship is still new. She busies her hands by pouring water and slicing lemon wedges. She could work at a catering company with how detail-oriented she is.

"I take it today wasn't good?" I ask, not completely sure I should be approaching the topic with her, but a bigger part of me is convinced she needs to get it off her chest.

She sighs and attaches the wedges on the rim of the glasses. "It's just happening so fast." She sounds so dejected. "Apparently, I don't qualify for alimony, so I don't know how I'm going to afford the house."

"You don't want to look for a job?"

"I don't really have any skills except organizing and cleaning, and I'm busy doing that in my own home. Plus, Trevor would have to go to daycare, and he's very susceptible to germs. He gets enough exposure at school. I don't know how to navigate this predicament."

"There's a market for that kind of thing, you know. Organizing and shopping? And you can work around your schedule."

She leads me into the living room, making sure to bring the monitor with her. Trevor has broken out into a terrible child-like rendition of "Sexy Back" he's singing as "Soapy Back". I suspect Deborah doesn't know the real words to this song. She'd probably have a conniption if she did.

Sitting on the couches that are as comfy as they look, she makes sure to face me, but not before placing two coasters on the table in front of us. Still, it's a comfort level I haven't seen from her before this moment.

"I've never heard of a work-from-home job that wasn't a scam before."

"I actually know a few people who've tried some of them. There are things like personal shopping where you drop groceries at someone's house. Or one of those stylists for the clothing box things people order online. You always dress really well. I bet you'd be good at that."

She smiles shyly at my compliment. "Well, thank you. First impressions are always the most important."

I don't tell her the first impression she gave me was when she was denying Trevor the joys of grilled foods.

"I'm serious, Deborah. You should look into something like that. You don't have to make a ton of money. Just enough to supplement your child support."

She glances away, her expression changing. I can't be sure, but it's almost as if she's having a realization that she has more skills than she knew.

"I think… maybe there is something I could do. You think I can really do this?"

"Absolutely," I say with no hesitation. "I have no doubt at all that you're going to be fine as a single mom. You're strong and inventive. You'll find a way. And if you get stumped, I'll help you figure it out. That list worked out well, right?"

"It did." Deborah looks down and wipes the invisible lint off her pants. I suspect she's trying to avoid looking me in the eye. "How are you so sure? I mean, you don't really know me, so how do you know I can do all of this?"

Looks like I'm going to have to come clean on how I really see her. She's nowhere near ready to date, but I'm sure she'll figure out my interest at some point, and she may not believe that my intentions aren't nefarious if I'm not totally honest from the beginning.

Taking a quick sip of my extraordinarily tasteless water, and I mean that in the best way possible, I put my glass down and shift my body at an angle so I can see her better.

"I know you're right at the beginning of this divorce and anything can happen. He could come back, or drop dead or, hell, there are so many possibilities."

"Language."

Her interruption scatters my thoughts as I try to figure out what she's talking about. "What?"

"You said H-E-double-hockey-sticks."

"Oh. I'm sorry. Can Trevor hear us?"

She shakes her head. "No. I just don't like bad language. It's kind of a pet peeve of mine. I know it's weird," she looks embarrassed saying that, "but it just seems disrespectful to me. Not that I think you were being disrespectful because you said it. I mean when other people do it. Oh no," she groans. "I'm doing it again."

"No, you're not." I laugh. "You're allowed to have opinions and preferences. I understand. Language isn't a big deal to me, more of a bad habit. I can make an effort for you if it's something that bothers you so much."

Deborah bites her bottom lip, but I can see the hint of a smile. If I'm not mistaken, she's starting to understand why I keep making an effort to see her.

"As I was saying, anything can happen and you are nowhere near ready, but someday, when it's time, you're going on a date with me."

The same lip she was just worrying drops when her jaw opens in shock. "A-a date?"

"Yeah."

"With me?"

"With you."

"But… why me?"

I could answer any number of ways. Because I like it when she gets flustered. Because she has a nice butt. Because the remixed chicken enchiladas are officially my new favorite meal. But that would only be giving her part of the reason. She needs more than that. She needs honesty and truth. She needs swoon-worthy. "Because you aren't perfect. No one is. But in my eyes, you're perfect exactly the way you are."

Her back goes ramrod straight and I can practically see the gears turning in her head. "I think… um…." She clears her throat and stands up. "Can you give me a minute? I need… I'll be right back."

Quicker than I can stop her, she disappears through the door into what I assume is her bedroom.

That didn't go exactly as planned. Fingers crossed my Thai noodles can change her mind.

CHAPTER
Seven

Deborah

Looking at myself in the mirror, I take deep, steadying breaths, trying to get my heartbeat under control.

Am I really going to do this? I like Aputi. He's kind and genuine and thoughtful. He's like no man I've ever met before, and I feel safe around him. In all my years of marriage, I can honestly say I never felt like that. But does that make this okay?

I've never been a girl who has one-night stands. Getting naked with someone I don't know, who might live in a dirty house or have bedbugs in their clothes never seemed appealing. Not that anyone has those kinds of goals, but those thoughts always stopped any womanly desires I may have had right in their tracks.

But this—this is so much more intimate than sex. So much more revealing. And yet, part of me wants this more than anything. And it's all because of Aputi.

He is so different from anyone I've ever known. Aputi is a protector. A provider. And I've been in his house, so I know he doesn't live in filth. Maybe there are too many chemicals, but no bedbugs. He's the kind of man who would take care of a woman forever, even if she got sick or fat or was in a bad car wreck. He's one of the good ones. And he likes *me*.

Before I can second guess myself, I turn the faucet on and begin getting ready for him. He doesn't know I'm doing this, doesn't have a clue. But I hope my actions tell him everything he needs to know about what I hope for the future.

Funny how a few weeks ago, I was perfectly happy with my present. Earlier today I was lamenting my past. And yet suddenly, I'm hopeful and, dare I say excited, about my future. Aputi helped me do that. He helped me see that maybe I was settling for a life that was settling for me. I'm not sure I want things to be that way anymore.

Tonight doesn't mean I'm offering Aputi forever, but it means I'm offering myself something more. As nervous as it makes me, this is the kind of intimacy I need. Aputi has made me crave it.

It takes a few minutes to get ready, but mission now complete, I stand with one hand on my bedroom door. Taking a deep, steadying breath, I ease the door open and walk through it into the light of the living room.

Aputi clicks off his phone and looks up, freezing immediately when he catches sight of me. The moment seems to go on and on and on. Finally, I can't take it anymore.

"I feel really naked right now, can you please say something?" I blurt out, tugging at my oversized T-shirt.

"You took off your makeup."

I blink back tears I didn't know were coming. No one has seen me without makeup in at least a dozen years, maybe more. I didn't expect to be so emotional about this moment.

"Deborah."

"It's not weird, right? I mean, I know I have some scarring on my face. I had really bad acne as a kid, so I usually cover it up. But is it hideous? You know what, don't answer that. I'll be back."

"Deborah." Aputi's tone is more forceful, causing me to stop before I finish turning around and disappear again. "You look amazing."

"I do?" I ask softly, not sure I heard him correctly. "I don't think I like my hair pulled up in this messy bun thing. It pulls weird at the top."

"I like it down too. But if you like it up, it doesn't bother me. It shows off your neck."

"Oh. Um. I… yeah."

"Deborah."

"Yes?"

"Turn around."

Slowly, and not really sure why, I comply. It's not as if he has power over me. It's as if I know he'll never hurt me. Such a strange thing to know only a few weeks after becoming, well, whatever this is. Friends, maybe. But I suppose when you finally realize you've been hiding behind perfection out of fear for as long as you can remember, realizing the fear is gone gives you the strangest sense of freedom.

He doesn't say anything, so I finally look up at him. That's when he speaks.

"I know how intimate this is for you. I'm so honored that it's me you are sharing it with. I'll never take advantage of that."

Once again, I have to blink back tears. For so many years, I've been doing everything in my power to make my husband look at me just like this. I thought I was doing something wrong. I thought I wasn't good enough. Turns out, I was trying too hard for the wrong person.

I open my mouth to tell him as much when Trevor comes racing through the room, singing about the Santa Spiderman on his jammies. When he sees me, he stops dead in his tracks.

My sweet boy blinks a few times, and for a split second, I wonder if he doesn't recognize me. It doesn't take long to realize he's actually having his own moment.

"Mommy." His voice is so low it's almost a whisper. "You look beauuuuuutiful."

My heart melts and yet feels full all at the same time. It's something I'm not used to, but it's something I never want to end.

"The boy's not wrong," Aputi confirms as Trevor loses his train of thought and runs out of the room again.

"Thank you. Not just for saying that, but for everything." I sit back down next to him on the couch, wearing my brand new yoga pants. I've never worn them before, but I've seen Elena and Callie both wear them, so I thought I'd try something new. So far, the comfort level is living up to the hype, which is unexpected. But everything about this night is a surprise at this point.

I don't know where this relationship is going. I don't know if or how it will end, but it's already one of the best things that has ever happened to me. Somehow, I know it's as close to perfect as it will ever be. Summoning my newfound confidence, I decide it's time to let go just a little bit more.

"I can't date you."

Aputi blinks a couple of times and his face falls. Immediately, I know I started this conversation wrong.

"Wait. That's not what I mean." Taking a deep breath, I give myself a moment to put my words in the right order. "I would like to go on a date with you at some point, but not yet."

A small smile graces his very handsome face. "I know it's too soon."

I nod, relieved that he, yet again, understands. "I know my marriage is over, and I'm surprisingly okay with that." I can't help but shake my head a bit at that realization. "With the exception of having to call myself a divorcée from now on, which is going to elicit a lot of whispers at the next PTA carnival, the idea of not being married to Rick isn't as sad as I would have thought a couple weeks ago. But I still don't think it's appropriate for me to date while I'm legally married. Separated or not."

Aputi's long arm comes up and rests on the back of the couch. It reaches so far, he's almost touching me. I can practically feel the heat from his skin on my cheek. Suddenly, I'm ready for the divorce to be finalized so I can touch him for real.

Ooh! I need to slow my hormones before I turn into a tramp. If I'm not careful, I'll end up with a tattoo right at the base of my spine.

"I'm not here to pressure you, Deborah. You've got a lot of life changes ahead of you. I'm just here to be your friend. For now." The quirked eyebrow gives me no doubt that he's just biding his time until I'm a single lady again.

Soon, Aputi, I think to myself. *I'll be single soon...*

Epilogue

Deborah
Six months later

"The court calls to order the Dickson case."

I stand and smooth my hands down my skirt then follow my attorney through the small swinging door and stand in front of the judge.

"Are you ready?" Kendall asks quietly as the judge reads through her paperwork. I assume she's refreshing herself of the details of our mediated settlement.

We signed off on everything a month ago. Thanks to Kendall's hard work, I found out we had many more assets than I realized. With the generous amount of child support I'll be getting and my portion of the other accounts, I'll be okay. Plus, Aputi is really good at keeping a balanced budget and helped me figure one out.

Yes, I have to work a bit, but being an on-line fashion consultant for a subscription clothing box has turned out to be a lot of fun and not very time consuming at all. Plus, I'm good at it. My customer satisfaction rate is well above the consultant average which means getting more jobs. I work them into my schedule, which hasn't changed all that much.

I'm really enjoying the job. And best of all, it means Trevor doesn't have to go to daycare.

Peeking a glance over at Rick, I don't think I've ever been so ready to move on with my life than I am right now. He looks terrible. He's gained more than a few pounds and the blemishes on his skin indicate he's reverted back to eating foods chock-full of additives and preservatives. Old college habits don't look good on him.

"I've been ready for months," I say with a wide grin. I can't help it. I'm really excited for today. Nothing will really change, except I'll be free from the stress of lawyers and retainer fees and trying to find parking downtown. Who in the world thought not having an elevator in an eight-story parking garage was a good idea? Thank goodness for Steve Madden and his obsession with making a comfortable heel.

The judge finally looks up, giving each of us the once-over. I know it's irrelevant that I wore my best Vera Wang blouse today, but I can't help hoping she's a fashionista and appreciates the effort I put into dressing respectfully for this occasion.

"Mr. Dickson. Mrs. Dickson. I'm glad to see you both here. Shall we begin?"

She makes quick work of swearing us in and asks a few basic questions about why I'm opting to keep my current last name, which I answer honestly—it's Trevor's last name too. In a matter of minutes, she declares us divorced and sends us on our way.

A few quick words from my attorney about calling me next week when she has certified copies of all the paperwork, and back through the swinging door I go. Unable to contain my smile, I grab my purse from Aputi just as he rises from the bench and follows me out the door to the hall.

"How do you feel?" he finally asks when we're safely beyond the quiet zone of the courtroom. Aputi is always asking me that question. At first, it unnerved me a bit. I didn't understand why he was asking. Was I going to give him the wrong answer? Would he eventually get tired of me expressing my emotions? The more it happened, though, the more I realized he was genuinely interested in my thoughts. He didn't want me to hold anything in. He wanted to help me through the hard things.

Very quickly, I began reciprocating the question. Now, it's not even something I think about anymore. We ask each other how we feel. We listen to each other's answer. We talk through the hard stuff. We move on. And we've become best friends because of it.

"Like I'm free," I say with a smile. "Like a new chapter is finally starting, and I'm so excited to see where the story is going to take me. And like I really don't want to walk up eight flights of stairs to the car."

"That's exactly how you should feel. About your divorce *and* the stairs." He chuckles. I love the sound of his laugh. It always makes this warmth spread through my whole body, like a favorite blanket you just want to snuggle with. Or maybe I'm just very aware of the fact that I'm officially single. Looking down at his watch, he adds, "How long until we have to be back for Trevor? Do we have time to grab a bite to eat?"

"Um…" I glance at my own wrist and begin calculating. "Elena is on stand-by just in case, but we should be fine. We have three hours and forty-two minutes—"

Those are the only words I get out before I hear my name being called by a familiar voice.

"Deborah."

There it is again. I'd know that voice anywhere.

Lowering my hand, I turn slowly to see Rick approaching. He looks disheveled and out of breath.

"Deborah, I'm so glad I caught you."

An odd statement, considering he has my phone number and could have texted me.

"Can I help you with something, Rick? Wait, you're not cancelling on Trevor, are you? He'll be so sad if he doesn't get to stay in the apartment this weekend. He loves the playground in your new complex."

Yes, Rick has moved away from the beach. Practically the minute the ink was dry on the beach house lease and six-months rent was paid in advance, the new girlfriend kicked him out. Decided she wasn't meant to settle down at such a young age.

I was shocked when Rick told me, yet I couldn't find it in me to sympathize with him. I did, however, applaud the other woman's skills in the art of the con. She swindled him into paying rent on a pretty fancy place.

He shakes his head vehemently. "Oh no. I'm not cancelling. I'm looking forward to my weekend with him. Actually," his tone turns a bit sheepish and that puts me on guard immediately, "I was kind of hoping we could make it a family weekend."

Behind me, Aputi half coughs, half chokes. Apparently, he wasn't any more prepared for that than I was. His warm breath tickles my ear when he whispers, "I'm going to give you a little privacy."

Quickly, I whip my head around to look him in the eyes. "You don't have to do that."

He smiles reassuringly. "I'm not leaving you. I'm going to be right here."

I nod slowly and watch as Aputi walks to the wall a few feet away and leans against it. The confidence he has is so opposite of the waves of nervousness practically flowing off Rick. As it should be. We were declared divorced less than five minutes ago, and he's already pushing for reconciliation? There seems to be more in his processed foods than just dyes and coloring because somehow he appears a bit delusional.

"Rick, are you suggesting we take a weekend to see if we could be a family again?"

He shrugs nervously. "I mean, yeah. Why not?"

Cocking my head, I can't believe what I'm hearing. Surely, I'm misinterpreting all of this. We just spent seven months and thousands of dollars on mediations and legal proceedings. Why in the world would he not have brought this up sooner?

And then I realize there is one thing I brought to court with me that I never brought to mediation—Aputi.

I want to be enraged over the fact that I wasn't "good enough" for Rick until someone else found me worthy. Oddly, though, it never comes. I'm not angry over what Rick thinks because I just don't care enough to feel anything at all. I'm well and truly indifferent to his thoughts and opinions beyond how it relates to our child.

Huh. I wasn't expecting that at all.

I could say all that, but one thing I'm still not is vindictive. Instead, I revert back to logic. "I appreciate the invitation, but I don't want to confuse Trevor. I've read quite a few books about children of divorce, and they all agree that setting good boundaries is essential for a healthy transition."

Rick's shoulders slump and I can tell he doesn't like my answer, but once again, I don't have feelings one way or the other to have the slightest bit of guilt. What I do have, however, is a strong desire to get out of this building and go home.

"I'll see you tomorrow night for pickup."

I turn to find Aputi no longer against the wall but standing close enough that he can listen to our conversation without obviously eavesdropping. It delights me to know he's protective enough over me to inch closer when I'm not looking.

"Are you ready to go, Aputi?"

He looks up, pretending to be startled that I'm finished with Rick already, but he's not fooling anyone. "Uh, yeah. Where do you want to eat?"

"Actually, if it's okay with you, I think I'd rather go home, scrub this makeup off my face, and watch a movie with you. Would that be okay?"

Rick gasps, and the tiniest bit of validation rolls through me that he has finally figured out Aputi knows me better than he ever did. His loss.

"Sure," Aputi says with a shrug as we walk toward the elevators. "Last week, I brought over some of that all-natural air-popped popcorn you like. It's in the pantry."

"That sounds wonderful. But there's one more thing." He looks at me, eyebrows furrowed. "About that date you promised me…"

The widest smile I've ever seen breaks across his face, and I know beautiful things are happening here. And it's perfect.

ME CARTER

THE
End

ABOUT THE *Author*

Mother, reader, storyteller—ME Carter never set out to write books. But when a friend practically forced a copy of Twilight into her hands, the love of the written word she had lost as a child was rekindled. With a story always rolling around in her head, it should come as no surprise that she finally started putting them on paper. She lives in Texas with her four children, Mary, Elizabeth, Carter and Bug, who sadly was born long after her pen name was created, and will probably need extensive therapy because of it.

You can follow her on Facebook at
https://www.facebook.com/authorMECarter,
on Twitter at https://twitter.com/AuthorMECarter,
Instagram at authorMECarter
(https://www.instagram.com/authormecarter/?hl=en)
or email her at AuthorMECarter@gmail.com

Other Titles by M.E. Carter

Hart Series

Change of Hart
Hart to Heart
Matters of the Hart

Texas Mutiny Series

Juked
Groupie
Goalie
Megged
Deflected

#MyNewLife Series

Getting a Grip
Balance Check
Pride & Joie
Amazing Grayson

Charitable Endeavors Series with Andrea Johnston

Switch Stance
Ear Candy

www.ingramcontent.com/pod-product-compliance
Ingram Content Group UK Ltd.
Pitfield, Milton Keynes, MK11 3LW, UK
UKHW020819310325
5234UKWH00042B/691